THE GOLIATH CODE

A Post-Apocalyptic Thriller (Book One)

SUZANNE LEONHARD

BOS

THE
GOLIATH
CODE

SUZANNE LEONHARD

This is a work of fiction. The characters, incidents, and dialogues are products of the author's imagination and are not to be construed as real. Any resemblance to actual events or persons, living or dead, is entirely coincidental.

BOS

basically
our story

Cover Art: indieauthordesign.com

ISBN-13: 978-0-9993922-2-5

For RRL

Acknowledgments

I've always wanted to write a book about the end of the world. I'd like to think it's because I long to give the most "tragical" story in the history of the universe a happy ending, but it could also be that I'm a bit of a drama queen —and what could be more dramatic than the apocalypse? The idea for The Goliath Code rolled around in my head for years before I finally started writing it and, once I sat down at my keyboard, writing through the eyes of a sixteen year old girl didn't come easy. There were a lot of people that encouraged me along the way and kept me going, so bear with me while I thank them.

First, Robert Leonhard. Bob stepped into my life at just the right moment. Not only is he a brilliant military strategist, he's a gifted writer, and an invaluable sounding board for stubborn plot points. On those days when I felt the story overwhelming me, he was always in my corner holding the spit bucket. I owe my persistence, as well as all the military references in this book, to the man I was smart enough to marry.

Then there are my priceless Beta Readers—brave souls that step into the fray of mediocre writing to encourage and redirect writers that, adorably, mistake a first draft for a final manuscript. For me those people were Rebecca Duffy, my sister in emojis, who gave the book its first thumbs up; Kadey Kerns, who got so angry at the original ending that I changed it immediately in fear for my life; Rachel Cole, who was instrumental in helping me organize the noisy chorus; Danielle DeSousa, who fell in love and demanded more; Heather Pontius, who encouraged me with lots of exclamation marks; Hazel Hickman, who gave me permission to be proud of this one; and my granddaughter Rosie Witter, who stayed up all night reading the book. All of you will never know how much your enthusiasm motivated me and kept me going through all the doubts.

Of course, no book would be complete without a magnificent cover, and I have Sean Lowery of HighImpact-Covers to thank for this one. His patience with my perfectionism says a lot about his character.

Finally, thank you to my editor Rosanne Catalano. Not only is she knowledgeable about the infrastructures of bridges and the lifespans of cheeses, she is a divinely gifted wordsmith.

And now...let's begin.

Prologue

I raced through the snow-covered forest, ignoring the biting cold. Sunbeams filtered through the pine canopy over my head, casting scarlet bands of dancing light across the frozen landscape. The scene reminded me of a book my mother read to me when I was little, about a magical world forever trapped in winter. Mom was gone now. So were happy endings.

The shouts behind me grew louder.

I glanced over my shoulder at the perfect set of boot prints I'd left behind in the snow. Two fresh, powdery inches had fallen the night before, slowing me down, leaving a visible trail, and making the soldiers' jobs that much easier.

I veered around a dead stump and crashed through a tangle of ferns. The muscles in my legs complained. I dug deep and ran on, letting the forest close in around me. My boot caught on a branch winter-welded to the forest floor. I stumbled but stayed on my feet.

Finally, I burst from the tree line and into a bright, snowy clearing where the brilliant red sky blinded me. *Apoca-*

lypse red. The words rang in my head. That was my grandfather's description of the ruddy Devastation sky.

The reminder twisted my stomach into a familiar knot of grief and guilt. I could still hear his gruff order. "Be smart. Stay tough. Protect them at all costs."

I squeezed my eyes shut against memories that always left me feeling desperate and alone. They say time heals all wounds, but mine had only festered.

The two men crashed out of the forest behind me. I took off running with a renewed energy. I dashed across the clearing into the shelter of the trees beyond. I dodged rocks, ducked branches, leapt fallen logs, and shot through a thick wall of blackberry bushes, no longer caring where I placed my feet. I ran from more than just the soldiers now; I ran from the crush of memories that threatened to overwhelm me.

A patch of ice did me in.

I landed hard on my back, knocking the air out of my lungs. The cold soaked through my coat and jeans, but I stayed on the ground. Everything had gone quiet—no more shouts, crunching snow, or snapping branches, just the sound of my heart thumping in my ears.

I've lost them.

I took a moment to catch my breath, pushing my black cap high on my forehead to stare up at the swaying green canopy above me. Nothing moved in the forest. Most of the animals had either died during the Devastation or been hunted to extinction.

I missed the birds the most. They'd been the first to die. One by one they'd fallen from the sky like fat, feathered hailstones, leaving swarms of mosquitoes to multiply. The deer and elk died next. Thousands of them went blind, developed lung diseases, starved, and wasted away. Then the predators fell: bear, mountain lion, wolves, coyotes. Except for the persistent buzz of insects, the forest had become an empty, lonely place.

Male voices broke through the silence. I lifted my head; the two soldiers stood in the trees thirty yards away. I hadn't lost them after all.

Good.

I smiled to myself and rolled to my feet. It would have spoiled the fun if our game had ended too soon.

I brushed the snow from my pants, lingering long enough for the men to spot me. The fat one saw me first. "There!" he shouted. Then I headed off at a steady pace, careful to run slower this time.

A few minutes later I found myself in a familiar glade where a crooked elm grew sideways over a rotten stack of firewood. I stomped around in the snow, making a confusion of tracks, then shimmied up to the highest branches of my favorite hemlock tree to wait for the fun to begin.

I spotted the soldiers easily from my vantage point. They shuffled along beside my tracks and, after a few moments, entered the glade to puzzle over my hodgepodge of foot-prints. I looked down onto their heads, watching them peer in one direction, then the other.

Finally, the tall soldier called out to me in accented English. "Ve know you are here, boy." He had gold bars on the collar of his ocean blue uniform, gold braided epaulets on the shoulders of his long overcoat, and a gold officer's insignia pinned to the beanie perched on the side of his head. He was a centurion, the obvious leader of the two. "Ve vill not hurt you."

I rolled my eyes at the lie.

The fat soldier tried coaxing me out. "We got some bread and fresh water for ya, lil' fella."

Violence flared in me. The man's Southern accent branded him a traitor, which made him worse than the invader standing next to him.

I fingered the sharp hunting knife in my pocket and imagined hurling it straight into the top of the private's large head—right through the fabric of his Europa beanie. It would be such poetry to kill him by skewering the symbol of his betrayal to his skull.

He who is prudent and lies in wait for an enemy who is not, will be victorious. It was my enemy's favorite quote, one I'd taken to heart and used to my advantage.

A distant howl snapped me back to reality.

The sound grabbed the men's attention, too.

"It's that thievin' wolf from camp," the Southern soldier grumbled.

The centurion scanned the tree line, his rifle at the ready. "Enjoying our food, I am sure."

"I told you," the private snapped, "the animal attacked me. What was I s'posed to do, Kovac, get myself killed over a sack a potatas?"

Anxious for the party to start, I shifted my weight off the branch. I wrapped my arms and legs around the thick tree trunk, hugging it tightly to my chest, and waited for the perfect moment.

Then my foot slipped.

I scrambled for a better hold, doing my best to stay quiet, but the slippery bark betrayed me. I came crashing down the tree in a hard rain of wood and pine needles. The centurion dove out of the way, but the fat Southerner had slower reflexes. I landed on top of him, knocking him to the ground. We grappled, each trying to get the upper hand. I kicked my bootheel into his face and sent him backwards, crying out and holding his nose.

I sprang to my feet, ready for whatever might come next. The cold steel of an automatic rifle barrel pressed against my cheek. "Do not move," the centurion ordered.

Every ounce of my training demanded I disarm him, but Europa soldiers were a heartless bunch of dogs—they shot first and asked questions later—so I fought down the impulse. Deciding on the "frightened child" approach, I scurried back against the hemlock tree.

"That's right, boy," the centurion sneered. "I am ze vun in charge here."

The private, his hand clamped over his face, wailed in agony. "Webel twash bwoke my dose!"

Keeping his weapon trained on me, the centurion kicked at the private. "Get up! You do not need your nose to stand!"

The private staggered to his feet. Blood oozed from between his fingers, dripping over his lips and chin. It was hard to hide my satisfaction. The fat man picked up on it immediately, grabbing me by the throat and shoving me back—hard—against the tree. "I'll teach you, ya scrawny runt!" he spat.

He hauled back his hand and cracked me across the face. Sparks shot through my jaw. I shook my head to clear the ringing in my ears, but, before I could stabilize, he struck me again. I staggered. One more blow and he'd knock me off my feet.

My hand shifted to my pocket, to the knife. I could put him back on the ground in a second.

The private moved to hit me again—my fingers curled around the smooth hilt—but the centurion grabbed his arm. "Halt!" Assessing me with narrowed eyes, he shoved the private away. "Vhat is your name, boy?"

The centurion had a rigid, pitiless face. When I didn't

answer, his stare intensified. He was trying to intimidate me, but it wouldn't work. Then he yanked the black cap from my head and freed my tangle of hair. I gasped, feeling instantly vulnerable.

The private's eyes practically leapt from his skull. "God almighty!" he shouted. "He's a her!"

He took hold of my chin, jerking my head from side to side.

I clenched my teeth. *Stay calm.*

"Wait a minute. Wait one mother-lovin' second." The smile on his blood-caked face widened.

I'd been made.

"It's her! We found her!"

The centurion peered harder at me, wrinkling his nose. "Vhat is your name, girl?"

But they already knew the answer.

"It's her, Kovac! I will tell you somethin', mister, the praetor better give me a promotion for this. I am *done* traipsin' through the wilderness roundin' up his lab rats." He cackled, patting me on the cheek. "This little lady is gonna make sure Melvin Calhoun gets exactly what he deserves."

"Ziss isn't America anymore, Private," his superior dismissed. "Ve do not give promotions to men for simply doing zeir jobs."

Calhoun gave him a calculating look. "Well, then. Maybe it's time I found more advantageous employment." He directed his weapon at the centurion.

This sudden change of events didn't surprise me at all —once a traitor, always a traitor—but the centurion's pinched face turned scarlet. "Vhat are you doing, you idiot?!"

"I'm takin' the girl." The private grinned. "Black

market'll pay top dollar for a comfort girl with copper hair."

He's going to sell *me?* The knife in my pocket called again. One quick strike to his kidney; that's what Melvin Calhoun deserved.

A branch snapped on the other side of the glade, followed by a subtle, steady rustle through the snowy underbrush. The soldiers were too busy arguing to notice.

"C'mon, Kovac," the private coaxed. "I'll cut ya in for a share. We can't waste prime girl flesh like this on the praetor's cracked experiments."

Kovac puffed out his chest. "You cannot bribe me——"

"Forty-five percent."

The centurion blinked. *"But is it really her?"* he breathed.

Calhoun took me by my coat sleeve and gave me a shake. "Go ahead. Tell 'im your name."

A large, hairy shape appeared in the woods behind the men. I smiled and looked the private in the eye. "You can call me bait."

"You see?" The centurion huffed. "She says her name is Bates."

The private scowled. "No…she said *bait.*"

A low, rumbling growl filled the glade. The soldiers turned. A hulking white wolf stood in the underbrush ten yards away.

Calhoun whimpered. "K-Kovac?"

The animal's black lips curled back into a terrifying snarl.

"Quiet, you idiot!" Kovac hissed.

The wolf raised his hackles. His thick body coiled. A glimmer of imminent death reflected in his cold amber eyes.

I cocked my head at the vicious beast. "You're late," I chided.

The centurion scrambled to turn his weapon on the animal. With a savage growl, the wolf was on him. Centurion Kovac went down in a riot of screams and sharp, snapping teeth.

The private shrieked at the wolf and raised his weapon. I moved into action, lashing out with a perfect crescent kick —one that would have made my grandfather proud. The private's weapon flew from his hands and flipped, end over end, against the red sky. I caught it in midair, spun, and slammed the stock into his chest, adding broken ribs to his cracked nose. He fell to the ground, moaning in pain. I snapped the weapon to my shoulder and pointed it at his left eye. He looked up at me, sputtering. Like my victims before him, the private was having a hard time reconciling my sudden transformation from scrawny runt to guerrilla fighter.

His breath came quick and shallow; he was calculating whether I was capable of shooting him. "You can't—"

"I can." Thanks to men like Kovac and Calhoun, my skills had been refined in the unforgiving fires of war and vengeance.

I stared down the rifle sights at the private's sweaty brow. I could hear the wolf enjoying his centurion lunch and, judging by the look of horror on his face, Private Calhoun could hear it, too. I pressed the rifle barrel against the soft, fatty flesh of the man's forehead, shifted my finger to the trigger, and slowly let out my breath—

"Seraphina!" the private shouted.

I hesitated.

"That's yer name, right? I-I have somethin' for ya."

He eased his hand down to his uniform belt and slipped a piece of paper out from beneath the brass buckle. He handed it to me with trembling fingers, its glossy surface faded and worn by time. The past and present collided. Hot tears flooded my eyes. Everything I was—everything I'd been forced to become—came crashing in and rage welled up inside me.

"Where did you get this?" I demanded.

The private snorted. "Thought that might get yer attention."

My eyes narrowed. "Not the kind you were hoping for."

I swung back the rifle stock and bashed him in the side of the head.

Part I

Chapter One

The world ended on the last Monday in September, three days after my sixteenth birthday.

I sat between my mother and my twin brother on a hard pew in the Roslyn Bible Church, a stone mausoleum built in the Dark Ages, watching my cousin Felicity marry Roger Freeman. I barely knew the bride. I'd never met the groom. As far as I could tell, neither of them cared whether I was there or not.

I cared.

The forecast called for snow that night, so my best friend, Alyson, and I wanted to grab a quad ride up to Crystal Creek before the park service closed the trail for the season. But, thanks to my mother, I had to sit through this lame religious ceremony first.

While the happy couple stood beneath a wedding arch of baby's breath and white roses, pledging their undying love, I stared at the back of my hand and tried to figure out if a tribal or a color tattoo would look better against my pale skin and faint freckles. My mother noticed and nudged me

SUZANNE LEONHARD

with her elbow. I clenched my jaw, turning a dark scowl back to the spectacle in front of me. Why did anyone even bother with marriage anymore? It never lasted. Case in point: my own parents. They weren't exactly happy these days.

My mom had taken my four-wheeler hostage to force me to this wedding. That had been—in baseball and felony terms—her third strike. Her second strike had been refusing to let me go to homecoming with Eric Hawk, something I'd never forgive her for.

No, because she said so.

I pictured myself—a sophomore—showing up at homecoming with Eric—a senior—in his black Mustang, his red-tailed hawk tattoo peeking out from under his rolled-up sleeve. It would have been awesome. Nope. My mom had found the perfect cruel and unusual punishment.

I wasn't in love with Eric or anything. Like most high school jocks, he was kind of a jerk, but the day he'd asked me to homecoming, I'd gotten twenty-three new follows on Trill.

Mom used to be more chill. She had a 24/7 open-door policy, which meant my brother and I could talk to her about anything, anytime. But talking to her hadn't helped much lately, not since she'd started going to church. That had been her first strike.

None of us understood why she'd done it, not even Dad. She'd been a rational human being her entire life, then one Sunday she'd gotten out of bed and gone to a service. My parents fought about it all the time. Dad tried to make her see reason; he asked why she needed religion, why we weren't enough for her. Mom always answered the same way. She encouraged him to go to church, which none of us would ever do.

14

Her conversion really messed things up for me and my brother. She disapproved of everything we did: our music, our movies, our friends. She insisted on praying over every meal—even in restaurants, even in McDonalds. It was humiliating. If anybody from school ever spotted her praying over my McNuggets, I'd never hear the end of it.

I'd told her that last week when she asked why I refused to eat out with her anymore. At that point, she'd threatened to pull me and my brother out of Cle Elum-Roslyn High School and enroll us in Mountain Christian Academy. They wear uniforms and take Bible classes *every day* at that school.

I just didn't get it. They say Christians have family values or whatever, but Mom's new religion was tearing our family apart. Lately, my dad practically lived at work, my brother rarely came out of his cave in the basement, and I spent most of my time at Alyson's house. At least my friend's mother respected her kids enough to let them live their own lives.

Up front, the pastor—we'd heard a lot about Pastor Rick lately—droned on and on about love, commitment, faithfulness, and mercy. Every now and then the wedding guests shouted a passionate "Amen!" I passed the time wondering what my mom would do if I came home with a red-tailed hawk like Eric's tattooed into the back of my hand.

Probably cut my arm off.

According to my mother's new religion only heathens wore tattoos, which probably explained why she wouldn't let me go to the dance with Eric. Thanks to Jesus and people like Pastor Rick, I was destined to remain a nobody who'd had a fleeting shot at popularity. My life was a wasteland.

I slumped down in the pew.

When the pastor started reading from the Bible, my

brother David shifted beside me. He'd been fidgeting and chewing his nails since we sat down. He wasn't any happier to be there than I was, but at least mom hadn't forced him to wear an ugly purple dress she'd pulled off a discount rack. She'd even found a pair of flowery shoes to match the baby roses she'd jammed in my braided hair. I looked like a cake.

In contrast, David wore a classy pair of blue pants and a gray button-down shirt. Mom had even let him wear his black sneakers because she couldn't find dress shoes to fit him. On rare occasions, my brother's condition worked in his favor.

Although David had been granted the distinct honor of entering this world three minutes and twenty-three seconds before me, he'd been born with a rare bone disorder called achondroplasia. Among other things, it causes dwarfism. My twin brother stood only four feet four inches tall. I almost always felt guilty about being bigger, stronger, and more coordinated, but it was okay. His resentment balanced things out.

His back was too bent to play sports, his legs were too bowed to climb trees, and his arms were too short to ride a quad. But what my brother lacked in physical ability, he made up for in intelligence. He'd read his first book at two, become a chess master at ten, and made himself a fully functional jetpack at twelve. My brother David was the smartest person I knew. Since our father was a Nobel Prize-winning geneticist, that was saying something.

David caught me staring at his legs, which stuck straight out from the pew, and kicked me hard in the knee. He didn't like being stared at. But I wasn't trying to be mean, I was imagining what his legs would look like when they grew as long as mine, when our father finally finished working on the cure he'd been promising David for years.

My brother dreamed of growing straight and tall like me. Now Dad was close to completing animal trials. If all went well, David might begin treatment by the end of the year. Last week I'd caught him looking at basketball hoops on Amazon. Yeah, my brother was a little bit excited.

I retaliated by jamming my elbow into his ribs. He whimpered like an abused puppy, earning me a stern look from our mom. I expected my parents to take David's side; they usually did. Today it gave me one more reason to be mad at Mom and I ran with it.

When the ceremony finally ended, the bride and groom kissed, turned to accept their applause, and then paraded up the aisle, arm in arm.

Our mother stood, gesturing for us to do the same. "Everybody stands when the bride and groom walk by," she whispered.

Rolling our eyes in unison, my brother and I reluctantly stood. "Dead man walkin'," David whispered. I bit my lip to hide a laugh.

BOOM! The deep sound broke the air. It shook the church, rattling the enormous stained glass window behind the stage. The giant bell banged in the steeple high above my head. I grabbed the pew in front of me, craning my neck upward. The plaster ceiling cracked.

The bride and groom stopped in the middle of the aisle. Felicity's eyes went wide with shock; she dropped her bouquet.

Her new husband bent down to pick up the flowers. "Sorry, God," he drawled. "It's too late to protest now."

The congregation fluttered with nervous laughter.

"It's just a fighter jet from McChord, folks," Pastor Rick assured us. "Nothing to worry about."

A low rumble started beneath the floorboards. My feet tingled with the sensation. David looked down—he felt it, too. The rumble grew louder; the vibration grew stronger. Everyone in the church started talking at once.

David leaned past me and grabbed Mom's hand. "We need to leave." The urgency in his voice made the hair on my arms stand up.

Mom nodded, shuffling us toward the aisle. The shuddering lurched into an all-out roll that knocked us back down onto the pew.

Car alarms wailed outside, sirens blared, shrieks went up from the wedding guests. The bride and groom fell to their knees halfway to the exit doors. No one knew whether to sit, stand, or run.

"Ladies and gentlemen," the pastor called from the front of the church. "Please try to stay calm. We seem to be having a minor earthquake."

I looked at David, staring into wide green eyes identical to my own, and a chill raced up my spine. My brother looked pale, nervous. That's when I got scared.

We got back on our feet again. The bell over our heads clanged like crazy; the ground beneath us sounded like an engine accelerating. I half-expected a freight train to come barreling through the floor.

"This church has been here for a long time!" the pastor called out a bit louder. "We are perfectly safe!"

Perfectly safe?

The deep rumble of the quake surged up through the foundation of the building and bounced it like a toy. I watched, amazed, as the stained glass window behind the man of God rippled like a living thing. It expanded and contracted; its blue, green, and gold colors rolling like a shimmering wave.

"Mom!" David shouted above the roar. "We have to get out of here!"

The pastor lifted his Bible over his head. "The Lord is my shepherd, I shall not—"

The stained glass window exploded from its casement. It shattered into a million pieces, a sharp hurricane of glass knifing across the stage toward the pews. Mom shoved us to the floor, then fell on top of us. My bare knees dug hard into the vibrating, polished wood. I heard screams—a baby crying—people praying. My brother's ragged breathing echoed in my ears.

I squeezed my eyes shut and willed it to end. But this was only the beginning.

Mom pulled us to our feet. I steadied myself as the church rocked all around us. "Are you two all right?" she shouted over the thundering noise.

She gave us a frantic once-over, then turned toward the exit. She had tiny pieces of glass embedded in her back and shoulders. Droplets of blood oozed through her beautiful print dress and slid down her slender, bare arms. I opened my mouth to tell her, but she pulled us toward the aisle again.

Wailing, crying people, most of them covered in stained glass and blood, froze in shock. Others stared at the pastor, who had gone quiet.

My brain screamed not to look at him, but I did anyway.

Pastor Rick Cole had fallen to his knees, his Bible clutched in his hands, his eyes and mouth open in a look of surprise. For a moment I thought he was okay. Then I saw the long, jagged piece of golden glass jutting from the side of his neck. He gurgled and toppled to the stage.

That's when all hell broke loose.

Screaming parishioners shoved each other aside and charged the aisles. Roger Freeman tried to escort his wife to the door, but the wedding party stampeded over her. A loud groaning pulled my eyes upward. The ceiling was gone. It lay in heaps all around us. I stared into the steeple—into the deep, dark underbelly of the heavy iron bell clanging madly against its frame. It rocked. It shuddered. And then it fell.

My mother grabbed the ruffles on the front of my dress and yanked me into the aisle beside my brother. The bell flew past, stealing my breath. It crashed down through the pews where we'd been sitting and into the basement.

The church was coming apart.

My instincts turned me toward the back of the building. Screaming people stacked up against the exit, pounding at doors that had shifted and refused to open. My mom hauled my brother onto her hip and pulled me in tight with her other arm. She dragged us down the aisle in the other direction. We clambered onto the platform where the elegant wedding arch had been, stepping on white roses and baby's breath scattered across the crimson puddle of Pastor Rick's blood.

Mom heaved open a trapdoor in the floor, revealing a deep baptismal font, and slipped my brother down inside. I went in next. The cold, hard porcelain bit into my legs as I scrambled in. My brother curled up in a tight ball. I felt the earth jolt, felt the font shift, and wondered if it would ever end.

A long, brassy note blended into the noise around me. I could barely hear it above the roar of the quake, but it grew in volume until it sounded like the piercing blast of a thousand trumpets. I crawled to where David huddled against the side of the font, molded myself against him, and covered my ears to shut out the terrifying noise.

A large piece of stone tumbled through the trapdoor. It slammed into the bottom of the font, filling the air with dust. I peered through the darkened gloom, wondering why my mom hadn't closed the trapdoor behind her and sealed us all in. Suddenly, a white-hot light lit the font like a starburst. I flinched and shielded my eyes as it illuminated my brother's grimy red hair and tear-streaked face. I turned to check on Mom. She wasn't there.

David shot me a frantic look.

I scrambled to the trapdoor, thrust my head out, and froze. The earthquake blast kept coming, but I barely noticed the steady shower of dust and plaster falling all around. My eyes fixed on the horrifying scene playing out in front of me. The painful brightness came from everywhere and nowhere. It felt too hot against my skin; I wanted to crawl back under the floor and hide. My mother stood just feet away, surrounded by a bubble of snow-white peace that felt threatening and alien. Her lips moved. For a bizarre moment, I thought she was singing, but I couldn't grasp the words.

Then she turned her head to look at me with an odd mixture of joy and regret glistening in her eyes. "Endure," she called out.

I realized, with a jolt of panic, that she was saying goodbye.

I would not leave her.

Determined, I moved to climb out onto the stage. The white bubble rose, lifting my mother with it. A crack of thunder split the air. The earth shuddered. What remained of the ceiling above my head detached in free fall. I tumbled backwards into the font.

The bright light winked out. The trapdoor slammed shut. The world went quiet.

I lay there in the darkness, gasping, struggling with what I'd just seen. The light had left...and it had taken my mother with it.

Chapter Two

I opened my eyes to pitch blackness. The lurching and shuddering had stopped, blanketing the world in an unnatural silence that made my heart ache. I couldn't see my brother, but I could feel his small body curled against mine. I could hear his breath hitching. He was crying.

"Mom?" he whispered.

I shook my head, still trying to work through what I'd seen.

"Sera?" he pressed.

He couldn't see me shaking my head in the darkness. He couldn't see my bloodless face, my haunted eyes, or my trembling hands.

He took hold of my arm. "Sera, did Mom get out?"

I tried to inhale past the constriction in my chest, but that only lodged it deeper. How could I tell him? Finally, I managed one simple word. "No."

It was enough.

I held him as he sobbed. I felt numb, lifeless. Ten minutes ago, I was sitting next to her on a pew, counting strikes. Now, she was gone.

The font shuddered. I held my breath as the rumbling started beneath us again, swelling on all sides.

David sniffled. "Aftershock."

CRASH! BANG! It sounded as if the world was trying to fall out from beneath us. I'd heard that aftershocks could be stronger than the initial quake, so I knew we weren't out of danger yet.

I pulled myself together, sat up, and took off my shoes.

"W-what are you doing?" David stammered.

"Mom—" My voice cracked; I took a deep breath. "Mom risked her life to save us. I'm not going to just sit here and wait for the church to finish us off."

I set aside my grief, knowing it would be waiting for me later. I rolled to my knees and felt above my head for the edges of the trapdoor. I pushed upward, but the door wouldn't move. "Help me." The air tasted stale. It was becoming hard to breathe.

I heard my brother stand up beside me. I planted my feet, put my palms against the door, and pushed with every-thing I had. "Puuuuush!"

David grunted and wheezed. "It's stuck," he groaned.

I adjusted my position and used my shoulder as leverage. "Again!"

We pushed and heaved until we were both exhausted, but we couldn't budge the door.

David finally sat down with a thud. "Something's blocking it. We're safer down here, anyway."

"I am not dying in here, David!" I bent forward, put my back against the trapdoor, and used my legs to push as hard as I could.

"We aren't going to die." His irritated tone did nothing for my growing anxiety.

Determined, I pushed and pushed some more, until my

muscles ached and my legs went weak. The door wouldn't move.

I sank back down onto the cold porcelain. "We're trapped," I breathed. Panic coiled itself around me. "Nobody knows we're here. How are they going to find us?"

"We're fine."

"We're going to die!" I shouted back. "Right here! Right where we're sitting!"

"Just stay calm—"

"I can't breathe." A dark fog clouded my vision. The world slipped sideways. I clawed at the high neckline of my dress.

"You're hyperventilating. Slow your breathing. Take slow, deep breaths."

I was gasping, desperate for air. "I can't—"

"Sera!" he shouted. "If I can breathe, you can breathe! Take slow, deep breaths!"

My head reeled. *Nobody's going to find us. We're going to die in the dark. Our bodies will rot here. Wild animals will tear us to pieces.*

I lurched upright, slamming my head into the trapdoor. Everything went black....

I'm floating in the water. A deep blue sky. Her silk print dress. A mountain of gold. A dragon rises from the sea. Red eyes burn through me. Sharp teeth sink into my neck.

I woke with a start, my throat dry, my heart pounding. The unexpected darkness disoriented me.

"Welcome back."

"David?" I croaked. I tried to shake off the disturbing dream, but I could still feel razor teeth against my skin. "W-where am I?"

"The font. You panicked and hit your head."

I rubbed the painful lump on the top of my scalp and it

all came flooding back to me. *The wedding. The earthquake. My mother.*

Fresh tears stung my eyes. "How long was I out?"

The light on David's wristwatch flared red, reminding me of burning red eyes. I saw the quick illumination of his face, dirty and dripping with sweat. "About twenty minutes," he replied.

"The air—"

"We have plenty of air, Sera. It's full of dust, but it'll last forever."

Forever? "I don't plan on being down here that long." A board creaked above my head like a ghostly footstep. I lunged to my knees and started pounding on the underside of the stage. "Help! Help us! We're down here!"

Almost in answer to my shouts, something crashed above us. It shook the font, sending a rain of dust falling onto our heads. I shrieked. "What was that?!"

"The church—what's left of it, anyway. It isn't stable. Like I said, we're a lot safer down here than wandering around up there."

"But there could be people out there looking for us."

"I've been beating on that door for the past twenty minutes." That explained his sweaty face. "There's nobody out there right now. Nobody alive anyway."

Panic nudged at my brain again. "They're going to find us, though, right?"

"Of course. We just have to stay calm and wait it out."

Stay calm, I coached myself. *Wait it out.* I sat down and began dividing out a strand of my hair. "How...how big do you think the quake was?"

"Based on the damage, the movement, and the fact that we live on a mountain made of volcanic rock—I'd say pretty big."

I braided my hair with trembling fingers. "Gimme a number," I pressed. If I was going to stay calm, I needed him to keep talking.

"I'm not a seismograph."

"Guess."

"I don't guess."

"Then hypothesize."

I heard an echoing thud and figured he'd slammed his hand against the font. "I don't know!"

Like me, he was processing a lot. Unlike me, he preferred to do his processing in silence.

We sat quietly for a moment, my fumbling fingers working and reworking the braid. The darkness pressed in. I started to imagine the world above me, annihilated and filled with bodies. My mouth went dry.

"What kind of jet do you think it was?"

"Jet?" David repeated.

"The pastor said the big boom was a fighter jet from McChord."

"Probably a Raptor. In dry air, they're capable of breaking the sound barrier at—" He cut himself off.

"At what?" I reached for him in the dark. "David?" I hated that I couldn't see him. "What is it?"

"Nothing." He sounded distracted. "It…it was at least a seven."

"A seven?" I realized he was talking about the earthquake now. "Seven… That sounds big."

Silence threatened again.

"What time is it?" I asked.

He sighed. The red light flared on his watch. "Five seventeen."

Another question popped into my head. I opened my mouth, then hesitated, not sure I wanted to hear his answer.

He must have heard me take a breath. "What?"

"Do—" I swallowed hard. "Do you think Seattle's okay?"

His answer was quiet. "Dad's building is built to withstand earthquakes."

"Can it handle a seven?"

"Definitely."

The universe wouldn't be cruel enough to take our mom and dad on the same day, would it?

Moments ticked by, turning into anxious minutes. My thoughts went to my mom, bringing hot tears to my eyes. I swallowed hard. "Do you think Ms. Hutchins will give us time to finish our History—"

"Enough, Sera. Conserve your energy and try to sleep."

I felt him roll away from me and knew he was taking his own advice, but sleep wasn't an option for me. I was too afraid I'd close my eyes and wake up dead.

I heard his deep, even breathing and fought the urge to reach out and pinch him for leaving me alone in the dark. I pulled my knees to my chest, trying to think about something pleasant—something other than crumbling buildings, bloody faces, and eerie white lights that stole mothers away from their children.

A while later I checked David's watch, thinking an hour had gone by since the last time he'd checked, but only minutes had passed. I clenched my fists and closed my eyes, trying to focus all my energy. I willed rescuers to find us. Thoughts of my mother eventually crept in again; I ended up sobbing quietly in the darkness.

Two hours later, David shivered against me in his sleep. I could feel cold air drifting over my skin. The sun must have gone down outside. I fumbled in the dark for my shoes and tugged them on, then huddled against my brother's back to keep us both warm.

A low rumble made my heart leap into my throat. I braced myself, imagining the font tilting sideways with the roll of another earthquake—until I realized the rumbling came from inside of me. I hadn't eaten since breakfast, but, with my stomach tied up in knots, I doubted I could. I licked my dry lips. A glass of water sounded amazing, though. I thought of Mr. Beckham, our science teacher, who'd taught us the rule of threes. The average human body could survive three minutes without air, three hours without shelter, three days without water, and three weeks without food.

Thinking of what would happen to me after being trapped in the font for three days made me shudder. What would it feel like to die?

At around one in the morning, my ears perked at the sound of a faint voice. At first I thought I imagined it, but then the voice came again, louder, and this time it woke David.

"What's that?" he murmured.

"It sounds like somebody calling out. Hello?" I called back.

"Hello!" came the excited female reply. "Yes, help me! I-I'm over here! My legs are trapped! I can't move!"

My heart sank. It wasn't a rescuer. It was someone trapped in the dark like us.

"What's your name?" David called back.

"Felicity," she whimpered. "Please. Please help me."

Our cousin had survived and now she lay out there in the dark, in the shifting church with the carnage. Images of smoldering wreckage and death filled my mind; suddenly the font didn't seem like such a bad place to be.

"We can't help you," David called back.

"Don't tell her that!" I snapped.

"I'm sorry, Sera, was it supposed to be a secret?"

"Saying it like that will just upset her."

"The woman is trapped under a church. I'm pretty sure she's already upset."

"Hello?" Felicity called to us.

"Let me do it," I told him. "Felicity?" I called sweetly. "It's your cousin Sera. I'm sorry, but David and I are stuck, too. We're under the stage and we can't get the trapdoor open."

"Ohhh. Oh, nooo." Felicity moaned. She started crying again, then screaming. "Help! Somebody help me!"

"You were right as always, Sera," David said dryly. "Your way was so much better than mine."

I scowled at him in the dark. "It's okay, Felicity," I called out. "We'll be rescued soon."

David grunted. "Now who's saying things they shouldn't?"

"It's true," I insisted. It had to be.

Felicity kept yelling. I could hear her struggling against whatever had her trapped.

"Try not to move," David advised her. "The building isn't—"

There was a CREAK, a GROAN, and then a loud BANG! I felt the sound jolt through my body.

"Stable," he finished.

Felicity's pleading stopped.

I held my breath. "Felicity?" There was no response— not even a whimper. Tears filled my eyes. "Hello?"

David squeezed my hand. We didn't hear from our cousin again.

At some point, I must have finally fallen asleep because I woke a few hours later to David nudging me. "Sera?"

"Hm?" I woke up groggy and disoriented.

"Listen."

Several cracks of sunlight now filtered down between the floorboards, offering enough light to make out the shape of my brother's dirty face. He looked like he'd been through a war. I cleared my head of sleep and listened. It was faint, but I could hear the distinct sound of something scraping above our heads.

My heart lurched. My brother and I locked eyes, then launched into a flurry of shouts. "Help! Help us!"

Excited, muffled voices echoed above us.

"We're here!" I screamed.

"Under the stage!" David cried.

We pounded on the trapdoor, beating on it with everything we had.

We heard a flurry of activity—banging, scraping, voices yelling. The light filtering down between the boards broadened and intensified. Plumes of dust fell into our eyes and drifted into our mouths. We kept pounding.

Finally, the trapdoor opened above our heads. We blinked in the blinding light of morning.

"Here!" someone bellowed.

The world became a blur of faces, lights, hands, and shouting. And then green eyes, capped by shaggy silver brows, stared down at us. *Grandpa Donner.* His sheriff's uniform was caked with dirt and sweat; worry and fatigue shadowed his face. When he spoke, the bushy ends of his thick silver mustache twitched with emotion.

"My God," he rasped. "They're alive."

Chapter Three

Several pairs of hands reached in to pull us from the font. The moment we stood on our own feet, Grandpa dropped to his knees and hauled us into a powerful hug. "I thought I'd lost ya both," he croaked.

David and I cried hysterically out of sadness and relief. Grandpa was here. He would keep us safe. He would know what to do.

I buried my face in his broad shoulder and never wanted to let go.

Finally, he shifted back. He wiped the tears from his own face, then looked us over carefully. "Are ya hurt?"

We shook our heads. Scratches crisscrossed our exposed skin and I had a lump the size of a walnut on the top of my head, but, other than that, we were both fine.

Grandpa looked past us, at the workers still shining their flashlights into the dark font. "Anybody else in there with you?" he asked us.

I glanced at David. His chin quivered. He opened his mouth to speak, but no sound came out.

"No," I rasped. That single word again. Small, but devastating.

Tears pooled in my grandfather's eyes. I forced down a sob. He pulled us both close again. David's chest shook with heavy emotion and I bit my bottom lip to keep from crying. I was the only one who knew the truth. And the truth was so much more horrible than either of them could imagine.

Grandpa took a breath and pulled himself together. "Let's get you two someplace safe, okay?"

David and I each took hold of one of his big hands, letting him lead us from the tangle of lumber and stone that had once been the Roslyn Bible Church. I glanced back only once. The stage we'd been hiding beneath was unrecognizable. The force of the quake had twisted and smashed it, just like the rest of the church. Everything was destroyed —except the font.

We left the church parking lot in the early morning light. The sun, just above the horizon, cast a dim glow over a totality of destruction like nothing I could have ever imagined. The historic neighborhood around us was in shambles, like a wrecking ball had bowled through it. Fires burned up and down the streets; hazy, black smoke shadowed the southern horizon and concealed the snow-capped mountains.

Sirens screamed through the city.

We headed down North Second Street, sidestepping ragged fractures in the road where the asphalt had thrust upward, leaving deep, angry rips in the earth. We wove through downed trees tangled in dead power lines and skirted around cars crushed by debris. I made the mistake of looking into one of the cars. When I saw the dead woman behind the wheel, I almost threw up. I didn't look into any more cars after that.

All the old houses on First Street were piles of kindling. Even the newer structures like Cascade Dental had suffered collapses. I saw Lisa Butler, a local realtor, sitting on her lawn, rocking her dead dog. A few houses down, hardware store owner Mike Jorgenson stood on his sidewalk, staring blankly at a large sinkhole that had swallowed his house whole. When we crossed onto Idaho Street, a loose horse charged out from a side yard and almost trampled us before racing off down the block.

The world had come unglued.

Grandpa led us toward the city hall building, which, aside from a few broken windows, had sustained very little damage from the quake. He ushered us through the shattered glass front doors, propped open with two heavy wooden desks, and led us toward a first aid station set up by the curving staircase. People in various stages of shock and despair packed the rotunda, lying in cots, slumped on metal chairs, and sitting in groups on the floor. I stared at the familiar faces as we passed, wondering if any of them had lost someone they loved in the flash of a bright white light.

Otto Reinkann, our family doctor, looked up as we approached. Normally a cheerful, friendly man, the doctor looked ashen and exhausted. He tried to smile when he saw us, but the effort got lost in the lines of fatigue drawn on his face. "How are my two favorite patients?" He sat us down in a couple of metal folding chairs and quickly assessed our health. "Some blankets and water, please?" he called out.

Across the room, a group of kids from school manned a table stacked with blankets, boxes of granola bars, and bottles of water. The town had obviously been busy while David and I were trapped in the font. It wasn't uncommon for snow and ice storms to take out the power in the winter, so people living in a town like ours, at the top of a mountain pass, knew how to pull together in times of need. I'd never seen anything like this relief effort, though.

A petite blonde turned our way. Milly Odette, a sopho-more like me, had her hair pulled back in a neat braid and still had on her cheerleader sweater with the big 'W'—for Warriors—on the front. I rolled my eyes and sank in my chair. The very last person I wanted to deal with right now was the annoyingly cheerful Texas transplant who, even in the aftermath of an apocalypse, still managed to look perfect.

Milly hurried over to us, carrying thermal blankets and two bottles of water. I ignored her.

Doctor Reinkann shined a penlight into David's eyes. "Do you have any pain?"

David shook his head.

Milly draped a shiny Mylar blanket over my shoulders, did the same for David, and then hurried off to help someone else.

The doctor's light glared into my eyes. "And how about you, Sera?"

I squinted. "Just here." I touched the sore spot on the top of my head.

He sifted through the hair on my scalp and probed the wound mercilessly. I grimaced. "Yes, I bet that does hurt," he said. Finally, he turned to Grandpa. "Water, food, and rest."

Grandpa nodded. "Give everybody what they need, Doc, but go easy on the supplies." In a low voice, he added, "We still don't have any idea how far-reaching this thing is."

I looked around the room full of people. Some were sobbing inconsolably. This wasn't anything like an ice storm or even the blizzard two winters ago that knocked out our power for ten days. It would take a long time to recover from this.

Two young men barreled through the front doors carrying a man on a stretcher. One of those young men was Tim Odette, Milly's older brother. "Unconscious man!" Tim shouted.

Tim—or, as my best friend Alyson liked to call him, tall, tasty, and Texas—had a bruise the size of a plum on his cheek, but it only made his eyes look bluer. He still had on his number five jersey. That, plus Milly's cheerleader sweater, told me the quake must have hit during football practice.

The doctor, already halfway across the room, called out, "More blankets!"

They placed the stretcher on a long table and, even from across the room, I could see that the man was in bad shape. As the doctor worked, a shocking flow of blood streamed onto the tile floor at his feet. I watched the crimson pool funnel into the grout and wondered if it would stain. Would people point to it in years to come and say, "That's from the day of the big quake."

The injured man started screaming.

A bottle of water appeared in front of my face—my grandfather's way of getting my attention. He pulled up a chair in front of me and David, then sat down. I snatched the bottle from his hand and drained it in several gulps.

Grandpa gave me a gentle look. "Can you tell me what happened to your mom?"

David's eyes settled on me. Panic tightened my chest. *The blinding light. Her whispered words. The crushing loss.*

Tears clogged my throat and I lowered my head.

"It's all right, sweetheart." Grandpa smoothed back my hair. "It's all right. We'll do our best to find her."

But they never would.

The injured man finally stopped screaming. I was afraid to wonder why.

"Mom saved us," David rasped. "She...she put us in the font and saved our lives."

Grandpa gave a tremulous smile and dashed at the moisture on his face. "That doesn't surprise me a bit."

"Have you heard from Dad?" David asked.

I watched my grandpa's face, looking for any sign that he was keeping something from us. He shook his head. "Phone and power are out. Can't even get a cell signal." David's expression fell and Grandpa patted him on the knee. "Seattle's built to withstand stuff like this. On top of that, I raised your dad to be tough as old leather. I'm sure he's okay."

Eliza Cole drifted past, wrapped in a blanket, her face red and splotchy from crying. She was the school nurse, but she was also Pastor Rick's wife. I'd never liked her. She was one of those Christians who walked around acting like their halo was shinier than anybody else's, but everybody knew she was having an affair with Coach Stephens. A picture of her husband flashed through my mind—on his knees, Bible raised, glass jutting from his neck—and I squeezed my eyes tight against the image.

"The pastor hasn't been found yet," Grandpa explained.

"He's dead." David wiped his nose on his sleeve. "In front of the window, three feet, maybe four, from the font."

Grandpa shook his head. "We only found you two in that area. Maybe he crawled off."

David frowned at me. We both knew Pastor Rick hadn't been in any condition to crawl anywhere.

Dirty, injured people continued to drift in through the front doors. I wondered about Alyson. She lived in an older home near Cedar Gulch and, based on what I'd seen in town, older homes hadn't done well in the quake. And what about Eric? I had no idea where he lived.

Deputy Jim Hester, a nice man who'd worked for my grandfather for as long as I could remember, called out to him from the front entrance. "Sheriff? We could use you outside. Mayor Skaggs is talkin' about callin' off the search at the library on account of the storm and a lot of folks are gettin' pretty upset."

Grandpa sighed and shook his head. "I'll be right there, Jim."

My heart lurched. I grabbed my grandfather's callused hand. "You're leaving?"

"There are still a lot of folks missing, Sera," he said. "But if you need me to stay, I will."

I imagined other kids out there, alone, buried beneath the rubble, wondering if they'd be found before their "rule of threes" ran out. I knew I couldn't stop him. Still, it took me another long minute to let go of his hand.

"I'll be back," he said. "I promise."

David shrugged off his thermal blanket. "I'll help."

Grandpa stopped him, and readjusted the Mylar back around his small shoulders. "The best thing you can do for me, son, is stay here with your sister." He gave us both serious looks. "Stay put and get some rest. I'll be back in a few hours." He kissed us each on the head and left.

David slowly climbed back up into his chair. He took everything as a slight against his capabilities and I could tell Grandpa's words had affected him.

"He didn't mean it like that," I said.

David stared at the floor. "Yes, he did."

Raised voices drew my attention to the door. Several bearded men barged into the rotunda, followed by a woman in a white bonnet. All four of them were draped in brown canvas ponchos with large yellow crosses embroidered on the front. They were CBCers.

They marched over to the man lying on the stretcher. It looked like the man's bleeding had stopped, but, instead of thanking Doctor Reinkann, the CBCers started shouting at him.

"You had no right to put your hands on him!"

"You have defiled my husband!" the woman wailed.

"Apostle Phillips," Doctor Reinkann began, "without treatment this man will die."

The tall, bald man, leader of the Cascadia Baptist Church, insisted on being referred to as the apostle. He led a group of religious preppers who lived in a commune outside of town. They didn't use technology and refused to associate with anyone who did—especially doctors.

"That is not up to you!" the apostle bellowed. He looked at the other two angry, bearded men. "Pick up Brother Eric."

The two men moved into action.

Doctor Reinkann protested. "You can't take him—"

The apostle stepped in front of the doctor and gave him a murderous glare. "We can! And we will!"

I held my breath, waiting to see if the doctor would insist. CBCers could be brutal when it came to protecting their own. A kid at school had found that out the hard way when he'd stolen a poncho off an elderly member. They'd jumped him in an alley two days later.

The doctor wisely backed down, allowing the apostle and his people to take the dying man away.

Tim Odette wandered over to us, shaking his head. "Poor fella. His family won't let the doctor help him."

David grunted. "They think their God will heal him."

Tim sat down in Grandpa's vacated chair. "So how you doin', Double D?"

David scowled and pulled his thermal blanket tighter around his shoulders. He hated Tim's nickname for him—Double D for David Donner.

"I'd be doing a lot better if I had a cellphone in my hand."

"Wouldn't do you any good." Tim downed a bottle of water. "Power and cell services are out. Nothin' but a shrieking tone on the landlines. Our folks flew to Texas two days ago; Milly and I haven't been able to get ahold of 'em yet."

"What about FEMA?" David asked. "Or the National Guard."

"Haven't seen any soldiers. Just a lot of sad, hurt people. And looters—I've seen a lot of those." Tim broke into a smile, smacking David on the shoulder so hard he almost knocked him out of his chair. "I sure am glad you're all right, Double D. You, too, Sera. Your grandpa was worried sick about y'all last night."

David exhaled his irritation and righted himself. For some reason—unknown to anyone but him—when Tim had arrived from Austin he'd decided to be David's best friend. Unfortunately, my brother had been punched, shoved, tripped, and mocked his entire life by guys like Tim. So, naturally, he assumed Tim was just setting him up for a big embarrassment down the road.

Milly walked up, wiping her hands on a paper towel. "If one more person comes in here bleedin', I am runnin' from this building screamin' my fool head off."

Her assessing blue eyes fell on David. "Did you get somethin' to eat?"

David's attention dropped to his lap.

"They've got fruit and sandwiches in the cafeteria." She arched her brows at his lack of response. "I'd be happy to fetch ya some."

David shook his head and muttered something that sounded like, "No thank you." I'd suspected for a while that my brother had a crush on Milly Odette; now the fact that her presence suddenly struck him mute confirmed it.

Milly looked at me. "Sera?"

"I'm fine." I was starving. I wasn't sure why I'd lied— maybe I just didn't like the idea of Milly Odette doing me a favor. It was too late to take it back, anyway.

"Well, you look just horrible," she declared. "That dress is—" She looked me up and down and grimaced. "Come with me." She turned on her heel and headed toward the back hallway.

I gaped at David, who shrugged, clearly not caring that his twin sister had just been insulted by Hillbilly Barbie.

"She's in drill sergeant mode," Tim warned. "You best go with her before she comes back lookin' for ya."

I scowled at Tim. In what universe did I jump because Milly Odette said so?

"I hear there's some donated clothes in the cafeteria," Tim added.

Clothes? The idea of finally getting out of the filthy, ruffled dress overrode any issues I had about Milly. "I guess it wouldn't hurt to check it out."

I pulled my Mylar blanket tighter around my shoulders, grateful it covered the dress, and trailed after Milly.

She led me past several empty offices, then into the cafeteria where dozens of people sat at long tables eating sandwiches and apples. My stomach growled at the smells, but food wasn't my priority at the moment.

Milly stopped in front of a table piled high with grocery

bags overflowing with clothes. I saw pants, shirts, socks, shoes—even underwear.

She slid a couple of bags my way. "Folks started bringin' in donations yesterday."

I dropped my blanket, no longer caring about the dress I had on, and started tearing through the clothes.

"There's bound to be somethin' in there that'll fit ya." She wrinkled her nose at me. "That dress is awful."

Something Milly and I could both agree on.

I quickly found a pair of jeans, a Washington State Huskies sweatshirt, and pair of worn running shoes—all in my size. "I'll take these."

Milly nodded. "Follow me."

She walked me into the ladies room, where a large frosted window lit up the small space. The jagged hairline fracture in the glass must've been a gift from the earthquake.

"Water's not on," she told me, "so don't use any of the toilets. They've set up Porta Potties out back if you need one."

With clean clothes clutched in my hands, I could feel my spirits beginning to lift. And then I caught a glimpse of myself in the mirror.

I stared in shock at my reflection. My hair had come loose from the updo my mother had painstakingly styled for the wedding. It now fell in a tangled, coppery, mess around my head. A thick layer of dirt coated my face, making my eyes look big and haunted. Muddy tearstains ran from my lashes down to my cheeks, and over my jawline. My nose was red and chapped where I'd been wiping it on my sleeve.

The ruffled dress was ruined. The front ruffle was torn where my mother had grabbed it to pull me away from the plummeting church bell; dirt and sweat stained the purple fabric. I knew the red splatters across the front had to be my mom's blood.

Unable to stop myself, I covered my face with my hands and cried.

After a few moments, I heard Milly pull several paper towels from the dispenser on the wall. "My mama says that when people encounter real tragedy in life, they divide into two groups, the quitters and the fighters." I heard the glug of a bottle of water as she continued. "She says, 'And it's up to you, Milly Lynn Odette, to decide which team you're gonna be on.' Here." I sniffled and peeked through my fingers. She held out a wet paper towel. "Let's get you cleaned up."

I wiped my face and scrubbed my arms and legs, trying to scour the tragedy off my skin, while Milly pulled out a brush and started working on my tangled hair.

"Our house is completely gone," she told me. "Ground swallowed it right up. 'Course, it swallowed up that godawful shed out back, too, so there's your silver lining. Did your mamma do your hair? I can tell it was real pretty before the quake got it."

"My mom——" My voice cracked. "My mom is…. She's missing."

Milly's eyes met mine in the mirror. "I'm so sorry." Her face turned pink. I thought she might start crying, which would have been an emotional disaster for us both. Instead, she swallowed hard and continued brushing. "There's a lot of people missin'—mostly kids. Folks have started tapin' pictures of them on the Miner's Memorial outside."

She pulled my hair back into a ponytail and secured it with an elastic band. "There. You're all set."

My reflection almost looked like a live person again— even if I didn't feel so alive on the inside.

Milly gave my shoulders a steadying squeeze. "Hang in there, Miss Sera. You're not as alone as ya feel."

Before I could start crying again, I took my donated clothes into one of the stalls and closed the door. I kicked off my pointy flats, then couldn't get out of the filthy purple dress fast enough. But, just as I was about to toss it to the floor, I had second thoughts. I pictured Mom sifting through the discount rack and finding it. As much as I hated the shiny fabric, the over-sized ruffles, and the washed out lavender color, something about it had appealed to Mom. She'd been thinking about me. She'd bought it just for me.

After I put on the jeans, sweatshirt, and running shoes, I left the stall with the purple dress in my hand. For almost twenty-four hours I'd been desperate to get rid of it and suddenly I couldn't part with it.

Milly looked me over, then nodded her approval. "Welcome to Team Fighter, Sera Donner."

That's when I decided to stop hating Milly Odette.

We left the ladies room together, heading back to the rotunda. I felt clean, human again, ready to take on the world—and then I saw the crowd gathered outside the front doors. *More drama?* My heart squeezed at the thought.

Milly paused. "Now, what's that all about?"

I tossed the purple dress onto a chair and we hurried over to see what was happening.

Everybody was staring up at the sky. I peered over the broad shoulders in front of me and saw an enormous, dense wall of black clouds rolling in from the east, churning with frightening intensity and speed. It was a monster storm; unlike anything I'd ever seen.

"Yikes," Milly said. "That's a soaker."

Doctor Reinkann stood at the front of the crowd, urging everyone back inside. "All right now. Everybody back into the rotunda, please. We are likely to see lightning strikes and some sizable hail from a storm this size. Come on, now. Back. Back inside where it's safe."

A shock of alarm shot through me. I looked around the crowd. "Where's David?"

Milly pointed at a blond head near the door. "I see Tim."

We pushed our way through the crowd toward him and I took hold of his arm. "Where's my brother?"

Tim looked down at me, his face weighted with worry. "He ran off."

"He *what?*"

"He took one look at the sky and said he had to find your grandpa."

My heart lurched. The wind was picking up. Things were getting bad fast.

Tim shook his head. "I shoulda stopped him."

"It would have been easier to stop the storm," I grumbled. "I have to find him."

"We'll help you," Milly insisted. "I need a break from blood and bandages."

Ignoring the ominous threat hanging in the sky above, the three of us hurried through the courtyard and out into the street. I looked both ways—past the earthquake wreckage—but couldn't see David.

Milly pulled her brother around to face her. "Which way did he go?"

Tim shrugged. "I dunno, Mills. He's pretty quick for a little guy."

Then I remembered what Deputy Hester had said. I knew exactly where my brother was heading. "The library."

We took off running up Idaho Street, past Marko's Place, past the Brick Bar & Grill, and past Suzy's Sundries—

all of them demolished by the quake. It didn't take long before I spotted David up ahead of us. He galloped through the rubble at an alarming pace for somebody whose short, bowed legs barely bent at the knees.

We caught up with him as he turned onto Dakota.

"Grandpa told us to stay put!" I shouted. *How dare you scare me like that!* I wanted to add.

Though out of breath, David didn't stop. He simply pointed up at the sky.

"Yeah," I griped. "Another reason to stay in city hall."

David refused to slow down, leaving us no choice but to follow him.

We found our grandfather standing with Deputy Hester and Mayor Skaggs outside the shell of what had once been the Roslyn Public Library. Rescuers in protective masks swarmed the site. The roof had collapsed. The walls were cracked and crumbling. There were books scattered everywhere.

We rushed up to them as Mayor Skaggs mopped his forehead. "...about fifteen minutes before the storm hits."

"We have a problem," David blurted.

Grandpa frowned down at him and then at me. "I thought I told you two to wait at city hall."

David, gasping, pointed at the sky. "See that?"

"We are aware of the storm," the mayor replied.

David, trying to catch his breath, shook his head. "It's... not a storm."

The mayor smirked. "All right, son, we don't have time for—"

"Now, hold on a minute, Frank," Grandpa Donner interrupted. "Let's hear the boy out."

David took a deep breath. "Did you hear the sonic boom before the earthquake?"

Grandpa nodded. "I heard that."

Deputy Hester frowned. "It was a fighter jet from——"

"No." David cut him off. "When a jet breaks the sound barrier, you don't hear one sonic boom."

All the color drained from my grandfather's face. "You hear two." His attention flew back up to the darkening sky. "My God."

The mayor looked up. "Well, if it's not a storm, then what the hell is it?"

David's answer sent a chill racing through my body. "It's an ash cloud."

Chapter Four

We raced back toward city hall, the dark, ominous ash cloud looming high above our heads. We'd been given permission to take supplies from Jorgenson's Hardware, so now Tim hauled a four-foot bundle of heavy plastic over one shoulder. Milly and I carried large cardboard boxes of protective masks, and David had rolls of duct tape slipped over each of his short arms with several box cutters jammed in his pockets.

The streets were empty. All rescue efforts had been stopped, the people ordered to seek shelter from the danger rolling in from the east. Thanks to my brother, a lot of lives would be saved that night.

A distinct smell hung in the air. It made my throat burn.

Milly's nose twitched. She sniffed. "What is that?"

"S...Sulfur," David answered.

Tim grimaced and coughed. "How bad is this gonna get?"

"'Pends...on the wind." David, out of breath, was having a hard time keeping up. We'd had to stop and wait for him a couple of times.

"Is it Mount St. Helens or Rainier?" I asked.

David shook his head. "Neither."

"Wait." I scowled. "What do you mean *neither*?"

He stopped to catch his breath. "Mount St. Helens is that way." He pointed to the south. "Rainier is that way." He pointed to the west. "Do the math."

"And what's that way?" Tim pointed to the cloud rolling in from the east.

David was getting frustrated. He didn't have a lot of patience for amateurs like us. "Yellowstone."

Tim started laughing. "The *park*? Double D, that ain't a volcano."

David gave Tim a death glare. The only crime worse than questioning my brother's ability was questioning his intelligence. "Yellowstone is the largest volcanic caldera *in the world*," he answered tightly. "The last time it erupted— 640,000 years ago—it caused an *ice age*."

Tim blinked. "Well, that don't sound good."

Milly shifted the large box in her hands. "Can we keep goin', please?"

We took off running again, weaving through the empty, decimated streets. By the time we made it back to city hall, the sky had gone as dark as a moonless night. We found hundreds of people tucked inside the building, bracing themselves for the expected thunderstorm. And Mayor Skaggs didn't want them thinking any different. To prevent what he called "widespread panic," we had orders not to tell anybody about the eruption.

Despite the size of the crowd in the rotunda the noise level hovered at a low murmur. Somebody had placed hand-cranked LED lanterns around the cavernous room, which cast creeping shadows against the marble walls and added to the unnatural mood. David and Tim recruited people to help them tape heavy sheets of plastic over the broken windows and glass front doors. Milly and I handed out protective masks.

If asked what the masks were for, we said what the mayor had told us to say, "Mayor Skaggs will be here soon. He'll answer your questions then." But, really, there was too much trauma in the room for anyone to pay much attention to what we were doing. Injuries ranged from bumps and bruises, to missing limbs and deep comas. Most had either lost someone in the quake or knew somebody who had.

I climbed to the middle of the open staircase and sat down on a cold marble step to keep an eye out for Grandpa. He'd promised to meet us back here before the ashfall started. Milly soon joined me, then the boys sat down two steps below us. I focused my eyes on the oversized portrait of the governor of Washington hanging on the two-story wall and wondered if the rest of the state was bracing for the worst—if they even understood what was coming.

A few moments later, the mayor and my grandfather shoved past the sheets of plastic now draping the front doors. They brushed a dusting of fine gray powder from their clothes, then Grandpa ordered the plastic sealed tight behind them. His eyes searched the crowd until he found us perched on the staircase. He nodded in our direction.

The mayor climbed up onto a chair in the center of the rotunda so everyone could see him. "Ladies and gentlemen?" he called out. "May I have your attention please? As of this moment, we still have not received any contact from agencies outside our community. But we do have some information regarding the storm currently enveloping our town. It is, in actuality, an ash cloud."

That revelation pulled people from their stupors. Heads

turned with interest, and patients sat up on their cots. As the news sank in, the murmur in the room rose to a steady buzz.

"Is it Mount St. Helens again?" somebody called out.

"I have no further details at this time," the mayor replied. "But the windows and doors are sealed, so we are perfectly safe in here."

My stomach lurched. *Perfectly safe.* Pastor Rick had said that right before he was impaled by a stained glass window.

"Did the eruption cause the earthquake?" somebody else asked.

"I have no information on that."

David grunted in front of me. He'd given the mayor plenty of information, but the mayor chose to discount it. It was because David was a kid, but my brother assumed it had more to do with his condition than his age.

"There are sandwiches and bottles of water available in the cafeteria," the mayor reminded everyone. "The town's water main was disrupted by the quake, so please don't use the restrooms. There are Porta Potties set up outside the back service door if anybody has the need. When we have any more information, we will let you know."

"This is a direct result of our government's secret weapons testing!" a ragged voice called from the back of the room. Mr. Victor was in his eighties and not shy about voicing his opinions, no matter how ridiculous they might be. Last month he'd raised a stink about the new RFID scanner guns at the Roslyn Market. He believed they were government tracking devices.

"Are you sure it wasn't aliens, old man?"

The muscles in my brother's back tightened beneath his grimy shirt. That voice belonged to Steve Skaggs, the mayor's son, a senior at our school. Steve had a nose like a toucan, but that didn't stop him from making fun of everybody else's flaws. David had become one of Steve's favorite targets on the first day of our freshman year.

Steve was standing with two of his buddies, Cody Richmond and Luke Milton—both equally repulsive. I couldn't help noticing that their leader, Micah Abrams, was missing. Had he been killed in the quake? My heart sank a little at the thought.

Mr. Victor defended himself. "Our government knows more than they're tellin', young man."

"That's a relief," Cody shot back, "because you sure don't." He laughed and high-fived Steve.

"All right," Grandpa said. "Let's keep it civil."

The boys offered my grandfather mock salutes, then laughed and moved on to harass somebody else.

Tim leaned closer to David on the step. "So, Yellowstone? Is that bad?"

"It's bad," my brother replied.

Milly pursed her lips. "I don't s'pose you could elaborate?"

David surprised me by turning toward Milly. To my knowledge, it was the first time he'd ever looked her in the eye. "It's extinction bad," he clarified.

Milly snapped her mouth shut and looked at me. I shrugged, not sure what I was supposed to add. My only knowledge of Yellowstone came from an eighth-grade field trip and all I remembered was mud pits, geysers, and David running around with a Junior Ranger kit.

"I read all about Mount St. Helens in history class," she retorted. "And *it* wasn't the end of the world."

David closed his eyes and rubbed his forehead. He had to be really stressed if Milly was getting on his nerves. "Mount St. Helens was like a firecracker; Yellowstone is like a nuclear explosion." He pivoted so he could better make his point. "Mount St. Helens released less than three cubic kilometers of debris. The last time Yellowstone blew, it ejected over twenty-five *hundred* cubic kilometers of material into the air. That's enough ash to bury Texas ten feet deep. The volume of material Yellowstone could potentially shoot into the stratosphere would put the entire world in a volcanic winter for seven years."

Milly gaped at him. "How did you get so smart?"

David, suddenly remembering who he was talking to, flushed a brilliant shade of red and spun back around, front and center.

"What's the heck's a volcanic winter?"

Tim's question made David's shoulders droop.

"It's a reduction in global temperatures," I answered. "Volcanic ash and sulfuric acid block the sun's rays, which makes the earth cold." Milly stared at me in surprise. "What?" I said in response. "He's not the only Donner who reads."

My stomach rumbled noisily. I still hadn't eaten anything. Remembering the delicious smells in the cafeteria, I stood and picked up a nearby lantern. "I'm getting some food. Anybody want anything?"

"Good here," Tim said.

"I'm fine," Milly responded.

"Whatever you're having," David mumbled.

I headed down the staircase, thinking I might take a couple of turns around the hallways to get rid of some nervous energy. As I walked past the front doors, I noted the fine layer of gray powder forming on the threshold, and paused. It looked like off-color talcum powder. I bent to touch it, wanting to know what it felt like, wondering if we'd have to shovel it like snow and leave it in piles at the end of our driveway.

Suddenly, the plastic covering over the doors flew open and a large gray animal burst inside. I screamed, scrambling backwards—and then I recognized Peter Williams, the school bus driver. Ash covered him from head to toe. The stuff even wafted in behind him, drifting across the slick tile floor in a misty gray cloud, prompting several people to rush forward and reseal the plastic over the door.

"They're gone!" Mr. Williams shouted. Tears smudged his ash-covered face. "All of 'em! Gone!"

Mayor Skaggs hurried over to him. "What are you talking about, Williams? Who's gone?"

The big bus driver took a fistful of the mayor's royal blue windbreaker and pulled him to his face. "My family!" His voice cracked with a sob. "They're all gone! Every last one of 'em. Taken!"

People started murmuring.

"Taken?" Grandpa asked. "By who?"

Mr. Williams spotted my grandfather and hurried over to him. "Sheriff!" he cried. "Sheriff, they're gone! *They're gone!*"

"It's okay, Peter." Grandpa put his hands on the man's shoulders and looked him in the eye. "It's all right. Who took them? Who took your family?"

"The white light!" Mr. Williams wailed. "It was the white light!"

I dropped my lantern.

It clattered to the floor, rolling to a stop by a pair of boot-clad feet. I looked up. Micah Abrams, head bully, stared at me from the shadows. He wasn't dead after all.

His broad shoulders shifted as he bent down to pick up my lantern and hand it back to me.

Heart lodged firmly in my throat, I managed to whisper thanks as I took it from him.

SUZANNE LEONHARD

He didn't say a word back. He just stood there, watching me.

I scowled at him and turned away. My feelings for him unsettled me enough without him staring at me like he'd never seen me before.

"It shot down from the sky and sucked them all into the air!" Mr. Williams continued to wail. "I couldn't—" His voice broke. "I couldn't hold onto 'em! It's comin' for us!" he shouted to the crowd. "It's comin' for all of us!"

Panic rippled through the room. Everybody started talking at once.

"What's he talkin' about, Mayor?!" somebody shouted.

"Who's coming for us?!" somebody else yelled.

Mayor Skaggs stepped forward. "All right, Peter," the mayor said. "We're gonna get you all taken care of." He stuck a needle into the bus driver's arm and the man dropped like a sack of potatoes.

My grandfather caught Mr. Williams before he hit the floor. "Was that really necessary?" Grandpa Donner demanded.

Mr. Williams moaned and tossed his head, but the sedative had drained the fight out of him.

"We've got a lot of frightened people in here, Sheriff," Mayor Skaggs replied. "The last thing we need is Williams, or anybody else for that matter, panicking them with stories of people getting sucked into the sky."

"Sounds like the work of aliens to me!" Steve Skaggs laughed.

I turned to see what Micah Abrams thought of his buddy's remark, but Micah was gone. The shadows, from which he'd so mysteriously appeared, had swallowed him up.

"Maybe it was the rapture!" Cody Richmond jeered.

Several people chuckled.

"I hardly think so." Eliza Cole, standing a few feet away with Coach Stephens, seemed recovered from her husband's passing. She flashed her standard condescending smirk. "I think I'd know if it was the rapture."

"Probably the Russians!" Mr. Victor bellowed. "They've been workin' on a tractor beam for years!"

"I vote we give Mr. Victor one of those shots," Steve taunted.

"All right," Grandpa called out. "Let's settle down. We've got a lot of injured people in here, so please be courteous to your neighbors."

The mayor gestured to two men standing nearby—Cody and Luke's dads, not much nicer than their sons. "Lem? Andy? Why don't you find Mr. Williams a nice private office where he can sleep it off?"

The men took possession of Mr. Williams, hauling him off down the dark hallway. As I watched them disappear into the shadows, I vowed that I would never say a word to anyone about what had really happened to my mother.

I'M FLOATING in the water. Warm. Safe. My feet touch the beach. White sand between my toes. A roar from the water. Red glowing eyes. Sharp teeth sink into my neck.

I woke with a start. I lay tucked beneath a warm blanket on a small sofa in the city assessor's office. A lone lantern lit the room. Its bright glow painted the walls an icy white and illuminated a large pendulum clock. It was 5:00AM.

I shook off the disturbing dream and sat up.

Before turning in for the night, the boys had snuck out the back service door and measured less than an inch of ash on the ground. This meager amount surprised David, but it gave the rest of us hope that he'd overstated his predictions of doom and gloom.

I wondered if the ashfall had stopped yet.

I pushed aside the blanket and eased my legs out over the edge of the sofa. Milly lay sound asleep on the floor a few feet away, still holding the red teddy bear Tim had found for her in one of the offices. She'd let me have the sofa—in fact, she'd insisted on it after I'd spent the previous night trapped in a giant porcelain bowl. The Odettes had been in town for six months and, the whole time, I'd assumed they were fake southern snobs. I was wrong. Tim and Milly were the real deal.

I left the room and padded down the hallway, glancing into the cafeteria as I passed. A few people were up and milling about, but most were still sound asleep, stretched out on the floor, or sprawled on the long tables and benches.

I made my way to the back service door to check out the ash and use a Porta Potty. Before I could push open the door, a voice brought me up short.

"Oh, good."

When I turned around, Eliza Cole stood in the hallway behind me. She was wearing a pink velour jogging suit. Her eyes were still puffy, but she'd tried to dress them up with concealer and mascara.

"Be a dear and take this to Mr. Williams in the county clerk's office." She held out a plate of food.

Mayor Skaggs had insisted that Mr. Williams remain locked up until he stopped ranting about abductions. Doctor Reinkann had assigned Eliza the task of looking after him because of her nursing background.

The very last thing I wanted was to face Peter Williams and his white light ravings. "Isn't that your job?" I asked.

Her eyes flashed. She shoved the plate into my chest. "Do as you're told."

I took the plate and watched Eliza saunter off toward the kitchen, probably to sit and whisper with Coach Stephens.

I followed the hallway to the county clerk's office. The door was locked, but I found the key in the knob and twisted it to open the door.

A single lantern threw long shadows over a tall bookcase and upholstered love seat. Mr. Williams sat in a leather chair, behind a large wooden desk. He didn't move when I came in. He just kept staring out the single window into the darkness beyond. It was creepy.

I took a deep breath and closed the door behind me. "Mr. Williams?" At first, I was afraid the sound of my voice might startle him, but he didn't move.

Then his answer filtered through the room, weak but calm. "Yes?"

I edged toward the desk. "I…I have some food for you."

He turned in his chair to stare at me from a gray, drawn face. He looked like he hadn't slept.

When he saw me, his bloodshot eyes flew wide and he lunged forward in the squeaky chair. "Did you see it?" He shouted so loud that I felt sure the entire building had heard it.

I took a step back. "What?"

"The *light!*"

"N-no." As much as I wanted to say yes—to finally admit to someone what I'd seen—I wasn't willing to take the chance of being locked up in my own private room.

He calmed down and sank back in his chair. "I had an uncle who disappeared near White River twenty years ago," he muttered. "Friends said they saw a bright, white glow

SUZANNE LEONHARD

over his tent that night." He paused and stared at me with glassy eyes. "Fella in Naches went missin' for thirteen days back in the nineties. Folks thought he was dead. 'Til he showed up walkin' along Highway 12 thirteen days later without a stitch a clothes on. Said a bright white light had picked up his whole truck and pulled him into the sky."

His eyes grew shiny with tears. "They were makin' dinner. My daughter and granddaughter were over for the weekend. My wife was cookin' their favorite. Beef Stroganoff. When the quake hit, we all headed out to the backyard and sat down in a circle on the grass, holdin' hands, just like they tell you to do."

His chin quivered and my heart clenched.

"It took my granddaughter first. She was just four years old. Floated up like a feather. I tried to hold onto her, but I…" He lowered his head. "I couldn't. My wife and daughter went next. There was…there was nothin' I could do." He sniffed. "They were both smilin' when it happened." His eyes lifted and met mine. "How am I supposed to endure without 'em?"

He started sobbing, then turned his chair back to the window to stare out into the darkness. "Maybe in thirteen days we'll find 'em walkin' down the road without a stitch of clothes on," he murmured. "Just like that fella in Naches."

Chapter Five

The ash stopped falling on the second day, leaving just four inches on the ground—a far cry from the apocalyptic amounts predicted by my brother. David stood by his theory about Yellowstone, however, citing wind change and blind luck to explain away the lower ash totals.

Mayor Skaggs, on the other hand, insisted that it was Mount St. Helens, assuring people that aid was on the way. Though I'd never admit it to my brother, I was in the St. Helens camp. Clearly the eruption had been smaller than David had expected. Surely help would come at any moment. But *any moment* stretched into two long weeks without a single word from the outside world.

It didn't help that phone and power lines were still down, and shortwave radios couldn't penetrate the ash-choked sky. The citizens of Roslyn may have been spared the worst on the ground, but it was an entirely different story in the sky. Ash clogged the upper atmosphere, blocking light from the sun, the moon, and the stars, leaving the town cloaked in heavy darkness day and night. Even at high noon you couldn't see your hand in front of your face without a flashlight. According to David, this suffocating darkness could last for months.

Out of the city's population of 2,893, the sheriff had declared 964 dead or missing. Of those, only 413 bodies had been recovered, including Alyson. My best friend and her family had been found on the fifth day, beneath their collapsed house. But 551 people remained unaccounted for, including, oddly enough, every kid under the age of twelve.

The strange case of the missing children seemed to give Peter Williams' claims of a white light abduction more cred —which really pissed off Mayor Skaggs. People were starting to listen to the bus driver, prompting more and more claims of family and friends being carried off by a mysterious white light. Several neighborhoods started buddy systems. Some people were even locking themselves in their homes to keep from being abducted themselves.

Finally, after a tense week, Mr. Williams led a small group that stormed the sheriff's office, demanding an investigation into the "White-Light Abductions." Mayor Skaggs had shut the group down fast, citing a city ordinance that prohibited public incitement. He'd demanded that my grandfather lock up every one of the agitators. Rather than go to jail, the people had quickly recanted their claims and dispersed, ending the white light conspiracy movement— and any hope I had of finding answers.

My mother was among the 551 missing.

Grandpa believed she'd fallen through the floor and into the basement, where her body now lay buried beneath tons of stone and rubble, too deep to be recovered. I didn't correct him. Mr. Williams' story about the man from Naches was never far from my mind. Maybe someday Mom would come walking back into town without a stitch of clothes on.

David and I were living with our grandfather now, in his

house on Third Street. With their own home destroyed and their parents out of town, Milly and Tim had decided to stay with us. Every night, I had the same nightmare about oceans and dragons and, every morning, I woke to darkness and forced myself to think of a reason to get out of bed. Today, I got up hoping that we'd finally clear a path to the interstate.

I stepped back from my shovel to adjust the mask covering my nose and mouth. All able citizens had been split into four groups: search and rescue, forage, cleanup, and support. I was on cleanup. My team was part of the main effort to reconnect Roslyn with I-90.

A massive landslide on South Avenue had obstructed the outlet at the neck of the valley. A team had been using dynamite on it for most of the day, so every now and then I'd hear a loud *BOOM!* It shook the ground beneath my feet, bringing back memories of the quake. After several hours, my nerves were raw.

Using snowplows, front loaders, backhoes, shovels, and sometimes bare hands, cleanup teams like mine slowly dug out the town, loading the ash and debris into trucks, then dumping it into the Willamette Ravine. It was a filthy, miserable job, made more difficult by the protective masks we had to wear.

Doctor Reinkann had declared the masks mandatory for cleanup crews in particular, to protect us from something called silicosis, some horrible lung disease that caused a lingering, painful death. The sweaty, smelly masks made it impossible to be heard without shouting. Over the past few days I'd seriously considered ditching the miserable thing and taking my chances with the lung disease.

I picked up my shovel and started back at it. My team was working on a winding part of Bullfrog Road that ran alongside Prospector Golf Course. Crank lanterns lit the zone and, between those and the headlamp Grandpa had given me, I could almost pretend it was daylight. By the time actual night fell, the hard, tedious work, always left me drained. I just kept telling myself that every shovel I lifted put me one step closer to Seattle and my dad.

David walked up, pulling a large cooler strapped to a wagon. The lanterns threw shadows across his face, deepening his scowl. He'd been assigned to the water purification team, arguably the most comfortable job to be had. With the power out and the pumps down, the city's only water source was the Cle Elum River, currently a useless sludge of ash.

Of course, David assumed he'd been given the job because he lacked the size or strength to do anything else, not because he was one of the few people in town smart enough to operate and maintain the city's complicated water purifiers. While the rest of us were sweating and hauling ash, my brother spent most of his time clean and indoors— and grumbling about discrimination.

He handed me a ladle of water. I clicked off my headlamp, tugged my mask down around my neck, and drank. The cool, clear water felt good going down my gritty throat. I wanted to tell David how much I appreciated it, but I knew better. Thanking him would only give him an excuse to launch into another tirade about how a monkey could do his job.

I handed the ladle back without a word.

Mr. Chaney, our vice principal, walked up. He and I were on the same cleanup team, along with Milly, Grandpa, Tim, and several other people. "How are you, Sera?"

"Okay," I replied. *Miserable*, I thought.

The vice principal lifted his mask to drink the ladle of

water David offered. A big man, he savored his drink with one hand while mopping sweat from his brow with the other. Finally, he sighed. "Thank you, David." He handed the ladle back.

"You're welcome," David grumbled, but it was hard to hear him through his mask. He might have said something rude, which wouldn't have surprised me a bit.

"I wanted to thank you, young man, for alerting everyone to that ash cloud," Mr. Chaney said.

Although Mayor Skaggs had tried to take credit, Grandpa made sure that everybody knew it was David who'd sounded the alarm.

David fidgeted with the cooler.

"You saved a lot of lives," Mr. Chaney added.

My brother's silence became awkward. Finally, I spoke up for him. "He was glad to help."

The vice principal smiled at me, then pulled his mask up over his nose. "Well. Back to work." He ambled off toward the dump truck.

I turned on David. "You could at least be polite."

"Don't play holier-than-thou with me, Sera," he replied through his mask. "I'm not in the mood."

"*You're* not in the mood?" I retorted. "I end every day with ash caked to my skin and my clothes, and stuck between my teeth! But, hey, it could be worse—I could be on the water purification team!"

He tugged down his mask. "I saved these people," he growled. "And the only reason I'm not cleaning Porta Potties right now is because my arms aren't long enough."

He was determined to be miserable, so I started to walk off and leave him to it. Then Steve Skaggs strolled up with his mask down around his neck, Cody and Luke in tow.

The look in my brother's eyes changed from irritation to seething hatred.

Steve snatched the ladle from David's hand. "Hey, Little Stinker, you helpin' the girls out with water? Where's your dress?"

Cody and Luke laughed.

"I left it with your makeup case," my brother replied.

Steve loomed over him. "What did you say to me, Little Stinker?"

David glared up at him. My brother had never backed down from a fight in his life—not even when Micah Abrams had dropped him in a dumpster on the first day of school. Micah had come away with a broken finger, though David had ended up spending a full class period sitting in rotting garbage before somebody'd finally fished him out. That incident earned my brother the nickname Little Stinker.

Raising my shovel in front of my chest like a polearm, I stepped between my brother and Steve. "Leave him alone, Skaggs."

Steve cocked his head at me. "Look, guys, it's Little Stinker's dog."

I felt my face go hot. "This dog bites," I retorted. Hopefully he wouldn't call my bluff and find out that I could never hit him or anybody else with a shovel.

Steve reached out to touch a strand of my hair. "Is that a promise, Red?"

"Just let 'em do their jobs, Steve," a deep voice called out.

Micah Abrams stepped into the circle of lantern light. Tall, dark-haired, and broad-shouldered, he stole all the air out of my lungs. I hadn't seen him since that first day in city hall. I knew I shouldn't be—and my brother would hate me if he guessed—but I felt relieved that he was alive.

Steve sneered at his friend. "What's your problem now, Abrams?"

Cody shoved Micah backwards. "I think that quake shook some screws loose."

I looked on in surprise, realizing there was trouble among thugs.

"Maybe we shoulda left him in that hole," Luke jeered.

Micah gestured at my grandfather working a few yards away. "The sheriff's standin' right over there, guys."

The three boys looked over to where my grandpa and Mr. Chaney were pushing a car to the side of the road. They immediately adjusted their postures from menacing to casual.

"Unless you feel like spendin' the night in jail," Micah added, "you should probably leave the sheriff's grandkids alone."

Steve jabbed his finger into Micah's chest. "I've about had it with you, bro."

Micah raised his hands. "Just lookin' out for ya, man."

Steve glared at Micah, and then turned to his two cohorts. "Come on, guys."

Cody and Luke sniffed at Micah, then followed Steve off into the shadows.

Micah turned his attention on me, his hooded, dark eyes revealing nothing. I instantly remembered why I'd had such a big crush on him in middle school. He was two years older than me and Jewish, which, to a white atheist girl, seemed incredibly mysterious. I spent all of sixth grade daydreaming about Micah Abrams.

But then he'd gone to high school and started hanging out with Steve Skaggs. I heard all the rumors about drinking, fighting, robbery. My grandfather had personally arrested Micah five times. But I could get past all that. Then he'd dumpster-dunked my brother the first day of our freshman year and the make-believe romance between me and Micah Abrams ended abruptly.

Micah nodded at David. "Sorry about that, man." He sounded sorry, but what he'd done in the past made that hard to believe.

David wasn't buying it. "Are you looking for applause?"

Micah shrugged. "Just tryin' to do the right thing."

"Yeah, right," David sneered. "I guess it was too much to hope that they'd find you buried at the bottom of a ravine somewhere."

I gasped, shocked that my brother could say something so hateful. I looked at Micah, expecting him to say something vicious back, but he just stood there, as if waiting for more.

"No mask, Abrams?" David quipped. "Well, maybe we'll all get lucky and you'll die slowly from the inside out."

"David!" I gasped.

My brother's steely glare cut me to the bone. "Do you have something to add, Sera?"

Yes and no. I didn't know what to say. I stood there with my mouth working. No sound coming out.

A loud scream saved me from myself. It cut through the heavy air and echoed all around us.

I dropped my shovel and took off running; it sounded like Milly. She and Tim had been working beside a wrecked lumber truck, trying to move a large pile of plywood from the middle of the road. I hurried up beside them.

My grandfather charged up. "What happened?"

Pale and shaken, Milly pointed at a wide crack in the asphalt.

I edged closer and peered down into the fissure. The glow of lanterns danced over a figure sprawled inside.

Milly had found a body.

I clicked on my headlamp, illuminating a long, male arm. I bent closer. My heart froze. A scarlet tattoo of a red-tailed hawk swooped down the length of the lifeless limb.

I HID behind the shattered timbers and dented white siding that used to be the Sportland Minimart and bawled my eyes out. I gasped and huffed through my mask until I finally tore the thing off my face. I had managed not to cry for two weeks, but seeing Eric Hawk dead in a hole had shattered my record.

The moment I'd seen the tattoo on his cold, dead arm, I'd known the truth. We were all going to die.

Nobody was coming to help us. The food would run out. The water purifiers could only last so long. We could barely breathe the air, even with our masks on. We would all end up like Eric, dead in a dark, ashy grave.

I pulled my knees to my chest and tried to calm myself. I felt like I was trapped in the font again with no hope of rescue. Who were we kidding? Two weeks with no word? David was right. Civilization was gone.

A throat cleared.

I opened my eyes. A baseball-shaped object floated under my nose. I quickly wiped the tears from my face and switched on my headlamp. It was an apple, clutched in a large, dirty hand. Micah Abrams was crouched in front of me.

"Have it," he said, like taking something from him was the easiest thing in the world. He wiggled it enticingly. "Go ahead."

My stomach growled in response. Grandpa was only

allowing us two meals a day, just in case we needed to stretch our food supply longer than expected. Without even touching it, I could taste the apple's sweetness on my tongue.

But I knew it would be a bad idea to accept something from Micah Abrams; my brother definitely would not take it well. Besides, why would Micah offer me his precious piece of fruit? It had to be a trick.

"Don't trust me, huh?" He grinned. "Don't blame you." He sat back on his heels and took a crisp bite out of the apple.

He still wasn't wearing a mask. "We're supposed to wear masks."

"And that is very good advice." He took another bite, making me regret my decision not to accept the apple. "You should definitely follow it." He swallowed. "I'm sorry about Eric Hawk. So, you really liked him, huh?"

He was *sorry*? Why all these apologies all of a sudden— first David and now me? Well, I still didn't believe him. Bullies were never sorry. They fussed, sniveled, and gave in when they got caught, but they never really felt bad about anything.

"Why are you talking to me?" I demanded.

He smiled. "You're direct. I admire that. Why am I talking to you?" He shrugged. "Because you're upset and I wanna help."

I snorted.

He finished the apple and tossed aside the core. "Listen. I heard about your mom."

All my defenses shot up. "My mom is none of your business."

"They found my parents yesterday." The sudden emotion in his voice surprised me, as did the tears he quickly blinked away. "In the hole where my house used to be."

"At least you know where they are," I retorted. It was a mean thing to say, and I instantly regretted it.

He looked me straight in the eye. "You don't know where your mom is?" An innocent question, but his cool expression implied something more. "Are you sure about that?"

I narrowed my gaze. "What do you want, Micah?"

"I told you. I wanna help."

I didn't want his help. I wanted him to go away. The dark stare that I'd found so appealing now suddenly felt like a probe rummaging around in my head, trying to dig up secrets.

"Terrific!" I snapped. "The world ends and I draw the school bully as my personal savior." I bit my lip to hold back a new round of tears. *No!* I screamed inside my head. *You will not cry in front of Micah Abrams!*

"What happened to your mom?"

With that one question, he'd gone too far.

"Why do you care?" I screeched at him. "She'll never be found—is that what you wanna hear? You wanna know all the sordid details of my life, Micah? My dad is in Seattle where I can't get to him! I've spent the past two weeks digging through piles of wreckage and ash and...and *dead bodies!*" I forced out. "Oh, but sure, an apple will solve everything. It'll find my father! It'll—" I choked up. "—it'll bring my mom back! Go!" I spat at him. "Get out of here! Go find somebody else to shove your fruit at. I don't need your help, and I don't want it!" I pushed him so hard he fell backwards onto the ashy pavement.

He lay sprawled there for a moment while I caught my breath. *What have I done?* Micah Abrams was no longer the boy I'd fallen for in grade school. He was a cruel bully and he would retaliate. Would he throw me in a dumpster, or worse? And then it dawned on me that I hoped he'd come after me in some way. Being angry felt so much better than being sad and afraid.

"And you can tell your friends that they better leave my brother alone!" I added for good measure, "because next time I'm going to hit Steve Skaggs right over the head with that shovel!"

Micah sat up. I steeled myself for what I felt sure would be brutal revenge. "Seraphina," he said firmly. "It's going to be all right."

I blinked. Of all the things I thought he'd throw back at me, reassurance was not one of them.

"Listen to me." He looked into my eyes. "It's going to be all right."

Tears spilled down my cheeks. "That's a lie," I gritted out. "Nothing will ever be all right again."

He reached for me. "Seraphina—"

I slapped his hands away hysterically. "Don't-don't touch me—don't you *touch* me! We're dead! We're all as dead as Eric!"

Ignoring my protests, he pulled me into his arms. I fought him, but not hard—I was exhausted, emotionally, and physically. I longed for the white light to shoot down from the sky and steal me away. I wanted the ground to open up and swallow me whole. I needed to wake up from this nightmare.

Micah held me tighter. Somehow, he knew that, in spite of my protests, I needed someone to wrap themselves around me and stop my world from flying apart. He felt warm and solid and, with one big sob, I slipped my arms around his neck, pressed my face into his shoulder, and cried harder than I ever have in my life. I cried for my mother and for Pastor Rick. I cried for Felicity and her husband of five minutes. I cried for David and all of my friends. And then I cried for myself, for the life that had been stolen from me in one great ashy explosion.

Micah never said a word. He just sat there quietly and let my tears soak his coat. When I was done, when I felt like I could finally breathe again for the first time since being trapped beneath the stage, I stayed right where I was—in Micah's arms. He was an unexpected anchor in the middle of a surging storm and I couldn't bring myself to let him go.

A loud shout broke the moment. "Get away from my sister!"

A small body slammed into us, knocking Micah—and me—to the ground.

Horrified, I untangled myself from my brother's bitter enemy and surged to my feet. "David, wait—"

"You don't touch my sister!" David raged.

Micah stood. At almost six feet tall, he towered over my brother like a colossus.

Undeterred, David glared up at him, his headlamp casting ghoulish shadows over Micah's face. "Ever!" With nothing else for a weapon, my brother hurled the ladle at Micah. It hit the taller boy in the face and bounced to the ground.

Micah clenched his fists. Thinking he was about to surge forward in retaliation, I reached for his arm, but he surprised me once again by taking a step backwards.

His retreat only made David more confident. "If you ever," David seethed, "come near my sister again, I will—"

I made the mistake of stepping in between them. "Micah wasn't hurting me!"

My brother looked at me with a mixture of disgust and betrayal. "You're *defending* him?"

"No! I...I mean—" I glanced at Micah. What did I

mean? "I was upset and he——"

"I was trying to help," Micah interrupted. "No harm done."

David lit into him again. "You don't get to decide what harm looks like!"

"Shut up, David," I gritted. He didn't know when to quit and he was pushing his luck with a boy three times his size. I turned to Micah. "Just go."

"Are you gonna be okay?" he asked me.

It was a sweet question, and I felt my cheeks heat up. "I'll be fine."

He nodded. "Okay, then. I'll see you later."

"Over my dead body!" David shouted past me.

I watched Micah walk away and the world went dark again. I turned on my brother. "What the *hell* is wrong with you?!"

"What's wrong with *me*?" David seethed. "I come looking for you to share some good news and I find you wrapped around that son of a bitch!"

I could see the situation through David's eyes. He wanted me to give him a reasonable explanation for being in a body lock with his mortal enemy, but I didn't have one—at least not one that he'd understand.

"He was helping me," I said weakly. It was the best I could do.

"Helping you what?" David sneered. "Get over your dead boyfriend?"

"That is a horrible thing to say."

"It's a horrible thing to do."

He turned to leave, then I realized what he'd said. "Wait! What good news were you coming to tell me?"

"The landslide's cleared." He threw the words back over his shoulder. "We're heading out to find Dad."

Chapter Six

The next morning, we set out for Seattle.

Grandpa had no illusions that the interstate would look any better than our local streets, so he planned to drive as far as he could and then we'd hike the rest of the way into the city. We loaded backpacks full of water, MREs, and flashlight batteries into the Kittitas County Sheriff's SUV, and climbed into the cab—the boys in the back seat, Milly and I in front with Grandpa. We headed to the Shell station near the roundabout on Highway 903 to siphon gas and meet up with the rest of the convoy.

"Whacha got there, Double D?" Tim asked in the back seat.

"It's a yellow scarf I found in the donations box. Did you know that in tenth-century France, they painted traitors' doors yellow to warn decent people to stay away from them?"

I rolled my eyes. David hadn't spoken to me since the Micah incident. I didn't blame him. If I'd caught him wrapped around Naomi Laswell—the girl who'd called me carrottop for years—I'd have a hard time forgiving him, too.

The right thing to do was apologize to him. The problem was that I'd felt better since crying all over Micah. I'd slept without nightmares for the first night in two weeks. I wasn't sorry for finding comfort in Micah's arms. Not one little bit.

"Nossir, I did not know that," Tim replied. "But why'd ya bring it?"

"I was thinking Sera might need it."

Milly gave me an odd look. I shrugged and played dumb.

We rumbled through town with our high beams cutting through the darkness. The plow on the front of the truck made easy work of the little bit of ash and debris still on the streets, but we had to drive slowly and cautiously anyway. Cleanup crews had cleared the big stuff, but occasional fractures in the asphalt required some creative steering.

All of us sat in reverent silence as we followed Washington Avenue past the Eagles Lodge and the burnt-out remains of Marko's Place. We drove beneath the tattered banner for Coal Miner Days stretching from sidewalk to sidewalk, then swerved around the fallen, ten-foot totem pole that had overlooked the Snohomish Woodcarvers shop. We slowly passed the Brick Pub—now just a mountain of red bricks—and rolled by the collapsed Purple Anntix store. I started fingering a length of my hair, braiding and unbraiding it, trying to keep my mind focused on something other than the wreckage lit up by our high beams.

Several vehicles waited for us in the parking lot of the Shell station. Deputy Hester was there in his Dodge pickup with the dented fender from hitting a bear last spring. Vice Principal Chaney leaned against the door of his ancient Chevy Suburban. Charlie Eagle and Vivica Davis were riding together in Charlie's CRV—because they had a secret romance that the entire town had known about for months.

We waited in the cab while Grandpa got out of the SUV to coordinate with Deputy Hester and the others. I could hear Tim and David talking in the back seat about what they planned to do in Seattle. Tim hoped the phone lines would work so he could get ahold of his parents in Texas. Like me, my brother just wanted to see our dad.

A Jaguar came zipping into the parking lot and jerked to a halt. The driver's door popped open and Steve Skaggs got out.

My heart sank. *Just what I need.*

Then things went from bad to worse. The passenger door eased opened and Micah slid out of the car. I heard David exhale loudly. I couldn't catch a break.

"What're *they* doin' here?" Milly questioned.

Tim snorted. "Probably hopin' Seattle Cannabis is still open."

"Or maybe," my brother added smoothly, "Micah is hoping to make out with Sera again."

I squeezed my eyes shut, knowing that Milly would not let this one slide.

"What?" she blurted. She gave me a dramatic, slack-jawed look. "And how long has *this* been goin' on?"

"Yes, Sera," David said, "how long?"

"Wait," Tim interjected, "I thought she had a thing for Eric Hawk?"

"Yes, but he's dead now," David replied.

Milly looked confused. "Wasn't it Micah who put you in that smelly ol' dumpster?"

"One and the same," David quipped.

Tim grunted. "I guess the heart wants what the heart wants."

"Could everybody just shut up, please!" I shouted.

Stunned silence filled the cab. I slumped lower in the

seat, burning with embarrassment. I couldn't deny that Micah and I had shared a moment, but I wasn't about to explain myself either. So, I sat there like a guilty lump, silently detesting my brother.

Grandpa climbed back in behind the wheel. "We all set?" Nobody answered. He looked around at each of us. "What'd I miss?"

"Ask Sera," David replied.

Grandpa's eyes settled on me. "Sera?"

"Nothing," I snapped back. "Everything's just fine."

His mustache twitched at my tone. "All right." He threw the SUV into gear and headed toward Interstate 90 and the Issaquah Valley, the other vehicles following close behind.

I kept my eyes focused out the front windshield. Soon I'd be with my dad, safe, warm, fed. The nightmare of the past two weeks would be nothing but a distant memory we all tried hard to forget. Milly reached over to pat my hand, smiling her kind smile when I looked over at her. However it had happened, I was glad Milly and I were now friends.

When we finally took the entrance ramp onto west Interstate 90, my heart dropped. Milly let out a breath. The freeway was an obstacle course of wrecked cars, fallen trees, and bent light poles—like an apocalyptic demolition derby. I stared at the dented green sign that read *Seattle 77*. Seventy-seven miles might as well have been a million.

"Difficult," Grandpa said, "but not impossible."

Our convoy rumbled forward, weaving through the frozen traffic, pausing often to clear obstructions and push aside cars. Most of the vehicles were empty and we scavenged what we could from them—food, water, car batteries, treasures from gloveboxes. Although we found signs that people had been camping in their cars, we didn't see anybody else on the freeway.

The ash covering the ground got shallower the further west we drove, but the darkness only seemed to deepen. Every turn of the tires weighed heavier on my hope. I wasn't sure what I'd expected to find outside of Roslyn, but it wasn't this bleak, lifeless landscape being revealed, bit by bit, in front of me. When our headlights finally illuminated the next sign for Seattle, we all groaned. We'd been at it for hours and the city was still forty-five miles away.

We passed a Traffic Advisory Sign:

TUNE IN TO 1610 AM FOR TRAVELER INFO

There wasn't a signal in Roslyn; I doubted there'd be one out here. I reached for the radio anyway.

"It won't work," David warned from the back seat.

"It never hurts to try," Milly answered. "Go ahead, Sera."

I clicked the knob. Static filled the cab. Afraid to hope, I held my breath, punched the AM button, and slowly turned the knob until the display read 1610. Nothing but static. My heart sank and I clicked off the radio.

"Told ya." My brother never knew when to shut up.

Several hours later, we reached the east summit of Snoqualmie Pass. The number of abandoned cars on the freeway multiplied, creating a winding maze that separated the vehicles in our convoy. Most of the vacant cars we passed were wrecked and piled on top of each other, but some just sat in the middle of their lane as if they'd been parked there.

"Where did the drivers go?" Milly murmured.

"That depends on who you ask," David grunted.

Tim sniggered. "Haven't ya heard, Mills? A big white vacuum cleaner came and sucked 'em all up."

Milly threw him a look over her shoulder. "That doesn't help, Tim."

While the boys laughed in the back seat, I kept my attention glued out the front window, anxious for any sign of life beyond our truck. It felt like we were the only people left in the world. For the first time I started to worry about what we'd find in Seattle. A few minutes later, we cleared the car maze. Nothing but dark, empty road stretched out in front of us. I frowned and glanced at Grandpa. He was focused on his rearview mirror and the fact that he couldn't see the headlights of the cars behind us anymore.

Our headlights flickered over a wide shadow ahead of us on the pavement and I narrowed my eyes.

What is that?

And then I knew. "Hole!" I shouted. "Hole in the road!" I grabbed the dash and braced for impact.

Grandpa Donner slammed on the brakes and yanked the wheel hard to the left. The SUV jerked, lunged, did a three-sixty in the slippery ash, before slamming sideways into the center divider. We came to a jarring stop.

"Sorry—sorry! Is everybody okay?!" Grandpa asked.

Heart pounding, I stared out the front window at the long dark gap of missing pavement just feet in front of us. I did a quick mental check of all my limbs. Other than a tweaked neck, I felt fine. I looked over at Milly. Her eyes were wide and she was breathing hard, but she looked okay, too.

"We're good," Tim said from the back seat.

"Yeah," David said. "Fine."

Grandpa threw on his siren and flashing lights to warn the others coming up behind us. We all spun in our seats to see if everybody got the signal.

Deputy Hester, in his Dodge pickup, had been behind us

since leaving the Shell Station in Roslyn. His headlights flickered as he emerged from the car maze. The lights bounced, then shifted sharply to the left. We heard the roar of an engine as his four-wheel drive kicked in against the slippery ash. His truck thrust forward and screeched to a stop behind us.

Mr. Chaney's suburban swerved, as did Charlie's CRV, then they both pulled up in line behind Deputy Hester.

Steve Skaggs was another story. His Jaguar emerged from the maze of cars and, instead of slowing down, picked up speed. He raced right up to the hole—as if the rest of us pulling to the side was an invitation for him to take the lead. When he finally slammed on his brakes, it was too late. With a high-pitched squeal, his tires tried to gain traction in the slick ash. The car fishtailed. His headlights shimmied, then dropped out of sight. His taillights shot up like red UFOs and held there, bouncing in midair.

I sucked in a breath. *Micah!*

I couldn't get out of the car fast enough.

Multiple headlamps flared to life as everybody swarmed the site. I hurried to Steve Skaggs' car, the smell of burned rubber and asphalt filling my nose. I couldn't believe my eyes. Steve's rear mag wheels were smoking and hanging in midair, six feet off the ground. His Jaguar had dropped forward through the hole in the freeway. Its undercarriage had caught against the thick, jagged pavement—that, and the way the Jaguar's fragile hood propped precariously against the opposite lip, had saved him. But it wasn't over yet. The whole mess creaked like it was about to give up the fight.

I could hear wind whistling up through the hole in front of me. My mind formed an image of a deep, jagged ravine lying directly beneath my feet.

Vivica Davis said what I was thinking. "Dare we hope it's only a few feet down?"

Charlie Eagle cracked a yellow glow stick and tossed it into the hole. We craned our necks and watched it drop until it disappeared.

Definitely more than a few feet deep.

Shouts came from inside the car. I turned my headlamp toward the cracked driver's side window and saw Steve dangling from his seat belt. He had a death grip on the steering wheel and he was sweating grenades. "Shut up!" he screamed at the top of his lungs. "Shut up! Shut up!"

Grandpa and Deputy Hester fired up some crank lanterns, lighting up the site with an eerie blue-white glow. I skirted around the back of the car to the passenger side to check on Micah. He was sitting calmly in his seat with his feet braced against the dash. Though dangling over certain death, he looked completely relaxed. In fact, if not for Steve's shouts, I'd have thought they were just two friends having a casual conversation.

Milly crouched down beside me to look in at Micah. "What's he sayin'?" she asked.

"I don't know." I couldn't hear his calm words over Steve's wailing.

"Whatever it is," Tim said, "Steve doesn't like it a whole lot."

Micah turned his head and looked at me through the window. He gave me an easy smile and a confident thumbs-up.

I scowled at him.

"That boy is just odd," Milly stated.

No kidding.

The adults scrambled around the Jaguar with their headlamps and flashlights, trying to solve the problem before it ended in tragedy. Finally, Mr. Chaney came up with an idea. "I think we should all climb onto the back of the car and force the back wheels to the ground. Then we can just pull the vehicle back from the hole."

"That would be extremely stupid," David spoke up. He'd been quiet up till then—most likely hoping the car would hurry up and fall, taking Micah and Steve with it.

"The kid's right." Charlie was shining his flashlight on the road beneath the Jaguar's undercarriage. "Look at the cracks in the pavement over here. The combined weight could break it away and send this whole bridge into the ravine."

As if in response, the car creaked and shifted, the nose of the hood denting under the added pressure.

"Okay, everybody," Grandpa called out. "Let's move back a bit."

Charlie Eagle owned his own construction company. If he said the entire bridge could go, then my grandfather wasn't taking any chances.

Fear gripped my stomach. I cast one last look at Micah —who'd gone back to talking to Steve—and then hurried across the bridge to join the others.

Vivica crossed her arms. "Well, somebody has to do somethin'."

Grandpa nodded. "We're gonna pull 'em out." The other adults gave him a skeptical look. "Anybody got any better ideas?"

Charlie stared over at the car bathed in lantern light. "The slightest shift could dislodge that hood."

"Then we best be careful," Grandpa replied. "Charlie, you open the door on the passenger side. I'll pull Micah free. Tim, you open the door on the driver's side, and, Jim, you pull Steve free. We do this slowly and together."

Everybody scrambled into position while me, Milly, David, and Vivica watched from the sidelines, our four headlamps glowing brightly against the underside of the car.

"Let's do it," Grandpa called out.

With a metallic click and then a steady groan, shadowed figures on both sides of the car eased open the doors. The car complained—creaked—shifted—but stayed put.

Milly grabbed my arm. I fought the urge to look away.

"Slow and steady, fellas," I heard Grandpa coach. "Slow and steady."

They got the doors halfway open; it looked like the plan would work. And then Steve panicked. He shoved open his door and lunged for Jim Hester's hand. The entire vehicle teetered off balance. Jim pulled Steve free. The car lurched as the hood screeched off the pavement's lip.

The Jaguar began a slow, grinding slide into the black abyss below.

I held my breath. The world spun in slow motion. Charlie Eagle flung the passenger door open. Grandpa reached inside. The car dropped through the hole with an ugly groan, taking Micah and my grandfather with it. I heard Milly gasp, followed by the angry crunch of metal on rock far below me.

I felt numb. My legs tried to buckle. The sound of people shouting broke through the hum in my ears, and I pulled my eyes open. *When did I close them?*

The Jaguar was gone.

The four of us rushed forward to where Mr. Chaney lay splayed on his stomach.

He had hold of Charlie Eagle's belt.

Charlie had hold of a pair of legs in jeans and black cowboy boots.

Grandpa.

My heart lunged as I looked down. My grandfather hung halfway through the hole in the bridge, saved only by Charlie Eagle's quick thinking and iron grip.

Tim and Jim scrambled in, carefully taking hold of Grandpa. They slowly pulled him up from the hole...and Micah appeared. I almost laughed with joy. Grandpa Donner had his hands locked into the front of Micah's jacket.

Milly broke into wild applause.

Viv whistled and clapped her hands. "Nice job, gentlemen!"

Tim slapped David on the back. "Your grandpa's a superhero."

David nodded quietly. I knew he felt relieved that our grandpa was safe, but I was equally sure he felt annoyed that Steve and Micah hadn't done a header into the ravine with the Jaguar.

We created a barrier of cars in front of the bridge to prevent anyone else from driving into the hole, then back-tracked to Exit 52. From there, we drove the wrong way on the eastbound side of the freeway. With Steve's Jaguar gone, he and Micah rode with Deputy Hester. Micah seemed unfazed by his brush with death, but Steve was badly shaken. Pale and sweating, Steve kept muttering something under his breath, but nobody could quite make out the words.

We proceeded at a crawl toward Seattle, on high alert for gaps in the pavement. It took constant weaving in and out of cars, trees, and occasional rockslides, but every mile forward was progress.

Several hours later, we reached the outskirts of Preston

and saw a green interstate sign tipped sideways on the shoulder.

SEATTLE
22

Milly and I fist-bumped each other. *Twenty-two miles.* I almost cried from relief. The Issaquah Valley lay just ahead of us.

And then David said three words. "Where's the glow?"

Grandpa squinted through the windshield. "Good question."

Milly focused her eyes into the inky black distance ahead of us. "Whaddya mean?"

Grandpa pointed into the darkness beyond his headlights. "We should see the glow from the city on the horizon there."

Tim leaned forward from the back seat to get a better look. "Are we close enough?"

"Maybe the ash in the air is too thick," I suggested, but uncertainty was growing in the pit of my stomach.

"Maybe," David muttered.

We sat quietly in our seats, eyes peeled out the windows, each of us anxious to get that first glimpse of city lights. *Just a little closer*, I told myself. *It'll be just around the next bend.*

Five minutes later we came to the end of the road. The Lake Creek Road overpass had collapsed onto both sides of the freeway. Three semitrucks lay sideways across the rubble, wrapped around each other like metal pretzels.

The convoy stopped and Grandpa got out of the SUV to meet up with the other drivers. We watched their headlamps bob as they walked around the scene, surveying the situation.

"There's no way around this mess," David announced.

"Are we close enough to walk?" Milly asked.

I nodded, hoping. "Maybe." We'd come too far to turn back now.

The adults gathered together. There were a lot of heads shaking and my heart sank deeper into my stomach. Finally, Grandpa came back and opened the driver's side door.

"Please don't say we're givin' up," Milly whispered.

He shook his head—"Nope"—and climbed back into the cab. "But we've gone as far as we can on the freeway."

He threw the SUV into gear, wrenched the wheel to the left, and drove around several cars until he was rolling slowly along the shoulder of the freeway. He took the exit and followed an access road for about a mile before pulling into a gravel parking lot. The other drivers rolled up beside us, their headlights reflecting off a wall of trees that hid a deep forest beyond.

"Get your packs," Grandpa told us. "We hike from here."

I scrambled from the truck, grabbed my stuff, and congregated with the others on one of the railroad ties bordering the parking lot. My nose tickled and I fought off a sneeze. There wasn't much ash on the ground here, but it was enough to bother me.

I clicked on my headlamp and stole a peek at Micah. He looked relaxed and focused, definitely not like somebody who'd almost died a horrible death a few hours ago. Steve, on the other hand, still looked dazed—and he was still muttering. I moved closer to my grandfather, hoping to avoid them both.

Charlie shined his flashlight toward the tree line, searching. "There." He lit up the face of a National Parks sign.

TIGER MOUNTAIN TRAILHEAD
ELEVATION 3005 FEET
SUMMIT 9.3 MILES

We all turned to look. The beams of our headlamps bounced off trees and dense underbrush before converging on the park sign and, beyond that, a well-marked trail through the woods that disappeared beyond our lights.

Grandpa moved forward. "All right, everybody, stay together."

We followed him into the forest.

The darkened trail picked its way along the mountain ridge, pausing occasionally at signs for places like *Carl's Hollow* and *Betty's Cove*. It wound around moss-covered boulders and cut through prickly blackberry thickets, leading us higher and higher into the Northern Cascades. The adults gravitated to the front of the group, leaving the four of us to straggle along at the back, with Micah and mumbling Steve bringing up the distant rear.

Milly moved up beside me. "What happened between you and Micah?"

I gritted my teeth, but tried to be polite this time. "Nothing important."

She cast me a skeptical glance. "But somethin' *did* happen?"

"Why is this such a big deal to you?"

She blinked at me. "Because we're friends. And friends are supposed to tell each other stuff."

We were friends now, weren't we? Come to think of it, Alyson would have been mad at me, too, if I'd kept something like this from her.

"Hey, you guys?" Tim called. He and David moved up beside us. "Skaggs is seriously givin' me the heebie-jeebies."

David snorted. "The world would be a better place if he'd fallen into that hole."

Milly gasped. "David Donner, what a terrible thing to say."

David's shoulders drooped. Besides my parents, I'd never met a soul in the world who could prick my brother's conscience, but Milly Odette had just done it with one gasp.

"I know Steve isn't the nicest person in the world," Milly continued, "but that doesn't give anybody the right to wish him harm."

"Speakin' of harm," Tim remarked, "what's up with Abrams? He hasn't called Double D 'Little Stinker' once this entire trip."

"Maybe he's changed," Milly offered. "What do you think, Sera?"

Milly and Tim looked at me expectantly—they were driving me crazy. "How should *I* know?" I retorted.

David grunted. "People don't change. They just get better at faking it."

"Bridge here," Grandpa called out. "Watch your step."

We came to a narrow wooden bridge across a wide mountain creek. Tim crossed first. I followed, but the sound of distant, roaring water stopped me in the middle. I moved my head around, shining my light into the woods, trying to get a better look at what I was hearing.

Milly and David scooted past me. The bridge creaked under their weight.

In the shadowy, yellow light I could just make out the shape of a cove fed by a high waterfall that tumbled over rocks and bushy ferns. The bridge, obviously a lookout, offered what must have been a spectacular view in full daylight.

Taking advantage of the moment, I closed my eyes and

listened to the tranquilizing sound of the rushing water. I let myself forget where I was. No eruption. No earthquake. The sun was bright. Mom and dad were behind me on the trail—

The bridge shifted. I opened my eyes. Micah stood beside me at the railing and my deceitful heart stuttered.

"Enjoying the view?" he joked.

I snorted. "Breathtaking." I looked up the trail and saw the bobbing lights of the others walking on ahead of us. If I ever wanted my brother to speak to me again, he'd better not see me standing alone with Micah.

"Listen, I'm sorry if I got you in trouble yesterday," he offered. "I know your brother doesn't like me very much."

"Understatement of all time," I replied under my breath.

Steve Skaggs scooted past us, still muttering to himself.

I waited until Steve had crossed the bridge and then turned to Micah. "What, exactly, is wrong with him?"

"Who, Steve? He's surrendering."

"Surrendering? To what?"

Micah arched his dark brows enticingly. "Truth."

I laughed. "What truth?"

Micah's eyes crinkled. "What truth?" He had a cool confidence that I found seriously distracting. "There's only one, Seraphina. But most people don't like to hear that—people like Steve. And then one day it hits them right in the face. *Bam!*" He slammed his hands together and I jumped. "Suddenly everything comes down to just one, quick choice." He leaned closer and for one horrifyingly thrilling second, I thought he might kiss me. "When your moment comes," he whispered, "choose wisely."

This was the Micah I remembered from grade school: charming, hypnotizing, irresistible. We stood there looking at each other, the lights from our headlamps blending into one magical glow around us, and I suddenly felt the urge to tell him about my mother.

"Micah——"

I heard my Grandpa shout my name. "Sera? Keep up!"

David's mocking voice drifted back to me. "She's hanging out with her boyfriend."

And, just like that, the magic was gone.

I stepped away from Micah, shocked by what I'd been about to reveal to a boy who, up until a few weeks ago, had spent his free time using my brother as a piñata.

"What were you about to say?" he asked.

"Nothing." I turned to leave, but he grabbed my pack and yanked me backwards against him. He startled me so badly I almost fell off the bridge. "What are you doing?!"

"Listen to me," he rasped in my ear. His urgent tone was frightening. "Stay close to me at the top. Promise."

Maybe Micah hadn't changed after all.

I wrenched myself away from him. "I'm not promising you anything. And don't you ever grab me like that again."

"Seraphina, you——"

"*Ever again.*"

I hurried across the bridge and up the path toward the bobbing line of lights—away from Micah, past the other kids—until I was walking safely beside my grandfather. One tearful hug in the dark hadn't earned Micah the right to put his hands on me or to tell me what to do.

Grandpa glanced over at me. "What was the holdup back there?"

Charlie Eagle grunted. "They were trying to decide which one of us to eat first after we get them good and lost."

"No contest," Deputy Hester called out. "Eat Chaney."

The vice principal hitched up his pants. "That's right,

pick on the fat man. I'll have you know this here is one hundred percent pure muscle."

"Chaney's not fat," Steve Skaggs quipped. It surprised me to see him walking casually beside the vice principal as if he hadn't been muttering incoherently to himself for hours. "He's just short for his weight."

The adults laughed at his joke. *I guess he's finished surrendering to truth,* I thought with a grunt.

"Some women like a little meat on a man," Viv responded. I liked Vivica Davis. As head of the city council, she'd led the effort to build a trampoline park for the local kids instead of another golf course for tourists.

The deputy chuckled. "I think ol' Don passed *little* quite some time ago."

"Don't pay any attention to that skinny fella, Don," Viv retorted. "He's just jealous because he's so hard to see in the dark."

We crested the peak of the trail and broke through the tree line. The path spilled out onto a vast, pitch-black meadow, stretching forever into the darkness.

I took a step forward. Out of nowhere, a powerful, frigid wind kicked up and hit me full in the face. It stole my breath, knocking me back a few steps.

Steve Skaggs rushed past me, like a sprinter heading for the finish line. He was muttering again, but this time I caught a portion of what he was saying. "…will of the father," he whispered.

A few yards out, he turned to face us all. "I'm at the top!" he shouted. He walked backwards with his hands in the air, like he'd just won a race. He laughed and pointed at Micah. "I'm still here—"

The world became a snapshot. I remember the wind rushing in my ears. The tangy smell of sulfur in my nose. The mushy feel of ash beneath my feet. Steve Skaggs uttered a sharp, short cry. And then nothing. He vanished—as if the ground had swallowed him whole.

We all stood there, boggling, trying to understand what had happened.

Grandpa took charge. "You kids stay here."

He edged forward, followed closely by Deputy Hester, the vice principal, Vivica, and Charlie Eagle. Without thinking, I tried to take a step forward, but Micah had hold of my backpack again and wouldn't let me move.

"Wait," he whispered to me.

My first thought was to defy him, since he obviously hadn't learned his lesson from the first time he'd grabbed me. But then I realized—if not for that blast of frigid wind —I would have been the one walking out first into that dark meadow. Maybe it wouldn't hurt to wait just a few more seconds.

I saw my grandfather stop short. He stood still for a moment, then slowly sank to his knees.

The others lined up next to him.

Deputy Hester's shoulders slumped. "What the…"

Vivica started crying. Charlie Eagle put his arm around her shoulders to comfort her.

Don Chaney was shaking his head. "How?"

"What's happening?" Milly whispered beside me.

"What is it?" Tim called to them.

David moved forward first, followed by Tim, and then Milly. They all stopped in a neat row, beside the adults. Nobody said a word.

I finally shook Micah off. He let me go and I hurried forward.

When I reached the spot where Grandpa Donner was

kneeling, his arm shot out in front of me. "Stop!" he ordered.

I froze. And then realized I couldn't take another step even if I'd wanted to. There was no other step. I stared out over nothingness, over an abyss, with thousands of bouncing red lights spread out in the distance. Micah stepped up beside me, slipping his arm through mine to steady me.

"Is that the valley?" I asked. *Why is it moving?*

"No," Grandpa rasped.

The sound of rushing water floated up to my ears. We all looked down. Our headlamps bounced off dirt, rock, roots, until finally illuminating a churning, angry surf. We were standing on the edge of a jagged cliff with angry waves crashing a hundred feet below.

"It's the Pacific Ocean," David answered.

Confused, I raised my eyes and looked out at the red lights. For a moment I thought we'd gone off course, that we'd missed a turn somewhere and walked all the way to the shore. But then I realized I wasn't looking at lights. They were fires, bobbing on an ocean choked with debris.

And, in the distance, illuminated by the flames, waves cascading over its proud, gold dome, was the top of the Seattle Space Needle.

Chapter Seven

I stood in the center of the churning crowd at city hall, watching the play of light on the rotunda walls. Dozens of crank lanterns lit the large room, giving the illusion of a bright, white day. Heavy plastic still sealed the doors and windows against blowing ash, but someone had scattered comfortable furniture around the room in an attempt to make everything look normal. But everything wasn't.

Seattle lay at the bottom of the Pacific Ocean and the citizens of Roslyn were having a hard time dealing with that fact. The entire town had packed into the rotunda, all demanding answers.

Grandpa stood on the second step of the staircase, trying to calm the crowd. Mayor Skaggs was understandably absent. He'd just been told about his son's death, not six months after he'd lost his wife to cancer. We probably wouldn't be seeing the mayor anytime soon.

So far I'd managed to hold it together, but Milly was a blubbering mess. She was standing directly beside me and I knew I would burst into tears if I even looked at her. Tim was doing his best to console her, but if she didn't quiet down soon, I would have to find another place to stand.

David hadn't said a word since Tiger Mountain. Like me, he was wrecked by the loss of our father. But Dad's death meant more than the loss of another parent to him, it also meant the loss of the cure for his condition. This disaster had not only taken our dad, it had taken my brother's hope of being made normal. In David's mind, he'd just been given a life sentence of inadequacy.

Micah, who had come in with Cody and Luke, stood at the back of the rotunda. My mind kept going back to that moment on the bridge, when he'd told me to stay close to him at the summit. It almost seemed as if he'd known what we would find when we got there. If not for that wind….

The crowd was amping up.

"Just tell us what's goin' on!" John Voss shouted. He was a bank teller from Cle Elum, but he now wore a gun on his hip.

"Based on what we saw," Grandpa answered, "we believe the Cascadia fault slipped during the eruption and subsequent quake. It looks like Seattle and its surrounding communities are a total loss."

The room exploded in gasps and shouts. I got jostled to the side and accidentally stepped on Milly's foot. "Sorry, Milly," I muttered. She was so lost in grief, I wasn't sure she'd even felt it.

Deputy Hester put his fingers to his lips and let out a shrieking whistle, bringing the crowd up short.

"What happened to Steve?" shouted Cody's dad. He was a small man with a big snarl.

Grandpa cleared his throat. "During the course of our hike, Steve Skaggs fell over the precipice. His body could not be recovered."

Andy Milton—Luke's dad—jeered. "Did you even try?" Mr. Milton worked at Harper Lumber, reeked of beer, and always had a cigarette tucked behind one ear.

Lisa Butler raised her hand. "Did you see anybody?" I remembered her sitting on her lawn, rocking her dead dog, the day Grandpa had led us from the church to city hall. Now she wore pajama bottoms and her short hair was so greasy that it lay flat against her head.

"No. But that doesn't mean there aren't survivors."

Several people shouted questions at once.

"One at a time!" The deputy bellowed.

Grandpa pointed to Sharon Webber, the Roslyn Grocery manager. All her stock—along with everything the foraging groups found—was being kept in a large, community warehouse off Arizona Street. "What about Bellingham? I...I have a sister there."

"We don't have specific information on Bellingham or any of the other coastal cities."

Grandpa pointed at Robert Ormann. He and his wife Jenny owned the local farmers market. "My dad broke his hip in the quake. He needs long-term senior care. We need help. If this is such a big crisis, why haven't we had any contact from federal agencies?"

Grandpa's eyes found us in the crowd. It was time to let the town in on the whole truth behind our situation. "David? Would you come up here, son, and tell the folks what you know?"

David wormed his way to the front and climbed to the sixth step on the staircase. The room fell quiet. "Good morning," he said sheepishly. When no one answered, he cleared his throat. "Yellowstone is made up of a chain of large lava pools called calderas," he began. "Scientists have mapped out about fifteen of them stretching from the north-west corner of Wyoming to the southeast corner of Oregon. These lava pools interconnect with several smaller pools throughout Nevada and California. An intricate maze of fault lines weave across these calderas—" He held up his hands, lacing his short, round fingers to illustrate his point. "—including our own Cascadia and the San Andreas in California. An eruption at Yellowstone has the potential to trigger earthquake swarms in all the major fault lines across the North American continent, from Vancouver to San Diego. If that has happened…then the entire west coast could be gone."

Everyone in the room stared at him in stunned silence.

"As for the rest of the country, we're talking tidal waves, extreme weather, and inches—if not feet—of ashfall. It is possible," David continued, "that the entire country, maybe the entire world, has suffered a cataclysmic multi-event, which would explain why we haven't heard from FEMA. Because there is no FEMA. Not anymore."

"This is ridiculous!" Lem Richmond bellowed. "Everybody knows it was Mount St. Helens that erupted!"

"Get this kid outta here!" Andy Milton sneered. "Just because his daddy is a bigwig scientist, doesn't mean we have to listen to him! Where are the experts?!"

"In Seattle," Grandpa responded.

The room hushed again.

"Listen, people," he continued. "I admit that the scenario my grandson is describing is dire, but we're gonna keep sending out patrols in the hopes of connecting with cities outside our county area. We need to get past the shock and start thinkin' fast if we expect to come outta this thing on the right side of daylight."

"What good are patrols gonna do us?" Lem Richmond spat.

"Our mission here in Roslyn hasn't changed, Lem," Grandpa stated. "We need to get basic services and utilities up and running. We need to start rebuilding. And we need to reconnect with the outside world. But everybody has to work together or we're all gonna be lost."

A deep voice boomed from the doorway. "Well, thank you, Sheriff Donner!"

I was shocked to see Mayor Skaggs walk into the rotunda, followed by several very large men who stationed themselves by the door.

"Appreciate the speech," he continued, "but it lacks flare." He crossed the room and climbed one step higher on the staircase than David. "I'll take it from here, kid." The menacing look he gave my brother sent a shiver down my back.

Then the mayor turned to the crowd. "Good people of Roslyn," he began. "The sheriff is right. It has become clear that our entire country has been hit by a devastation greater than anything this planet has known since the dawn of recorded history. It's time to face the facts. We are on our own." He gave my grandfather an intense stare. "So, before any more of us *die*," he said pointedly, "we're gonna need a plan."

"That's right!" Eliza stated.

"We're gonna run out of food and water pretty soon," John Voss added.

"My pantry is almost empty," eighty-two-year-old Ava Gorski whimpered. Her husband of fifty-five years had been killed during the quake.

Grandpa held up his hands. "Folks, we've got teams out gathering food and supplies from abandoned homes and buildings every day—"

"And how long do you think that's gonna last, Sheriff?"

Mayor Skaggs demanded. "A week? Maybe a month? We are in a crisis, people! A crisis with no visible end! Ash is choking the life out of our world. Animals are dying—birds are literally falling from the sky. Lemme add this up for you folks." He held up his fingers and counted off. "We have zero sunlight. That equals zero plants. Which equals zero animals. Which equals zero food for you and me. Zero food equals zero people. This is an extinction level event, ladies and gentlemen! And we need to decide, here and now, if we are going to be victims of this devastation or *survivors*!"

He said this last word with such enthusiasm that the entire crowd cheered. I had to force myself not to join in. It was inspiring to hear so much passion after feeling discouraged for so long.

"That's what we're here for, Mayor," Grandpa spoke up, "to come up with a plan. But a plan isn't going to solve anything if we don't work together as a community."

"Well, now, Sheriff, as the duly elected mayor of this town, I have already come up with a plan." He looked out over the crowd. "Wanna hear it?"

"Yes!" they all shouted.

The mayor held up one finger. "Stay alive."

We all looked at each other.

The mayor chuckled. "That's it, people. Do whatever it takes, but stay alive."

Vivica Davis crossed her arms. "All due respect, Mayor, but that doesn't sound like much of a plan."

"That's the beauty of it, Viv—its simplicity! There is one simple rule: survival of the fittest."

"Which means exactly what?" Charlie Eagle asked in a measured tone.

"Which means makin' some hard decisions, Charlie."

His eyes fell on Lisa Butler. "Miss Butler. How's your elderly mother doing?"

Lisa gave him a wary frown. "Fine."

"And how much insulin does she have left?"

She hesitated, then muttered, "Three days."

"And how long do you suppose your mother will live beyond those three days?"

Lisa glared at him. "One, maybe two days, unless we can find—"

"How many of you would like to give some of your food to Lisa's mother who will be dead in five days?"

Everyone in the crowd shrank back a bit.

Robert Ormann sputtered. "Are you actually suggesting that we stop feeding Lisa's mother?"

"I am suggesting, Mr. Ormann, that your sickly father not be allowed to take food out of the mouth of Andy Milton's healthy son."

Andy Milton squared his shoulders and glared a challenge at Robert Ormann.

"Bring it on, Milton!" Robert Ormann challenged back.

"I'm not saying this is gonna be easy, people," the mayor continued. "But feeding all the sick and the dying in the infirmary will only harm the rest of us in the end."

"I hear those Cascadia Baptist freaks have a lot of food stored up!" Andy Milton announced.

"And the weapons to protect it," John Voss reminded.

The mayor smirked. "Yeah, we'll be takin' those, too."

"Mayor," my grandfather said carefully. "I think you need to go home and get some rest."

Frank Skaggs' expression went stone cold. "Said the man with the invalid grandson."

My grandfather blanched; my heart dropped to my

stomach. I felt Milly squeeze my hand. The world was turning itself inside out right in front of my eyes.

"Mr. Richmond?" the mayor called out. "Would you like to give your son's food to the sheriff's grandson?"

Lem Richmond crossed his arms and puffed out his chest. "Hell, no!"

The crowd erupted into jeers and cries of outrage. Familiar voices sounded strange, twisted with greed or horror. People started yelling and pushing.

I saw my grandfather rush up the stairs to protect David as many in the crowd tried to get their hands on Mayor Skaggs. The men the mayor had brought with him surged forward in a violent wave that left several people bloodied and on the floor. Deputy Hester tried to step in. John Voss landed a punch that knocked the deputy sideways. Lem Richmond joined the fray, sending John Voss backwards into Mike Jorgenson and knocking Jenny Ormann to the floor. Robert Ormann jumped on John Voss, and soon everybody was pushing and shoving everybody else.

A shoulder jammed into my stomach, knocking the air out of me. A heel landed on my foot. I panicked when I lost sight of Milly and Tim; I got shuffled to the back of the room where the rioting crowd swallowed me up. Punches and elbows were being thrown all around me. I stood in the middle of the brawl, watching neighbor turn against neighbor, and I wanted to scream at all the madness.

Micah pulled me out.

He moved me back against the far wall and stood over me, his broad back and strong arms a cage that kept the others out. I stared up into his determined dark eyes, knowing I was safe.

"You all right?" he asked. The crowd moved in blurry chaos all around us.

I nodded, my heart hammering. "You?"

He shrugged. "Been better."

Suddenly the deputy's ear-splitting whistle cut the air. The crowd froze. Micah and I turned toward the staircase.

Grandpa Donner's voice boomed out over the crowd. "Enough! Is this what we've become in just two weeks? A group of people willing to beat the tar out of each other to survive?"

Frank Skaggs, his face bloody and his hair tousled, looked completely insane. "And your grandson is the first one on my list!" Enraged, he pointed at my grandfather. "My son was your responsibility! A life for a life!"

"For God's sake, Frank," Deputy Hester implored, "Steve's death was an accident."

"There are no accidents, Jim! Only failures to lead!" Skaggs' hateful stare settled on David. "That this monstrosity lives while my perfect son is dead! That is true injustice!"

David's flushed face went white and a searing fire sparked to life inside me. I moved to step around Micah, intending to defend my brother, but Micah blocked my way. "Quick to listen," he whispered. "Careful to speak. Slow to anger."

My grandfather responded in measured tones. "Regardless of what happened to Seattle, this city will continue to abide by the laws and governances of the United States of America."

"America's gone!" Skaggs shouted. "So is Judge Holmes and so's the courthouse! We're livin' in a brave new world where only the strong will survive! Why should we feed the dying? Why should we give our precious resources to helpless people like that—" He pointed at David. "—when the boy is just going to die anyway?"

Several people shouted out their agreement and I felt the world slip out from under my feet. These were our neighbors, our friends.

My grandfather's mustache twitched. "Listen to me, people. I know things seem bleak and I know you're scared, but if we start fightin' each other, none of us are gonna survive."

"That's a touching sentiment, Sheriff." Skaggs jeered. "But I think I'll take my chances. What about the rest of you?! Are you with me—or against me?"

Many in the room cheered.

"Then let's get to it!"

The mayor turned on his heel and walked out of city hall, his goons following him. He left with a full third of Roslyn's citizens in tow. It was a devastating loss.

Micah sighed. "This isn't good."

"I can't believe he said that about my brother."

"He's a broken man, Seraphina—"

"That doesn't give him the right to deny anybody food," I countered.

Cody and Luke swaggered up to Micah. Both of their fathers had just walked out the door with Frank Skaggs.

Cody sneered at me. "You comin', Abrams?"

"Yeah." Luke snorted. "We're done wallowin' in ash with these losers."

"I'm staying," Micah replied.

I blinked at him.

"You're what?" Luke demanded.

"And you'd be smart to do the same," Micah added.

Cody and Luke exchanged a smirk. Then Cody pointed his finger at Micah's head, like pointing a gun at his victim. "Later, Abrams." He pulled his pretend trigger and both boys left the building.

Micah took me by the hand. "Come on."

My palm tingled down to my fingertips as he pulled me through what was left of the crowd to the staircase. We emerged in front of my grandfather, who looked relieved to see me safe.

"Micah," Grandpa Donner said. He looked back and forth between the two of us, clearly not sure about the young man he'd put behind bars more times than he could count.

Micah met his eyes. "I'm sorry about how things went today, sir."

Grandpa clapped him on the shoulder. "Thank you for lookin' after my granddaughter."

"It's my pleasure. Anything I can do to help."

David scowled at us from the stairs. "You can start by taking your hands off my sister."

Micah looked down—as if he'd forgotten we were holding hands—and then let go of me.

Milly hurried over with Tim. "Sera," she gasped. "Are you okay? When I lost ya in the crowd, I—" She noticed Micah standing beside me.

"See," Tim said to her. "I told ya she was all right."

Her face red and puffy from crying, Milly still managed to smile slyly at me. "Nothin' important, huh?"

She wasn't going to be satisfied until I spilled my guts to her about Micah. Welcome to life with Milly Odette as my best friend.

Deputy Hester approached, rubbing his sore jaw. "Some of us were talking, Sheriff. If Skaggs is bold enough to attack Apostle Phillips at the commune, he's likely to try the city food storage next."

Grandpa sighed, his face drawn with fatigue. "Take

some volunteers with rifles down to the warehouse and keep watch."

"I'd like to help," Micah offered.

Grandpa gave him a serious look. "Have you ever fired a weapon, son?"

"More times than I'd care to admit to the sheriff."

Grandpa chuckled. "All right, then."

Micah turned his gaze on me. "You gonna be all right?"

I nodded, even though I wasn't sure. Each day only seemed to get worse.

"Don't be afraid," he whispered.

With those words, Micah headed out with Deputy Hester and several others to protect the community warehouse.

David's face was tight and red. "Well, I'll certainly sleep better knowing Micah Abrams is guarding my food."

Grandpa Donner set his big hand on my brother's shoulder. "David, forgiveness is the first impulse of a fearless heart."

David scowled. As far as he was concerned, Micah's crimes would never go unpunished.

Tim squared his shoulders. "Grandpa Donner? I'd like to guard somethin', too."

"Me, too," Mike Jorgenson spoke up.

"Count me in," said Lisa Butler.

One by one every hand in the room rose into the air, young and old, men and women.

Grandpa looked out over his eager volunteers, nodding with pride. "Looks like we're gonna need more guns."

ONLY A HANDFUL of people in the state knew about the old National Guard armory outside the city limits of Roslyn. My grandfather was one of those people.

We drove up Cedar Gulch Road in the sheriff's SUV, none of us saying a word. All our heads were still spinning over what had happened in the city hall rotunda. Skaggs had divided the town in a matter of minutes, but the law-abiding citizens of Roslyn were not going to sit back while he and his followers looted the town.

We pulled into a potholed parking lot, the headlights illuminating a familiar stone building.

"Why are we stoppin'?" Tim called from the back seat.

Grandpa threw the SUV into park. "Because we're here."

I squinted at the building. "Are you sure?" There'd been a cave-in on the left side, probably from the earthquake, but otherwise the building looked just like it had ever since I could remember.

"Isn't this the old roller rink?" David asked.

Grandpa got out of the truck and headed up the buckled paved walk choked with weeds. I stared at the building, the setting of countless elementary school birthday parties.

Tim gave me a confused look. "I thought he said he was takin' us to an armory."

"Maybe he's lost," Milly suggested.

I nodded. "All these crumbling buildings look the same in the dark."

"Maybe you should all stop yammerin' and follow me," Grandpa called back.

We clicked on our headlamps and followed Grandpa up the cracked cement walk to the side of the building, where a twenty-foot chain-link fence, shrouded in thick vines, stared us in the face.

Tim looked stumped. "Now what?"

Grandpa started climbing.

We all shrugged at each other, then followed.

The ragged links of the old fence cut into my fingers as I moved up and over the rattling obstacle. Tim and Milly dropped down beside me on the other side. We stood in a large courtyard that had been a smooth slab of asphalt before the years, weeds, and earthquake had gotten to it. It was empty, except for something big and fat squatting near the back of the fence.

Milly flashed her headlamp at it. "What is that?"

"It's an M-1." Grandpa helped David off the fence.

She wrinkled her nose. "What's an M-1?"

"It...It's a tank," David said reverently.

Tim lit it up with his headlamp. "What? That big bush over there?"

Grandpa was already moving toward the building. "It's covered with a camo net."

"Tell me we're taking it," David begged.

Grandpa grunted. "The batteries are dead, the fuel is likely contaminated, and we'd need transmission fluid and oil for the final drives—not to mention grease for the tracks. And with no 120-millimeter ammo...it's basically a seventy-ton paperweight."

David grumbled his disappointment.

We followed Grandpa along the back of the building until he came to a place in the wall where the stone ended and the structure became smooth. He pushed aside the weeds and overgrown bushes, revealing a tall, black, iron door.

Tim smiled. "Ladies and gentlemen, Grandpa Donner is, in fact, James Bond."

"You ain't seen nothin' yet." Grandpa pressed his fingertips into a groove in the door and a panel popped open, exposing a ten-digit keypad.

David shook his head. "That's not going to work. No power."

Grandpa gave him a smug look. "Wanna bet, smarty pants?" He punched in a code. "It's not electric." The door clicked open. "It's push button."

David gaped. "How old is this place?"

Grandpa shoved open the heavy iron door. "Older than your Great-Aunt Patty." He ushered us all inside a long, dark hallway. "I was the custodian here when I joined the ROTC thirty years back. They closed it not long after that. Locked up the doors and turned the top floor into a roller rink. But they never bothered to change the key code."

Tim snorted. "Well, thank you very much, incompetent Uncle Sam."

We walked down the long corridor, our footsteps echoing against the painted cement walls. We passed military posters, cork assignment boards, offices, storage rooms, utility closets, bathrooms, and even a small kitchen.

I couldn't believe my eyes. I'd attended a dozen skating parties on the hardwood floor above our heads and not once had I even imagined what lay beneath my rolling wheels.

"Should be just in here." Grandpa pushed against an old wooden door. It creaked open into a dark, musty expanse that felt empty and dead. Then our collective headlamps lit up an immense room full of floor to ceiling green metal shelves.

Tim sucked in a breath. "Anybody else gettin' goose bumps?"

David gaped. "Long past that stage."

My stomach clenched. Automatic rifles loaded down every shelf.

"There's enough firepower in here to start a war," David breathed.

A chill crawled over my skin. Is that what we were planning to do? Start a war?

Grandpa pulled a dusty tarp off an old piece of machinery. He pushed a button, turned a crank, and the machine sputtered to life. Like magic, the lights overhead lit up like a Christmas tree.

It was such a relief to be standing in the warm, secure glow of electric lighting after weeks in the dark that I just stood there, unmoving for several seconds.

We all took a good look at the room around us. There were bins of grenades, caches of rocket launchers, and walls full of armaments I'd never seen before. There were helmets, boots, uniforms, and stacks upon stacks of automatic weapons.

Grandpa threw open the lid on an old metal tool box and pulled out a pair of wire snips. "I'm gonna go make a discreet door in that fence out there. You kids start grabbing guns and ammo."

Grandpa left, and David and Tim started loading their arms with weapons. Milly found an empty storage bin and started filling it with ammo clips. But I hung back.

Finally, Tim looked up at me. "Come on, Sera."

I shook my head. "This isn't a good idea."

David glared at me. He was holding two automatic rifles in his arms. "Don't even start, Sera."

Milly paused in her ammo gathering. "What? What's wrong?"

The Goliath Code

"Sera doesn't like guns," David jeered. "But we don't have time for her gun control soapbox right now."

"These people are our friends," I reminded them. "Our neighbors."

"Is she kiddin'?" Tim asked.

David straightened. "Did you even hear what Skaggs said about me?"

"Every word. But are you really going to shoot him over it?"

"If I have to."

Milly hesitated. "Surely they wouldn't really hurt David."

Tim grabbed another weapon. "I don't plan to find out."

"You shouldn't pick up a gun unless you're willing to use it," I said. That was a direct quote from Grandpa Donner and I had no intention of ever shooting anybody.

David glowered at me. "First your new boyfriend and now this? I'm starting to wonder who's side you're on, sister dearest. Anybody with half a brain can see right through Micah's Good Samaritan act. He should have gone with his Skaggs-loving buddies, so I'd have a good excuse to shoot him."

I clenched my fists. "Like Grandpa would ever give *you* a gun!" I shot back.

I'd hit him right where he lived and I regretted it instantly.

He turned his back on me and continued to load up.

Milly was starting to look skeptical. "Maybe we should—"

Grandpa marched back in through the doorway. "What's the holdup?"

"Sera," David ground out.

I swallowed hard. "I don't like guns. I'll help some other way."

"I don't like guns either." That surprised me, coming from a former Navy SEAL. "But a wise man once said that the only thing necessary for evil to triumph in this world is for good people to do nothin'." He walked up to a shelf and started collecting automatic rifles. "I took an oath—long before you kids were even born—that I would prevent evil from spreading in this great nation. And that oath doesn't end if the evil happens to be my neighbor. I will protect my family, Sera. With my last breath, if need be. You'll have to decide for yourself the part you're willin' to play." He turned and left the room with half a dozen weapons slung over his shoulders. David and Tim, their arms full, followed him.

I wasn't convinced that Frank Skaggs and the others were evil, but I trusted my grandfather more than anybody else in the world. He'd seen three wars and nine deployments. He wasn't the type of man to take conflict lightly.

Milly stood over her crate half full of ammo clips, watching me, waiting.

I grabbed an empty storage crate and started filling it up.

A few minutes later, Milly and I squeezed through the "door" Grandpa had made in the chain-link fence, taking our twin crates of ammo out to the SUV. When we came around the building, David and Tim were staring up at the sky.

"What are you doing?" Milly asked. We set our bins in the back of the truck and joined them.

Tim pointed up. "You see it, Mills? It's right there?"

It took me a moment, but then I gasped. Hanging over the trees on the ink-black horizon was the faint but unmistakable glow of the moon.

Chapter Eight

One week later the sun came out—a giant crimson ball against a hazy crimson sky—much dimmer than before. Grandpa Donner called the sky color "apocalypse red"; it reminded him of the oil fields he'd seen burning in Saudi Arabia. It cast a peculiar shade of filtered light that never quite warmed your face. Some people took the sun's reappearance as a sign that things were getting better. All I saw was an unfamiliar orb in an alien sky that reminded me the world would never be the same again.

Despite the sun's reappearance, we still couldn't get a radio signal in or out. David had a hard time explaining it. He said rain or snow might help clear the ash from the lower atmosphere and improve the signal, but we hadn't seen any rain since the eruption.

The acidic ashfall had burned all the vegetation. Now, without normal sunlight, plants refused to grow back and animals began to die. Predators wandered into town in search of food. A mountain lion had dragged off Ken Sheridan's dog, so people figured it was only a matter of time before they started dragging off people, too. We weren't much better off than the animals. Hunting was poor. Food was scarce and, with five of us to feed, Grandpa's pantry was nearly empty. Like a lot of people in town, we had to ask for food from the community food bank to survive.

We'd heard that Frank Skaggs and his people were still alive. The day after the meeting at city hall, they'd raided the CBC commune. Shots were fired and people were killed, including Apostle Phillip. In the chaos, the entire commune had burned to the ground, taking all of the CBC food stores up in a blaze of fire and smoke. Nobody had seen or heard from Skaggs since. Rumors claimed that he'd set up camp at his hunting cabin near Curry Canyon, while his people were living in tents and eating bugs. I didn't worry too much about them attacking us. If they got it into their heads to challenge the citizens of Roslyn, they'd find themselves outgunned. Grandpa had sworn us all to secrecy about the armory, but people had been so desperate to get their hands on a gun that nobody asked where they'd come from.

Things began to settle in to what Milly called "a new normal." Since we had daylight again, we started the task of rebuilding. Smaller outlying communities like Lakedale and Driftwood Acres had reached out to us for support, so there were construction projects going on all over the area. Don Chaney and Charlie Eagle had been tasked with finding a way east to Ellensburg. They'd attempted the trek several times by road, once down I-90, once down State Route 10, and once down Highway 97. Each time, they were stopped by several feet of ash.

Everybody had a job. Tim and Micah helped Vivica at the food warehouse, providing security and keeping records of who got what. David had been assigned to the team trying to design a better water purification system. We needed to clean the ash from the water more efficiently without wearing out the filters so fast. Of course, David resented what he saw as an unheroic job, but he begrudgingly did it anyway.

Milly had convinced Doctor Reinkann to let her work at the hospital, one of the first buildings repaired after the quake. She'd begged me to work there with her, insisting any best friend would do it. So now I spent my days giving sponge baths, cleaning bed pans, and changing sheets. Being friends with Milly could be challenging at times but, in those dark moments when I started to feel hopeless, I was glad I had her to talk to.

We were seeing a lot of cases of what Doctor Reinkann called "early onset silicosis," especially in older people. This confused the doctor. According to him, the disease usually took decades to manifest and normally responded well to removal of the irritant. But even in the clean environment of the hospital, these patients were getting worse.

I worried about Micah. I didn't know where he was living and whether he was working in the ash or not—and I'd never seen him wear a mask.

"You're thinkin' about him again."

I was making a bed at the end of my shift. I looked up to see Milly in the doorway of the hospital room, smiling at me. *She might be getting to know me too well,* I thought.

"I haven't seen him for almost a week." Not since Tiger Mountain and city hall. I thought about him a lot, though. I wondered if he ever thought about me.

"We haven't seen much of Tim either," she replied. "Viv keeps them pretty busy at the warehouse. Don't worry." She winked. "I'm sure Micah misses you, too."

My cheeks heated. "He probably just sees me as an annoying kid." He was eighteen after all.

"Mama always says bees can't ignore honey. And,

believe me, girl, when Micah looks at you he sees a big ol' pot."

I gave her a sideways look. "I'm not sure how I feel about that comparison."

Milly laughed. "I need to check on Mr. Ormann. Meetcha out front in ten minutes."

I went back to changing the bedsheets, but looked up again when I heard the door close. Sharon Webber stood there, her clipboard hugged to her chest. With the Roslyn Grocery demolished and Sharon out of a job, Doctor Reinkann had taken her two months of pharmacology school into consideration and assigned her the task of dispensing medicine.

She gave me a serious look. "I've been hoping to talk to you."

I shook out the top bedsheet. "About what?"

"Your mom."

My hands hesitated over tucking in the corners, but I recovered quickly. "Oh?"

She came toward me. "There's something you don't know—something I've only told a handful of people. My family didn't die in the quake."

I straightened and frowned at her. "You said your house collapsed and they—"

"They were taken," she said, then added in a whisper, "by the white light."

I refocused on finishing the bed.

"Just like Mr. Williams' family, Sera, mine was taken."

"I'm sorry to hear that." My hands started to shake. The town still treated Peter Williams like a lunatic and this was a subject I avoided at all costs.

She wandered over to the window and looked outside at the brilliant purple sunset. "Mom and Dad were standing with me on the sidewalk, holding my sweet Sarah Jane." Her voice wavered. "A blinding white light shot down from the sky, and they were just—"

"Gone." The word slipped out of my mouth. I instantly regretted it.

Sharon spun toward me. "Ava Gorski said your mother is unaccounted for." Even silhouetted against the window with the setting sun behind her, I could see the unmistakable look of hope in her eyes. "I was wondering if maybe you… if maybe you might have seen the same thing I did."

I took a deep breath and delivered my lines. "My mom died in the church. She fell through the floor and into the basement. She's buried under tons of rock and debris; there's no way to recover her body."

Sharon's expression sank. I felt terrible lying to her.

"I'm sure there's a logical explanation for what you saw, though," I added to soften the blow.

She gave me a sober look. "We know what it was."

Now it was my turn to hope. "You do?"

"Aliens."

Aliens? I cringed. *Great. A whole new way to sound crazy.* Then I realized what she'd said. "Wait. You said *we?*"

"Ava Gorski's husband disappeared the same way," Sharon revealed. "She told folks the oak tree in their front yard killed Ted, but she's since admitted to the White Lighters that the white light took him." She clamped her lips shut and blinked at me, as if she'd revealed too much.

"The White Lighters?"

She paused, then admitted, "The White Lighters Society. We meet on Friday's at the old Moose Lodge on West Utah. But you can't tell a single soul, Sera Donner."

I shook my head. "I would never." And I meant it. The

last thing I wanted was to connect myself to anything related to the white light.

"The building's a bit crumbled," Sharon went on, "but it's private and secure.

They actually have a club? I thought. "How many of you are there?"

"There's me, Ava, Peter, of course, and several other people whose names I don't care to mention right now. Nine in total. We were hoping to make you an even ten—after all, you're the sheriff's granddaughter. If you came forward about the white light, then people would *have* to listen." She was still hoping I'd change my story, but I focused on hers.

"Why would aliens want to kill people in Roslyn?"

She laughed like I'd asked the dumbest question she'd ever heard. "Our families aren't *dead*. The aliens just want us to *think* they're dead so that we won't go looking for them." She flashed me a smile. "Endure."

I frowned. "What?"

"That's what people say when the white light takes them. Endure. Why would they tell us they're going to endure if they're dead?"

My head was spinning. *Aliens?*

Sharon's eyes narrowed on my face. "Did your mother say something to you? Before she...*fell through the floor?*"

I opened my mouth to tell another lie.

A sharp, loud *POP!* interrupted me. The large window behind Sharon shattered, and her face expanded outward in a blast of red. She crumbled to the ground.

I stood there, stunned.

Bullets were suddenly flying all around me, embedding in the walls and ceiling. One zinged past my ear. I scrambled for cover under the bed.

Gunfire in the hallway. People screaming. The hospital was under attack.

"Pledge or perish!" someone shouted.

Feet running. More gunfire.

The attackers were moving from room to room. It was only a matter of time before they found me.

Something dripped into my eyes. I reached up to wipe it away and my fingers came back warm and sticky. I looked down at my hand—at my clothes—I was covered in Sharon Webber's blood.

A scream crawled up my throat. I clamped my hand over my mouth. Fighting panic, I took a shaky breath and tried to think clearly. *More gunfire in the hallway.* I had to get out of the building.

The window.

I slipped out from beneath the bed, doing my best to avoid looking at Sharon Webber. Her blood was spreading into a dark red pool around her body. The thick, metallic smell made me gag. I crawled to the shattered window, careful of the glass on the floor. *Another scream. More shots.* The gunmen were getting close.

I stole a quick look out the window. The ground was six feet down. Another bullet blew past my head. I dropped to the floor and stared into what was left of Sharon Webber's face. Muffled voices came from the room next door. I was running out of time.

The cafeteria lay just down the hallway to the right. I remembered seeing an access stairwell from the kitchen to the parking lot. That's where I needed to go.

I slid across the floor. The voices had gone quiet again. Hand shaking, I turned the knob, cracked open the door and peeked out. The hall was empty.

Careful not to squeak the hinges, I slipped out of the room. *More gunshots.* I scrambled toward the cafeteria.

A cold, familiar voice stopped me in my tracks. "Hello, Sera."

I turned. Cody Richmond and Luke Milton stood at the other end of the long hallway, holding handguns.

"We were hopin' for your brother," Cody sneered, "but you'll do."

I squeezed my eyes shut. I wasn't ready to die.

Cody fired.

CRACK! The shot shocked me so badly I ducked. I felt the aggressive, violent sound deep in my teeth. The vinyl floor at my feet splintered.

Cody was a terrible shot.

I took off down the hallway at a full sprint. The boys kept firing, their bullets tearing up the linoleum and digging into the walls.

I reached the cafeteria, weaving around tables and counters, then dove through the creaky swinging door into the dark kitchen. The boys charged after me—I could hear them knocking over chairs.

I barreled past the row of ovens toward the exit at the back of the room. I found the door in the dark, grabbed the knob, and pulled. It didn't move.

I used both hands, braced my foot, and pulled with all my might. It was stuck. I felt along the panel of the door and found a long board nailed across its width. The outside staircase, damaged in the quake, hadn't been fixed yet.

I heard the creak of the kitchen door and shrank into the shadows. I folded myself up behind a wheeled metal rack stacked with boxes, covered my mouth, and tried not to breathe.

"Seee-ra," Cody sang.

My heartbeat sounded like thunder in my ears.

I could hear more gunfire outside the kitchen. This was an organized attack. We'd been worried that Frank Skaggs and his people might raid the food warehouse, but it had never occurred to anyone that they would stoop to attacking a hospital full of sick people. Why not? Frank Skaggs was making good on his threat that only the healthy and strong would survive.

I shut my eyes against burning tears. Sharon's dried blood itched on my skin. And then I heard Luke's creepy whisper in my ear.

"Hey, Sera."

I shrieked and turned my head. His gun was in my face. This time he wouldn't miss.

"I'll say goodbye to Micah for ya."

I slammed my eyes shut.

BANG! BANG!

The smell of gunpowder filled the air. I waited to feel the searing pain of a bullet entering my brain. Instead, I felt the weight of Luke Milton toppling onto me and knocking me backwards. The metal rack tipped over, clattering to the floor. I stared into Luke's dead eyes and screamed.

"Luke?" Cody sounded uncertain.

Two more shots cracked through the air. And then I was pulled out from under Luke. I fought and kicked at the dark form dragging me to the back of the room, but it did no good. I was shoved into a dark space between two stoves, where a shadow draped itself over me. It surrounded me. It shielded me. It could only be one person.

"Are you hurt?" Micah whispered softly.

I started to cry. "Micah?"

"Seraphina," he breathed. "Are you hurt?"

"N-no," I choked out.

The gunfire outside the kitchen grew louder. I heard running in the cafeteria next door and panic fired in my brain.

"They're coming!" I rasped. "Micah, they're coming!" My instinct was to run. But Micah had me trapped.

And then it was too late. I heard the squeak of the kitchen door swing open.

"Stay still," Micah whispered. He pressed his forehead to mine; I felt his breath against my face. "Not a sound."

There were footsteps all over the room. "There's an exit here somewhere," somebody growled.

"Find it! Before the sheriff and his buddies find us!"

I tried to push back further against the wall. I was tucked between the stoves, but Micah huddled in plain view, hidden only by changeable shadows. If they spotted him, we were both dead.

"Look at this," a voice said nearby.

My breath caught.

"It's the Richmond boy."

They'd found Cody.

"The Milton boy's over here," another replied.

"Gonna be two pissed papas."

"I told Skaggs it was stupid to do this in daylight."

"Yeah, he's not exactly all there these days."

"Find the door."

That last voice was so close it startled me. I twitched, slamming my elbow into the side of the metal stove. The sound boomed through the room like a drum. My heart stopped.

That was all they needed to pinpoint our location.

Shots exploded in the room. Bullets ricocheted against the stoves and the racks above our heads, embedding into cabinets and walls. I heard several dull thumps, felt Micah tense—heard him grunt—and knew he'd been hit. But he held his position in front of me.

The gunfire intensified, grew louder, more pronounced, like there were suddenly a hundred guns firing in the room. Then everything went quiet.

The smell of gunpowder burned my nose. I tasted blood. Was it Micah's? Someone charged toward us. I squeezed my eyes shut against another barrage of bullets. A flashlight clicked on.

"Sera?" It was Grandpa Donner.

To my amazement, Micah stood up, tall, straight—uninjured. "She's okay," he said.

"Thank God." Grandpa Donner lifted me to my feet and pulled me into his arms.

The kitchen lit up with additional flashlights as Don Chaney and Charlie Eagle came in. I saw five bodies laid out, including Cody Richmond and Luke Milton.

Charlie checked them over. "These are Skaggs' men."

I looked around the room, at the chaos, at the bullet holes in everything. Micah had saved my life.

I blinked at him. "Are you okay?"

He shrugged. "They're terrible shots."

"Yeah," I said, feeling dazed.

Grandpa led me and Micah out of the kitchen. Bodies of the sick and the elderly were scattered throughout the long hallway. Betty Granger, Dean Lawson, George Ormann, Rose Myers. I grabbed my stomach, turned my face to the wall, and vomited.

We headed for the exit stairway as Mike Jorgenson and Ken Sheridan, armed with M16s, went room to room. They were looking for survivors and making sure all of Skaggs' men had been cleared from the building.

Milly was waiting on the sidewalk outside, wrapped in a

blanket. Her eyes rounded in horror when she saw me. I rushed toward her; we held onto each other and cried. David came bounding up with Tim and Vivica Davis. They stopped and stared at me.

"Sera?" David breathed. "Are you all right?"

"It's not her blood," Grandpa Donner told them. He wrapped a blanket around my shoulders. When I shivered, he pulled me in close.

I gazed around at the growing crowd, looking for Micah. I spotted him talking with the Ormanns. I still couldn't believe he hadn't been shot.

Deputy Hester came screeching up in his cruiser, lights flashing, siren blaring. He scrambled out of his car, weapon in hand, and ran toward my grandfather. "What happened?"

"Skaggs' men hit the hospital. Micah sounded the alarm."

"*Abrams?*" David blurted.

"How did Micah know?" Deputy Hester asked.

Grandpa shrugged. "Kid's got a sixth sense."

A large, frightened crowd was gathering. Word of the attack had spread fast through town. It seemed the war we all thought we'd avoided had started.

Don Chaney, Charlie Eagle, Mike Jorgenson, and Ken Sheridan came walking out of the building, looking glum.

"Survivors?" Grandpa asked.

Charlie shook his head. "They were thorough."

Jenny Ormann fell into her husband's arms, crying.

"We need to hit them back!" Robert Ormann shouted. "We need to attack their camp and kill every last Skaggs scum we can find!"

Many in the crowd shouted their approval.

Don Chaney leaned in to my grandfather and murmured, "Maybe he's right, Sheriff."

Mike Jorgenson agreed. "We need to protect our food stores."

"If they take the food warehouse," Charlie warned, "we're done for."

The crowd grew larger and more worked up. They raised their fists in the air, chanting, "Kill the Skaggs! Kill the Skaggs!"

"We have to fight back!" Robert Ormann shouted again.

As Grandpa Donner considered the options, a faint buzzing sound tickled my ears. Others heard it, too, and the crowd's chanting died down. I looked up into the red sky and saw something I never thought I'd see again.

An airplane.

Big and gray, it came toward us over the treetops. I blinked, afraid I was seeing things, but everybody else was seeing it, too. We all watched, stunned, as it roared over our heads like a giant winged angel, then ejected a fluttering blue cloud in its wake.

The entire crowd erupted into cheers—Jenny Ormann even stopped crying.

We're saved, I thought.

A cloud of blue leaflets fluttered onto our heads like bright butterflies. People jumped up, catching fistfuls of them in midair. Others danced in them, kicking up piles with their feet.

One fell on my shoulder. I pulled it off to get a better look. Big gold letters ran across the top of the paper.

EUROPA
HUMANITARIAN AID

Below that were words written in a language I couldn't read. I handed the flyer to Grandpa. "Europa?"

He looked at it. "It's German," he said. "It says they're going to give us food and water."

The crowd exploded into whoops and shouts. The people started chanting, "Europa! Europa! Europa!"

Tim whistled, dumping an armload of fliers over my head. He and David did a do-si-do.

But my grandfather didn't look happy.

"This is good, right?" I asked him.

"Depends," he said thoughtfully.

"On what?"

He looked up at the plane quickly disappearing into the distant horizon. "On the price."

Chapter Nine

"Take the weapon, Sera."

I stared at the M16, my whole body shaking. I'd barely slept and hardly eaten for three days. The image of Sharon Webber's face exploding played in a slow-motion loop through my head all the time, and I couldn't seem to get the smell of her blood off my skin.

The Skaggs had only gotten bolder since the hospital massacre. They'd raided four homes in the past two nights, stolen everything not nailed down, and killed three more people. Their attacks made it clear that, no matter how many guards we posted on the food warehouse, they would find other ways to take whatever they wanted from us.

Now, with the Europa supply drop due in thirty minutes, my grandfather and I were in a standoff. He refused to let me stay home by myself, but he wouldn't allow me in the truck until I took the M16 out of his hands. I didn't want to carry the gun. I could barely stand looking at it.

"Sera," Grandpa said patiently, "if you don't take the weapon we're gonna be late."

If my grandfather arrived at the drop zone even a

minute behind schedule, it could be disastrous for the entire town. No one had food. We were scratching by on rations from the food warehouse and those would run out soon. If the local communities didn't show up in an organized force, with their sheriff leading them, the Skaggs would likely march in and take everything.

"Everyone else has a gun," I complained. "Why do I need one?"

"Because you're part of a team, Sera. A team where everyone watches everyone else's back."

David was tired of me. "Seriously, Sera. Stop being so dramatic and just take it."

My brother, along with Tim and Milly, stared out at me from the bed of Grandpa Donner's pickup. None of them were having any trouble holding their own weapons.

Even Tim was irritated with me. "We need to go *now*," he stated.

David checked his watch. "Twenty-five minutes."

"C'mon, Sera," Milly encouraged. "It'll be fine. We'll stay together."

I stared at the M16, hating it. I wasn't capable of shooting anybody, but I also couldn't be responsible for people losing their Europa supplies.

I took the weapon from my grandfather's hands and climbed into the truck bed. I refused to acknowledge the cold, heavy weight of it. Instead, I stared off into nothingness as we drove away from the house.

By the time we reached the field of Cle Elem-Roslyn High School, several hundred people had already gathered. Instead of parking in the lot, Grandpa drove around the back of the school and parked on the baseball diamond. He opened the tailgate and everybody spilled out. I left the M16 behind in the bed.

Tim assessed the crowd. "Looks mighty peaceful."

Grandpa wasn't as optimistic. "Never underestimate a hungry crowd."

He reached into the truck bed for the M16 and put it in my hands. "Keep it with you. Tim, you're with me. Sera, Milly, David, stay with the truck."

David gaped. "But——"

Grandpa cut him off. "This is no time for pride, son. Do what you're told."

David scowled as Grandpa walked away with Tim.

I watched them approach the churning crowd and fought down a rush of anxiety. The field was too open. Anything could happen.

Then I spotted Micah. He pushed past several people to shake hands with my grandfather. I relaxed a little. I hadn't seen Micah since the hospital massacre, even though he'd tried to visit me several times. My brother would barely speak to me as it was; inviting Micah into our house would create more conflict than I wanted to deal with. But things seemed to work out whenever Micah was around. I leaned back against the side of the truck and tried to will my knees to stop shaking.

Milly moved up beside me. "It's okay to be scared, Sera."

It didn't feel okay. It felt pathetic and weak.

"Mama says being scared just means you're doing somethin' brave."

I opened my mouth to tell her I was getting sick of hearing what her mama said about everything, but then I saw my own fear reflected in her eyes. It reminded me that she'd been in the hospital that day, too, but, unlike me, Milly had gone back the next day to help with cleanup. Unlike me, she hadn't hidden in the house for the past three days.

This Texas girl had more grit than anybody gave her credit for.

"Watch it!"

I looked up, realizing I'd accidentally pointed my weapon at David.

He shoved the barrel away. "Do you even know how to use that?"

"Point and pull the trigger."

Milly laughed.

"Give me that." David snatched the weapon out of my hands. The thing was almost as long as he was tall. "Pay attention, before you shoot yourself—or me. You stand squared like this." He illustrated the proper stance. "It gives you better stability against the recoil." He pointed the weapon toward the tree line. "Your support hand goes on the forestock here. Keep your head up. Place the butt of the rifle near the centerline of your body, high on your chest. Press your cheek to the side of the stock like this. Look through the scope. Center the crosshairs on your target. And, when it comes time, press the trigger—don't pull."

I scowled at him. I wasn't dumb enough to believe that his elaborate lesson was for my benefit. He wanted to show off for Milly, not to mention vent some of his anger that he'd only been given a handgun.

"I was in the same gun safety class as you."

He shoved my weapon back into my hands. "I stayed till the end."

I clenched my teeth and sat down on the truck's tailgate. My grandfather had made attendance in his weapons safety class the price of getting a gun from the armory. We'd all attended, but, at the first sound of a bullet exploding from the end of a gun, I'd run from the room in a panic. It was humiliating and David was a jerk to even bring it up.

More people filed onto the field, a large combined group from the towns of Lakedale and Driftwood Acres. Everyone seemed friendly. Some people even danced in a circle, singing about a big jet airliner. Everyone had agreed that all the supplies would be divided between the towns according to population and everybody seemed happy with that arrangement. But, as Grandpa kept insisting, hungry people were unpredictable.

The rumble of airplane engines rose in the distance. The people on the field, alerted, grew restless. They packed in tighter. I stood up in the truck bed to get a better view. Grandpa, Tim, and Micah were in the back of the large crowd from Roslyn congregated near the center of the field. The Lakedale and Driftwood Acres group had carved out a location at the back near the chain-link fence. Everybody searched the sky.

The heavy droning of the approaching propellers grew louder, until, finally, the plane appeared. A cheer went up as blue parachutes blossomed in midair. People separated from their groups, trying to predict where the crates would fall.

And then a large group of men emerged from the woods to the left of the field. My heart stopped. Frank Skaggs had come with about fifty of his people, all armed.

The Lakedale-Driftwood Acres group spotted them first and the atmosphere on the field changed instantly. Warning shouts rang out. The Roslyn group shifted, moving as one on an intercept course.

The violence was sudden and brutal. With the gently swaying crates hovering above them like dangling carrots, all three groups collided. I saw the impact of fist to jaw, rifle stock to skull. People I knew collapsed to the ground.

There was one gunshot—and then rapid gunfire. People

fled in every direction like startled birds. The crates hadn't even hit the ground yet.

Hands reached into the air. Desperate cries, insisting on ownership, were drowned out by screams of pain and more gunshots. I saw Eliza Cole snatch a box out of the hands of another woman. The woman started to rant and Eliza backhanded her. The woman hit the ground, her hands empty, and Eliza walked off with her prize. So much for loving thy neighbor.

People knocked each other over, throwing elbows and fists to claim their fair share. Crates were torn open as fast as they hit the ground, the contents looted and taken away.

Lisa Butler, carrying a single case of Europa water, hurried past our truck toward the parking lot. Her clothing torn, she was bruised and crying. She got tackled from behind by John Voss—a man twice her size—and fell, face-first, into the ash and dirt. Her case of water tumbled out of her hands. Voss snatched it up, kicked her in the ribs, and then hurried off with his prize.

Lisa climbed to her feet and caught sight of me, standing in the truck bed with an automatic rifle and a good vantage point. I hadn't done a thing to help her. A hot surge of shame shot through me as she turned and limped back to her car, empty-handed.

I looked back at the crowded field, fighting the urge to run. Instead, I searched for Grandpa, Micah, or Tim. The chaos had swallowed them whole.

"Where are they?" Milly crouched beside me in the truck bed.

I spotted them, thirty yards out. "There!" Tim and Grandpa had their arms full. They were weaving through the clash with Micah guarding their backs.

I turned to David. "They're coming—"

But David was gone. Panic hit me. "David?" I scrambled to the other side of the bed and looked around the truck. "David?"

I scanned the fringes of the crowd, fighting panic, afraid one of Skaggs' men had grabbed him. Then I saw him. He'd made it to a discarded crate twenty yards out and found a single overlooked item.

"David!" I screamed.

He looked up, holding a case of Europa water, and flashed me a grin. I should have known he'd never settle for standing silently in the background.

He ran for the truck. I held my breath, silently urging him on as he dodged fights and scrambled over people laid out on the ground. For the first time in my life I felt grateful that he was small and easily overlooked. He owned the field like a miniature Super Bowl running back. He was going to make it.

And then a loud shot rang out. Blood erupted from his leg. He stumbled. I watched my brother go down in a cry of agony and disappear beneath the jostling crowd.

I was out of the truck bed before I even realized I'd moved. I could hear Milly shouting at me as if from a long way off. I shoved through the warring crowd until I finally saw my brother clinging to a case of water, blood oozing from his thigh.

Lem Richmond had his rifle pointed at his head. "Hello, Little Stinker," I heard him say.

Desperate and in pain, David shoved the case of water at Lem and tried to scoot away. "Take it!" he cried. "Just take it!"

David had surrendered the water, but that didn't matter. I recognized the look on Lem's face. I'd seen the same look on his son's face three days before at the hospital. Richmond didn't care about the water. He wanted to shoot my brother, just like Cody had wanted to shoot me.

My vision narrowed to a tunnel with Lem Richmond at the center. The violent sound of the crowd muted to a low, dull hum. My thoughts turned sharp. I saw Lem Richmond's face framed by a small round circle.

CRACK!

The sound exploded in my ears. The weapon in my hands jerked back against my shoulder and Lem Richmond fell, motionless, at my brother's feet.

I stared down at the man for a moment. *Was I dreaming?* Pulling the trigger had been such a simple thing, just a quick motion of my finger.

David lay gasping on the ground. I threw down the rifle and pulled him to his feet. He tried to pick up his case of water, but somebody else grabbed it first. I took a tight grip on the back of his coat and ran him toward the truck. If I'd been strong enough to pick him up I would have. The wound in his leg was bleeding badly and he stumbled after only a few yards. The crowd surged in around us. I pulled him upright again, but he lost consciousness and dragged us both to the ground.

The violent crowd pressed in. We were stepped on and kicked. I looked around, desperate for help, but saw nothing but rage and violence in the faces around me.

And then Micah appeared. He lifted David over his shoulder, grabbed my hand, and we ran together through the crowd to the truck.

Grandpa, already there, took one look at David and his expression hardened. "Everybody in the truck!"

With the scene around us going from bad to worse, we loaded David into the pickup bed and left the drop zone behind. I didn't remember the drive home, except that my brother was unconscious and Milly had tied a tourniquet around his thigh.

It was growing dark by the time we turned into the driveway. Everyone scrambled out of the truck to accompany David into the house, but I couldn't find the will to move. I stared at the two boxes of supplies we'd managed to carry away from the drop zone and wondered how they could be worth someone's life.

I touched my forehead. It felt tender where I'd been kicked. My head was starting to ache.

"You should have your grandfather take a look at that."

I glanced up at Micah, approaching from the house. He hopped up on the tailgate and eased down beside me. "Milly says David's gonna be okay," he continued. "The bullet went through skin and muscle. Didn't break the bone."

Just a couple months ago, Micah had been the one trying to hurt David. Now, genuine concern for my brother reflected in his warm, dark eyes. *Why are you so different?* I wondered.

He pushed a piece of hair back from my face. "What's going on in your head right now?"

"I don't like guns." My voice surprised me. It sounded distant and raw, not my own.

"I understand, but you—"

"No, you don't." Emotion welled up in me, making my chin quiver. "Four years ago my best friend's brother shot himself."

Micah grew quiet.

"Alyson found him. Out back. Behind her house. She never got over it."

"Difficult times will come," he murmured.

"Grandpa says the only thing evil needs to succeed is for good people to do nothing." I looked him in the eye, afraid of how he would react to what I was about to say. "I'm not sorry I killed Mr. Richmond. His son tried to kill me. He tried to kill my brother. They started it. I ended it."

Micah's expression softened. He placed his hand over mine and our gazes locked. The electric contact of his skin erased any fear I had that he would judge me for what I'd done. His nearness pulled at something deeper inside me. I realized that I should thank him for, once again, saving my life. And then I thought I might kiss him instead.

At that moment, Grandpa Donner came marching out of the house with a cigar clamped between his teeth and Tim in step behind him. Micah cleared his throat, removing his hand from mine.

"I don't think I've ever seen that much blood in my whole entire life," Tim was saying.

Grandpa shook his head appreciatively. "That Milly's got a gift."

Tim grinned. "She's watched a lotta hospital dramas."

"So what's goin' on out here?" Grandpa asked. He looked back and forth between me and Micah.

Tim, seeming to sense that they'd intruded on a private moment, reached into the truck bed for a Europa box. "I'll get this stuff inside." He headed back to the house.

My grandfather pinned me with a serious look. "Milly told me what happened out there. I'm proud of you, girl."

Tears tightened my throat.

"I know it's hard. But you were given a choice and you made the right one."

He hoisted the other Europa box up and out of the truck bed, then paused. "Micah, you've been in my jail so many times I was about to start chargin' you rent."

Micah grunted, looking chagrined.

"But it looks like we owe you another thank you." He

extended his hand. "It's good to see you finally comin' into your own."

Micah stood and shook his hand. "Thank you, sir."

"Now you two best get inside." Grandpa turned and carried his box toward the house. "Not a good night for stargazin'."

I waited until he'd disappeared inside, then turned back to Micah. "You should stay." The idea of him heading off into the night alone worried me.

"What, here? Naw. I'm fine where I'm at. The Skaggs won't bother me. I don't have anything they want."

I shook my head at him. "Doesn't anything scare you?"

He gave me a long, searching look and I realized that he was the only person in existence who could make my heart stop and start at the same time.

"I'm sorry I didn't come out when you came to see me," I said.

He held up three fingers. "Three times."

I smiled. "I'm sorry three times."

"You have a beautiful smile." He winced and looked down, as if he'd said something he shouldn't.

"Thank you."

He held out his hand to me. "You should definitely go inside. Unless you were planning on sleeping out here in the truck."

He had a point. I certainly couldn't stay out there all night.

I stared at his broad fingers, knowing that taking his hand meant standing up. It meant making the decision to move forward from the hospital massacre and the drop zone. I wasn't sure I knew how.

As if reading my mind, he answered my thoughts. "You're stronger than you think, Seraphina."

He stood there quietly, holding out his hand, waiting for me to make the choice. I suddenly felt like I could do anything.

I slipped my hand into his and allowed him to pull me to my feet.

He helped me down off the tailgate and we walked to the porch, hand in hand. He paused on the bottom step, his eyes locked with mine, his lips slightly parted. I felt like there was something else he wanted to say. I held my breath, waiting.

Finally, he frowned and looked away. "Sleep well."

I felt a pinch of disappointment as his fingers slipped from mine. He turned to go, but I couldn't let him leave—not like that. "Micah?" He looked back at me. "Will...will you come see me tomorrow?" We could sit on the porch; David never had to know.

His mouth curved into a warm smile. "Absolutely."

I stared after him as he headed off down the street, watching even after he'd disappeared into the cold, dark night.

MICAH DIDN'T VISIT the next day. Or the day after that. I considered going out to find him, but the Skaggs had upped their game at the drop zone and Grandpa insisted we stay close to the house. I kept busy helping Tim repair the cellar walls and reinforce the door, just in case we needed a safe room.

Instead of putting David in the hospital and making him an immediate target for Frank Skaggs, Doctor Reinkann had put Milly in charge of my brother's rehabilitation. From David's point of view, this was just about the best thing that had ever happened to him. Under Milly's gentle care, he was healing.

Days passed with no word from Micah. The Skaggs kept my grandfather and his deputy busy with nightly raids throughout the area. The demand for guns grew, spreading into the outlying communities. The Skaggs had made off with most of the supplies from the Europa drop, so food grew scarce in town again. Fights in the streets over rations weren't uncommon. People were getting desperate.

Then a large, well-organized group of Skaggs attacked the Lakedale City food warehouse, killing the town's mayor and six other people in the process. Grandpa'd had enough. He gathered all the community leaders together and told them it was time to fight back. So the 1st Cascade Militia was born. Their mission, guard and protect the citizens of Kittitas County against all enemies, foreign and domestic. Tim was the first person to sign up.

Finally, seventeen days after the first Europa crates drifted down to the ground, a plane flew overhead and released more blue leaflets into the air, announcing a supply drop the very next day. This time the town's citizens stayed in the safety of their homes and let their new militia take charge.

The 1st Cascade, at an impressive three hundred strong, ended up securing all thirty-five crates without a single ounce of blood spilled. The Skaggs had made an appearance, but they'd beat a hasty retreat once they'd seen what they were up against. It was a proud day for the militia and for the entire county.

With the militia on duty and people walking around with satisfied bellies, the town calmed down, making it safe to finally leave the house again. While David recuperated at home, Tim went back to guard duty at the food warehouse and Milly returned to work at the hospital. Finding Micah became my number one priority.

I scoured the city for him, then broadened my search to the outlying communities. In the end, I even checked the morgue. I found no sign of him anywhere. No one had seen him since the first Europa drop. I knew in my heart that the Skaggs had captured him.

Micah had been missing for over three weeks when I stopped by the hospital to pick up fresh bandages for David. "How's he doing?" Milly asked.

"He's David and he's incapacitated," I grumbled. "How do you think he's doing?"

Suddenly Tim burst through the hospital doors carrying a large man over his shoulders. "Need a little help, here!" he called out.

Milly grabbed a nearby gurney and Tim lowered the unconscious man down onto the sheet. She began checking his vitals. "What happened?"

The man was beaten and bloody and, judging by the angle of several of his fingers, he likely had a few broken bones.

"Found him in a ditch by Crystal Creek," Tim answered.

Though badly swollen, the man's face looked familiar. Then it hit me. "That's John Voss," I said. "He's one of Skaggs' men."

Tim and Milly exchanged a look. Milly carefully pulled back the neckline on Voss's dirty, blood-stained shirt. I gasped at what that revealed. He had an angry, blistering brand burned into his chest: TRAITOR.

Milly's jaw set. "Another defector."

"Another?" I repeated.

"He's the second we've seen," Tim answered. "It's nice

to know a few are havin' second thoughts, but Skaggs ain't lettin' 'em go easy."

"The man is a monster," Milly ground out.

"Pledge or perish," Tim said wryly. "That is their motto."

Milly unlocked the wheels on the gurney and started rolling Voss away. "I'll get him taken care of."

Once Milly left, Tim turned to me with an uneasy smile. "Can you take a look at somethin' for me?"

"Sure," I replied warily.

He lifted his shirt. "I'd ask Milly, but I don't wanna freak her out." He showed me a blotchy red rash on his stomach.

Fear seized my heart. I bent closer to get a better look.

Tim hesitated. "Is it…?"

I breathed a sigh of relief and shook my head. "It's not viridea. It looks like poison oak."

Tim let out a thankful breath, then laughed. "I guess that won't kill me."

"Probably not."

With the bird population dwindling, disease carrying mosquitos were multiplying. The result of that was a new, more virulent form of the West Nile virus. Victims suffered from a rash, encephalitis, convulsions, and eventually death. We'd lost four people to it in just the past week.

"Mix some baking soda with a little water," I told him. "Use it as a paste. It'll help the itch."

"Gotcha. Listen, Sera, there's somethin' else. Might be just a rumor. But I'm not so sure I should keep it from ya."

He was worrying me again. "Heard something about what?"

"About Micah."

My heart stopped. Part of me wanted to grab him and force him to tell me everything. Another part of me wanted to run from the hospital as fast as I could, before he told me something I could never unhear.

"I was talkin' with some of the men from the militia they put together over in Ronald," he went on. "One of 'em said that the Skaggs had captured a Jewish kid from Roslyn the night of the first food drop. Sera, their description sounded a lot like Micah."

I reminded myself to breathe. "What…what happened to him?"

"He's likely being held in one of their detention camps. They ain't pretty."

Tears stung my eyes. I should have never let Micah leave that night. I should have insisted he stay with us at the house. This was all my fault.

I sniffled. "How do we get him back?"

Tim shook his head. "We don't. Not 'til this damn war ends."

That night I went home and sat at my bedroom window, staring out into the dark night. I thought of Micah, beaten and alone, trapped behind the razor wire of a Skaggs prisoner of war compound, and a fire grew in my belly until it blazed as hot as the sun. I was going to make every single one of those Skagg bastards pay for what they'd done—to me, to David, to Micah. I wouldn't rest until he was home.

One month after Micah had gone missing, I walked into City Hall and joined the 1st Cascade Militia.

Part II

Chapter Ten

I ran down Highway 903 with my M16 clutched in my hand. Ben Turner stayed close behind with his own weapon at the ready. He had two seized weapons slung over his shoulder and extra ammo clips stuffed into his jacket, but he was still managing to keep up with me—one of the benefits of having a high school linebacker as my spotter.

It was almost midnight with a full, red moon rising on the distant horizon. That, plus the burning remains of a pickup truck, cast an eerie glow over the scene. We charged through the parking lot of the Cle Elum Walmart, dodging wrecked cars and toppled shopping carts. Bullet holes pitted the store's walls, shattered glass filled its windows. The contents of its shelves had been looted months ago. It was early May, eight months after the Yellowstone eruption.

The Skaggs were pushing hard against our defenses. Heavy snows into the early spring had minimized the fighting, but, with a lull in the weather, the enemy was back in full force. Their ranks had risen dramatically since the initial conflict at the first Europa drop. Their every-man-for-himself motto had attracted all the disillusioned from the outlying communities around us, forcing Roslyn and Cle Elum to band together with Lakedale, Driftwood Acres, Pine Glen, and Easton, if only to match the Skaggs in numbers.

The never-ending war had few rewards. Everyone fought desperately over the Europa humanitarian drops, but they were infrequent and inadequate; both sides constantly ran low on food and supplies. I hadn't eaten three squares a day in over four months. To top it off, we had yet to encounter a single Europa representative. All we'd ever seen of Europa were their planes and their crates of supplies.

Ben and I leapt over a dead Skagg. Normally we'd pause to see if we knew him—nine times out of ten we did—but tonight we had information that couldn't wait. We continued our headlong charge toward the barricade at the end of the street.

A board swung back as we raced inside. There were more than thirty troops positioned behind the salvage wall made up of cars, old appliances, furniture, metal sheeting, and tires, among other things. They were men, women, teenagers—anybody capable of carrying a weapon was welcome in the 1st Cascade Militia.

"They're coming!" I shouted.

A barrel fire set near the center of the fortification illuminated the determined faces staring back at me. Though cold and exhausted from holding the line for the past few days, we would not falter in the defense of our town and the people we loved.

Grandpa emerged from the rickety shed converted into his headquarters. Several days of dirt filled the lines around his eyes. He gave me a tired look. "Tell me."

"They have the tank."

He cursed and kicked a stack of tires. He'd made a

mistake in not securing it that first night he'd taken us to the armory. Now one of the Skagg scouts had found it and, somehow, made it operational. At least they hadn't found the armory itself.

"We couldn't verify ammo," I added. "But Skaggs is riding in the turret."

Grandpa shook his head. I could tell he was beating himself up over his mistake, but he'd led us well over the past six months and nobody blamed him. "Well, let's hope they didn't find an ammo supply point somewhere and all we're really dealin' with is a seventy-ton battering ram. How many troops?"

"We count forty-seven," Ben replied.

A shout came up from the ranks. "Skaggs incoming!" It was Jude, Ben's brother. He was on sentry duty, wearing his nightvision goggles.

The Turner brothers had become a permanent fixture around our house, ever since a recon team found them trying to survive on an abandoned farm four miles outside of town. I'd hardly known the two of them in school—Ben was a sophomore on the football team and Jude was the senior class president—but now they were like brothers to me. Grandpa Donner said war could do that; it turned strangers into family.

I clambered up onto a sideways refrigerator and a broken chair to peer over the top of the barricade. Down the street I saw marching silhouettes flickering in the light of the distant truck fire. I lifted my weapon and peered through the nightscope. The vehicle fire washed out the scene, but with each step, the Skaggs' numbers became clearer. I could hear the rumble of the tank.

"Forty!" Jude hollered. "Maybe fifty!"

Charlie Eagle climbed up beside me and peered over my shoulder. "Tank's in the rear!"

"Hold 'em back!" Grandpa ordered.

Charlie tapped my shoulder. "You're up."

I steadied my weapon, chose my shot, and fired. One of the silhouettes fell.

Weapons fire broke out all along our line. The Skaggs, ducking for cover at the sides of the road, returned fire, but they couldn't do much damage through the barricade. We picked them off one by one. They mostly fought with hunting rifles and handguns, no match for our M16s. If the battle had been soldier against soldier, we would have won the day.

But then the tank lined up.

I glanced back at my grandfather watching from the hood of a car. Our lives all depended on the hope that they didn't have ammo in the big gun. The turret swiveled around toward us. I held my breath. It lined up on our position, then let loose with a heart-stopping *BOOM!*

The 120mm shell blew our fortification to bits.

Ben and I slammed to the ground. His elbow drove into my cheek. I tasted blood. We stared at each other, wide-eyed, slowly realizing we were both still alive. He shouted something—I saw his lips move—but I could only hear the ringing in my ears. And then my hearing came back with a high-pitched whine—slow and then sharp.

"Charlie!" Ben shouted.

Charlie Eagle lay facedown a few feet away from us, his arms at odd angles. We both scrambled to our feet and rushed over to him, but I could already tell there was nothing we could do. Ben turned him onto his back. Dead eyes stared up at us. One more stone piled onto my heart.

One more name added to the list of people I'd lost to the Skaggs.

Grandpa bellowed behind us. "Fall back!"

Ben grabbed me by the sleeve of my coat and pulled me away. The Skaggs poured in.

We saw Tim helping Mike Jorgenson out from beneath a large piece of sheet metal. We paused to help them, then we all took off running. Bullets whizzed past my head and zinged off the asphalt behind me. Following my grandpa, we barreled into the Chevron tire store and dove into the dark shadows behind the racks. A volley of shots hit the building. A mirror hanging on the wall behind me shattered. We returned fire.

The tank plowed over the remains of our barricade and crushed the fire barrel. Then it paused, adjusted its heading, and started moving toward the tire store.

We were about to get hit again.

"Here!" Grandpa shouted from the back of the store. He threw open the rear door, spilling in red moonlight. We piled out into a back alley, slipping away as another tank shell exploded the store.

Grandpa led us west, skirting through parking lots and winding our way through darkened backyards. He finally stopped just outside the old wastewater plant, allowing us to regroup and catch our breath.

"What's the plan?" Tim asked.

"We're falling back to the fortification at the round-about," Grandpa replied.

Jude balked at that idea. "But, sir, if we fall back, they take control of the Drop Zone."

"I know that, son," Grandpa replied. "But if we pull back now, we live to fight another day. Sera? You with us, girl?"

I blinked at him. My ears were still ringing and I was having a hard time getting the image of Charlie Eagle out of my mind. He and Vivica had been married for only three weeks. His loss would crush her.

"Sera?"

"I'm fine," I replied.

Jude slapped his gloves against his thigh. "How the hell are we going to fight off a tank?"

Tim snorted. "Don't s'pose anybody's got a tank trap in their pocket."

A look came over my grandfather's face that I'd seen many times in the past few months. He had a plan. "Everybody follow me."

I slung my rifle over my shoulder and we all took off into the night.

He stopped us at the top of Widowmaker Hill on the southern outskirts of Roslyn. The blind hill had a slight jog to the left where there'd been several head-on collisions over the years. "This is where we make our stand," he said.

Out of breath and frustrated, Jude shook his head. "I don't get it."

"How does Widowmaker Hill stop a tank?" asked Ben.

"Ever heard of an abatis?"

We all looked at each other.

"That a Starbuck's drink?" Tim joked.

Grandpa grunted. "Skaggs is gonna wish it was. I want every troop we've got, from the roundabout to the café, onsite within the hour. The rest of you, I need six chain saws and thirty Molotov cocktails. Can you do that for me?"

"Yes, sir!" we all shouted.

"They lost a lot of soldiers in that fight, so they're gonna want some time to regroup. That's gonna be our window of opportunity. Now, everybody head out!"

The troops scattered into the darkness.

"Sera? I want you and Ben to scout south. Report any movement. Do not engage."

Ben and I took off through the dark forest. I wove through the trees and ground cover in the direction of our last stand at the Walmart and, with no extra gear weighing him down this time, Ben kept up with me easily. The snowpack was shallow and we had our determination to keep us warm.

"Watch your three," Ben whispered.

Noting the break in cover to our right, I moved more deliberately until I'd regained the trees.

"You think this abatis thing is gonna work?" he asked.

"We're gonna find out."

"Guess that wrecks our wild plans for the night."

"What wild plans are those?"

"Bark tea at the café?"

I shook my head. If Grandpa knew how much time Ben spent flirting with me in the field, he would assign me a different spotter.

"Is that a yes?" Ben persisted.

I ignored him and kept moving.

He puffed his breath. "It is colder than a whore's heart out here."

"Next time wear the long johns."

"They're too constricting."

Something caught his eye and he pulled up short. We both dropped down into the snow. He pointed to our one o'clock, then held up two fingers. I lifted my head and saw two Skaggs peeing against trees fifty yards ahead of us. Beyond them, what looked to be the entire Skaggs army made its way down Highway 903, with the tank leading. They'd regrouped faster than expected and they were moving ever closer to the city limits.

"Looks like double what they had at the barricade," Ben whispered.

"They must have merged with another group."

"Ronald," we both said at once.

"They turned on us over a lousy bag of rice," Ben muttered.

"The good citizens of Ronald deserve what they get."

We watched the enemy in silence, trying to get a good feel for their numbers and capabilities. Every foot the tank rolled forward made me more uneasy. I started forward. "We have to stop that thing."

Ben grabbed my leg. "G-Pa said not to engage."

My grandfather was a smart man, but I was not going to just sit back and let seventy tons of metal roll over my town. "Then stay here."

I crawled through the snowy underbrush on my belly until I'd maneuvered onto a rise overlooking the highway. I propped the muzzle of my M16 on a rock and evaluated the situation through my nightscope. The Skagg soldiers appeared to be no better off than our own: ragged, gaunt, battle-worn. The men and women, mostly in their twenties, looked as hungry as we felt.

We'd heard rumors that the Skaggs ate their dead. Like Grandpa always said, never underestimate a hungry man.

A female fighter near the middle of the group slipped on the icy road and fell to one knee. I zeroed in on her, recognizing Naomi Laswell. She'd cut her brown hair short and traded in her designer jeans for a pair of camos, but it was definitely the girl who used to call me carrottop.

A hand reached down to help Naomi to her feet. Somebody lit a cigarette, illuminating her rescuer's face and I froze.

Large brown eyes, a long straight nose, a chiseled chin and a crooked smile—a smile that used to melt my heart.

Micah.

I gasped and jerked away from my scope, feeling like I'd just been struck in the chest. It couldn't be.

I pulled in a shaky breath, blinked to clear my eyes, and then took another long look through my scope.

I watched him move casually alongside Naomi, trading a few words with the man walking on his other side. It was definitely Micah. Naomi said something and Micah laughed. He laughed with our enemy as they pushed forward to destroy us. He wasn't tied up or under coercion. He marched with our enemy willingly.

I would have preferred to find him dead.

Tears sprang to my eyes, blurring my vision. What had he done? Had he walked away from me that night and joined the Skaggs? I'd spent all those months, missing him, *crying* over him and he'd been conspiring with our enemy the whole time—an enemy who invaded our homes, stole our food, and murdered our citizens.

David was right; people didn't change.

Something shifted inside me. All my heartbreak fled, replaced by a rage so potent I could taste it in the back of my throat. I set Micah's face in the crosshairs of my scope and nestled my cheek against the stock of my rifle. I eased my finger over the trigger, letting out a slow, steady breath.

"How's it look?"

My muscles twitched in surprise. Ben had crawled up next to me.

I came to my senses, realizing what I'd been about to do.

"What?" Ben asked in response to my expression. "Did

you really think I was gonna let you have all the fun?" He raised his own weapon to look through his scope.

I stopped him. "It's just a bunch of useless Skaggs." That wasn't a lie. "We need to report this."

We had a tense walk back through the dark to our new field position on Widowmaker Hill. My silence wasn't lost on Ben. He probably thought he'd done something wrong; I wasn't in the mood to correct him.

Fifteen minutes later, we heard the rumble of chainsaws echoing through the forest. We moved quickly to clear the woods. Then we saw trees being cut down along the reverse slope of Widowmaker. They were felled carefully, one at a time and at an angle, so that their trunks interlaced with their tips pointed toward the top of the incline. My grandfather was a genius. The trees would make an impenetrable wall that the tank could not see until it crested the top of the blind hill.

We found him instructing snipers positioned in the trees on the far side of the highway. "He's gonna have vehicles following behind his tank," he was telling them. "Aim for the drivers."

He turned to us. Meeting his bloodshot eyes, I wondered how long it had been since he'd slept. "How many?"

Ben answered him. "At least eighty."

He nodded. "They got reinforcements." He looked at me, sensing something was wrong. "What else?"

I shook it off. "Just tired."

"If this works," he replied, "we're all gonna sleep well tonight." He pointed to the east side of the road. "I need you two on the other side of the road in those trees over there. You're looking for bolters—soldiers going to ground in the woods. Nobody gets away. This ends today. Capture or kill. Got it?"

We heard the roar of the tank's engines. They were coming. *Micah* was coming.

"Positions!" Grandpa yelled.

Ben and I headed back into the woods. "You gonna tell me what spooked ya out there?" he asked, checking his weapon.

"Nope."

He snorted. "Figures."

"Just do your job, Sergeant Turner."

He found a thick copse of trees with adequate cover, overlooking the road. I moved thirty yards south and positioned myself behind an old shed. I tried to focus on my mission, but I couldn't get Micah's face out of my head. How could he have done this to us—to me? I raised my weapon, zeroed my nightscope on the road, and waited.

Will I be the one to kill him?

The thought popped into my head just as the tank appeared in my scope, roaring like a gray monster down the road toward Widowmaker Hill. *Or will it be somebody else? Ben? One of the snipers lying in wait on the other side of the road?*

Five SUVs followed the tank, along with eighty or so armed footsoldiers. Dirty snow churned beneath tread, wheel, and boot. The faces passed in a blur...until I saw him.

Everything came into sharp focus. He looked directly at me, as if he knew I was there, sighting on him from fifty yards out. My mouth went dry as I waited, breathless, to hear the first shot that would signal our attack.

Then it came. One loud, lone shot sent the world into chaos. I flinched, but kept Micah in my sights. I watched him through my scope and pictured his warm brown eyes. The way he smiled. The feel of my hand in his and the way my heart tripped at his touch.

Do it!

But I couldn't. I couldn't bring myself to squeeze the trigger.

I lowered my weapon.

The sound of gunfire split the night; the soldiers around Micah ducked for cover along the road. He didn't move. He just stood there like an idiot who wanted to die.

A heavy rain of bullets bombarded the Skaggs' SUVs, sending two of the vehicles screeching and skidding into a collision with each other. One of them exploded in a spectacular orange ball of fire, knocking Micah to the ground. He ducked his head just as one of the doors shot past him.

He was going to get himself killed.

Without thinking, I ran toward him. I leapt over prone Skaggs—some dead, some firing into the tree line—without a thought for the bullets flying around me. The Skaggs, busy shooting wildly into the woods, paid no attention to me.

I reached Micah just as the second SUV exploded. As the blast knocked me off my feet, I dove on top of Micah.

He blinked into my eyes. "Seraphina? What are you doing?"

"Saving you!" I shouted back.

A bullet whizzed past my head.

"Who's saving *you*?"

I took him by the sleeve of his jacket and pulled him to his feet. Ahead of us, the tank lumbered on toward Widowmaker Hill, despite heavy losses among the foot soldiers. Frank Skaggs obviously felt invincible hidden deep inside the belly of his armored vehicle. He was about to get a rude awakening.

The sound of shattering glass drew my attention to the three SUVs that made it through the initial onslaught. One of them suddenly erupted in a splash of red-hot flames, forcing me and Micah back several steps.

Molotov cocktails.

The second wave had started.

"Come on!" I dragged Micah off the highway toward the trees, just as a barrage of flaming glass bottles filled the air.

We dropped to the ground in the safety of the woods and watched as the Skaggs still alive on the highway suffered a crushing rain of hellfire. Their screams echoed through the night. The smell of their burning flesh filled my nose and gagged me. I had to look away.

From our vantage point, I watched the tank crest Widowmaker Hill. I imagined Frank Skaggs sitting inside, thinking he had won the day.

The tank's heavy gun and nose dipped down the far side of the hill, where it met the front of the abatis. The vehicle came to a screeching, grinding halt.

A half dozen chainsaws flared to life. A half dozen more trees fell, this time behind the tank. The driver threw the armored vehicle into reverse, only to slam into the points of the abatis there.

The tank groaned and screeched as the driver continued to switch gears, trying to maneuver out of the mess he'd found himself in. And then, with a grinding, banging, clunk, the left tread spilled off the tank. It was trapped.

The tank driver panicked and went full throttle, attempting to escape. Instead, the seventy-ton vehicle slid to the right and managed a half-turn before the tread on the right snapped off.

More Molotov cocktails filled the air. One by one, the homemade bombs hit the tank; a fine stream of flame crawled up one side. The fire crept into the exhausts and smoke poured from the vents. The top of the turret popped open and several men, including Frank Skaggs himself, stumbled out and fell to the ground, coughing. They were captured and dragged away.

Finally, a loud explosion split the night. The entire turret blew off the tank, soaring forty yards into the air. The armored vehicle had turned into a giant welder's torch, burning hot blue and yellow in the middle of the highway as the remaining ammo caught fire and exploded.

Cheers sounded from every direction. We'd done it. We'd taken out their tank and captured their leader.

I pulled Micah to his feet.

"Congratulations, Seraphina, your side just ended the war. Of course, you had to kill dozens of men to do it."

"You wanna live?" I growled. "Keep your mouth shut."

He looked at my weapon, then at me. "I'm not your enemy."

The sound of a bolt being thrown on an automatic rifle stopped me cold. I turned to see several clean-cut soldiers dressed in ocean blue BDUs pointing AK-12s at our heads.

Micah scowled. "They are."

Chapter Eleven

After months of fighting battle after bloody battle, Frank Skaggs had become a mythical figure in my mind, one with fangs and claws and fire shooting from his eyes. It was bizarre to see him beaten and tied up, when he'd once been the terrifying man who'd demanded my brother's head on a platter. He looked out of place standing in the mayor's office with the civilized people.

My eyes landed on the man standing behind Skaggs' old desk. I suspected his broad, friendly smile was all for show. "Come in, come in," the man said to me and my grandfather, as if we were all old friends.

My thoughts rushed back to the day before when I'd stood on the curb lining First Street, standing within a crowd of more than a thousand people, trying to ignore the biting cold. We'd all left our weapons at home—to prevent any misunderstandings—and I'd felt naked without my M16 slung over my shoulder.

They'd marched past us, one by one, a sea of ocean blue in even rows of twelve, their blue and white flags, embossed with a circle of ten gold stars, snapping in the frigid mountain wind. Grandpa Donner had said for months that our benefactors would one day name a price for their random and miserably inadequate supply drops, but nothing could have prepared us for the force we saw—soldiers, trucks, tanks. We'd defeated the Skaggs only to be occupied by a bigger, stronger, and much more dangerous force.

Europa.

And this cheerful, smiling man standing behind the mayor's desk commanded that force.

He wore a smart blue uniform with polished brass buttons on the front and three shiny gold stars on his shoulder epaulettes. The number of medals pinned to his chest spoke to his high-ranking position in the Europa pecking order. His hair was a dark brown, shot through with silver, and he wore a day's growth of beard over deep lines etched in by a persistent smile. But his eyes drew most of my attention. They were small and dark as night, like tiny black marbles inside the head of a creepy doll.

His hands landed on the desk in front of him. A gun rested there, inches from his fingertips. We'd come without weapons, not even a knife tucked into a boot. I wondered if my grandfather regretted that decision now.

Frank Skaggs snarled. "Don't trust him—"

The larger of the two guards rammed his gunstock into Skaggs' stomach, doubling him over, and I flinched. The guard's casual violence was terrifying.

The man behind the desk wagged his finger at Skaggs. "Now, now, Mr. Skaggs, we'll not have you spoiling our little get together today. You will remain quiet if you wish to participate."

The man's European accent sang in my ears, reminding me of scholarly and refined things. My instincts knew better.

I suspected his accent was as much a weapon as his never-ending smile.

He turned that smile on my grandfather, where it was completely wasted. "You must be General Donner."

"I'm no general. I'm a workin' man."

The man laughed. "Yes, of course. But I would not be mistaken if I were to say that you lead the Cascade Militia?"

"You would not."

The man clapped his hands. "Excellent. I am Christoph Stanislov, Praetor Stanislov to my men. You may call me Christoph, because we are going to be great friends, you and I." His small eyes fell on me. "And who is this lovely young lady?"

"You asked to see my family. Me and my granddaughter's all that's left."

We'd left David hidden away at home. Grandpa didn't want the praetor knowing about David. After Frank Skaggs, he wasn't about to take the chance that Europa might also consider my brother a liability.

The praetor nodded grimly. "This is very sad to hear. I, myself, lost a brother in the eruption. He was visiting your Air Force Academy in Colorado when the caldera blew."

He paused as if waiting to hear our condolences. When we offered none, he came around the desk toward us, his head cocked, his lips pursed. My eyes dropped down to his shiny black boots. It had been a long time since I'd seen shoes that weren't caked in ash and mud.

"You do know what has happened here?" he asked us. "That there is nothing left of your country?"

My knees went weak. After so much time with no contact from the outside world, we'd certainly assumed the worst. Yet hearing it said aloud was heartrending. I had so many questions, but I wasn't allowed to ask even one.

Grandpa Donner had given me explicit orders not to utter a word unless asked a direct question. And I should only give yes or no answers. He doubted that Europa had helped us out of the goodness of their hearts. Until he'd figured out what they wanted, I had to play the part of a harmless girl who knew nothing about war—something I hadn't been for a while.

Grandpa stuck out his bristly chin. "No, sir, I do not."

"You do not what? You do not know or you do not understand?"

"I don't know."

The praetor sat on the edge of his desk and spread his hands wide. "Well, it is a complete ruin. New York, Chicago, Atlanta, Los Angeles, your own Seattle. And D.C.," he added pointedly. "You live on an island surrounded by an endless sea of gray ash. Hundreds of millions of people are dead. Your government has disintegrated. America has been laid bare. She is no more. When I heard the news—I tell you the truth, I wept for days. Truly I did."

Tears burned my eyes. I bit my lip to keep it from trembling.

"But Roslyn!" The praetor leapt from the desk, grinning again. "Roslyn has survived! Was it the will of God? Perhaps. But Europa—*Europa* has fed you and kept you alive all these months. Why? Because we love America! Isn't that right, George?"

He looked over at the taller soldier guarding Frank Skaggs. The guard grunted. The praetor shrugged. "George is a man of few words."

I glanced sideways at my grandfather. The news of America's destruction was affecting him, too. His mustache was twitching.

The praetor paced in front of us, the heels of his

polished black boots clicking against the hardwood floor. "Now," he continued. "Let's talk about your little conflict. Mr. Skaggs? This is where you will be allowed to talk." He wagged his finger at Skaggs as if he were a naughty child. "You have made quite a mess of your community, sir. We give you food, we give you medicine, and you repay us by fighting with General Donner—" He laughed at himself. "Forgive me. You repay us by fighting with *Mr. Donner, the working man*, whose people believe in sharing equally with all. Am I correct with my facts, gentlemen?"

He was spot on and I wanted to say so but my grandfather's stony silence kept me in check.

Skaggs coughed before answering. Considering the bruises and swelling on his face, I was surprised he could speak at all. "You must really think you're somethin'," he rasped, "prancin' around in your shiny prissy boots."

The praetor scowled down at his own feet.

Skaggs continued, "But you got yourself into all kinds a trouble when you dared set foot on U.S. soil."

The praetor made a show of looking wide-eyed and stunned.

"This is America," Skaggs snarled. "The home of the brave, the land of the free. We don't like strangers comin' in and tryin' to run things their way."

"*My* way?" The praetor gestured at himself. "Oh, no. I'm certainly not in charge. We are a confederacy of ten nations, Mr. Skaggs. I answer to my superiors who, in turn, answer to the people of Europa."

Skaggs spit a stream of blood onto the floor and growled, "The people of Europa can kiss my ass."

The praetor's smile vanished. He blinked at my grandfather. "I can see why you fought with this man. He is arrogant, vulgar, and extremely ungrateful."

Frank Skaggs wasn't finished, though. "Ungrateful? You kept us all half-starved. But that was your plan all along, wasn't it, Stanislov? Keep us hungry and fightin' with each other. Then you could swoop in at the last minute and claim—"

The praetor picked up the gun from the desk and shot Frank Skaggs between the eyes.

I let out a startled cry. Blood splattered the two guards, but they didn't even blink. I stared, wide-eyed, at my grandfather. *Who are these people?*

As the guards dragged the body of Frank Skaggs out of the office, the praetor took a breath and set the gun back on the desk. Then he looked directly at me. "Forgive me. I cannot abide a blowhard." Then he cocked his head. "I'm sorry, my dear, I didn't get your name."

"Se-Seraphina."

Grandpa cleared his throat. I'd responded without thinking.

"Ah, the Hebrew name for fiery angel." He examined me. "And Donner. The proud German word for thunder. This is an odd name for such a quiet American girl." Then he smiled again. "Are you Jewish?"

This time I remembered the rules. "No," I replied.

The question made me think of Micah. He'd been heavy on my mind over the past couple of days. I hadn't seen him since the battle of Widowmaker Hill, where I'd handed him—along with the other captured Skaggs—over to Europa. I assumed he'd been locked up with the rest of them.

"Is your brother named after a Hebrew angel as well?"

"No." Too late I realized my mistake. "I mean—"

The praetor smiled at me. I glanced at my grandfather.

"Sera's brother's name is David," Grandpa conceded.

"Wonderful. The mythical David from the Bible. Does he brandish a slingshot and slay giants?"

"He keeps to himself mostly."

"But you didn't bring him with you today. Am I to assume that this is because of his condition?"

My heart sank. Despite our efforts, he already knew about David.

Grandpa's mouth tightened. "He's a little person."

"Aren't we all, on the inside?" the praetor replied. "And this *condition* of his, have doctors been consulted?"

I could tell that my Grandpa didn't like this line of questioning. Neither did I.

"It's genetic. It's just who he is."

"Certainly he's under a doctor's care? Your son's, perhaps? Dr. Jason Donner? I've read his work. He is a brilliant geneticist."

"My son is dead. And David is perfectly healthy."

The praetor pursed his lips and paced. Finally, he stopped directly in front of me. I stood motionless, my eyes locked on his boots. "Are there any other members of your family tucked away at home, Sera?"

"No," Grandpa answered.

"I would prefer to hear the answer from the young lady." He slipped his finger beneath my chin, lifting it until my eyes met his. It took everything I had not to recoil from his touch. There was a malevolence behind his gaze. He camouflaged it with pleasantries, but it was there just the same. "We are going to be friends, you and I. And friends are always honest with each other."

"No," I answered.

"No...?" he encouraged.

I swallowed. "No. There aren't any other family members at home."

He smiled. "Yes. Very good friends." He stepped away. I took a breath. "Now, Mr. Donner—may I call you Mark?"

Grandpa didn't respond. The praetor didn't seem to expect him to. "*Mark*, we are going to have a very special celebration at week's end. It will commemorate a covenant of friendship between Europa and Roslyn. There will be roasted venison, boiled rabbit, and barbecued cow for a more local flare—I do so love your barbecue. There will also be…" He wagged his brows at me. "Cakes and pies and all manner of sweets. How does that sound, Sera? Good?"

Good? I'd barely had time to hear the menu before my mouth started watering. I'd eaten nothing but Europa's boxed rations for as long as I could remember. I felt confident I could eat an entire barbecued cow all on my own.

"Yes," I said—not because I felt compelled to reply, but because if I didn't say something he might hear my stomach rumbling.

"Excellent. From you, Mark, I need a list of all the soldiers in your 1st Cascade Militia."

And there it was. The price we'd pay to eat.

Grandpa didn't respond. In fact, he clenched his jaw as if to say *Over my dead body*.

The praetor laughed and clapped him on the shoulder. "Don't look so worried, my friend! We want to give them medals for their brave service. Your cause is now our cause." He gave him the kind of serious look a father gives a child. "Can I count on you?"

My grandfather hesitated.

If he refused to answer, I dreaded what the cost would be for his disobedience. Would the praetor shoot him the same way he'd shot Frank Skaggs?

And then Grandpa surprised me. "Absolutely."

My mouth opened in surprise.

"Excellent!" the praetor said. He pointed at me. "As for you—tell your brother that I expect you both to be at the celebration."

I blinked. I wanted to celebrate with all that food more than anything else in the world, but accepting a kindness from this man didn't feel smart.

"Ah-ah, I will not take no for an answer. There will be more food than anybody could possibly eat." He could see me weakening and waited for my response. "There will be music and games," he added, as if that would settle things in his favor.

I glanced at my grandfather, who kept his eyes straight ahead with his lips thinned. He didn't want me to say yes.

The praetor leaned back against the edge of his desk. My attention fell on the gun lying there. "We are friends," he asked, "are we not, Sera?"

I swallowed hard. "Yes."

He lunged upright. "Then it's settled! I will see you and your brother at the celebration. Oh, and Mark." He pointed at my grandfather. "Do not forget that list."

Chapter Twelve

Tim paused, his dart pulled back to throw. "A *list?*"

Ben stood twenty feet away, waiting his turn at the large bullseye hanging on the wall of the Roslyn Café.

Jude Turner grunted. "He actually expects Grandpa Donner to turn in a list of all the fighting men in Roslyn?" Jude sat next to Milly at the table we all shared. She was cleaning a deep scratch on his arm. "Ow!" He winced.

She *tsked* at him. "Hold still, ya big baby."

"He says he wants to give them medals," I replied. I stared down into my bark tea and tried to shake the feeling of foreboding that had gripped me since we'd met with the praetor.

Ben snorted and tossed his dart. "More like a bullet to the brain."

"This praetor must think G-Pa's got a nut loose," Tim commented.

Milly shrugged. "So, what happens if he doesn't give him the list?"

"The praetor will kill him." They all looked at me, their expressions slipping.

"That makes it easy then," David murmured.

My brother sat across from me at the table, playing chess by himself—something he did a lot lately. His leg had healed completely since the drop zone, but six months of isolation had made him bitter and withdrawn. While the rest of us fought for our town or, like Milly, worked at the hospital, David stayed home where he'd be safe from Frank Skaggs.

"What?" he said in response to our stares. "It's simple. There's no way to fight them, so we join them."

"This is America," Tim jeered, "not France."

"America is gone," David responded. "We should cooperate in good faith with Europa. Or would you prefer starvation and death?"

Ben shook his head, exasperated. "We can't just hand them the names of our fellow fighters."

"Why not?" David countered. "Europa food drops have fed us for half a year. What makes you think Praetor Stanislov doesn't intend to do exactly as he said and give all your friends medals?"

Tim and Ben broke into laughter, which only deepened David's scowl.

"You haven't met him," I replied. "He doesn't feel right."

"Oh. Well," David retorted, "everybody stop what you're doing. Sera's having a feeling."

I glared at him. "He shot Frank Skaggs without batting an eye."

David slammed his hands down onto the table, knocking over his chess pieces and startling us all. "*Good!*" he boomed. "Skaggs was a vicious, embittered megalomaniac who was responsible for the deaths of almost a hundred people! In seconds, the praetor kills a man you've been trying to kill for months, and you *criticize* him for it?"

"Skaggs said we shouldn't trust him," I gritted out.

David gave me a patient stare. "The enemy of my enemy is my friend, Sera." He climbed down from his chair, scooped up his game, and walked over to a nearby table to sit by himself.

"He's got a point."

We all stared at Jude.

"My brother the diplomat," Ben remarked.

Jude shrugged. "The praetor hasn't given us any reason to doubt him."

"David wasn't there," I snapped. "None of you were. Grandpa's convinced that Europa's reasons for being here have nothing to do with helping us."

"Then what do they want?" Jude asked. "Milly's MRE casserole recipe?" He pulled a face and shuddered.

Milly scowled and gave him a playful punch.

I glared at them both. Their infatuation with each other bordered on annoying.

"Whatever it is—" Ben tossed his dart at the board. "—they aren't gettin' it."

The bell over the front door rang as three people entered the café wearing clear plastic capes and carrying flashlights. One of them was Peter Williams.

"Great," Ben muttered. "The freak parade has arrived."

Every eye in the place watched them shuffle across the room to a table in the corner. We all knew what was coming. They'd start shining their flashlights in everybody's faces and shoving handwritten flyers at us. Their writing claimed the white light abductions were signs of an imminent alien invasion. They were a reminder of my mother and the last thing I needed today.

Milly scowled. "It isn't polite to stare."

"If you don't want people starin'," Tim answered, "then you shouldn't leave the house wearin' your shower curtain."

Ben dropped down into David's vacated chair across from me. "I liked it better when the White Lighters were afraid to show their faces in public."

"Like the Spathi?" Jude replied.

"Bunch of filthy cowards," Ben growled.

"I'd love to get my hands on a Spathi," Tim added.

The Spathi—Greek for 'Spears Of God' were anonymous. After Frank Skaggs had killed their apostle and burned down their commune, the remnants of the CBC changed. They hid in trees, camouflaged by their brown canvas ponchos, and sniped people in the name of their Lord. We'd lost five soldiers to them in just the past month.

The bell over the door clanged again. Milly looked up. Her eyes grew wide and fixed behind me. She leaned across the table and grabbed my arm. "Sera!" she hissed. "Look!"

I turned in my chair. A familiar figure with dark hair and dark eyes stood at the door. Micah. Part of me had hoped to never see him again.

"I know," I said.

She gaped at me. "You…you *know*?"

Ben scowled. "Isn't that Micah Abrams?"

Tim grunted. "In the flesh."

"I thought he was dead."

Tim clapped Ben on the shoulder. "Looks like yer outta luck, buddy."

I swung to my feet, slung my automatic rifle over my shoulder, and met Micah at the door. "You need to leave," I hissed.

Micah stared back at me with intense, mesmerizing eyes. I wanted to blacken them both. "We need to talk."

About what? I thought. *How many nights I cried myself to sleep after you disappeared? The moments my heart stopped, thinking I saw you in a crowd? Or maybe the day I learned you were captured and gave up hope?* "I have nothing to say to you."

I turned to walk away and saw my brother staring at us from across the room with a murderous expression on his face.

Micah grabbed hold of my hand.

"Let go of me!"

He pulled me out the door and into the red sunlight.

"What are you doing here?" I wrenched my hand from his grasp. "You made your choice—you're not one of us anymore!"

He looked frustrated. "You're judging things you can't possibly understand, Seraphina."

"You mean like lies? Cruelty? Betrayal? I hope spending some quality time with the people who starved and murdered us brought you a great deal of satisfaction." Then a thought occurred to me. "Did you break out of jail?"

He gave me an impatient scowl. "I told them I wasn't a Skagg and they let me go."

"Then the praetor's dumber than I thought."

"I am not a Skagg," he insisted.

"You're worse than a Skagg! You're a traitor!" I'd seen too much death to tolerate defectors. They were the worst of the worst, viler than the enemy themselves.

"We don't have time for this. There's a bomb in the café."

My breath caught. "A *what*?!"

"You need to leave."

"If there's a bomb, then why are you here?"

"To save you."

My treacherous heart skipped at his confession. I

covered it by narrowing my eyes. "Who told you about a bomb?"

"Seraphina," he warned, "I will carry you away if I have to."

I hooked my thumb through the shoulder strap of my weapon. "That would be a good way to get yourself shot."

He checked his watch. "Five minutes."

I stared at him, trying to read the truth in his expression. I didn't want to give him the satisfaction of acting on his warning, but my pride wasn't worth people's lives.

I charged back into the café. "Everybody out! Now!"

Ben jumped from his chair. "What's happening?"

"There's a bomb threat."

"A bomb threat?" Tim repeated.

Chairs toppled. People scrambled to their feet. A wave of clear plastic capes fluttered to the back exit.

"By who?" Milly asked.

"I don't know."

David slipped down from his chair. "Considering it's been a while since I've heard the ring of a telephone, I'm curious…exactly how was this threat made?"

I looked back at Micah who'd followed me inside. "He told me."

David laughed, then climbed back into his chair. "I believe I'll wait this one out."

"Micah's word is good enough for me." Jude held out his hand to Milly. "Exit stage left?"

Tim nodded. "I'm with you two."

Ben looked at me. "You coming?"

"Once the building is cleared."

He hesitated, glancing between me and Micah, then followed the others out the back exit.

My brother remained at his table.

"Don't be stupid, David," I said.

"I think you'll find out soon enough that you are the stupid one." He sipped his bark tea, glaring at Micah over the rim of his mug.

"Seraphina," Micah warned.

"I'm not leaving without my brother."

Micah checked his watch. "Fine." He marched toward David.

David was instantly suspicious. "What are you doing?"

"Saving your sister's life." He picked David up and threw him over his shoulder like a squirming sack of snakes.

"What the hell do you think you're doing?" David bellowed. He kicked Micah hard in the chest; Micah had to grab hold of his flailing feet to keep him under control.

Micah turned to me with his enraged bundle. "Out! Now!"

I moved quickly toward the exit of the café, my brother's curses ringing in my ears. We spilled out into the snowy courtyard, clambered through the wreckage of Harper's Lumber, ran across what used to be the Laswell family's backyard, and ended up on Washington Avenue with the others. David screamed bloody murder the whole time.

"Oh my stars," Milly commented when she saw David thrashing over Micah's shoulder.

Tim grunted. "This ain't gonna end well."

Micah set David on his feet and, wisely, took a few steps back. David's face was red, his mouth tight, and his eyes were bulging from his head. He looked like a bomb about to go off.

And then one did.

The explosion ripped through the air and popped my ears. We ducked behind the wall of the lumber building as a shower of debris rained down over our heads.

I glanced over at Micah. He didn't look happy about being right.

When the dust settled, we all hurried onto Second Street and stared down the block. The café was completely demolished. Again.

"Damn," Tim breathed.

David picked up a splintered board and advanced on Micah. "How did you know? *How?*"

"Whoa, now, Double D." Tim stepped in front of him and took away the board. "Let's not beat the messenger."

"The guy just saved us from being blown to bits," Jude interjected.

David looked around at everyone. "How can you all be so stupid?" he shouted. "He probably planted the bomb *himself!*"

That was an interesting theory. Micah had undoubtedly learned all kinds of new tricks from his friends the Skaggs. Before I could pursue it, though, the heavy sound of marching boots reached our ears. Our new protectors, the Europa Guard, were rushing in to save the day.

"Scatter!" I ordered. Until we knew Europa's true motives, it wouldn't be smart to get caught at the site of a bombing.

We took off in different directions. I raced up the alley toward Coal Mines Trail, glancing back only once to see my brother still standing in the middle of Second Street. He was refusing to follow my orders. I doubted they'd suspect him, but his determination to rebel against the rest of us worried me.

I reached the outskirts of Pioneer Park and slowed to a walk. I heard footsteps and knew Micah had followed me.

"Let's just cut right to the chase," I said.

He fell into step beside me.

"Who was your informant?"

"I can't say."

I gave him a direct look. "Because it's you."

He blanched. "Come on, Seraphina."

"Only a Skagg would know about a Skagg bombing, Micah."

"How can you be so sure it was the Skaggs?"

"Who else would blow up a well-known hangout of the 1st Cascade?"

He pointed at me. "Now *that* is a very good question."

My mind churned. Was he suggesting Europa planted the bomb? I opened my mouth to ask, but he suddenly veered left toward Fourth Street.

"Wait, where are you going?"

"I can't spend all my time saving you, Seraphina Donner."

I gritted my teeth. "You're not off the hook yet, Micah!" I called after him.

He responded by giving me a jaunty wave.

I watched him walk away, hating that I could still feel so drawn to someone who'd betrayed me so badly.

***

THAT NIGHT I had the nightmare again for the first time in months.

I'm floating in the water. A beach of shimmering white. A mountain made of gold. Micah. The dragon roars. Eyes so red. Teeth so sharp. Run, Micah! He smiles at me as the dragon devours him.

I woke up screaming.

Chapter Thirteen

On the morning of the Europa Welcome Festival, the sun struck the cloudless red sky with a beautiful blood orange and deep magenta dawn. For the first time in months, temperatures climbed a few degrees above freezing. But there wasn't a soul on the streets.

The Skaggs bombing of the Roslyn Café had people on edge. The big red 'S' painted on the sidewalk outside made it clear who'd planted the bomb. Pockets of insurgent Skaggs were still hiding out in the mountains, apparently refusing to give up the fight.

Regardless of people's fears, participation in the festivities at Pioneer Park was mandatory. The praetor and his men had gone all-out. Streamers of blue and gold decorated the gazebo and baseball diamond, highlighting the banners welcoming the "saviors" from Europa to our town.

They'd built a stage and podium. They'd even strung lights around the edge of the stage to complete the grand effect, although we didn't have the electricity to turn them on.

The White Lighters came out in full force with fliers and

bullhorns, shouting, "Endure!" Every now and then, they'd shine their flashlight into the wrong face and get it ripped from their hands and thrown back at them.

Most citizens went to the park to celebrate. They sat around the big bonfire, drinking mulled wine from Europa and waving miniature blue and white flags like it was the Fourth of July. Though I didn't like it, I understood Roslyn's love affair with Europa. They wanted their grim lives to get better, so they were willing to follow anyone who promised positive change. We just couldn't figure out what Europa wanted with Roslyn.

I sat on a picnic table with Grandpa, Milly, and the boys, toward the back of the large crowd. David stood in the center of the picnic table so he could see the stage over the restless throng. He had a tiny Europa flag clutched in his hand and he was smiling—something I hadn't seen him do in a long time.

A platoon of Europa soldiers marched onto the stage. David bounced on his toes, vibrating with excitement. "Here we go!"

The soldiers began to sing. I watched, astounded, as most of the crowd bowed their heads and fell into reverent silence.

Hail Europa, friend of all,
Thy mighty name makes nations tall.
Thy will alone be law on earth.
We welcome now thy kingdom's birth.

We pledge each day our hearts, our lives,
Our every care from thee derives.
We lay our lives down at your throne.
Protect, preserve our life our home.

Hail Europa!

A cheer went up from the crowd. Several people shouted, "Hail, Europa!"

"What a joke." Ben shook his head in disgust.

"We fought and died for these people," Tim added. "And now they lay down for Europa."

Grandpa patted Tim on the shoulder. "'To conquer a nation, one must first disarm its citizens.'"

"To accept the gift of kindness," David interjected, "one must first put down his weapons."

Grandpa grunted. "There's nothin' wrong with keepin' an open mind, son, so long as your brain doesn't fall outta your head in the process."

Like the rest of us, Grandpa tolerated David's adoration of Europa, but David was paying for his rebellion with a loss of access. He was no longer in the loop. The rest of us knew what Grandpa had planned for that day, but, as far as David was concerned, the praetor would get exactly what he wanted: a list of 1st Cascade soldiers.

Just the night before, under the cover of darkness, Vivica Davis had marched the 1st Cascade out of town. With the loss of her husband Charlie Eagle, she'd welcomed the opportunity to take command of the troops. She'd risen to the rank of captain in a matter of months. Grandpa knew his soldiers would be in good hands.

Grandpa had also insisted Doctor Reinkann and his family go with Vivica. As the militia's field surgeon, the doctor was in as much danger as the soldiers themselves. Doctor Reinkann had hesitated at first, but, for the sake of his wife and teenage sons, he'd agreed to leave in the end.

The Odettes and the Turners had refused to leave; they wouldn't even discuss it. Grandpa hadn't pressed them.

The crowd around us cheered. We stood up to get a better look as the praetor strutted across the stage like he was accepting the presidency. He wore an ocean blue long-coat with gold shoulder braids and brass buttons. The tall, furry white hat propped on his head made him look like an overdressed chef, in my opinion. But what flanked him on both sides really caught my attention; two enormous white wolves sat precisely at his feet. They eyed the crowd as he stepped up to the podium. They were magnificent and, without a doubt, lethal.

As usual, the praetor's broad smile was pervasive. He waited until the applause died down before speaking. Though we couldn't hear him, he kept talking as if we could.

"We can't hear you!" shouted the crowd.

The praetor smiled. Shrugged. Shook his head. Finally, he turned to his personal guard George, standing behind him, and gestured dramatically. It was all so overdone I felt like I was watching a bad high school play.

George handed him a microphone and the crowd chuckled a bit at that folly. Then we all gasped in shock as the loud, high-pitched squeal of microphone feedback cut through the cold morning air. I watched, stunned, as the praetor bent his head to the mic.

"Can you hear me now?"

His voice boomed out like thunder. His wolves startled and snapped at each other. And then the lights strung up around the edge of the stage lit up like a Christmas tree.

The audience lost their minds.

David thrust his hand in the air and cheered. "Yes! Yes!"

Milly and I stared at each other in shock. Europa had done it. They'd turned on the electricity.

The praetor's friendly, accented voice boomed out over

the crowd. "People of Kittitas County, I am Praetor Stanislov, the humble commander of the Europa Military Guard."

The crowd was going wild.

"Gotta give the man credit," Grandpa conceded. "He knows how to make an entrance."

The praetor nodded gratefully in response to the cheers, then waited for the crowd to quiet down. "For months, Europa has watched with deep distress as you have struggled," he began. "A timeless historical bond once linked the United States with the international community, but that bond was severed many years ago by your own inflexible government. For over a decade, Europa has worked to gain the proud confidence of the European people through the noble ideals of a One World government, while, here in America, your intractable leaders thrust you into a long, hard period of suffering and bitter adversity.

"Your government, by means of brutal terror and punitive, destructive economic measures, attempted to maintain an existence rejected by the vast majority of you, the American people. Thus, the world watched as a small minority, simply by seizing the necessary instruments of power, suppressed more than three hundred million people. And, if that were not bad enough, your political suppression and the deprivation of your freedoms led to an economic decline that was in shocking contrast to the blossoming life in Europa."

Grandpa grunted. "Europa propaganda."

I spotted a dark head near the front left of the stage and knew it was Micah. Last night's nightmare came back to me in a rush, along with all the emotion. The dragon had visited me every night for the past week, always waking me with a start. Now the recurring nightmare revolved around me saving Micah. He died every night in my dreams. How was I supposed to get him out of my heart if I couldn't get him out of my head?

"And who could blame you," the praetor continued, "if you looked toward Europa with longing eyes? We are the same people that your forefathers united with for so many centuries. The same people your ancestors once fought shoulder to shoulder with in terrible wars. Our culture is your culture. We share some of our most cherished values with you.

"We have felt your suffering as our own, the suffering imposed on you, our brothers and sisters here, first by your own government, then by natural disaster, and finally by hostile elements within. Therefore, it would be impossible— nay, inhuman—for Europa to simply watch as you die from hunger, lack of medicines, or unsavory aggressions. My good friends, this Devastation, as you call it, has reached to the four corners of the world. Europa has accepted more than four million refugees in through her hospitable borders. And now, we welcome *you*."

A great cheer went up from the crowd. The wolves onstage grew restless again, but one firm word from the praetor settled them down. Micah's tall, still figure caught my eye again. I hadn't seen him clap once and I wondered why he'd bothered to get a front row seat if he wasn't one of the devoted.

People around us were high-fiving and hugging; some even started weeping. David was in the latter group.

"Is he actually cryin'?" Milly whispered to me.

He actually was.

"Now," the praetor continued, "not everyone may feel inclined to accept our charity. There have been millions who have resisted our offer. They have become beggars, reduced to misery and poverty, but who can understand the depths of the human heart?"

The crowd chuckled.

"However, I'm sure that the people here are far wiser than that, far wiser than even your national leaders who have since blown away with the ash. We know that you will welcome our open hand of friendship. That is why we have conquered your enemy the Skaggs and left them as a footstool at your feet."

This announcement was met with roaring cheers from the crowd. We all blinked at each other.

"Did he just say what I think he said?" Ben questioned.

I closed my eyes and fought down a rush of anger. We had suffered, bled, and died for these people and Europa was taking all the glory.

"Unbelievable," Jude stated.

"The people are actually buyin' this," Tim remarked.

Grandpa chuckled. "Welcome to the rewriting of history, ladies and gentlemen."

David scowled at us, but kept cheering.

The praetor continued. "I, myself, as the praetor of the Europa Guard, will live here among you, to personally ensure the safety of your rights as free citizens of Europa. The world will see that, for the American people, these new days are filled with hours of blissful joy and deep emotion. Long live Europa! Long live a free America!"

The people in the crowd lost their minds. The sound level was deafening.

"Free," Jude snorted. "Free to do what Europa tells us to do."

I stared at my grandfather. He had an odd smile on his face. "You actually look impressed," I remarked.

Grandpa shrugged. "I am. That was a stunning rewrite of the speech Hitler gave when he invaded Austria."

David rolled his eyes. "Please tell me you are not actually going to compare him to Hitler."

"Why?" Ben shot back. "Will that hurt your feelings?"

"Because it's tired," David retorted. "Every alarmist since World War II has compared his rival to Hitler."

Tim laughed. "Well, if the swastika fits...."

As the Europa troops filed off the stage, the praetor commanded the microphone once again. "Ladies and gentlemen, I know that you are very anxious to get to all the yummy food, but first Europa would like to honor our American brothers and sisters who fought tirelessly along-side us against the Skaggs."

"Now we fought *with* them?" Ben growled.

Tim grimaced. "He's rewritin' so fast I'm gettin' whiplash."

To their credit, the crowd applauded, although not nearly as loudly as they'd applauded and cheered for the praetor.

"But I will need some help." Praetor Stanislov shaded his eyes and looked deep into the crowd. His gaze landed on my grandfather. "Ah. There he is." He smiled. "The hard-working Mr. Donner. Would you and your lovely family please join me onstage?"

Here it was. The moment I'd been dreading ever since the praetor had asked for the list of soldiers from the 1st Cascade.

David nearly stumbled as he hurried off the picnic table, while Grandpa and I moved more deliberately through the crowd on our way to the stage. The three of us climbed the four wooden stairs and approached the praetor at the podium. I could feel Micah's eyes following me; I hated that he was about to watch me play puppet to the praetor.

As we approached, the white wolves emitted low growls. They were bigger than they'd looked from the audience; their heads were enormous.

The praetor smiled effusively. He made a great show of shaking Grandpa's hand. "Mr. Donner, so good to see you." He turned his smile on me and shook my hand. "Sera, thank you for coming." His palm was sweaty and I resisted wiping my hand on my jeans.

The praetor's eyes landed on David and widened like a toddler ogling a new toy. "And this must be David. It is wonderful to meet you, young man."

David smiled so broadly I thought his face might split in two. "It's very nice to meet you, too, sir."

One of the giant wolves sniffed my leg and bared its teeth.

"Never mind my pets," the praetor said. "They take their job of protecting me a little too seriously sometimes." He ruffled the fur on the head of the wolf to his right. "Don't you, Hati?"

The wolf snapped at him and the praetor slapped him viciously on the snout, his smile faltering a bit. When the wolf cowered to the floor, the praetor's smile reappeared. "Bad tempered brute," he cooed.

I looked out over the audience. They were buying every counterfeit moment of the praetor's act. So was David. My eyes landed on Micah's stony face. He wasn't fooled a bit.

"Are those Ellesmere Island wolves?" David asked.

"Why, yes, they are. Aren't you a clever young man?"

David beamed.

The praetor turned toward the audience, who had been hanging on every word. "Ladies and gentlemen, Mr.

Donner has been kind enough to make me a list of the brave soldiers who fought with us in the 1st Cascade." He held his hand out to my grandfather. "Mr. Donner, if you would be so kind?"

My grandfather made a show of hesitating, then placed the piece of paper in the praetor's hand.

The praetor waved the list at the crowd. "If you hear your name, please come up and join us on the stage."

Soldiers removed the podium and set a small table next to him. Small, blue velvet boxes, stacked in precise, neat rows, rested on top of it. He looked at the list and glanced over the names. They had been carefully chosen, the letters neatly printed to avoid mistakes.

I held my breath and waited as he called the first name. "Jacob O'Neil."

The crowd broke into murmurs as they looked around, waiting for Jacob O'Neil to reveal himself. At first it seemed as if Jacob was absent. But then somebody shouted, "Here he is!"

David and I stepped back as a very reluctant young man shuffled up onto the stage and tried to hide behind the praetor and my grandfather. The guy was sweating bullets.

Grandpa Donner turned and saluted him. "Son."

Jacob O'Neil looked at my grandfather as if he'd never seen him before—because he hadn't ever seen him before. Jacob O'Neil was a Skagg, one of many who had infiltrated our community after the battle of Widowmaker Hill to avoid arrest by Europa.

Confused and alarmed, Jacob O'Neil didn't dare correct the mistake. He would soon be joined by thirty-seven other guinea pigs, all of whom would, unknowingly, help us test Europa and their intentions toward the 1st Cascade.

The praetor, wearing a broad smile, shook Jacob

O'Neil's hand. "Thank you, young man. Thank you for your fine service to this community."

He picked up a blue velvet box from the table, opened it, and showed it to the crowd. Inside, the polished gold medal had 'EUROPA' embossed in blue around the edge and a woman riding a bull imprinted in the center. It was all topped with a crisp blue and gold ribbon.

The crowd "oohed" and "aahed" over it, which pleased the praetor. He handed the medal to Jacob O'Neil and then directed him to stand at the back of the stage.

The praetor read out the next name. "Erica Cauldwell."

The crowd looked around for their next hero. Murmurs were heard here and there, but no one stepped forward.

"Come now," the praetor said. I could tell he was growing impatient and his wolves could, too. They both shifted restlessly. "Why so shy?" He tried to maintain his smile. "Where are you, Erica Cauldwell. Raise your hand. Up, up, up."

Finally, a single pale hand emerged from the crowd, slowly and with little confidence.

The praetor smiled. "Ah. There she is. Come up. Come up now. We have a medal for you." He turned to share a terse laugh with my grandfather. "Perhaps we should have offered confectionaries?"

The crowd chortled.

This went on for almost a full hour. The praetor would read a name, the crowd would fall silent, and then eventually the Skaggs would either reveal themselves or be revealed by somebody standing near them. Finally, thirty-eight Skaggs stood on the stage, all of them holding tiny boxes, all of them white as sheets.

The praetor gestured to them. "Ladies and gentlemen, the heroes and heroines of your 1st Cascade Militia."

The crowd applauded and cheered.

Grandpa made a grand gesture of saluting them all. "Thank you for your service."

They all looked so dumbfounded that I almost laughed out loud.

"And now," the praetor announced, "as is custom in Europa, we will leave the stage and allow the soldiers a few moments to be honored by the crowd."

We followed him to the stairs and exited the stage, leaving the Skaggs standing there staring awkwardly out over the cheering throng. We moved to the right and stood off to the side. I stole several glances at the praetor. He seemed completely fooled by the list.

David tugged on my arm. I bent down toward him. "What is going on?" he hissed in my ear. He'd met enough of the 1st Cascade to know that none of the people on stage were part of the militia.

I kept applauding. "Just smile and clap."

He did as I said, but I could tell he was angry that he hadn't been in on the plan.

A loud gunshot suddenly punctuated the whoops and cheers. The mood of the crowd changed instantly. Jason O'Neil separated himself from the others onstage. He'd shot one of the Europa soldiers standing in the front row.

He pointed his gun at the praetor. "Pledge or perish!" he shouted. He fired again.

Lucky for the praetor, Jason O'Neil was a terrible assassin. Unlucky for Jason, the praetor's wolves were not. Jason's shot went wide, hitting another man in the crowd, but the largest wolf broke free of his restraint and was on Jason in seconds. With a shocking ferocity, the animal dragged the man down and tore at his throat.

The other Skaggs attempted to flee, some even jumped

into the audience to get away from the vicious beast. The praetor barely had control of the second wolf and, for a moment, it seemed as if it, too, was going to break free and tear into the crowd.

And then an explosion ripped through the air, hitting my eardrums like nails. I felt it in my bones. It shook the ground and knocked us all backwards. I slammed into the dirt and snow. A hard, heavy rain of debris fell over the top of me. The smell of plastic, burnt wood, and gunpowder stung my nose.

After a few moments, I managed to sit up and look around. The world had gone muffled and sideways. Everything was in chaos. The stage was now a charred hole full of debris.

I stumbled to my feet, my ears ringing, my head throbbing, my vision blurred.

Micah.

I moved like I was dreaming, slow and fluid. Screaming people shoved past me, going the opposite direction, tripping over each other to get out of the park. I passed charred, mangled bodies, and images from the church on the day of the quake flickered through my mind.

"Endure," I heard my mother whisper.

I climbed over a mound of debris several feet high, his name rolling over and over in my head. *Micah. Micah.* My foot slipped and stuck in something soft and sticky. I looked down to see my shoe planted in the scorched remains of a man's chest.

I screamed and everything went black.

Chapter Fourteen

I woke up on the sofa in Grandpa's house. Staring at the ceiling, I blinked to clear my vision and moaned at the ache in my head.

Milly sat beside me. "She's awake."

Tim's face appeared in front of mine. "Did he say anything to you?"

I wasn't sure what he meant. "H-how did I get here?" The last thing I remembered was standing on stage as the praetor handed out medals.

"Give her a minute," Milly instructed.

"What the hell have you done?" David shouted. I squinted across the room and saw him pacing back and forth in front of the fireplace.

"Chill out, David." Ben, standing by the front door, slammed a banana clip into his M16 and lifted the edge of the curtain to look out the window.

Jude had his rifle loaded and shouldered. "Anything?" he asked his brother.

"Nothing yet," Ben replied.

I tried to sit up, but my head instantly rebelled and I laid back down. "W-what happened?"

My brother stormed toward me. "I'll tell you what happened! You just destroyed any chance this town ever had at survival!"

Milly surged to her feet. "At least give her time to catch her breath before you go blamin' her for the end of the world!"

I held my aching head and tried to clear the haze. "Could somebody please tell me what's going on?"

Milly turned and looked at me with tears pooling in her eyes. "They've arrested Grandpa."

The world fell out from under my feet. It all came rushing back: the festival, the stage, the bomb. I pushed into a sitting position, ignoring my spinning head.

"Arrested!" David yelled savagely. "*And for what?* Trying to kill a man who wants to help us!"

This time Jude stepped in front of him. "Calm down—"

"Calm down?" David laughed. "You blow up a stage full of people, and you want *me* to calm down?"

I stared at him in shock. "You think *we* blew up the stage?"

"Of course he does." Ben's opinion of my brother had hit rock bottom.

Tim couldn't believe it either. "How can you think we'd be capable of doin' somethin' like that?"

"Because his new best buddy is Europa," Ben snarled.

David threw up his hands. "I give up. *What* do you have against them? Is it the abundance of food and water?" He flipped the switch on the wall, turning on the lights over the fireplace. "The electricity, perhaps? Or are you just jealous that nobody needs the precious 1st Cascade Militia anymore?"

"They're an invading force!" Ben shouted at him. "Wrapped up in a pretty bow!"

David snorted. "Next you're going to tell me that the praetor planted the bomb, hoping to kill himself."

"It was obviously the Skaggs," Milly interjected. "They found a red 'S' painted on the roof of the park gazebo, just like at the café."

David laughed. "Well, score another one for mindless Milly. You think the Skaggs blew up a stage full of Skaggs?"

Jude bent down to look David in the eye. "You talk to her like that again and I'm putting my foot through your face."

David waved him off, but moved further across the room.

"David's right," Tim stated. "It don't make sense. Even if the Skaggs planted the bomb, they wouldn't set it off with their own people on stage. The praetor's obviously pretty fond of himself. I don't see him knowingly standin' on top of a bomb—even if the plan was to set it off after he left."

"But if the Skaggs didn't do it," Jude answered, "and the praetor didn't do it, then who the hell did?"

Milly chewed her lip. "If the 'S' doesn't stand for Skaggs, then what could it stand for?"

That's when it finally clicked in my head. "Spathi." They all looked at me. "It stands for Spathi."

"Spathi?" Tim repeated. "Where would Spathi get bombs?"

"Where do they get rifles and ammo?" I said.

"Off dead soldiers." Jude answered. "If they're the bombers, then they've upped their game."

Ben nodded. "The Skaggs certainly make a perfect scapegoat. We all suspected them."

"Then the Skaggs didn't blow up the café," Milly concluded.

"No, they didn't," I replied. Micah had been trying to tell me that on the day of the café bombing.

My breath caught in my chest. *Micah.* He'd been standing in front of the stage right before the explosion. A wave of nausea hit me so hard I thought I might be sick.

Milly saw it on my face. "Sera? What is it?"

"We need to tell Praetor Stanislov what we know," David stated. "If we tell him about the Spathi, he'll release Grandpa."

I pulled my thoughts together and tried to focus. "Why would he think Grandpa blew up the stage?"

"Because he knows your list was a fake, Sera!" David snapped. "He thinks Grandpa had all the Skaggs brought up onstage so he could blow them sky-high!"

My heart sank. Our list hadn't fooled the praetor at all.

A hard knock sounded on the door. Tim and Jude readied their weapons, then Ben pulled open the door. When I saw Micah standing there, looking haggard but safe, it took everything I had not to run into his arms.

I got to my feet. "You're okay."

His eyes locked with mine, his expression hollow—haunted. Something was wrong.

"What do you want?" David snarled.

"They're going to execute him," Micah rasped. "They're going to execute your grandfather."

I dropped back down to the sofa.

The room fell silent. We were all too stunned to move. Finally, Milly put her face in her hands and started to cry. Jude crossed the room to put his arm around her shoulders.

"Well, of course they're going to execute him!" David

exploded. "They think he's a damn terrorist because of that stupid fake list!"

I rubbed at the ache in my forehead. I needed to think.

"We need a plan," Tim said.

David snorted. "Because your plans have worked out so well up to this point."

"Here's a plan," Ben announced. "We call back the 1st Cascade, march into city hall, and kill every last damn blue coat we see."

Jude shook that off. "They'll only send more."

Milly sniffled and hiccupped. "We can't just…just sit here and do nothin'."

David grabbed his coat off the chair.

I straightened. "Where are you going?"

"To talk to Praetor Stanislov."

Micah blocked the door. "That's a bad idea."

David glared murderously up at him. "Get out of my way."

"They've imposed a curfew," Micah told us all. "Anybody caught out after dark will be arrested on sight."

"Then I won't be seen," David gritted out.

I shook my head. "David, the praetor is smart. He'll talk you in circles."

"Why," he sneered, "because he talked *you* in circles?"

Ben looked flabbergasted. "Why do you have to be such an ass all the time?"

"Because," Tim responded, looking gloomy. "Double D is only on the side of Double D."

David jeered at him. "When I need a hick's opinion, I'll ask Milly."

Jude lunged toward him, but Milly took his hand and steadied him.

"David," I began, "Grandpa made it very clear that we shouldn't underestimate the praetor."

"Sera, the praetor is just a man, a man who can be reasoned with like any other man." He turned for the door.

"Fine," I stood up again. "I'm going with you."

Micah vetoed that immediately. "Absolutely not."

I pulled on my coat. "If we're not back in two hours, I want every one of you out of town before dawn. Find the 1st Cascade and stay put."

Ben nodded. I knew he'd follow orders and make sure the others did, too.

"Seraphina, this is crazy," Micah pleaded. "At least talk with Deputy Hester. Or Charlie Eagle."

I gave him a hard look. "They're dead."

That knocked the wind out of him. Of course he didn't know. He'd been too busy making friends with the people who'd killed them.

David laughed at the shocked look on Micah's face. "She doesn't need you anymore, Abrams. She's replaced you with an M16." He marched past Micah and out the front door.

I grabbed my little Derringer from the table by the window and stuffed it into the back waistband of my pants. "Remember what I said. Two hours."

Refusing to even look at Micah, I followed David outside. The sun was already low in the sky. It would be dark soon.

"Seraphina, wait."

I stopped on the walk. When I thought he'd been killed by the stage bomb, I'd been hit with a kaleidoscope of feelings—some I was too afraid to name. I wasn't sure I trusted myself to look at him now.

"It's not like you to just charge in without thinking things through," he said.

Against my better instincts, I turned. The fear and concern on his face grabbed hold of my heart and made me doubt my determination to resist him. I reminded myself of his betrayal and threw his own words back at him.

"You're judging things you can't possibly understand, Micah."

I ignored the hurt look on his face and hurried after my brother.

It was a two-mile walk from our house to city hall. The streets were infested with blue coats, so David and I stuck to the alleys. In the cold, gloomy night, the smoke and smell from the stage explosion still hung in the air. I could hear the stomping of soldiers' feet as they marched in formation nearby. Were they preparing for an occupation? The stage explosion had given the praetor just the excuse he needed to take the town.

David had no idea what he was about to come up against.

"Stay impersonal," I counseled. "You don't want him in your head. Stick with yes and no answers—"

"You're being ridiculous, Sera. I'm a gifted debater and Praetor Stanislov isn't the three-headed ogre you and the others make him out to be. Mark my words, Grandpa will be coming home tonight."

A four-man guard detail paced the street in front of city hall. We couldn't possibly avoid them, so we approached with our hands in the air, hoping we could plead ignorance about the curfew Micah had mentioned.

"Good evening," David called out.

They responded to our greeting with the barrels of four automatic weapons.

"Keep your hands in the air," David whispered to me, "and don't make any sudden moves. I'm David Donner," he called out to the guards, "and this is my sister, Sera. We would like to speak with Praetor Stanislov if that is at all possible."

A very large soldier separated himself from the shadows surrounding the coal miners' memorial. George, the praetor's personal guard, barked out some orders in German, then two other soldiers came forward and took hold of us. They escorted us into the rotunda, where we were thoroughly patted down. They confiscated my Derringer. I noted that the flag of Europa—an enormous one—now hung on the wall in place of the governor of Washington's portrait.

George led us up the marble staircase to the offices on the second floor. He ushered us into the mayor's office, where the blood of Frank Skaggs still stained the hardwood floor, and then into the room beyond.

It became immediately clear that the praetor had taken over the mayor's suite as his personal living quarters. Another Europa flag stood in the corner, a watercolor portrait of Stanislov himself hung over the fireplace, and a quote had been stenciled in big black letters on the wall in front of us.

> *He who is prudent and lies in*
> *wait for an enemy who is not,*
> *will be victorious.*

The praetor entered the room, carrying a snifter of brandy, his surviving white wolf following in step behind him. A brief scowl darkened his face, but then it instantly transformed into a broad smile. "Stupendous. I certainly did not expect to have such wonderful company tonight. Please. Come. Sit down."

We sat on one of the matching red leather sofas.

"It's good to see you are both well after today's horrible tragedy." He sat on the opposite sofa, with a coffee table between us and his wolf at his feet.

"We're pleased you're safe as well," David replied.

One of us was pleased, anyway.

"Thank you, David. You are lovely children. Although, I must admit, I am a little surprised to see you both. This seems to be a job for someone a bit *older* than yourselves."

A plate of butter cookies sat in the center of the coffee table and my eyes kept wandering back to it. It had been a long time since I'd had a cookie.

The praetor eyed me over the edge of his brandy snifter. "Sera. Stop staring. Try one."

"No. Thank you."

He rolled his eyes at David as if they were old buddies sharing a private joke. "Come now, Sera. Coyness has its merits, but it does grow tiresome after a while." He leaned forward and pushed the plate toward me. "Both of you. Have one. They're delicious."

Before I could decline again, David reached out and took a cookie. He picked up the plate and held it out to me. I stared at him, making my disapproval obvious. He wasn't going to follow any of my suggestions at all.

I accepted the plate from him and set it back on the table without taking a cookie.

The praetor chuckled at David. "Women." Suddenly he sat forward on the sofa. "Oh, my goodness, where are my manners?"

He turned to George, who was standing nearby. "George, bring our guests some lemonade."

Lemonade? "No. No, thank you," I heard myself say.

The praetor shook his head, disappointed. "Good heavens."

"I'd love some," my brother piped up.

I scowled in response.

The praetor almost spit out his brandy laughing. "Oh, my dear, don't be too hard on your brother. Men are notorious pushovers when it comes to food and drink. George, some water for the lady and a tall glass of lemonade for this fine young man right here." He looked at me. "I trust that a glass of water won't be too much of a concession for you?"

My scowl deepened and he only laughed harder. I was tempted to accept the lemonade after all, but George disappeared before I could make up my mind one way or the other.

"Now. Let us get down to business, shall we?" He looked back and forth between us, his brows raised, and I held my breath. "There is the little matter of your grandfather. I'm sure that's why you are both here tonight?" He crossed his legs.

I nodded silently.

David crossed his short legs, mirroring the praetor. "Yes, sir. We were hoping to talk with you about that."

George reappeared with a glass of water for me and a frosty glass of lemonade for David. David smiled as he took his first sip. I wanted to reach over and slap him.

"How is it?" the praetor asked him.

"Perfect."

"Not too tart?"

David shook his head. "And not too sweet."

"Excellent. It's my mother's recipe."

David smiled. "Your mother is a saint."

The praetor laughed. "That she is."

Their blossoming friendship was too much for my empty stomach. I snatched a cookie from the plate and chewed it up without even tasting it. Try as I might, I could not picture this man with a mother. Weren't people like Stanislov made in laboratories somewhere, like other poisonous things?

The praetor's smile slipped. "You do realize your grandfather is being held on charges of murdering several of your own citizens in addition to three of my guards. Not to mention my poor Hati."

"He was a beautiful animal," David said solemnly.

I leaned back into the sofa, suddenly realizing I was nothing but a spectator watching two expert manipulators test each other's skills.

"Skoll and Hati were born on Ellesmere Island," the praetor told us, "in the far north, above Canada, not far from the Arctic Circle. The area is remote and usually completely encircled by pack ice, so the wolves have no experience with man or his violent, oppressive nature. They are quite curious and tolerant of us; their loyalty and ferocity cannot be matched." He rubbed Skoll's massive head. "Hati once tore out the throat of a young soldier who simply touched the sleeve of my jacket."

Looking into the wolf's black and amber eyes, I imagined him tearing out a man's throat. He bared his teeth at me and a shudder raced up my spine.

"It is best not to look him in the eye, Sera," the praetor warned. "Now." He clapped his hands and I almost jumped out of my skin. "I'm afraid your grandfather is a convicted terrorist and there is very little I can do about that."

I scowled. "Convict—"

"That's why we're here," David interrupted. "There are rumors…."

"Rumors?" The praetor leaned forward, arching a brow. "What kind of rumors?"

"About a resistance movement."

The praetor sputtered dramatically. "The Skaggs are no more. What on earth could anybody be resisting?"

"There's a God-worshipping hate group in the area that detests everything that has anything to do with the betterment of society."

"God?" he snorted. "How quaint."

"They call themselves the Spathi."

The praetor smirked. "Spear of God. Clever."

"We think the 'S' that was painted at the café and on the park gazebo stands for Spathi," David concluded.

The praetor smirked. "Because we all know it doesn't stand for Skaggs, don't we? Why would they blow themselves up? It was very clever of your grandfather to give me a fake list, by the way."

"He's old and tends to be suspicious of change," David replied.

I clenched my teeth, forcing myself not to respond to David's remark.

"Nonsense," the praetor waved him off. "I would have done exactly the same thing. I'm embarrassed that I didn't realize it until after the explosion. Now, if what you say is true, then we must ferret out these terrorists before they strike again."

"That would be wonderful," David replied. "But no one has any idea where to find them."

Enough about the Spathi. "Sir," I interjected. "About our grandfather?"

"Yes, of course." He paused. "I must admit, I am

relieved by your news of these Spathi. The idea that your grandfather would participate in such a heinous crime did come as a bit of a shock to me. He seems like such a sensible man. What could a man possibly gain by doing this? I asked myself that very question. Does Mark Donner really hate progress that much? Does Mark Donner really hate *me* that much? Tell me, what does your father think of all this?"

That odd question even silenced my brother; David's mouth slammed shut.

"Our father?" I asked.

"Yes," the praetor replied. "Your father, Jason Donner. He's done some astounding work with the human genome. Fascinating stuff. I read all about his cure for your condition in *Scientific American*. He is literally hoping to turn David into Goliath. It is poetic—almost lyrical. I would love to meet him."

David and I exchanged a look.

David shook his head. "I'm sorry, sir, but our father was in Seattle during the quake. He...he was lost with the city."

The praetor grimaced. "Now that is a shame. Because, you see, your father...he would be the perfect man to negotiate your grandfather's release tonight." He stared at us for a long moment, then flashed his smile. "But *c'est la vie*. Based on your information about the Spathi, I must reconsider the charges against Mark Donner."

Relief flooded through me. Could it be that easy? Was the praetor a reasonable man after all?

"Thank you," David said.

"Yes," I said, then reluctantly added, "Thank you."

The praetor shrugged. "It's the right thing to do. But." He gave us a wry grin and shook his finger at us. "If I am scratching your back, then you must be scratching mine."

I went cold. I'd forgotten about the price tag. What would it be this time? A promise? A secret? Another list?

David was foolishly unfazed. "Name it."

The praetor laughed. "Oh, I like you, David! So much arrogance and self-assurance in such a tiny little package."

David twitched, though his smile never faltered.

"I guess size really doesn't matter," the praetor quipped. He laughed so hard at his own joke that Skoll shifted nervously beside him.

Normally David would have skewered anyone who dared to say something so inappropriate to him, but now, for the sake of our grandfather, he had to sit there and take it.

The praetor finally sobered and wiped his eyes. "Ah, we have enjoyed this visit, eh Skoll?" He patted the wolf on the head. "I will not execute your grandfather. And, in return, the two of you will find me the leader of this terrorist group."

David blinked. "You want us to find the Spathi leader?"

I knew exactly what the praetor was asking and I suddenly realized that Micah had been right. Coming here had been a serious mistake.

"That's impossible," David added. "I told you, nobody knows where they are."

"You will bring me the person responsible for bombing my Welcome Festival and then I will let your grandfather go free."

A vise squeezed my heart. He had given us an impossible task. We hadn't won at all.

"You have one week," the man continued.

"But what if we can't find their leader?" David asked.

"Then, my dears," said the praetor, rubbing the wolf's ears. "I am terribly afraid that I will have to shoot your grandfather."

Chapter Fifteen

The next morning, I woke to the dull sound of a distant explosion rattling my bedroom window. Milly and I joined the boys in the front yard to see a fireball blazing on the western horizon. The Spathi had struck again. This time, they'd bombed a barracks full of Europa soldiers. Although I had no sympathy for the praetor and his men, everything the Spathi did would be blamed on Grandpa Donner. We had to find out where the religious fanatics were holed up and put an end to this before it was too late.

The praetor retaliated for the bombings by withholding food, water, and electricity from the community—in the name of "ferreting out the terrorists." His soldiers went door to door, handing out flyers that promised extra rations for any information on those responsible for the attacks. The day Europa marched into town, the people of Roslyn had been injected with a new hope. That hope was now being twisted into anger and paranoia as neighbor turned against neighbor and father against son.

The week wore on with more bombings, but no sign of those responsible. Soldiers raided homes, pulling people from their beds, interrogating entire families on their front lawns, and burning down suspicious houses. It was the Skaggs all over again, only this time we were outmanned and outgunned.

The five of us spent days turning the town upside down. We spoke to everyone—even offered them food from our own rations—but no one had any idea where the Spathi were hiding. The terrorists had done a flawless job of covering their tracks and the town was paying the price.

We were running out of time.

We'd heard rumors that Europa held its detainees at a fenced self-storage compound off Whitehead Road, so we decided to take matters into our own hands.

That night, we crept through the dark, cold, snowy field that used to be Miller's Dairy and crossed the old Pacific Northern railroad tracks. Tim and I took point, Milly and David followed a few yards back, and the Turner brothers brought up the rear. We moved carefully and quietly, avoiding notice. The Europa Guard was out in full force again that night and none of us could afford to be arrested.

As we got closer to the compound, I heard a voice coming over a loudspeaker. I caught words like "American" and "misguided" despite the heavy accent, but I couldn't make out full sentences.

Tim and I aimed for a dark place along the enclosure, where the floodlights didn't quite reach. We assessed the fence. Eight feet up, thick coils of razor wire looped along the top of the heavy chain link. The subdued, shadowy compound had patches of brightly lit areas beneath the floodlights, and the open storage units were giving off a dim glow.

I peered through the links. I could see shapes of people drifting around inside.

"See any guards?" Tim asked.

I shook my head, then turned and gave the signal for David and Milly to join us.

David scurried up beside me, out of breath. "Where is he?"

"Hopefully someplace warm," Milly said, rubbing her hands together against the cold.

The Turner brothers joined us.

"Numbers?" Ben asked.

"Twenty, maybe thirty prisoners," I answered.

Jude scanned the compound. "I don't see any soldiers."

I pulled back the bolt on my weapon. "They're in there."

Tim pointed at a familiar figure walking beneath one of the compound lights. Vice Principal Chaney had been taken the night before in a raid on Nevada Street. Chaney approached two other prisoners, who turned out to be Robert Ormann and Mike Jorgenson.

"We need to free them, too," Milly said.

"No time, Mills."

"We can't just leave 'em here."

It broke my heart to say so, but we had no choice. "We stick to the mission," I ordered.

Milly's lips tightened. "Change the mission, Sera."

"We'll be lucky to get G-Pa outta there before they sound the alarm," Ben replied.

"We can come back for them later," Jude told her.

"We grab G-Pa and skee-daddle," Tim asserted.

I held up my hand. "Shh!" The voice on the loud-speaker grew clearer. I wanted to hear the words.

"The United States has no poets," the staticky voice said, "no painters, no architects, no composers of world prominence. Whatever culture it has, it has borrowed from

Europe. The country lacks its own language, culture, and civilization. It has borrowed everything, debasing it by Americanizing it, but never improving it. Americanization creates cheap imitations that give sound cultural values an American stamp, turning a mature language into slang, a timeless waltz into jazz, a work of literature into a crime story."

"It's old propaganda audio from World War II," David said. "The praetor does seem to favor the era," he added, ruefully.

We heard footsteps and all five of us trained our weapons on the intruder.

It was Micah, approaching along the fence. "They blast that stuff day and night," he said quietly. "To demoralize them."

We all lowered our weapons. Except for David, who held tighter to his handgun.

"What are you doing here?" my brother growled.

"Visiting a friend."

That's when we realized that Micah wasn't alone. Grandpa was walking along beside him on the inside of the fence. My heart surged, but then I saw my grandfather's face. He'd been beaten so badly that I wouldn't have recognized him without his shaggy silver hair and bushy mustache. A tight rage coiled within me. The praetor would pay for this.

As the others pressed against the fence like eager puppies, trying to touch him through the chain-links, I pulled the bolt cutters out of my coat. If we moved quickly, we could all be out of town before daybreak.

Micah moved close to me. "Don't," he murmured.

"Don't what?" I hadn't seen him since I'd set him straight on the porch four days earlier. I'd begun to think he'd left town again, but now I had a strong impression that he'd been spending a lot of time here at the fence, talking with my grandfather. I wasn't sure how I felt about that.

"Whatever you have planned," he answered.

"I'm not leaving him in there."

"It's not your decision, Seraphina."

I glared at him. "I suppose you think it's yours?"

"Sera?" I looked up at my grandfather. "I'm sorry if I'm ruinin' your plans, sweetheart, but there's not gonna be any great escape here tonight."

I frowned at him, confused. "What are you talking about?"

Tim clarified the situation. "We're here to getcha out."

"It'll be fast," Ben assured.

Jude pulled a second pair of bolt cutters out from under his own jacket. "We brought two."

Grandpa took hold of the fence. "I appreciate the effort, kids, really I do. I'm sure you've all worked hard on every detail of your plan. But I can't leave."

"You can't stay here," David breathed.

Milly sniffled. She held tightly to Grandpa's fingers through the fence. "You have to come with us."

"I want to, Milly. But if I let you kids break me outta here, there will be hell to pay for everybody else tomorrow —inside and outside of this compound. I won't be responsible for that."

The beatings had obviously knocked something loose in his head. "You have less than three days." I clamped the blades of my bolt cutter around a link in the fence. The tears in my eyes made it hard to see. "There is no discussion."

"Sera."

I looked up into his battered face, my hands poised on

the handle grips. "Please." My voice was hoarse with emotion. "Please let me do this."

His mustache twitched and his eyes filled with tears. "I won't be saved at the expense of others."

"But—" David's voice choked. "They're going to kill you."

"Greater love has no one than this," he replied, "to lay down one's life for one's friends."

I shook my head. *How could this be happening?* "You're not making any sense."

"I'm needed here, Sera."

"But *we* need you!" I rasped. "*I* need you. You can't just—"

A shrill scream came from somewhere in the compound, freezing my words in my throat. Two guards burst from the large office and held the doors wide.

Grandpa gripped the fence. "We don't have much time. I expect you to be strong and protect each other. You're a family now. Don't ever give in and don't ever lose hope."

Milly was sobbing. "You're coming with us."

Another scream sounded. Praetor Stanislov came marching out the office doors with his wolf at his side. A tall soldier, who could only be George, followed him, dragging a squirming woman by the arm. "Robert!" the woman screamed. "Robert!"

It was Jenny Ormann.

Robert Ormann was still standing with Vice Principal Chaney and Mike Jorgenson beneath a distant floodlight. "Jenny?" He rushed toward his wife.

Grandpa's expression hardened. "Go. Now."

"No," David bawled. "Not without you."

Jenny Ormann screamed again and George struck her viciously, knocking her to the ground.

"Now, dammit!" Grandpa gritted out.

Tears streaming down his cheeks, Tim hauled Milly away from the fence and hurried her across the field. The Turner brothers, their faces screwed up with emotion, backed away, then took off after Tim and Milly.

David pressed his face against the fence. "This is my fault," he choked out. "I shouldn't have met with him."

"You bought me valuable time, David. Now go," Grandpa ordered. "Catch up with the others and look after 'em. They're gonna need your wisdom to get through this. Don't let 'em down, son."

David backed away from the fence, then turned and disappeared into the dark night.

Grandpa turned to me. We linked fingers through the fence.

Tears spilled from my eyes. "I'm not leaving." My throat was so tight I could barely breathe. I could hear the soldiers shouting at Robert Ormann in the background.

"Do you remember the cabin I took you and David to when you were little?" he asked.

Nodding, I wiped my nose on my sleeve.

"Take them there, Sera. Be smart. Stay safe. Protect them at all costs."

"Not without you."

"Leave tomorrow." His voice caught. "First thing. Promise me."

"The praetor might change his mind—"

"He won't. He wants something we can't give him. And when he's done with me, he's coming after you and David. Promise me."

"But if we find the Spathi—"

Jenny screamed again. The guards had taken hold of

Robert Ormann, shoving them both up against a cinderblock wall.

Suddenly a flashlight lit up the back of my grandfather's head. "You zere!" a guard shouted. "Get away from ze fence!"

"Micah!" Grandpa growled. "Get her out of here!"

"No!" I held onto his fingers, crying hard as Micah slipped his arm around my waist. "No, no, no!"

Grandpa's eyes filled with tears. "I'm sorry." And then he let go of my hand.

Micah hauled me across the field. My grandfather was swallowed up by the darkness. "Promise me," I heard him call out one last time.

I saw a muzzle flash—heard the sharp crack of rifle fire. The screaming finally stopped. They'd shot Robert and Jenny Ormann.

Chapter Sixteen

We didn't leave for the cabin the next day. Or the day after that. Regardless of promises, we couldn't bring ourselves to abandon Grandpa while we still had hope that he might be released. We just needed one lone Spathi and this would all end.

I investigated leads in Lakedale and Driftwood Acres, while David and Tim questioned White Lighters on street corners. Milly and the Turner brothers dug through the burnt-out shell of the old CBC commune, hoping to find something that might help us. We all came up empty handed again. It was like the Spathi had just disappeared.

The morning before my grandfather's execution, I woke to the sight of two Europa soldiers positioned on the sidewalk outside the house. Their presence ended any possibility of us leaving town as Grandpa had ordered. The praetor was making sure we stuck around; I felt both angry and relieved.

I'd snuck back to the compound fence on my own the night before, with the bolt cutters under my coat, hoping to finally convince my grandfather that he needed to escape. I couldn't find him. Micah was there, though, lurking in the darkness, whispering to prisoners through the fence. I wondered if he'd told Grandpa that we hadn't left, that I'd disobeyed him. Somehow that thought made everything feel so much worse.

I dressed, then braided my hair with shaking fingers. A stranger stared back at me from the small chipped mirror over my dresser. Large green eyes, hollowed out cheeks. I looked gaunt, grim, much older than sixteen. I remembered a time when all I'd cared about were clothes and school dances. I cringed at the memory, but longed for those simpler days.

I stepped into the kitchen. Everyone was eating a silent breakfast around the table, nobody saying what all of us were thinking. We had twenty-four hours.

"Did you see them?" Milly's face was pale. She had dark circles under her eyes. I'd heard her tossing and turning all night. She wasn't sleeping any better than I was.

"Yes." I grabbed a bottle of Europa water from the cupboard and sat down to drink it for breakfast. I hadn't had much of an appetite lately.

"Guess we're staying," Jude murmured.

"As if we would have left," Ben retorted.

David took a deep breath and set down his spoon. "We need a Spathi."

"Got one in your pocket?" Tim grumbled.

David scowled. "Let me rephrase that. We need to invent a Spathi."

"Invent?" Ben frowned.

"Yes. We grab a lowlife off the street and tell the praetor he's the terrorist."

Milly glared daggers at him. "You'd turn in an innocent person?"

David sighed, impatiently. "Everybody is guilty of something."

And then Tim spoke up. "I think we should give 'em Harold Victor."

Everybody stared at him in surprise.

"*What?*" Milly breathed.

Jude looked confused. "But he's, like, eighty years old."

"Exactly," David interjected. "He's perfect. He's old and his entire family is gone. His son died during the quake. His wife died from silicosis."

Ben looked around the table, nodding slowly. "He's got arthritis. He can't work."

Tim shrugged. "Nobody would miss him."

"Nobody needs him," David added.

Milly was aghast. "So we're Skaggs now? We judge people's right to live based on their age and ability?"

David's glare drilled into her. "You'd rather they shoot my grandfather?"

"I don't want 'em shootin' anybody, David!" she cried. "But we can't just start turnin' in innocent people."

Tim slammed his hands down onto the table. In the entire time I'd known him, I'd never seen Tim lose his temper. "Welcome to reality, Milly!" he shouted. "Innocent people are gettin' shot every day at that compound! Nobody is safe! Not even *you!*"

Milly put her face in her hands and broke into quiet sobs. The table fell silent. We were each struggling with what to do. Milly was right, this would make us no better than the Skaggs we fought to defeat. But not doing it meant giving up Grandpa, our only compass in this lost world.

Ben slowly raised his hand. "I vote for Mr. Victor."

David's hand shot up. "So do I."

All eyes fell on Jude. He looked at Milly. From my seat across the table I could see her silently pleading with him.

Jude shook his head. "Milly's right. It's not who we are."

David grunted and rolled his eyes.

Tim looked at me. "Sera?"

Now I bore the weight of their stares. Did I kill a stranger or let my grandfather die?

David saw my hesitation. He arched his brows. "Tell us another way."

There was no other way. But if I raised my hand, Harold Victor would be executed. My fingers twitched in my lap. I just had to hold my breath, raise my hand, and my grandfather would live.

The front door burst open and Micah walked in. "Pack up."

David clenched his teeth. "Who the *hell* does he think he is?"

"Leave behind what you can live without. I've got a truck parked in the alley between Idaho and Washington. We're leaving."

I stood up from the table. "What are you doing?"

"What you couldn't."

A judgment if I'd ever heard one.

Tim folded his arms. "We're not goin' anywhere without G-Pa."

Milly brushed the tears from her face. "They want to exchange Harold Victor for him."

"*What?*" Micah looked at me, shocked. "*Why?*"

"Because Mr. Victor is old!" Milly was disgusted with us all. "And apparently useless."

Micah's jaw tightened. He looked directly at me. "Your grandfather made it clear that he was not going to save himself at the expense of anybody else."

"What're you, his lawyer?" David shot back.

Ben blinked back tears. "We have to do something."

Milly folded her arms. "Killin' somebody else isn't the answer."

"The praetor would be the one doing the killin', Mills."

"Don't play that game," Micah countered. "You'd be killing Mr. Victor whether you pulled the trigger or not."

David sneered. "Oh, how profound."

"It's the truth!" Milly stated.

"At least take responsibility for what you're planning to do," Jude joined in.

"We're plannin' on savin' G-Pa's life!" Tim bellowed.

"You heard Micah!" Jude shouted back. "He doesn't want to be saved if it means other people will die!"

"So now we're listening to Abrams?" David demanded. "Am I the only one here who remembers he vanished for six months? Convenient how he came back after the fighting ended."

"Enough!" I stood from the table. "I vote no!" I looked at Micah. "And we're not leaving. So that's settled, too." I grabbed my coat and stormed out of the house.

I had one day left to save my grandfather, and I didn't plan to waste it sitting around a table arguing like a bunch of children.

I searched from the east side of Ronald to the western edge of Cle Elum. I spoke with former Skaggs and followed leads into condemned buildings. In the end it was always the same; nobody knew where the Spathi laid their heads at night.

The sun was sitting low in the sky by the time I returned home. I found Micah camped out on the front porch, waiting for me. My heart was breaking. I didn't have the energy to go another round with him.

"He's at peace with it, if that helps."

Tears tightened my throat. "It doesn't."

I walked past him into the house.

DAVID SHOOK me awake in the middle of the night.

Confused, I pushed the hair out of my face and sat up. "What? What's going on?"

"No questions," he whispered. "Just get dressed."

He led me out the back door and into the cold night air. We walked up the back alley, through the old elementary school parking lot, and between the two fences that bordered Clark Woods. Eventually I found myself heading toward the rubble of the old Roslyn Bible Church.

I hadn't been back since the quake and my hands shook as we crossed the street toward the ruin. It looked much the same as it had the day Grandpa led us away. The roof was gone, like most of the outside walls. Large timbers from the rafters lay everywhere, tossed around like toothpicks.

"Why am I here?"

"Shh," David whispered. "Follow me."

We crept inside, careful where we placed our feet. The building was still unstable and the last thing we needed was to get trapped there again. As we moved deeper into the church, I was surprised to see the glow of soft lantern light coming from a distant alcove.

David gestured for me to stay quiet, then directed me toward a large pile of stones and lumber. We moved behind it, keeping to the shadows, and peered around the side.

I stared into an office space that had been cleared and swept clean. At least thirty people sat on the floor in a semicircle. All of them faced one familiar, dark-haired person who sat on a large desk, commanding their full attention.

Micah.

"There's no hope in the system as it is right now," he was saying. "People are lost in chaos and the only thing that will solve it is to eradicate the existing order."

A prickly wave of uneasiness washed over me.

The group nodded and murmured. I recognized a few faces.

Ken Sheridan sat near the front, along with former Skagg John Voss. "Yesterday's bomb took out thirteen soldiers," Ken said.

"Many more will die," Micah responded. "What we do here, now, in this small town, is all part of a greater plan. We are holding up the standard that generations before us have bled and died for. This world will be purged, cleansed with a righteousness born in blood."

Eliza Cole sat in the center of the group. "They're offering extra rations for people who turn in dissenters," she said. "My neighbor was dragged off to the compound this afternoon."

"Don't give into fear," Micah answered. "Remember, death means promotion. Defend your families and each other. Fight in your homes, in the streets, and anywhere else the enemy confronts you. Never give up. Never surrender."

A brown piece of canvas caught my eye, wadded up next to Micah on the desk, the edge of an embroidered yellow cross stitched into the fabric. It was a Spathi poncho.

I felt the dizzying sensation of my world spinning out of control. I looked at David. He was watching Micah closely. And he was smiling. His delight made my stomach turn. I pulled on his sleeve. I wanted to leave. He shook me off, wanting to see more.

"Brace yourselves," Micah continued. "You're about to witness a fire storm of destruction like nothing ever seen before. Be strong, so that a thousand years from now, people will remember and say that this was our finest hour."

We slipped out of the church with Micah's words still ringing in my ears. *A firestorm of destruction. Death equals promotion.* He was encouraging people to die for his cause. I couldn't help seeing the similarities of Grandpa choosing death over escape.

Once outside, David grabbed my arm. "So?"

I had to force out the words. "Micah is a Spathi."

"He's not *just* a Spathi, Sera, he's their *leader*—their spiritual guru!" He could barely contain his enthusiasm. "I kept telling everybody that he hadn't changed, but nobody ever listens to David." His exuberance sickened me.

I closed my eyes and tried to process everything I'd heard. When had Micah become a religious zealot? Was this just another thing that he'd claim I couldn't understand?

"Come on, Sera," David prodded. "This is perfect. This is exactly what we need."

He was right. Micah was perfect. The perfect replacement for our grandfather.

Chapter Seventeen

I sat on the porch step, my fingers absently working a tangled braid. I was waiting for the sun to rise.

Micah was a Spathi; an enemy of not only Europa but of decent people everywhere. For a week, he'd watched us search desperately for a Spathi terrorist who would satisfy the praetor, and the entire time we'd been searching he'd been manipulating my grandfather into sacrificing himself.

He would let my grandfather take the fall for him. I still couldn't believe it. I'd spent the past couple of weeks convincing myself that Micah didn't matter anymore, but this new betrayal had shattered me.

After seeing him at the church, I'd gone home, hidden in the cellar, and cried in the dark until my chest hurt. I felt devastated and stupid. He'd conned me, and my grandfather had almost paid with his life.

Eventually, I'd moved past sadness to anger, and then into unwavering resolve. I wished I'd never met Micah—wished I'd never fallen into his arms that day in the ashy darkness behind the Sportland Minimart. He was the terrible person my brother had always accused him of being, and if I'd only listened I could have spared myself months of heartache.

The horizon glowed with orange and purple light. Dawn was coming and, with it, reckoning. Micah planned to go with us to city hall when we informed the praetor that we'd failed to find a Spathi terrorist. I wasn't sure what I would say to him when he arrived. I only knew what I wouldn't say. I was not going to tell him I was sorry or ask for his forgiveness. He was the one who'd done horrible things. My childish delusions about Micah Abrams were over. We would tie him up, gag him, and then march him to city hall where he would be arrested in place of my grandfather.

The sky grew lighter. I saw Micah coming down the street and my stomach seized. The others were waiting inside the house. David had told them what we'd seen last night, and I'd finally told them all that I'd caught Micah marching with the Skaggs at Widowmaker Hill. David had been outraged that I'd kept that information to myself, but he'd gotten over it quickly, since he was about to be rid of Micah once and for all. Now, with everything that had come to light, even Milly agreed with trading Micah for Grandpa.

Micah strode up the walk and stopped in front of me. "Hey," he said. He looked sad, but I now knew it was only an act.

"Did you get any sleep?" he asked.

"I was up all night," I responded.

"Yeah, me, too."

I know exactly what you were doing last night, I thought.

He crouched down in front of me and took hold of my hands. The gesture surprised me and I found myself gazing into his warm, dark eyes. Suddenly, I remembered what it felt like to be held in his arms—comforted, safe. After today, I'd never feel that again. A surge of emotion washed over me and my confidence wavered. But I knew the emotion for what it was: the dying breaths of a childish infatuation.

"Seraphina," he said, "there's something I need to tell you."

I leaned back from him, afraid he was about to say something that would make me change my mind. He never got the chance. The others came out of the house, walked past me and off the porch.

Ben twirled a pair of Grandpa's handcuffs around his index finger, his expression tight with anger. "Hey, Micah."

Micah straightened. "Ben." He eyed the handcuffs. "What's going on?"

"That's what *we* wanna know," Tim replied.

They surrounded him.

"Is there a problem?" Micah asked.

Milly stared at him with red-rimmed eyes while Jude clenched his fists and glared.

"A problem?" David came out of the house wielding a baseball bat. "You could say that." He stopped beside me on the step. "Sera and I followed you last night."

Micah shifted, swallowing hard. "Seraphina, listen, I—"

"You're wasting your breath," David stated. "She knows who you are now."

Micah persisted. "This is what I wanted to talk to you about. I need to—"

"We thought you were one of us," Milly cried.

Micah shook his head. "No. That's just it. I want all of you to be one of *us*."

Milly gasped.

"You aren't even going to *try* to deny it?" Jude snarled.

Micah sobered and straightened. "We're doing God's work."

He was proud of himself, proud of all the hate and violence. How could I have been so wrong about him?

David lifted his bat. "We'll take that as a no."

I shoved open the double doors to city hall with one mission in mind. I would retrieve my grandfather and leave this godforsaken town behind. Let the praetor have Roslyn. I didn't care anymore.

Micah's hands were cuffed behind his back. Tim had stuffed a sock in his mouth and pulled a pillowcase over his head to keep him quiet, but none of that was necessary; he'd come along willingly. In silence, we'd walked him all the way to city hall, ignoring the stares. Considering David had hit him several times with the baseball bat before I'd intervened, I was amazed Micah could walk at all.

We arrived just in time.

The praetor was coming down the long hallway toward the rotunda with his standard guard—the white wolf and George. My grandfather, blindfolded, his hands tied behind his back, was led by two guards. As he got closer I realized he was staggering. He had new bruises on his face.

"Ah, the Donner bunch has arrived." The praetor smiled broadly, then gave Micah a surprised look. "And who is this?"

David spoke up. "Good morning, sir. As you requested, we've brought you the leader of the Spathi."

The praetor's smile wavered, then his eyes lit with a dark gleam. "Have you now?"

"No!" Grandpa rasped. "Don't...don't do this!"

George rammed his weapon into my grandfather's stomach. It doubled him over and his two guards struggled to keep him on his feet.

I lunged at George, but Ben grabbed me by the arm and held me back. "We don't need you getting arrested next," he hissed.

George leered at me. One day, I was going to kill him and his praetor.

"Sera," the praetor chastised. "Have your manners deteriorated so quickly since our last visit?"

"We've fulfilled our part of the bargain," I replied. "Now let my grandfather go."

Grandpa shook his head, adamantly, but, thankfully, he hadn't yet caught his breath enough to speak again.

The praetor held up a finger. "First, let us have a look at who we have here, shall we?" He pulled the pillowcase off Micah's head.

Micah blinked, squinting in the sudden light. When his eyes darted to me, I quickly looked away. In spite of all the horrible things he'd done, my heart wasn't strong enough to look him in the eye.

Grandpa Donner gasped and struggled against his bonds. "No!" he cried. "No!"

The praetor's smile broadened. "Now, this is interesting." He gave me a careful look. "I have been led to believe that this particular Zionist is a very special friend of your family. What a difficult choice this must have been for you."

"Not difficult at all," David assured. "My sister detests traitors."

The praetor looked, wide-eyed, at Micah. "Hell hath no fury, eh, young man?" He pulled the sock out of Micah's mouth. "Do you have anything to say for yourself? Any words in your own defense?"

Micah looked directly at the praetor. "Whether I live or

die isn't for you to decide." He was sweating and there was a little catch in his voice.

The praetor blinked, then laughed. "Oh my." His guards laughed with him. "You've really been stung by the martyr bee, haven't you? But I have some hard news for you, my friend, it *is* my decision whether you live or die. And, just between you and me, I made it the moment you opened your filthy Jew mouth." He turned to George. "Take him to the courtyard."

My heart stopped.

George reached for Micah. It took everything I had not to stop him. Like my grandfather, Micah would not be getting a trial. Before the Devastation, the courtyard at city hall had been a beautiful outdoor garden, with a sculpted fountain and wrought iron benches, where people could read or eat their lunch. Now it was where Europa lined up agitators and shot them.

As the soldiers led Micah away I glanced at my friends. All of them, except for David, looked as stricken as I felt. Yes, Micah had done terrible things, but being responsible for his death was more horrifying than any of us had expected.

Micah or my grandfather. We'd made our choice. Now we had to find a way to live with it.

The praetor looked at George and then gestured to Grandpa. "Let him go." The large guard pulled out a knife and cut the ropes binding my grandfather's hands.

"Come, now, children," the praetor urged. "Take your grandfather home. A deal is a deal."

Tim and Ben rushed to Grandpa's side. We had to get him out of there fast. I looked up to see Micah being led through the exit door at the far right of the rotunda. Before I could look away, he caught my eye.

"It's okay, Seraphina!" he called back to me. "I—" His voice hitched. "I forgive you!"

Something inside me shattered.

Micah was pulled out the door and disappeared into the courtyard.

Dazed, I turned to see the praetor grinning at me. "Aw," he said, "isn't that sweet."

If I'd had a gun, I would have shot him.

I heard Milly sob. I could feel myself coming unglued.

"Sera!" David's shout pulled me back into focus. "Let's go!" He was standing at the front doors, holding them open.

Jude took Milly's hand and pulled her toward the exit.

Tim and Ben each had one of Grandpa's arms but were making slow progress with him; he was too thin and weak to walk on his own and he was resisting them. "No," he muttered. "No." Tears were pouring down his battered face. He stumbled several times, but the boys kept him on his feet and moving forward.

"You have a very determined family there, Mr. Donner," the praetor called after us. "Not to mention, the teensiest bit ruthless."

I fixed my eyes on the exit, hoping that once I got outside I'd be able to breathe again.

Then I heard a loud voice call out from the courtyard. "*READY!*"

No, I thought. *Please, no.*

I moved faster, willing my ears to close.

"*AIM!*"

To shut out the sound of his death.

"*FIRE!*"

But the moment burned itself into my brain for eternity.

The discharge of three successive shots seemed to stop my own heart. The blood drained from my head into my stomach. A low, keening wail filled the rotunda. For a moment, I thought I was making the sound. Then I realized it was my grandfather. He'd fallen to his knees, wailing, "No! Please, God, no!"

Tim and Jude had to lift him off his feet and carry him outside.

I followed them out into the red daylight, hurrying past David who let the doors swing closed behind me. Tears blinded me; grief crippled me. I fought desperately to hold it all in. It had taken every bit of strength I possessed to walk Micah into that rotunda, knowing each step moved me closer to losing him forever. Why did he have to be so terrible? Why couldn't he have just been the mysterious boy I remembered from the 6th grade? I loved him then. I think I loved him now. But his betrayal had been brutal. Mine, however, had been absolute.

Chapter Eighteen

May blurred into June, then June into July. The sky was still red and the air lacked the usual warmth of summer, but the freezing temperatures had finally fled, taking most of the snow with them. We were left with a tepid, dead world where nothing thrived, not even hope.

The county of Kittitas, Washington, was an occupied territory. The praetor ruled with an iron fist, raiding businesses, conducting random home inspections, and making frequent arrests—all to protect us from future terrorist attacks. But the Spathi hadn't made an appearance since news of their leader's execution had been spread all over town. Ken Sheridan, Eliza Cole, and all the others I'd seen at the church that night, were nowhere to be found.

The praetor's fixation with my family had only intensified. He refused to let any of us leave town. We lived each day under intense scrutiny, our home subjected to weekly searches. None of us had any idea what he wanted.

That wasn't quite true; I felt sure my grandfather knew, but he was rarely coherent enough to answer simple questions, let alone explain the devious mind of Praetor

Christoph Stanislov. Grandpa hadn't recovered from his time in the internment camp. Bent and gaunt, he spent most of his time muttering over an old German book with a cover so worn it was impossible to read the title.

It was Citizenship Day, the day when everyone in the county would become Europans. I headed home from the hospital where I'd worked all night looking after soldiers who'd been stricken with viridea. Those who worked, ate, as the praetor liked to say, and we had seven mouths to feed. I didn't mind the work. I lived under the delusion that if I kept busy enough I wouldn't think of Micah. Even though I knew I'd done the right thing trading him for my grandfather, not a day passed without thoughts of him haunting me.

The streets were empty that morning, except for a few soldiers on patrol. A rumor had been spreading that everyone between the ages of seventeen and twenty-one were about to be inducted into the Europa Guard. Nobody felt like celebrating.

David and I were still sixteen, as were Ben and Milly, but both Jude and Tim had turned eighteen the month before. I couldn't imagine a day without them, and Milly was a wreck over the possibility of losing them both.

Compared to the rest of the town, Pioneer Park was swarming with people—soldiers getting ready for the big event. As I walked past, I noticed several long tables being set up, as well as lights being strung around the gazebo. The park that used to host Memorial Day barbecues and Fourth of July picnics, was now littered with Europa's blue and white flags snapping in the cool breeze. I heard the crackle of a microphone sound test and I knew the praetor would give another of his longwinded speeches. He wanted a party and the town would accommodate him out of sheer terror.

I walked past Mrs. Gorski's house. She sat on her porch,

a thick shawl wrapped around her stooped shoulders, watching the preparations with sharp, watery eyes.

"Good morning, Sera." She pulled the shawl tighter.

"Good morning," I replied, adding, "Be careful today."

She nodded. "May the blessed white light protect us all."

I gave her a patient smile, then continued down the sidewalk toward my grandfather's house. With its message of peace and promised deliverance, the White Lighter Society was fast becoming the religion of choice among the citizens. I had no use for it—or any other kind of hokey redemption plan meant to tranquilize the populace. We were prisoners in our own town and flicking flashlights on and off at each other wouldn't solve a thing.

I crossed the porch, walked through the front door, and entered chaos. George and his Europa goons were raiding our house again.

"You can't just show up here whenever you want and go through our stuff!" Ben shouted.

Jude snatched a partially carved block of wood out of a curious soldier's hand—he was making a gift for Milly. "You're not taking that."

The soldier held out his hand. "Ze knife."

"It's just a carving knife," Jude argued.

The soldier jammed his rifle into Jude's ribs.

Jude doubled over and gritted his teeth. He slipped the small knife from his back pocket and slapped it into the soldier's palm. So much for Milly's gift.

In the kitchen, George knocked dishes from the cupboards while Milly watched, helpless, as they shattered at her feet. "If you'd just tell us what you're looking for...," she said, close to tears.

George ignored her.

David sat in a chair by the fireplace, a *Scientific Journal* in his lap. He sipped his cup of bark tea. "Just stand back and let them do their job," he grumbled.

"I'm surprised you're not helpin' 'em." Tim lingered at my grandfather's door, guarding it. They never bothered grandpa, but we never knew what to expect from Europa.

The first time, it had been a door-to-door to confiscate weapons. We'd managed to stash a few of the smaller ones, like Jude's carving knife. The next time they'd showed up it had been for identification purposes, to get a census of the city and outlying communities. For most of Kittitas County, the unlawful intrusions ended there. But not for the Donner house.

Soldiers invaded constantly, at all hours of the day and night. They'd barge in just to see who was home. Sometimes they'd search specific rooms, like the attic or the cellar. Once they'd even torn up several of the floorboards in the bathroom. They never would say whether they were looking for something specific or just harassing us, but they'd confiscated books, prescription medications, photographs—once they'd even taken every scrap of paper in the house.

A large soldier came out of the hallway carrying David's school backpack. That got my brother's attention. "What do you want with that?" he demanded.

The soldier handed it to George, who promptly unzipped the pack and removed my brother's laptop. The praetor had long since turned off the electricity he'd so generously gifted to the community, but David still considered the laptop priceless. It contained all his scientific theories and the beginnings of an essay he hoped would someday get him into MIT.

George smiled at us. He'd obviously bagged his prize for this particular hunt. "*Lasst uns gehen,*" he muttered in German. The soldiers headed for the door.

David leapt from his chair and intercepted them. "That's mine!" he bellowed.

The soldiers laughed. One of them put his hand on David's forehead and held him at arm's reach. "Not anymore," he replied in precise English. Then he gave my brother a shove that sent him backwards to the floor.

As the door closed behind them, we stood in silence. David had been completely humiliated and we all felt embarrassed for him—except for Ben who'd given up on being patient with my brother.

"How do you like Europa now?" Ben taunted.

His jaw clenched, David stood up and dusted himself off. "I blame each of you for this."

"Us?" Tim blurted.

"I can't wait to hear this," Jude remarked.

Milly came out of the kitchen, arms folded, and stared at David.

"They single us out because of what you did at the Welcome Ceremony."

"Oh for Pete's sake," Tim growled.

David pressed his point. "Because of that fake list, they think they can't trust us."

"Well, they *can't* trust us!" Ben shouted. "They've at least got that right."

Milly shook her head at David. "For the life of me, I can't figure out whose side you're on."

"His own," Tim remarked.

"Just because I think logically, instead of charging in with guns blazing—"

"As if you'd ever charge in," Jude sneered.

David glared at him. "Who negotiated with the praetor for my grandfather's release? I didn't see any of you volunteering to go."

That's when they all started yelling at once.

"All right!" I interjected over the noise. "Enough!" I let out a shrill whistle and they all finally fell silent. "It's over. Let's move on." I looked at Milly. "How's he doing today?"

"Still babblin' about numbers." She angled a look at David. "Stickin' that Citizenship Day flyer under his nose last night was probably not the best idea."

David had taken it upon himself to tell our grandfather about the ceremony and Grandpa had become extremely agitated. He'd started mumbling about numbers and calculations, but nothing that made any sense.

"I don't need some backwoods hick telling me what's best for my grandfather," David snapped at her.

Milly's nostrils flared. "I'm fixin' to put you through the floor, David Donner!"

"Then it'll be my turn," Jude warned.

Scowling, David climbed back into his chair and pretended to read his magazine.

Milly turned to me. "I took him breakfast, but he didn't eat it."

"I'll check on him."

I walked down the hall and knocked softly on my grandfather's door. He didn't respond, but then I didn't expect him to. He hadn't communicated directly with any of us since we'd brought him home from city hall on that horrible day in May.

I eased open the door. "Grandpa?" As usual, he sat in the creaky rocking chair by his bed. He was pale and thin, unrecognizable as the man he used to be. I wondered if he ever slept.

I sat down on the edge of his bed. He didn't look up. I wasn't sure if he even knew I was there. He just kept reading his old German book.

"Grandpa Donner?"

His lips moved as his eyes drifted over the whisper-thin page.

I set my hand on his knee. "I wish you would look at me."

Then he started whispering the same words he'd been muttering since seeing the Citizenship Day flyer. "Calculate the number. Calculate the number."

He kept repeating that over and over. I ignored it and started talking to him instead, hoping that something might draw him out.

"The soldiers were here again. They took David's laptop."

"Calculate the number."

"Milly's worried that Tim and Jude will be conscripted into the Europa Guard."

"Calculate. Calculate."

"I hear that instead of an ID card, Europa gives you a tattoo." I looked at the back of my hand. "I used to want a tattoo—"

My grandfather lunged forward and grabbed my arm. He looked me right in the eye. "It's the number...of a man," he rasped.

My breath caught. "Grandpa? Grandpa, can you hear me?"

"Calculate the number." His grip tightened.

"You...you're hurting me."

I stood. He stood with me. He wasn't letting go.

His voice got louder. "It's the number of a man." He started shouting. "A man! It's a man!"

Tears of pain and fear burned my eyes. "Grandpa, let go!"

Ben came charging into the room, followed by Tim and Jude. By then my arm felt like it was breaking.

"What's going on?" Ben demanded.

"Calculate it!" Grandpa shouted.

"I-I don't know," I stammered. "He just grabbed me."

Tim tried to catch my grandfather's attention, but he wouldn't take his eyes off me.

"A man!" Grandpa shouted. "It's a man!"

Jude took hold of Grandpa's arm. "G-Pa? Let go of Sera."

"You're hurting her," Ben added, hoping to break through.

"Calculate the man," Grandpa muttered at me.

His grip tightened again. I winced.

"Okay," Tim said. "No more asking nicely."

It took all three of them to pry my grandfather's fingers off my arm.

Once free, I ran from the room, hurt and confused. Five finger-sized bruises were already appearing against the pale skin on my forearm.

The boys came out a few moments later. "He's calmed down," Tim said.

I looked past him to see Grandpa in his rocking chair, quietly reading his book as if nothing had ever happened.

Two HOURS LATER, people filled Pioneer Park, trying to pretend they were having a good time and not scared out of their minds. They all stood in deep lines at long tables set up by the gazebo, organized according to the first letter of their last names. The party came complete with balloons and streamers, bowls of sweet punch, trays of delicate cookies and cakes, and Europa guards with AK-12s.

I stood in the line closest to the gazebo, in front of the placard with the letters A-F written on it, with David directly behind me. I could smell the food, meant to appease the masses, and my treacherous stomach grumbled.

The praetor wore his counterfeit smile and, flanked by the white wolf and George, stepped up to the microphone perched at the top of the gazebo steps. "Ladies and gentlemen," he began. "Welcome to our Citizenship Day Celebration, where you will all be made official members of the Europa Confederation of Nations."

People cheered and applauded, but their effort was half-hearted and their smiles didn't quite reach their eyes.

"Citizenship Day has become a proud and noble tradition among our allied members. It is a time of renewal and celebration, a time to break free of the old and embrace the new. Now, the soldiers seated at the table in front of you will gather some of your personal information, and then you will take the oath and sign your citizenship certificate. After which, you will receive your Biotat identifying you as a citizen of Europa and eligible for all the privileges and benefits that come with your new status.

"Once your swearing-in ceremony has concluded, I invite you to gather around the bonfire for unlimited food and drink. I'm sure you will find, as others before you have discovered, that Europa is a kind and generous mother." He took a step away from the mic, then remembered his manners. "Thank you and have a nice day." His smile flashed quickly, like a bullet.

The ceremony began. Thomas Bradley was at the front of my line. His dad, John Bradley, used to own the local Quick Mart. Thomas had been a grade behind me in school, where he'd spent his lunch hours shooting spitballs at the teachers.

He raised his right hand, as instructed by the soldier, repeated the oath to Europa, then signed the paper placed in front of him. They ordered Thomas to stick his right arm into a large metal tattoo machine. It began to hum. He yelped as a lightning fast needle buzzed over the back of his hand like a swarm of angry bees. It was over in seconds. He stepped aside, rubbing his offended appendage. I tried to get a look at the Biotat, but when he walked by me he was babying his hand like it might fall off.

The next in line, Alison Evans, a former postal worker, took her oath, signed her paper, got her Biotat, and stepped aside. And the line moved ever forward. Julie Davis, Michael Dunbar, Ron Franks, Christina Absalom.

I heard an engine and looked up. A troop transport truck rumbled from the road and onto the grass. It drove around the lines of people, then parked on the left side of the long tables. No soldiers got out. I craned my neck and could see that the back of it was empty. An empty transport truck could only mean one thing; they intended to fill it with something—or someone.

Two lines away I saw Tim step up to a table. "Name?" I heard the soldier ask in accented English. Milly stood behind Tim. She was barely holding it together.

"Age?" the soldier asked Tim.

"Eighteen."

Tim raised his right hand to take the oath. I flashed back to when he'd taken the oath to join the 1st Cascade and a profound sadness flooded through me.

Then I heard Milly screech. A soldier had sidled up to her, cooing at her in German and trying to touch her hair.

Milly slapped his hand away and he slapped her back —hard.

Tim reacted instantly. He threw a solid punch that knocked the soldier to the ground.

Everything happened fast after that. Several soldiers rushed Tim. He was hit and kicked, then dragged off toward a military car parked a few yards away. Before any of us could think what to do, the car sped off with Tim inside.

Milly was in hysterics and drawing a lot of attention to herself. Jude hurried over to calm her down before she ended up hauled off like her brother. My mind spun. Where were they taking Tim? Would they lock him up the way they had my grandfather?

"*Neem*," I heard.

"Sera," David hissed.

It was my turn at the table.

The soldier gave me an impatient look. "*Neem*," he repeated. His thick accent made the word sound foreign.

David pushed me forward. My throat had gone dry. "Sera," I responded. "Seraphina Donner."

He wrote down my name. "Age."

"Sixteen," I rasped.

He wrote my age by my name. "Raize your right hand."

I slowly raised my hand. I looked over at Milly. She was crying on Jude's shoulder.

"Do you swear to be faithful and obedient to the leader of the Europa Confederation of Nations and people, to observe the law, and to conscientiously fulfill your duties?"

I looked back at the soldier. "I…I do."

He shoved a piece of paper and pen in front of me. "Sign."

I looked down at the document. It was written in a language I didn't recognize.

"Sign," he repeated.

"W-what does it say?"

The soldier's eyes flashed. "Sign ze paper."

I picked up the pen, my hand hovering over the signature line. *Pen to paper*, I told myself. *And then move it to make letters*. It seemed so easy in theory, but my brain refused to obey. The soldier in front of me grew impatient.

David moved up next to me. "Sera. It's just a piece of paper."

"It's more than that," I hissed back.

"Sign. Ze. Paper," the soldier repeated.

"For God sake, Sera, sign it."

A real battle raged inside my head. Saying the words was one thing, but signing my allegiance over to Europa? How could I pledge myself to a country I detested? And what about Tim? Where were they taking him? There was no way I was putting my name on that paper.

I put the pen down.

The soldier in front of me reacted violently. He took hold of my shirt and yanked me halfway over the table. Pens and papers scattered onto the ground; the people in line around me gasped and stood back.

I felt the cold pressure of his gun at my temple. "Sign. Or I vill put a bullet through your thick American skull."

"Wait!" David held up his hands. "It's okay," he said to the soldier as he shoved a pen in my hand. "Just give her a second. She's going to sign." He gave me a hard, tight look. "Do it!"

The pressure of the gun drilling into my head made my eyes water. I grasped the pen. I could barely see the document from my position on the table, but I angled my eyes and watched my hand tremble as I put the tip of the pen onto the paper. My vision blurred. I couldn't see the line. The soldier's grip on my shirt tightened. He was going to shoot me.

Then a commotion drew the soldier's attention.

I heard David shift beside me. "Oh no," he whispered.

The soldier let go of my shirt and my feet landed back on the ground. He came around the table, staring at something behind me. I turned and froze.

My grandfather walked slowly toward the gazebo. He looked like something out of a horror movie with his hair matted to the back of his head, his clothes hanging from his thin body, and his old book clutched in his hand.

People parted to let him pass. He stopped in front of Praetor Stanislov.

"Mr. Donner. So good of you to join us. You look— actually, you look terrible." He laughed.

My grandfather dropped to his knees. At first, I couldn't tell if he'd fallen or done it on purpose, but then he raised his book high over his head and shouted in a voice that boomed stronger than anyone thought him capable of. "Watch out that no one deceives you! For many will come in my name claiming I am the Messiah!"

Fear shot through me. This scene looked too familiar. The image of Pastor Rick, standing on the stage in the Roslyn church, holding his Bible over his head, floated back to my memory. The pastor had been praying for deliverance from the earthquake, just before being impaled by a piece of stained glass window. Too late, I realized what book my grandfather had been poring over for weeks. He was holding a German Bible.

The praetor's smile faltered, then returned with full

force. "How sweet. Ladies and gentlemen, Mr. Donner has found God."

The soldiers laughed. The people around me stared, too stunned to do anything else.

"Nation will rise against nation!" Grandpa continued. "There will be famines and earthquakes!"

"The Gospel according to Saint Matthew, I believe. Chapter 24, no? But these things have been happening since the beginning of time, old man," the praetor replied. "It truly saddens me to see you brought this low."

"Haughty eyes! A lying tongue! Hands that shed innocent blood!" Grandpa shouted at him. "These things are an abomination to the Lord!"

The praetor's smile vanished. "Enough of this." He pulled his gun out of its holster and pressed the bore against my grandfather's forehead. "I have grown tired of these games."

I tried to move forward, to intercede, but the soldier beside me took a vicious grip on my arm and held me in place.

"You will answer me this time, old man!" the praetor bellowed. "Do you hear me? Where is your son? Where is Jason Donner?"

I felt David take my hand. How many times did we have to tell this man that our father was dead?

"You think your God can save you, old man?" the praetor sneered. "Go ahead! Ask your God to save you!"

"We must do the will of the Father!" Grandpa answered. *Will of the father*, I thought.

"Will of the Father!" Grandpa repeated.

That's what Steve Skaggs had been muttering the night he'd stepped off the edge of the world.

The praetor's face screwed into a mask of rage. He took

my grandfather by the back of his shirt and turned him around to face me. He pressed his gun so hard into his skull that it forced Grandpa's head sideways. "You! Sera!" he yelled at me. "Where is he? Where is your father?"

I couldn't breathe. My legs shook so badly I could hardly stand. What different thing could I tell him? What magical answer might spare my grandfather's life?

"What do you want from us?" David cried.

"I want the *truth*!" the praetor roared back.

"Sera," a soft voice called to me. It was my grandfather. "Seraphina? Look at me." My eyes shifted to his face. It was him—he was present again. "It's okay, honey. Don't be afraid. Just tell the truth."

"Yes, Sera," the praetor mocked, "tell me the truth."

I took a deep breath and tried to quiet the trembles in my body. I was so tired of being afraid. I swallowed hard and answered the praetor's question. "My father is dead."

The praetor blinked at me. And then he broke into laughter. "Good heavens. You actually believe that, don't you? Well, this is certainly embarrassing. It seems that I have been wasting my time in this cesspool of a town."

He shot my grandfather in the head.

My world stopped. David let go of my hand. The soldier's unrelenting grip on my arm kept me on my feet as I watched my grandpa crumble to the ground.

I heard someone screaming. It was me.

I tried to run to him, but the soldier wouldn't let me go.

The praetor stood calmly amid the chaos of terrified people fleeing the park. "Collect everyone under the age of twenty-one and put them in the truck," he ordered. "Shoot everyone else. I am done with this wretched town."

His command brought clarity to the riot in my head. People were cowering on the ground around me.

David had fallen to his knees, his face a pale mask of shock. Milly, devastated, tried to keep Jude from attacking the nearest guard. Ben shouted at me to move.

The soldier in me took over. My vision went into sharp focus. I spun toward the man holding onto my arm and yanked the AK-12 off his shoulder. Driving the barrel into his chest, I pulled the trigger.

Soldiers fired into the fleeing crowd. I fired back. Ben tackled one of the praetor's men across the table, took his weapon, and started shooting at the soldiers. Jude tipped over one long table, pulling David and Milly out of sight behind it.

I strode toward the praetor. He released his wolf. It raced toward me, jaws snapping. I raised my weapon and shot the animal dead.

In three quick strides, I had my weapon pressed against the praetor's ribcage. He pulled his side arm and I knocked it to the ground.

The park fell silent.

With most of his soldiers dead on the ground or hiding behind trees, the praetor put his hands in the air. "Careful, Sera," he said gently. "Guns can be very unpredictable things."

The citizens of Roslyn looked up from where they'd run for cover. Only a few had been injured. Ben had taken refuge behind a tree, while Jude, Milly, and David watched from behind the tipped table.

I looked at my grandfather laying on the ground and my heartbreak turned into a fury that threatened to consume me. I considered firing the weapon in my hands and, in one glorious moment, sending the praetor to hell where he belonged. But reason steadied my hand. If I killed him now, we would never get Tim back; we would never make it out of town alive.

From the corner of my eye I saw George, his weapon raised, edging closer.

I dug the bore of the automatic weapon into the praetor's ribs until he grunted in pain. I turned my head, leveling my gaze on George. "Please. Come closer," I growled.

George stopped.

The praetor's laugh was tense. "Honestly, George. You are being cowed by a little girl."

I raised the weapon and put a persuasive bullet between George's eyes. I'd never felt a greater sense of satisfaction as the big soldier stared at me, stunned, then toppled backwards to the ground.

I clenched my teeth. "I'm a sergeant in the 1st Cascade Militia, you son of a bitch."

The praetor's posture changed entirely. "Now *that* I did not see coming."

I looked over my shoulder at Ben and the others. "Get in the truck."

The four of them skirted the crowd behind me. Several soldiers watched them closely, but they didn't dare move as long as I had their beloved praetor in my death grip.

"What do we do with Stanislov?" Ben called out to me.

"We bring him."

The praetor tensed. "You will die," he breathed.

"You'll be *lucky* if you die. *Move.*"

Ben scrambled in behind the wheel of the truck while David and Milly clambered into the canvas-covered bed. Jude had my back. I forced the praetor over the tailgate with me. Jude climbed in after us.

"You are being stupid," the praetor spat out.

I shoved him down onto the bench seat. "Shut up!"

Ben put the truck into gear and plowed out of the park at full speed, bouncing over holes, knocking down barricades. We had to get out of town before reinforcements arrived.

Beside me, the praetor was sweating. It felt good to see him nervous for a change. Jude kept his weapon pointed at the man. We were both looking forward to shooting him.

David, pale and staring straight ahead, had yet to shake off the shock. He'd been so desperately wrong about Europa and the praetor.

"David," I said to him. He didn't respond. "*David.*"

Finally, he looked at me.

"Are you with us?"

He nodded, then went back to staring.

Next to Jude, Milly sat with her head down, her hair hanging in her face. She'd stopped crying, but I wasn't sure if that was good or bad.

The praetor stupidly decided that it was safe to open his mouth. "What do you hope to gain from all of this?"

I slammed the stock of my weapon into his nose, which exploded in blood. He stopped talking.

The truck skidded into a turn as we raced up Arizona Avenue. Ben would head down Highway 903 toward the interstate. I looked out the back at the scenery flying past. No one was pursuing us, but that wouldn't last. The soldiers of Europa wouldn't rest until they got their precious praetor back. First they'd give us Tim, then we'd return their leader —in several pieces.

Suddenly David came back to life. His gaze shifted to the praetor. "What is this sick obsession you have with my dead father?"

The praetor smirked. He dabbed his sleeve at the blood covering his face. "I find your naiveté quite charming."

"I can't wait to cut that smirk off your ugly face," Jude remarked.

The praetor's expression slipped.

Ben, not exactly an experienced driver, careened into a tight turn. The truck came dangerously close to tipping sideways. I fell back against the canvas. Jude, David, and Milly toppled from the bench and onto the floor.

That's when the praetor made his move.

Before I could react, he threw himself over the gate and out into the road below. I scrambled to my feet in time to see him limping for cover behind the old Chevron station. I fired at him, but the truck bounced, throwing off my aim.

"Stop! Stop the truck!" I shouted.

I gathered my courage and prepared to jump over the gate.

Jude grabbed me. "No, Sera! We can't lose you, too! He's gone—he's already gone!"

My heart felt like a stone in my chest as I watched the praetor disappear around the building. We couldn't afford to stop to pursue him.

With a savage cry, I hurled my weapon toward the back of the cab. A low growl of protest rumbled from the dark space.

Jude pointed his weapon at the sound. I edged forward and found a large covered box tucked into the corner. I lifted the canvas tarp, revealing a white wolf cub in a crate. It backed away and snarled at me. This had to be Hati's replacement.

"Kill it," David ordered.

That was my first thought, too. But then something in its brilliant amber eyes changed my mind. "No. It's not his fault."

This one perfect thing would live, in spite of the praetor.

The ride smoothed out and I knew we'd reached the interstate. Finally, the window to the cab slid open, revealing Ben's face. "Where am I going?"

I looked around at David, Milly, and Jude. Everyone was looking at me.

"Tim?" Milly said.

Jude shook his head. "They could be holding him anywhere."

"The praetor's gonna want our heads on sticks," Ben warned.

Jude nodded. "We need someplace to lie low and plan a rescue."

Then I remembered what Grandpa had told me through the fence at the compound.

Take them to the cabin, Sera. Stay smart. Stay safe. Protect them at all costs.

I'd let him down once. I wouldn't do it again.

"Highway 97," I told Ben.

He shifted into a higher gear and we headed into the back country of the Wenatchee National Forest.

Part III

Chapter Nineteen

I crouched behind a pile of wood in the ankle-deep snow and watched as the two soldiers prepared to break camp. They'd stamped out their fire and were loading their tents and supplies into the back of the truck. Soon they would load the children.

We'd been hiding in the wilderness of the northern Cascades for almost a year. News of Europa and its despicable activities filtered through to us via a growing network of rebel factions. Not long after we'd fled Roslyn, the praetor had abandoned our town for Ellensburg, just east of the Cascades. He'd set men to work digging out the Central Washington University complex, then claimed it as his central command. His soldiers now patrolled the communities of the northern Cascades, confiscating supplies, seizing property, and arresting people for fabricated crimes like "subversive language" and "aggressive demeanor."

Europa's biggest offense by far, however, was the abduction of American children. They forced some into military service. Some were never seen or heard from again.

They had five kids today, gagged, trussed up back to

back, and shivering in the cold. The group included a frail-looking girl who'd been crying most of the morning. Small, weak, she was not soldier material. I'd heard rumors that pretty young girls were being stolen from their families to work as concubines, comfort girls for the military. I wondered if that was to be this girl's fate.

Not on my watch.

Something cold and wet touched my cheek. I looked into a pair of bright amber eyes. Ash stood beside me. He was my constant companion; my partner in crime.

My relationship with the white wolf had suffered a rocky start. He'd bitten my hand several times and eaten my favorite pair of boots, but he was a magnificent animal, loyal, intelligent, fearless—everything the praetor had said the Ellesmere wolves were. Though only a year old, Ash was almost five feet long and already weighed more than I could lift.

I nodded, giving him the signal to begin.

Like an overzealous puppy, he bounded off toward the soldiers' truck with his tongue lolling out. I shook my head at his antics; he seemed to enjoy this game even more than I did. Knowing exactly what I expected, he hid beneath the rear suspension and waited for the right moment to spring into action.

The fatter of the two soldiers walked up to the open truck gate, his bedroll in one hand and a bag of potatoes in the other. Potatoes, a hot commodity, went for a full clip of ammo on the black market. I wondered what hungry family he'd stolen them from.

Ash sprang out from behind the wheels and slammed into the soldier's legs. The man yelped and dropped every-thing. While he spun in a tight circle, sputtering, trying to figure out what had happened, Ash took advantage of the confusion. He snatched the potato bag in his massive jaws and darted out of reach.

"Whoa! Hey there!" The fat soldier raised his arms and took a few steps toward the wolf, trying to startle him into dropping the potatoes. Ash, too seasoned for that ploy, skittered away and then stopped to stare back. The soldier tried again. Ash huffed, dancing closer to the tree line.

The taller soldier, a centurion, looked up from packing his bedroll to see what was going on. "Just shoot ze beast," he called out. He picked up his AK-12.

That was Ash's cue; he turned and galloped into the woods.

Not willing to give up the valuable food, the fat soldier grabbed his own weapon out of the truck. Both men gave chase.

I waited until they'd disappeared into the woods, then hurried across the camp. The kids' eyes rounded in terror when they saw me. I pulled off my face mask and held my finger to my lips, signaling for quiet. Relief flooded their expressions and they shifted with anticipation.

Taking the knife from my pocket, I sawed through the ropes binding the biggest boy. Once free, he joined me in releasing the others.

"Follow," I whispered to them.

I led them all into the forest and hid with them behind a wall of young pines.

"Thank you," one of the boys gasped. He couldn't have been much older than I was.

"Where are you from?" I asked quietly.

"Peshastin," he whispered.

"Dryden," another answered.

"Leavenworth."

"Me, too," said a smaller boy.

"I-I'm from C-Cashmere," the frail girl whispered, shivering. Her hands were bright pink from the cold.

I took off my gloves and handed them to her. "Here."

Tears filled her eyes. "Th-thank you."

I looked away, wishing I could do more.

I stared out across the camp at the distant tree line. Ash was out there somewhere, hopefully leading the soldiers far from camp. Sometimes they gave up on their stolen supplies sooner than planned, though, so I needed to keep my eyes peeled just in case.

Our game would have been much easier if ammunition weren't so precious; two quick bullets would have meant checkmate the moment I'd spotted their camp. It didn't matter, though. Ash and I had never lost. We made a good team.

I heard gasps behind me and knew the wolf was back. The sight of him always shocked people at first, but, as I often told David, he was only dangerous to dangerous people. I took the bag of potatoes from his mouth, then pulled him into a hug to show the kids they could trust him. I ruffled the fur on his massive head. A few of them got brave and reached out to touch his shaggy back.

I handed the bag of potatoes to the tallest boy. "Stay quiet," I told them, "and follow the wolf. He'll lead you to two boys named Jude and Ben. They'll take you to a logging road. Follow the road west to Winton. The people there will help you."

Winton had become a stop on an underground railroad of sorts. Rebels in the old mining town had no qualms about hiding enemies of the praetor or returning stolen children to their families.

The frail girl threw her arms around my neck. "God bless you," she whispered in my ear.

I flinched. It had been a long time since God had been mentioned in my presence. I preferred a simple thank you. "Sure," I muttered. Then I patted Ash on the back. "Go on, boy. Get 'em out of here."

The wolf huffed excitedly and padded off, the kids following behind. It would take them twenty minutes to hike to Ben and Jude. They would only make it if the soldiers, once they returned to camp, didn't go after them. That's where I came in.

I walked into the middle of the camp, stood by the embers of the dead fire, and waited. By now the soldiers had realized that they would never catch the wolf. They'd decided to call the potatoes a loss and get back to their captives.

I heard the two of them crunching through the snow long before I saw them. They ambled into the clearing. "... probably a whole pack of 'em," the fat soldier was saying.

"Vhite volves do not grow here," the centurion replied.

The fat one stopped cold. He'd seen me. "Hey!"

"You zhere!" the centurion called.

I took off at a gallop, running in the opposite direction from where Ash had led the kids. I had at least twenty minutes to kill before my backup returned.

THIRTY MINUTES LATER, I was staring down the rifle sights at the private's sweaty brow. I could hear the wolf enjoying his centurion lunch and, judging by the look of revulsion on his face, Private Calhoun could hear it, too. Breathing deeply, I pressed the rifle barrel against the soft, fatty flesh of his forehead and shifted my finger to the trigger. I slowly let out my breath—

"Seraphina!" the private shouted.

I hesitated.

"That's yer name, right? I-I have somethin' for ya."

He eased his hand down to his uniform belt and slipped a piece of paper out from beneath the brass buckle. He held it out to me.

It was a small photograph.

Curious, I yanked the picture from his fingers. My eyes drifted over the faded image. The edges were worn, the surface cracked, and there was a diagonal fold across the middle. But there was no mistaking the faces staring back at me.

They were sunburned, windswept, standing in the shadow of Sleeping Beauty's Castle. The short boy wore an LED necklace. The lanky girl held a half-eaten Mickey Mouse ice cream bar. Their parents stood behind them, flashing easy smiles. And their grandfather, the tips of his shaggy silver mustache stiff with sunscreen, wore a mouse ear hat with the name "MARK" embroidered in red on the cap.

I blinked back hot tears. My father always kept this picture in his wallet.

The private snorted. "Thought that might get yer attention."

My eyes narrowed on Calhoun. "Not the kind you were hoping for." I swung back the rifle stock and bashed him in the side of the head. "Tell me where you got this?"

He held his hands out in front of his face. "I-I'll only speak with David Donner."

"Wrong answer." I jammed the bore of the weapon against his squishy nose.

"I have a message for him—f-from your father!"

My breath caught. "My father?"

"That's right! B-but only for David Donner!"

"And what if I just shoot you right here?"

His eyes went wide. "Then you'll never know the truth."

Although it went against my better judgment, I tied Private Calhoun's hands behind his back, blindfolded and gagged him, then marched him up the mountain through the snow. If there was any chance my father was alive, I needed to know. If it turned out the private didn't really have a message for David from my father, then it would be just as easy to kill Calhoun at the cabin.

Ash kept his distance, preferring to watch our progress through the trees. Undoubtedly confused by this change in our routine, he followed along like a loyal soldier. Odds were good that he'd be having Calhoun for breakfast in the morning.

Grandpa Donner's hunting lodge lay deep in the wilds of the Wenatchee Forest near Colchuck Lake. By the time I saw the large cabin blending into the curve of the snowy, wooded hillside, the sun was already going down, painting the red sky in shades of turquoise and purple. The cottage was solar-powered, had its own well and indoor plumbing, and Grandpa had stocked it with enough food and supplies to last us another year.

Ash loped toward his shed out back, where he'd wait until I unlocked my bedroom window later that night. I'd have a bowl of cat food waiting for him by my bed, as usual. None of us knew why Grandpa Donner had stocked up on cat food—he didn't even like cats—but Ash had been raised on the stuff.

I pushed open the front door and shoved Private Calhoun inside. He fell to his knees with a muffled cry of pain, then rolled onto the circular brown rug. I shut the door against the cold and faced the room.

Milly straightened on the sofa, where she'd been mending a pair of socks. She took one look at the soldier on the floor and slipped the .45 out of the holster on her hip. She hadn't actually shot anyone before, but, if push came to shove, Milly could get the job done.

She stood up. "Sera's brought us a gift," she called to the rest of the cabin.

Ben charged in from the back hallway. "Where've you been?" He blinked at Calhoun. "You brought one home?"

Jude came out of the kitchen, wiping his hands on a dishtowel. His wary eyes landed on the private. "I can't wait to hear this."

The basement door banged open. David stepped into the room holding a jar of pickles. "Ben, I told you not to eat all the dill—" He stopped short when he saw Calhoun, then he glowered at me. "Have you lost your mind?!"

Jude folded his arms. "What happened to your number one rule?"

Ben's brows arched. "Never lead anyone home."

Milly glared at Calhoun. "Has he got a name?"

"Who cares what his name is?" David shot out. "We're not *keeping* him!"

Jude scowled. "It's a simple question, David."

"It's a stupid question, Jude!"

I pulled the photograph out of my coat pocket and handed it to my brother. "He gave me this."

David's eyes landed on the picture. His face turned splotchy and I thought he might cry. The others moved in to look over his shoulder.

Ben shrugged. "So they're looking for us. What else is new?"

David sniffled, then lifted his eyes to mine. "Where did he get it?"

"I don't know. He said he would only talk to you."

He looked down at the bound and gagged private. "Why me?"

Jude draped his arm over Milly's shoulders. "The praetor probably found the picture in the Roslyn house."

Milly agreed. "Every soldier's got a copy by now."

"No." David held up the picture. "This is from our father's wallet."

The others went quiet, finally understanding the seriousness of the situation.

I nudged Calhoun with the toe of my boot. "Get up."

Calhoun resisted, mumbling something from behind his gag.

Jude and Ben hauled him to his feet, dragged him across the floor, and dropped him into one of the kitchen chairs. They removed his blindfold. The man looked terrible. His nose was purple, crooked, and swollen; both his eyes were beginning to turn black. But he was going to look a lot worse if he tried to play games with us.

I pulled the gag out of his mouth. "Talk."

"Can I—" he croaked. "Can I get a glass of water?"

I kicked him in the leg. "Talk!"

"Owww! All right!" He took a breath and looked at David. "I got a message for ya from yer father."

David blinked. His expression changed from a foggy look of confusion to the shining hope of a little boy. "You do?" he rasped.

"Your dad sent me ta find ya. He wants his kids ta come be with him so y'all can be a family again."

"He's lying," Jude growled. "If you're friends with their father, then why are you wearing a Europa uniform?"

Calhoun's smile wavered. "Well…uh… That—that's a long story, son."

"Yep." Ben nodded. "He's lying."

Milly's lips curled. "He's just a cutthroat traitor tryin' to save his own skin."

Calhoun shook his head. "No, no! Now, that's not true, kids. I-I'm here ta help ya. If you'll just untie my—"

I kicked him again.

He cried out and griped some more. "I'm a friend of yer father's! I swear it!"

David stared intently at the soldier. He'd given up on life after he'd lost our father and his cure, but Calhoun had just punched a hole through the darkness and let in a small ray of sunshine.

Jude looked at me. "Is he telling the truth?"

"I don't know." Part of me hoped he was; part of me hoped he wasn't. I wanted my father alive, but not in the hands of the praetor. "I know how to find out, though." I gestured at Milly. "Open the door."

Milly nodded and crossed the room.

The color drained from David's face. "What are you doing?"

Calhoun laughed and coughed. "You gonna give me a cold, darlin'?"

Milly wrapped her fingers around the doorknob.

"No!" David stepped in front of me. "We agreed that animal would stay outside. And I'm not stupid—I know you sneak him in through your window every night."

David and Ash had a sordid history. David had tried to drown him not long after we'd arrived at the cabin. Ash had taken offense and given him a nice scar on his arm for his trouble. David hated Ash. The feeling was mutual.

I stared at my brother. "Do you want the truth or not?"

David hesitated. When it came to our father, he wanted the truth more than anything else in the world—even more than avoiding an animal that would eat him without a second thought.

Calhoun started to look nervous. "Okay, w-wait a second."

I looked around the room. "Anybody who hates the sight of blood should leave."

I mostly said that for effect. I didn't intend to let Ash eat Calhoun. Yet.

Ben shrugged. "I wouldn't mind seeing him splattered all over the floor."

"Now—now, hold on just a second." Calhoun tried to smile, but his lips trembled. "Nobody needs to be gettin' splattered."

Milly pulled open the door. David, scowling, immediately moved to a far corner of the room, which only strengthened my bluff. Jude and Ben edged behind the sturdy kitchen table, adding to the effect.

A blast of cold air swirled snow into the cabin, hitting Calhoun full in the face. He pressed back into his chair. "Wait! You don't gotta do this!"

I brought my fingers to my lips and let out a shrill whistle.

Calhoun squirmed against his chair, his eyes glued to the open doorway. "I-I'm sure we can come ta some kinda understandin'."

I was unmoved by his fear. "We don't want an understanding, Private. We want the truth."

Two intense amber eyes emerged from the cloud of blowing snow swirling just inside the threshold. A low growl filled the cabin. I heard Calhoun whimper. It wouldn't take long for him to break.

"Private Calhoun, meet Ash. Ash's pet peeves are blue and gold uniforms, traitors, and liars."

Giving a cursory glance to his surroundings—noting David in the far corner—Ash stalked slowly into the cabin, massive and terrifying.

Private Calhoun's feet skidded against the floor. He was trying to escape by pedaling backwards. "Just tell me what ya wanna know!"

"Did you get the picture from our father?" I asked.

His hesitation told me everything before he even spoke. "Y-yes!" he stammered.

The wolf raised his hackles and let out a menacing growl.

I leaned in close to the private. "Ash doesn't believe you."

Sweat dripped into Calhoun's eyes. "H-he's just an animal! H-he don't know nothin'!"

I looked at Ash. "He just called you stupid."

Ash lunged at the soldier.

Calhoun screamed. "Wait!"

The wolf paused, his sharp, snapping teeth inches from the private's face.

I raised my brows. "Yes?"

"I…d-didn't exactly *get* it from yer dad."

David stepped out of the shadows, his expression grim. "Then where, *exactly*, did you get it?"

"F-from the praetor. H-he made copies. We all got 'em."

"Like I said," Jude affirmed, "just a copy of a picture he got from the Roslyn house."

Calhoun shook his head. "N-no! H-he got it from yer father! I swear he did!"

Forgetting about Ash, David marched into the center of the room. "Where is my father?"

"In Ellensburg," Calhoun squeaked.

"Another lie," I asserted.

Ash reared up and slammed his enormous paws onto Calhoun's chest. The private froze. The wolf snorted hot breath into his face. "N-not a lie," the private stammered, barely breathing.

David moved closer. "Have you seen our father?"

"No, but the pra—praetor says we're s'posed to tell ya he's in Ellensburg and he wants his kids with 'im."

Finally, the truth. I flushed with anger and disappointment. This was just another of the praetor's elaborate schemes to flush us out of hiding.

David wasn't ready to give up, though. "Is my dad there or not?!"

Ben shook his head. "The praetor is playing with you, David. He's using your dad as bait."

Jude agreed. "He's just trying to lure us to Ellensburg."

Calhoun looked, wide-eyed, into Ash's deadly stare. "C-could somebody get this animal—"

Milly stepped in. "Have you seen my brother?"

Three days after fleeing Roslyn, we'd gone back to rescue Tim. We found the entire town abandoned and burned to the ground. We weren't sure who the praetor had taken with him to Ellensburg, but we'd found a lot of unmarked graves and hadn't had the heart to speculate. Tim was a capable, strong soldier, though, too good to waste. We felt certain they'd conscripted him and we looked for him in the face of every soldier we saw. Tim was out there, somewhere, and we were going to find him.

Calhoun frowned at her. "Who?"

"Tim. Timothy Odette. The praetor took him from Roslyn eleven months ago."

"I-I seen a lotta kids—"

"He's a big fella," Milly went on. "Football player. Blond hair. Square head. Kinda dopey."

The private shook his head. "Doesn't sound familiar." Ash growled and the man squeaked. "I ain't seen him!"

"Where do you take the kids?" I demanded.

Calhoun swallowed hard. "T-to the university in Ellensburg. Th-that's where they experiment on 'em."

I narrowed my eyes. "What do you mean, experiment on them?"

"I dunno. It's…it's some genetic thing. Makes 'em really big—really strong. Pr-Praetor calls it…uh…uh…the Goliath Code. Ya know, like Goliath in the Bible."

David sank down onto the sofa, hope flaring in his eyes again. The praetor was dangling the one carrot my brother would find irresistible: his cure. I should never have brought Private Calhoun back to the cabin. I should have snatched that picture from his fingers and shot him dead.

"David," I warned. "Don't jump to conclusions."

"Why not, Sera?" he demanded. "Why am I not allowed to hope? Why, for once in this hellish world, can't something go my way for a change?"

"Think!" I shouted. "The praetor is trying to manipulate you!"

He lurched off the sofa and jammed his finger up at me. "*You* think! Just *once*! About *me*!"

"He told us himself that he knows about Dad's work! He knows how important it is to you! Jude is right. He's just trying to lure us to Ellensburg!"

"And what if he really does have our father?"

"Don't be stupid." I dismissed the possibility. It was the wrong thing to say.

David glared at me, then turned and walked out of the room.

I glanced at the others. The three of them looked surprised by the exchange. They weren't aware of my father's work on the cure and were waiting for an explanation. I didn't feel like giving one. "I need some air."

Calhoun started whimpering again. "C-could somebody *please* get this thing off me?" he begged.

"Ash," I called. He was drooling all over the front of the private's coat. "Let's go."

Ash hesitated and looked back at me.

"Now," I snapped.

The wolf let out a disappointed whine, then dropped down from Calhoun's chest and padded after me to the door.

"Sera?" Milly questioned.

I gestured at Calhoun. "Get some rope and tie him up." Then I left the cabin with Ash at my heels.

It was a cold, clear night, with a brisk wind blowing off the top of the mountain. I zipped my coat and trudged across the clearing through the snow toward a car-sized boulder resting on the edge of a hundred-foot drop. I crawled up the knobby rock, dangled my legs over the side, and looked down into the dark valley below.

I wasn't naive enough to believe that my father was still alive. And, like me, David had seen Seattle. He knew the destruction the earthquake had caused. But the praetor had chosen his bait well. My brother was desperate to believe his lies.

I leaned back to stare at the blood-colored moon, letting the cold air wash over my face. David would be here any moment now. I needed to organize my thoughts. It would take a great deal of diplomacy to make him see reason. I needed to be understanding but firm. If I had to shackle every one of them to a chair, we would all be staying put at the cabin until the threat from Europa had passed.

Ash clambered up and sat down next to me. When I

didn't reach out to scratch him, he rested his muzzle on my shoulder and sighed in my ear. I grunted at his childishness and scratched his chest. He understood me better than anybody, a fact reflected in his ever-changing moods.

"Everything's fine."

He thumped his tail.

"I don't think you're going to get to eat this one, though."

He growled a little in response.

I smiled and ruffled his ears. "And I don't need your sass about it."

It had occurred to me that I could take the private down the mountain to the Chiwaukum Lake rebel camp. They might be able to get information out of him that could help their cause.

The wolf alerted, whipping his head around with a warning growl. David was behind me.

"Do you think the praetor has him?" he asked.

"David, Dad is dead."

"You know he always carries that photo in his wallet."

I turned toward him and took a deep breath. "I don't know how the praetor got the photo. But I know he wants us captured. And I know we can't trust Calhoun. Those are the two most important things informing our choices right now."

David's jaw tightened. "And what about saving our father?"

Ash growled at his sharp tone.

"Hush," I whispered to the wolf. I scratched his furry head and thought a moment. "What if Dad is alive? Do you think he'd want us risking ourselves to save him?"

David fell silent. I hoped that was a good sign.

I pressed my case. "If we leave this mountain now, we're

not only risking our lives, we're risking Jude's, Milly's, and Ben's."

Grunting, he looked away. "And the cure? What if the praetor has found a way to replicate it?" He stared up at me. "What if this thing he calls the Goliath Code is Dad's cure?"

"How in the world could a man like the praetor possibly succeed at something that took our father a decade of research to accomplish? Isn't it much more likely that this is all a ploy?"

He didn't respond.

"I am not going to gamble our lives on a possibility, David."

David looked at the ground and fell silent for a moment. "What do you plan to do with Calhoun?"

"I'm not sure yet."

"Well. You'll do what's best for everybody else, Sera." He turned and walked away. "You always do."

I watched him walk back to the cabin, knowing I'd failed to convince him. I was right, though, and the others would agree. David was just going to have to come to terms with that. We had too much at stake to let his vanity lure us out of hiding. Even if our father was alive.

I slipped out of bed early the next morning, wanting to get Calhoun down the mountain and be back before nightfall.

I yawned and looked over at Ash, sound asleep at the foot of my bed. "Time to get up, boy," I whispered. I ruffled the fur on his back and got a low groan in response.

Milly stirred in her bed across the room. She yawned and stretched. "What's happenin'?"

I stood up and pulled on my jeans. "I'm taking Calhoun down the mountain to Chiwaukum Lake."

She scrunched her face. "To the rebels?"

"Yeah. Just getting an early start. I'll be back before sundown."

"'Kay." She rolled over and went back to sleep.

I pulled on my boots and slipped into my coat, hoping it wouldn't be too windy out. Gusts coming off the mountain in the morning could reach subzero temperatures. I roused Ash again, then he and I headed out of the bedroom.

The living room sat in muted shadow. If I squinted I could almost see my grandfather sitting on the sofa, smoking a cigar. When David and I were little, he used to bring us up to the cabin on weekends to give Mom and Dad a break. Those were some of my fondest memories.

I clicked on the lights. "Wake up, Calhoun. If you need to use the——" I froze.

Private Calhoun was gone.

Ash reacted to my change of mood with a low, menacing growl. I glanced frantically around the room, then ran to check the kitchen. It was empty, too.

"Ben!" I called. He was supposed to be on guard duty last night. "*Ben!*"

Ash shadowed me as I hurried to the weapons rack by the front door and grabbed the M16. Calhoun's AK-12 and David's .45 were missing. My stomach clenched. I would not panic. I threw open the front door to a frigid morning. The sudden blast of cold air made my eyes water. I scanned the tree line. Nothing moved in the frost-covered pines. I looked for footprints leading off into the woods, but without fresh snow it was hard to tell the new from the old.

I went back into the cabin and closed the door. I checked out the room. There weren't any signs of a struggle.

Nothing was out of place. Even the big round rug on the floor was in the same position it had been in the night before.

I stared at the empty kitchen chair. The only evidence that Private Calhoun had even been there was a puddle of ropes on the floor.

He'd escaped.

The consequences of that hit me hard. I sat down on the sofa. Our time of sanctuary was over.

Jude and Milly wandered into the room, rubbing the sleep from their eyes. I must have woken them both when I yelled for Ben.

Jude yawned. "What's going on?"

"Calhoun's gone."

They were both instantly awake.

"What?" Jude hurried over to the empty kitchen chair. "That's impossible! I checked his ropes before I went to bed!" He held up a piece of discarded rope.

"It's been cut," I told him. "And Ben—"

A sleepy voice answered from the hallway. "Ben what?"

I looked up, surprised to see Ben standing next to Milly. I felt relieved, then enraged. "Were you *sleeping?*"

Jude pointed at his brother. "You were supposed to be on guard duty!"

Ben looked confused. "I— David asked to take my shift."

My stomach turned. I closed my eyes.

Jude gestured to the room. "Then where is he?!"

"How the hell should I know?" Ben shot back.

A cold feeling of dread was winding itself around my heart. Ash shifted restlessly at my feet.

Milly examined a hank of rope. "Maybe he's in the basement?"

I breathed deeply. She was thinking Calhoun had gotten loose and tied David up somewhere. I hoped it was true. The alternative was so much worse.

Jude headed across the room. He threw open the basement door and thudded down the stairs. "David?" His bellowing voice echoed below us.

We all listened, but Jude didn't get an answer.

He came back up the stairs, shaking his head.

The heartbreak was crushing.

Ash plopped his big muzzle onto my knees. He looked up at me with soft amber eyes; I absently rubbed his ears.

"Calhoun must have forced David to go with him," Milly said.

Jude took the rope from Milly's hand and held up the neat end. "How did Calhoun cut the rope?"

"He must have had a knife," she answered.

"He didn't have a knife," I murmured.

Milly's eyes filled with tears. "He must have," she insisted.

"He didn't!" Ben shot back. "I searched him myself before I went to bed."

The room fell silent. The truth was hitting us all hard. I had dangerously underestimated my brother's obsession. It hurt to realize that even the possibility of a cure mattered more to David than we did.

My chin trembled as I voiced what we all were thinking. "David set him free. They left together."

Milly eased down next to me on the sofa and took my hand. "He really thinks the praetor has your dad?"

My heart ached so badly I couldn't answer, but I knew this had very little to do with my father and everything to do with my brother's pride.

"How could he be that stupid?" Ben roared.

Milly tried to justify his actions. "It must have been a really hard choice for—"

"Don't," I interrupted. "It wasn't hard for him. We need to worry about ourselves now."

Jude nodded, pursing his lips. "We can't stay here anymore."

Milly winced. "You think David would tell Europa where we are?"

"Maybe, maybe not," Jude replied. "But Calhoun definitely would."

Her posture wilted.

I looked around the cabin. We had security, shelter, food, water—and now we had to walk away from it all. Because of David.

Ben's jaw tightened. "Well, that's great. Where are we supposed to go now?"

I shook my head. "I don't know."

"How much time do you think we have?" Jude asked.

Ash suddenly leapt to his feet and let loose with a mournful howl.

My heart thudded. "None."

Chapter Twenty

We watched them burn our cabin.

After looting our stored supplies, they broke the windows, tore the front door from its hinges, and set the roof on fire. The flames melted the snow from the shingles, licked down the cedar siding, and crawled under the floor-boards to consume everything inside. My grandfather's hide-away and our sanctuary went up in a thick, black cloud of smoke.

We'd barely had time to grab our weapons and our packs before the Europa squad arrived—nine men in all, plundering and vandalizing, joyfully laying waste to our refuge. We could only hide in the woods and wait for them to finish, then gather what little might be left before we set about finding another place to call home.

Milly and I crouched in the woods behind the thick trunk of a fallen pine. I could tell by her ragged breathing that her anger matched mine. I wasn't sure who I hated more—Private Calhoun, or my brother—but it would not go well for either one of them when they crossed my path again.

Jude and Ben hid a few feet away, on their bellies in the snow, peering over the top of a knoll. Ben had a tight grip on his M16; Jude's hand on his shoulder seemed to be the only thing keeping him from charging the soldiers.

Ash shifted beside me. He was on high alert. If not for him, we would have been captured or trapped inside the cabin as it burned.

Milly leaned close to me. "They haven't found the truck."

I blinked at her. I'd forgotten about the transport truck we'd stolen from Roslyn. We had parked it in the woods behind the cabin, concealed in a stand of tall blackberry bushes. It would be perfect for a getaway once the soldiers tired of their games and moved on. I felt sure it still had enough gas to get us down the mountain, maybe as far Winton.

The sound of an engine sputtering to life crushed my hopes. The large transport truck, blackberry brambles clinging to its canvas and sticking out from beneath its windshield wipers, came around the side of the smoldering cabin with two cheering soldiers in its wake.

I closed my eyes and threw my head back, wishing something would go right.

"Plan B," Milly whispered.

But there was no Plan B. There hadn't even been a Plan A. I wanted to lie back on the cold snowy ground and cry. David was gone, our home was gone, our transportation was gone. I opened my eyes, watching the black smoke from the cabin billow up into the distant clouds. I wanted to be like that smoke and float far, far away into the red sky.

A rock landed not far from me. I frowned over at Jude. He and Ben stared at me in horror, gesturing wildly. I looked to my left. Milly was gone. My eyes darted to the cabin in time to see her enter the clearing, heading straight toward the soldiers. My first impulse was to scream her name. Thankfully, I thought better of it.

I fumbled with my weapon, scrambling to get it ready. Hands shaking, I pulled the bolt, jammed the stock against my shoulder, and zeroed in on the men. *Nose to the charging handle.* I blinked to clear my eyes.

"Breathe. Slow it down. Breathe." The first person to touch my best friend was going to get a bullet between the eyes.

Milly's words took the soldiers—and me—off guard. "Have you seen my pretty bird?" she asked brightly.

They turned their weapons on her and my heart lurched. "Steady, boys," I whispered. My finger hovered over the trigger. If I fired, it would bring all of them down on our heads.

One of the soldiers shouted something at her in another language.

Milly kept ambling forward. "He's fluttered off without a word."

The men were confused by her. But, when they saw she was unarmed, they slowly lowered their guns.

"He took my heart with him, away." Milly twirled like a lunatic. "Will you help me find him, pray?"

The soldiers shared a laugh. Even the men who'd found the truck hurried over to join the fun. Pretty Milly had quickly gathered everyone's undivided attention.

"He has a tail of crimson red. A spot of white upon his head."

I crept toward Jude and Ben, keeping my eye on the men surrounding Milly. "We need to get to the truck."

Milly continued to talk and twirl. "His wings are soft and feathered so. And where he flies my true love goes."

Jude kept his weapon trained on the soldiers surrounding Milly, though his hands shook and sweat beaded on his forehead. "We have to get her out of there!"

"She's distracting them," I whispered back.

Ben agreed. "Look. They think she's crazy."

A soldier reached for Milly but she eluded him, twirling away to the other side of the circle of men. She was risking her life for us; we couldn't let her efforts go to waste.

"Follow me," I told them.

I crept around the base of the knoll and glanced back to see if the boys were following my orders. Ben was right behind me. Jude hung back, reluctant to take his eyes off Milly. I waved him forward. He gritted his teeth, gave up his position, and followed.

We skirted the trees, staying hidden until the rumbling truck was just twenty feet in front of us. Thanks to Milly, it had been left running and unguarded. We snuck up to the passenger door; Ben and Jude crawled in and onto the bench seat.

"Gun it," I told Jude. "Head for 97 and Winton.

Jude shook his head. "Not without Milly."

I peeked up over the hood. One of the soldiers had tired of Milly's games. He'd taken hold of her arm. *"Komm ihr hübsches Mädchen."*

"Go!" I snarled.

Ben reached his leg under his brother's and stomped down on the gas. The truck surged forward. I dropped flat in the snow. The vehicle raced toward the circle of soldiers, plowed over two of them, made a slight right, then careened down the logging road. Five of the soldiers ran after it, firing their weapons. The two that stayed behind had Milly.

The tall one spotted me. He wrapped his arm around

Milly's throat and, hand shaking, pressed his handgun against her temple.

The short soldier pointed his AK-12 at me. "On your knees!" he shouted in a heavy accent.

I rose up on my knees, lifting my weapon over my head with both hands. Ash peeked out at me from around the side of his shed. I shook my head; two soldiers with guns meant he'd get shot for sure. He ran off to watch from the safety of the trees.

I locked eyes with Milly, willing her not to do anything stupid. Hopefully the boys had gotten away and would be back to rescue us. In the meantime, the soldiers wouldn't hurt us if we kept calm and did as we were told.

But calm wasn't exactly Milly's style these days. She side-stepped, driving her fist backwards into the soldier's groin. He dropped his gun as she spun away from him, falling to his knees in the muddy snow.

The shorter soldier faltered, directing his AK-12 at Milly, then back at me. He wasn't sure which one of us posed the bigger threat.

Milly's soldier, still on his knees, moaned in pain. She eyed his handgun, lying just out of reach.

I didn't want her to do it—it was too risky. I tried to catch her eye, tried to shake her off, but she was too focused to notice.

She dove for the gun.

The short soldier turned his AK-12 on Milly. I rolled my weapon back into my arms, fired, and dropped him in the snow.

The soldier on his knees finally regained his composure and lunged for Milly. She pointed his handgun at his head. "Ah-ah. Don't be grabby, now."

She'd done it. I was impressed.

I stood to check on the unmoving soldiers that had been hit by the truck. Milly and I high-fived as I passed. The run over soldiers were broken, bloody, and very dead. I stuffed their ammo clips inside my coat.

"This one's name tag says Harris," Milly called to me.

I walked back to her. She had Harris on his knees with his own gun pointed at his head. Grandpa Donner would have been proud.

I sneered at the soldier. "You're an American."

"I...I'm a citizen of Europa."

He was a child, barely old enough to shave. I placed the bore of my weapon against the side of his head. "Tell me, citizen of Europa, where is my brother, David Donner?"

"H-he was brought in by Private Calhoun earlier this morning. He asked for amnesty. You can ask for that, too. Europa's been good to us. We owe them our—"

"Save it, Harris. Where are they going?"

"Where else?" he replied. "Ellensburg."

"Thank you for your cooperation." I stepped back to shoot him and Milly cleared her throat. I stared at her. "What? He's a traitor."

"He's a kid."

I exhaled in disgust, but I slammed the butt of my M16 into his head instead. He collapsed to the ground. "Make better choices!" I shouted down at him. I looked at Milly. "Happy?"

"We aren't animals, Sera."

"Yes, but they are, Milly."

Gunfire sounded in the distance, echoing off the canyon walls. We exchanged a panicked look. *Jude and Ben.*

The two of us took off through the woods, racing down the slope of the mountain with Ash bounding ahead of us. The logging road was full of hairpin turns; if we ran in a straight line we would eventually cross paths with the boys in the truck.

Several minutes later we spotted the transport truck below us. We ducked behind some trees. The truck sat at a dead, crooked stop, pointing in the wrong direction. There was no sign of Jude, Ben, or any soldiers.

I commanded Ash to stay put.

Milly and I crept from the cover of the trees, our weapons ready. We reached the truck and moved along the driver's side. It was riddled with bullet holes. They'd hit the gas tank, leaking diesel onto the dirty snow.

The driver's door stood open. Milly stifled a gasp. There was blood on the seat and more on the ground.

Several sets of footprints led off down the snow packed road.

"Come on," I told her. "They can't be far—"

Two grinning soldiers popped up from the other side of the hood, holding AK-12s. "Hands up, please," one of them said in accented English.

I clenched my jaw. I'd allowed my worry for the boys to distract me and hadn't checked the other side of the truck. Now Milly and I would pay for my stupid mistake.

The soldiers came around the front of the vehicle toward us. We dropped our weapons and raised our hands. One of them—Genc, his nametag said—was enormous, tall and well-muscled. The other soldier—Hogstadt—was particularly unattractive, with one long eyebrow and a crooked nose.

"The praetor will be quite happy to see you again, Miss Donner," Hogstadt said to me. He leered at Milly. "But perhaps I'll have some fun with this one first."

He wrapped a finger around a lock of Milly's hair. She

cringed and pulled away. "Good lord," she grimaced, "you could make an onion cry."

Hogstadt bared his teeth and took a fistful of Milly's blonde hair. She cried out in pain.

"Hey!" I shouted.

I went to lunge at the ugly soldier, but Genc jammed his rifle into my stomach, knocking the wind out of me.

Ash came hurtling out of nowhere. He'd always had a fondness for Milly, as Private Ugly was about to find out the hard way.

In a blur of snarls and white fur, Ash leapt at the soldier, taking him by the throat and dragging him to the ground. It was fast and it was brutal.

The enormous Genc pointed his weapon at Ash. I sprang forward, shoving the rifle barrel into the air. *CRACK!* It fired, but the shot went wide.

"Run, Ash!" I ordered.

I grabbed hold of Genc's weapon, wrestling for control. He was strong and he wasn't letting go, but neither was I. He tossed me around like an empty sack.

Milly jumped on his back. He flung her to the ground.

I glanced over and saw Ash dancing backwards toward the tree line, his muzzle dripping with Private Ugly's blood. His worried eyes were on me and I knew he was tempted to rush to my defense. I heard shouts and truck engines.

Reinforcements were coming.

"Get outta here!" I bellowed at him.

He turned and bolted for the woods.

The big soldier finally got the better of me; he threw me onto my back. He pointed his rifle at my face and pulled back the bolt. The ugly soldier lay on the ground beside me, gurgling in his own blood. I closed my eyes and prepared to join him.

The sound of the shot seized every muscle in my body. I waited for a searing pain that, strangely, never came. I opened my eyes to see Genc collapse to the ground. Milly stood behind him, holding Private Ugly's smoking AK-12.

It was her first kill.

She stared at her victim, her face turning a little green. She was dazed and breathing hard. I thought for sure she was going to throw up.

I scrambled to my feet and took the weapon from her hands.

I knew exactly how she felt. I could still remember what Grandpa said to me the night I'd killed Lem Richmond and I repeated it to her. "You were given a choice. You made the right one."

She smiled at me through a mist of tears.

A group of soldiers charged around the transport truck toward us. They looked down at the two dead soldiers on the ground, then scowled at me, the only one holding a weapon. One of them yanked the rifle from my hands, then clipped me across the jaw with it. Pain shot through my face and I fell to my knees. He hauled back the weapon to hit me again.

"No!" Milly shouted.

"Private Gunnar!" a man barked out. "Do not damage ze goods!"

Private Gunnar stepped back. The pain in my face left me dizzy. My jaw had gone numb.

A short, thin, weaselly man reached out a gloved hand to help me to my feet. He wore the gold bars of a centurion. I steadied my spinning head, and stood up on my own next to Milly.

"Red hair. Green eyes. Foul disposition," the centurion commented distastefully. "Mizz Donner, I presume?"

I stared at the man, but didn't respond.

He squinted at me, then threw back his head and bellowed. "Gunnar?"

The soldier who'd clipped me with the rifle stepped forward. "Yes, Centurion Dirvis?" In contrast to his shaved head and abundance of tattoos, Gunnar's French accent added a cultured quality to his words.

"Put zem in ze truck with ze others. Guard zem well, Mister Gunnar." He gestured at me. "Zis vun is precious to ze praetor."

They took our hidden weapons and then led us to a transport truck, stripped of its canvas. It was parked at the back of a long line of vehicles, all pointed south on the road. Private Gunnar forced us to climb into the back of the truck. That's where we found Ben and Jude.

Jude was laid out on the cold metal floor, pale and moaning in pain. He'd been shot in the side. Ben was using his own coat to stop the bleeding. My heart seized. *No,* I thought. *Not Jude. Please, not Jude.*

Milly hurried to his side. She lifted away Ben's coat to get a better look, revealing an angry, oozing hole just beneath his ribs. "It's not spurting," she said breathlessly. "That's good."

Ben's face was drawn and almost as pale as his brother's. "He's lost a lot of blood, though."

Milly unwrapped the scarf from her neck, folded it into a tight square, and gave it to Ben. "Use this. Press hard."

The truck bounced as Private Harris from the cabin climbed over the tailgate. He gave us a sullen stare, then sat down on the bench across from Private Gunnar. He had a nasty bruise on his forehead, but, thanks to Milly, he was still alive. Maybe we could get him to return the favor.

"Harris." Pain shot through my bruised jaw. I winced

and continued more carefully, "Our friend's been shot. He needs a doctor."

Gunnar snorted. "Friends of yours, Private Harris?"

Harris scowled at me, then looked away.

Milly was having none of that. "Are you deaf *and* stupid? We need a doctor, now!"

Gunnar grinned and pulled back the bolt on his rifle. "You screech at us one more time, *mon chéri*, and you will be the one needing the doctor."

Milly pulled back her shoulders, preparing to give Gunnar a piece of her mind, but I shook my head. They weren't going to help Jude. Pushing them would only get more of us hurt.

Engines revved and the convoy started out on a slow, bumpy course down the winding road. Jude moaned in pain with every bounce and jostle. Milly did her best to comfort him, but there wasn't much she could do without medical supplies. We could only keep pressure on his wound and hope that, wherever we were headed, we got there soon.

"Hey, traitor," I called to Harris.

He glared at me.

"Where are we going?"

"Ellensburg," he responded. "Where they'll put you and your friends in front of a firing squad."

So, they were taking us to Central Command. The praetor obviously wanted the pleasure of killing us himself. I wondered if he'd already executed David. Although I tried not to care, my eyes burned with tears at the thought of losing my brother. David had made his choice, though. He'd given himself up and made us all pay for it.

It grew warmer as we traveled further and further down the mountain. I paid close attention to our location. Escape was our only option. There were rebels hiding all over in the mountains, and our home would have to be with them now.

The snow became patchy until it finally disappeared altogether, replaced by a thick mix of mud and volcanic ash. Jude was getting worse with each passing minute. Milly kept talking to him and kissing his face, but he wasn't responding. We hit a bump. He moaned.

Gunnar glowered at him. "I did not join the guard to be a babysitter."

"No, you prefer *shooting* women and children," I mocked.

"I hear the praetor has particular taste when it comes to comfort girls," he jeered. "He likes the redheads."

I looked away and he laughed at me. I took a break from plotting our escape to imagine shooting both of our guards in the head.

We hit another bump and Jude moaned again. It broke my heart to hear him in so much pain.

"Oh, oh, oh," Gunnar mocked. "Shut him up already!"

No, a bullet to the head was too good for Gunnar. Maybe I'd feed him to Ash instead.

As if on cue, a flash of white appeared in the woods to my right. Ash was staying close. I longed to leap from the moving vehicle and join him, but it would be nearly impossible to get Jude out of the truck, let alone run with him through the woods. We would have to commandeer the vehicle.

Private Harris saw Ash, too. "What was that?" He peered off into the woods.

Gunnar rolled a cigarette. "What was what?"

"I saw something."

"Probably her dog," Gunnar dismissed.

"She has a dog?"

Gunnar shrugged. "A wolf."

Harris gaped. "There's a big difference between a dog and a wolf."

"I know. Hers tore the throat out of my best friend." Gunnar bared his gray teeth at me.

Gunnar and Private Ugly were besties? That explained the pain in my jaw.

Suddenly the woods around us came alive with sound, transforming from a dead, ash-choked forest into a jungle in the Amazon. I heard birds in the trees, elk crashing through the underbrush, crickets screaming like sirens. But there hadn't been anything like that in the woods for almost two years.

Gunnar and Harris raised their weapons. Gunnar pounded on the outside of the truck bed, signaling for the driver to stop. We came to a grinding, lurching halt. Jude moaned in response.

CAW CAW-CAW! The loud call echoed toward us.

"Did you hear that?" Harris asked Gunnar.

"Sounded like a parrot."

Harris shook his head. "Not in Washington."

The convoy in front of us rolled to a stop about a hundred yards away. I could hear Centurion Dirvis screaming orders all the way from the front. "Vhy did you stop?" He ran past the other vehicles and stomped up to our driver's lowered window. "Vhy?" he screeched.

"Private Gunnar signaled me to stop, sir."

The centurion looked up at Gunnar and Harris, still peering into the woods, their weapons ready.

The sounds had stopped.

"Vhat are you doing?" Dirvis screamed.

"Shh," Gunnar replied. "We heard something."

The centurion scrambled to get his own weapon into his

hands, then peered into the woods himself. "Who is zere? Come out!"

I exchanged a look with Ben. With the vehicle stopped, this could be our only chance for escape. The sun was hanging low over the tops of the trees, casting long, deep shadows over the road. If we could get beyond the edge of the woods, we stood a good chance of hiding in the gloom of a thicket.

I blinked and narrowed my eyes, focusing on the tree line. Was it a trick of the light or were there people standing just inside the forest, staring at us?

A loud crash came from the woods to our right. Startled, I jumped and banged my elbow on the side panel. Harris and Gunnar began shooting. The smell of gunpowder filled the air. I covered my ears. Milly and Ben threw themselves over Jude. Bullets were tearing through the woods, but nobody was shooting back.

"Stoppp!" Dirvis shouted. "Vhat are you shooting at?"

Gunnar and Harris stopped firing. When the air finally cleared, several trees had been mortally wounded and thousands of bushes had been brutally massacred.

"Idiots!" The centurion stamped his foot. "Get your truck moving! Now!"

Dirvis marched back to the front of the convoy. It was now or never.

I cleared my throat and looked at Milly. "How's he doing?" She glanced up at me; I raised my brows at her so she'd know what I was thinking.

"He's really weak, Sera." Meaning, she didn't think he could survive an escape.

My heart sank. Our truck lurched into motion again and Jude winced in pain. We'd lost our chance. If we didn't think of something soon, none of us were going to survive.

A few minutes later the convoy came to a fork in the road and rolled to a stop once again.

Harris looked at Gunnar. "Why are we stopping now?"

"Meh. The great Centurion Dirvis is probably lost again. He drove us around the mountain for hours yesterday. The man has the navigation skills of a retarded rhinoceros."

The temptation to leap from the truck was strong. I could run for help, maybe save us all—if Gunnar didn't shoot me in the back first.

The convoy ahead of us started up again—I was running out of time. Our truck lurched into gear. I looked down at the muddy road, working up the courage. And then I heard the whirring sound of spinning tires. We rocked, lunged, but didn't move forward. I smiled to myself. We were stuck in the sludgy ash.

I looked up and watched the convoy take the left fork in the road toward Winton—they hadn't noticed our truck's predicament. And if Dirvis hoped to make it down the mountain and out of rebel territory before morning, he was in for a big surprise. He was going the wrong way.

It was almost dark now and, considering all the strange sounds they'd heard earlier, Harris and Gunnar weren't comfortable being separated from their convoy. They both started pounding on the sides of the truck, demanding the driver get moving. But every time the driver stepped on the gas, he dug the tires in deeper. Finally, both soldiers climbed out to see what they could do.

This was the moment. We were taking the truck.

I nodded to Milly and Ben, signaling for them to be ready. I would go for Harris first; he was the smallest and the closest to me. I sensed Ash nearby and I knew he would take care of Gunnar. The driver would have to get out of the cab, so we'd have time to deal with him.

I took a few deep breaths to get my adrenaline pumping and lurched to my feet.

A gruff voice called out from the woods, stopping me in my tracks. "I want all weapons on the ground or I send every one of you straight to hell!"

Gunnar and Harris froze.

I heard the loud clanging sound of bolts pulling back on a hundred weapons and I knew we were surrounded.

A clunk sounded by the driver's door. I looked over to see that a weapon had been tossed out the window.

Gunnar and Harris didn't even offer up an argument. They threw their weapons on the ground, too, then raised their hands in surrender.

Ben stood up slowly. We both eyed the tree line. The dim twilight was working in the man's favor—I couldn't see a thing past the edge of the road. We put our hands in the air while Milly stayed in a crouched position, applying pressure to Jude's wound.

"You three soldiers," the voice continued. "Two in the back, driver in the cab. Start running."

"And how do we know you will not shoot us in the back?" Gunnar demanded.

"You don't! *Move!*"

Gunnar and Harris took off, joined by the driver as they sprinted down the road. I watched them take the left fork, in the same direction as the misguided convoy, before disappearing into the darkness. That left just us and what had sounded like a hundred invisible gunmen.

Ben looked at me cautiously from the corner of his eye. "Friend or foe?" he whispered.

"The enemy of our enemy…" I hoped I was right.

Suddenly the distant, echoing sound of heavy gunfire erupted in the woods ahead of us. We heard men shouting and muffled explosions. Only one faction besides Europa had that much firepower; the rebels were ambushing the convoy.

I stepped toward the tailgate, my hands still in the air. "We're guerrilla fighters," I called out. "One of us is injured."

A lone, tall figure emerged from the woods, dressed in dark clothes with a black bandana covering the lower half of his face. He moved with steady confidence, casually carrying his weapon in one hand. "Who's injured?" he said.

"My brother," Ben replied. "Jude Turner."

The man came toward us and stopped just behind the truck. The glow of the taillights illuminated a pair of large, dark eyes and a jolt of terror shot through me. I swallowed hard. It couldn't be.

He tugged the bandana down from his nose, revealing the strong angles of a face that had haunted me for more than a year. I took a step backwards, his name escaping my lips on a shaky breath.

"Micah."

Chapter Twenty-One

Micah was alive.

Head spinning, I blinked to clear my eyes. This couldn't be real. If not for the stunned look on Ben's face, I would have thought I was losing my mind.

"You-you're—" Ben stammered. "But you're…"

"Dead?" Micah supplied.

We'd watched them drag him off to be executed. We'd heard the countdown, felt the gunshots in our bones. But Micah Abrams had just walked out of the woods—alive and in one piece. I wasn't sure whether to be thrilled or terrified.

"How?" I yelled. With everything churning through my head, that was all I could manage to get out.

"I think the word you're looking for is miracle."

I stared at him, part of me afraid he might be telling the truth. "There's no such thing."

He grunted. "What good are your eyes if you never believe them?"

Then it all came together for me. "You made a deal with the praetor," I accused. "You…you've been working with him all along!" *And why not? He'd already been a Skagg and a Spathi, why not a spy for Europa?*

He gave me a frustrated look. "I just chased off three soldiers and saved you—*again*—and now you're gonna accuse me of working with the praetor?"

"You *are* a traitor!" I sounded hysterical, even to my own ears. But Micah was alive, and there wasn't anything more crazy than that.

"Could we possibly have this reunion another time?" Milly barked. "Jude is dyin' over here!"

Micah jumped up into the back of the truck. I immediately leapt over the side to the ground and snatched up one of the discarded AK-12s. I moved around to the lowered tailgate and pointed the weapon at Micah's back.

Ben stared at him and poked his arm with one finger.

"I'm as real as you are," Micah told him. He crouched down, placed his hands on Jude's stomach, and closed his eyes.

Milly gave him an odd look. "He needs a doctor."

After a moment, Micah sat back on his heels and sighed. "Yeah. He does."

"Do you know where we can find one?" Ben asked with a hint of hope.

"Leavenworth," Micah responded. "It's about three miles down the mountain."

Even with Jude lying injured in the back of the truck, I couldn't take my eyes off Micah. His hair was longer and he had a day's growth of beard. He looked leaner and more muscular, his thick shoulders and broad back stretching the limits of his jacket. He looked good.

He stood up, turning to Ben. "Help me get him out of the truck."

The leader in me came to life. I tightened my grip on

my weapon. "No," I said. Micah didn't get to come back from the dead and start ordering us around. "We drive the truck to the doctor."

"No," he countered, "we don't. This truck is a magnet for every patrol in the vicinity."

"The risk is worth it if it gets Jude there faster," I insisted.

But Milly was already preparing to move Jude. Ben stooped down to lift his legs. The two of them had decided who they would follow and it wasn't me.

Micah helped Ben carry Jude out of the truck bed and lay him carefully in the road. Jude didn't wake during the process. He didn't make a sound.

Ignoring me and the gun I still had pointed at him, Micah detached the strap from his M16 and slipped it around Jude's stomach to secure Milly's scarf to the wound. Milly watched with worried eyes from the back of the truck. "Milly," he called to her. "Grab the canvas cover in the storage locker under your feet."

She found the canvas beneath the floor of the truck bed and Ben helped her drag it down to Micah.

Micah pulled a long knife from the sheath on his hip. I flinched and steadied the rifle in my hands. If he intended to take revenge on us for handing him over to the praetor, he'd be dead before his blade touched skin.

He cut out a six-foot square of the canvas, then he and Ben placed Jude in the center of it. They used the tie-down cords to wrap Jude up like a burrito, then made a towing harness out of the remaining cords. The whole thing would slide along the ground easily while keeping Jude's legs slightly elevated. It was an impressive act of improvisation.

Milly moved past me, shoving my weapon out of her way. "Excuse me." She took off her coat and tucked it beneath Jude's head for a cushion. Both Milly and Ben seemed to have forgotten who Micah was.

"We go due north," Micah said. He slipped the corded harness around his chest. "Through these woods. We'll avoid the blue coats and be at the doctor's house in an hour."

Ben and Milly nodded, but I'd been fooled by Micah too many times to make the same mistake again.

"Wait." I moved in front of them all. "A year ago he was a terrorist and now we're going to follow him blindly into the dark woods?"

"I don't care if he's the praetor himself," Ben retorted, "as long as he can get my brother to a doctor."

Milly gave me a desperate but firm look. "Sera, if we don't find Jude medical attention soon he isn't gonna make it. We can deal with this other stuff later."

I looked down at my friend, bundled up in the canvas. Only his pale face was visible, but even in the waning light I could tell he was struggling. Micah was his only hope.

Tears burned my eyes. Life had been so peaceful at the cabin. Now my world was upside down again. And David was to blame.

Left with no choice but to trust him, I nodded at Micah. He moved past me and headed into the forest, dragging Jude, feetfirst, on the makeshift litter behind him.

We followed a smooth, rarely used hunter's trail at a rapid, determined pace, avoiding the logging road altogether. Jude's litter moved easily over the fallen pine needles. After a while, Ash came bounding up to walk beside me and I rubbed one of his ears. Micah seemed very sure of where he was going, even in the dark, giving me the impression that he knew the terrain. Was he working for the praetor? Or was he with the rebels now?

He seemed to switch sides as often as the wind changed directions.

We marched on in silence. Every now and then Jude would moan and Ben would reassure Milly that he was going to be okay. I hoped Ben was right. We had a lot riding on Micah, somebody who'd proven time and time again that he couldn't be trusted.

"Not much further," Micah announced.

Ash's ears perked at this new voice, but instead of taking off into the woods, he loped up the path to greet Micah. I watched, stunned, as Micah reached out and patted the wolf on the head—something that would have cost anybody else their arm. I'd never seen anything like it. Even Ash was on Micah's side.

The wolf paused to sniff a bush and I brushed past him. "Turncoat," I whispered.

When we finally reached the outskirts of Leavenworth, Jude had fallen silent. He was running out of time.

Micah led us to an old farmhouse in the middle of a meadow. We crouched behind a broken split rail fence and observed the main house in the red moonlight. I could see a thin trail of smoke coming from the chimney and the white hot glow of LED lantern light in the window. Somebody was home.

Ben assessed the house. "I don't see any sign of Europa."

Ash walked up, plopping down beside me with his ears flat and his eyes on the farmhouse. He panted, reacting to my nervous energy. I pointed to a large barn a few yards from the house. "What's in there?"

"An infirmary," Micah answered.

I gave him a direct look. "For who?"

"Europa soldiers."

I blinked. He'd led us right into the heart of our enemy. "Are you crazy?!"

"They've all got viridea," he added. "People stay away from this place."

Viridea? This just got better and better. "And so should we!" Viridea had become airborne and highly contagious.

"He's the only doctor I know." Micah slipped through the fence and headed off across the meadow, pulling Jude behind him. Ben and Milly followed without hesitation.

Left with no choice, I set off toward the house with Ash at my side. I kept my weapon ready, alert for any sign that we were being watched or followed. Ash acted as my early warning detection system. If anything moved out there in the dark, he'd be on it in seconds.

I caught up with the others on the porch. My first impression of the farmhouse wasn't a good one. The place was a wreck. There were broken boards, sagging siding, and cracked windows. The floor of the porch had a foot-sized hole in it.

Milly turned to Micah. "Are you sure a doctor lives here?"

The front door creaked open. The nose of a .22 rifle poked out. "State your business," a gruff voice demanded.

"A deep need for Hilda's cooking," Micah replied.

The door flew open, revealing a familiar tall, balding man with a grin on his face. "Micah!" he exclaimed.

My mouth dropped open. It was Doctor Reinkann.

The doctor took one look at the rest of us and his expression melted. "Oh, my heavens." He stepped aside and held open the door. "Come in, come in, all of you."

Micah pulled Jude's litter across the threshold, and Ben and Milly filed inside behind him.

The doctor's eyes fell on Jude. "Take him in there, Micah, by the fire."

I lagged back with Ash, doing a quick final scan of the meadow. Nothing moved. "Wait here," I told the wolf. Then I went inside and shut the door.

The inside of the house proved to be homier and more inviting than the outside. Nothing was chipped, peeling, or scarred with holes. Several crank lanterns lit the main room, throwing a white glow over an invitingly fat sofa and an overstuffed lounge chair. Both pieces of furniture were cozied up to a snapping fire built in a big stone fireplace. It reminded me of my grandfather's house before the Devastation and for a moment I thought I might burst into tears.

Though he'd left with Vivica Davis and the rest of the 1st Cascade, clearly the doctor had made himself at home here. There were pictures of his family on the walls, medical books lining the mantle, and amazing smells coming from the kitchen. At least we hadn't missed dinner.

The others left their weapons at the door, but mine was staying with me so long as Micah was around. I moved into the living room to take advantage of the warm fire.

The doctor gave orders; Ben and Micah unwrapped Jude on a cot by the fireplace. Milly's work had slowed the blood loss, but he was still unconscious and his face looked gray in the flickering light.

Dr. Reinkann peeled back Milly's saturated scarf to examine the wound. "I've seen worse."

"Is that good or bad?" Milly asked.

"Good. You did good." He sat down on a stool beside a wooden cabinet full of medical supplies and got to work. Milly hovered nearby, assisting him.

I moved away from the scene. It had been a hard day and the sight and smell of the blood made me nauseated.

"Where have you kids been?" the doctor asked.

"At the Donner cabin," Ben answered. "Near Colchuck Lake."

"I heard what happened to your grandfather, Sera." He shook his head. "I'm so very sorry."

I nodded back, preferring not to talk about it.

"Have you maybe seen Tim?" Milly asked hopefully.

"He's not with you?" the doctor responded.

Milly's lip trembled. "The praetor took him."

The doctor looked away. "I'm sorry to hear that."

My eyes drifted to Micah. He sat on the sofa, emptying his backpack onto the coffee table. A tin cup. A faded lighter. A pocket notebook and pencil. A ratty blanket. A Bible. Finally, he found what he was looking for—a small, nondescript packet—and tucked it into his shirt pocket.

In the middle of refilling his pack, he glanced up and caught me staring. I quickly looked away.

I heard a loud gasp behind me. Startled, I swung my weapon around, raised and ready to fire. A plump woman emerged from the hallway. It was Hilda Reinkann, the doctor's wife.

"Oh, Otto," she whispered tearfully. "They are so pale."

"Then feed them, my love," the doctor replied. "I'm sure they won't mind."

Micah cleared his throat at me. "It's considered bad manners to shoot your hostess."

Realizing I still had my rifle pointed at Hilda, I lowered it to the floor. "Sorry," I muttered.

Hilda spotted Jude on the cot. "Should I get your nurse, Otto?"

"No," the doctor replied. "She has her hands full with the patients in the barn. I have a perfectly capable nurse right here." He smiled at Milly.

Hilda clicked her tongue at us, gesturing toward the sofa. "Come. All of you sit, sit."

Ben dropped down at one end of the sofa and Milly sat down at the other. I eyed the only vacant place in the middle, beside Micah, and refused to comply.

"Sera?" Hilda asked. "Is that little Sera, Alice Donner's girl?"

Her words took me back to another time, when the world was whole and the sky was blue. Memories of my mother flashed through my head, flowing red hair and the smell of lavender and jasmine. I missed her.

"Sera," Hilda coaxed. "Come. Sit. I promise you, Micah won't bite."

She held out her hand to me. "Come." She wasn't going to take no for an answer. "And then I will bring the food."

Food. I supposed my issues with Micah could wait until later—at least until after supper. I laid my weapon on the coffee table beside Micah's pack, where I could grab it quickly, and sat down next to him on the sofa.

"Perfect!" Hilda exclaimed.

She grabbed a folded quilt from a nearby chest and shook it out. Then she spent a generous amount of time tucking us all in and fussing. "You must be tired." She gasped. "Look at them, Otto, they are white as ghosts. When was the last time you ate? Oh, poor things." Once we were all tucked in and warm, she stood back and surveyed her work. "There," she said. "Now. Who is hungry?"

The heat from the fire combined with the softness of the quilt and made me want to close my eyes and slip into a long, deep sleep. Yet the idea of food had my stomach wide awake. I didn't know about Micah, but the three of us hadn't eaten a thing all day.

"I could eat a little something," Ben answered

sheepishly.

"Me, too," Milly added.

Hilda broke out in a beaming smile. "I bet you could all use some *spritzkuchen*."

I didn't even know what that was, but my stomach assumed it was food and my mouth watered accordingly.

"I made it just this afternoon."

"Hey, Hilda." Micah pulled the brown packet out of his shirt pocket and held it out to her. It was a tea bag.

Hilda gasped and clapped her hands. "You remembered!" She took the tea bag, held it to her nose, and took a long, deep sniff. "Ahh. Honey lemon." She smiled at Micah. "You get extra tonight." She headed for the kitchen.

Micah turned back to the room, smiling. "Extra," he breathed.

The doctor looked up from where he was still working over Jude. "You'll spoil her."

"She deserves it."

Clearly, Micah had spent a considerable amount of time with the Reinkanns. That surprised me. The Reinkanns were decent people, not the kind to be socializing with a terrorist. But then I remembered they'd left Roslyn before the Welcome Ceremony, before the stage explosion, before the truth about Micah had come out. Micah was conning them just like he'd conned me and grandpa.

I could feel his gaze and knew he was staring at me. I turned to look at him. "What?"

"That looks painful."

I had no idea what he meant until he tapped his own jaw. I'd forgotten all about the bruise on my face. Considering how it had felt, I could only imagine what it looked like now.

"Bar fight?" he asked.

"Private Gunnar," Milly answered. "She fought him for his weapon."

Micah's eyes hardened. "Gunnar," he repeated.

Doctor Reinkann stood from his stool. "All right. I've removed the bullet, cleaned and stitched the wound. This is one very strong young man."

Ben leaned forward on the sofa. "Is he gonna be okay?"

The doctor pulled his stool closer to us. "He's going to need a lot of rest to heal properly. But he's going to be fine."

Ben and Milly smiled; all the day's tensions flowed out of me like a sigh. Finally. Some good news.

Doctor Reinkann looked at Milly. "And it's all thanks to you, young lady."

"Micah's the real hero," Milly said. "If he hadn't come along and helped us get Jude here…well, I'm just real grateful we don't have to think about that now."

Great, I thought. Now Micah was a hero. He had everybody fooled.

Hilda came back from the kitchen carrying a plate of food that smelled as sweet as heaven. She set it on the coffee table, then plopped herself down in the overstuffed chair by the fire. "*Spritzkuchen,*" she announced.

We stared at the plate of little donuts, then looked up at her. When she'd said she was going to feed us, I'd imagined MREs or some other slop pulled together from rations. Where had she gotten the milk, the butter, the eggs to make pastries?

"Europa," the doctor supplied. "We fix their soldiers, they pay us with food."

I looked at Milly and Ben. We were all thinking the same thing. Was it treasonous to eat food provided by the enemy?

Finally, I reached for one of the little donuts. I was too hungry to let principles—or the ache in my jaw—stop me from eating something that smelled so good. I shoved the *spritzkuchen* into my mouth.

"Jehovah Elohim…"

I stopped chewing and glared at Micah, who was praying with his head bowed.

"Bless this food that we are about to eat…," he continued.

Shocked that he would flaunt his Spathi beliefs so shamelessly, I looked at Milly, expecting her to be incensed, too. But both she and Ben had stopped eating and closed their eyes respectfully. Hilda and Otto even had their heads bowed.

"…heal our friend Jude…" Micah continued.

The rest of them may have been willing to compromise their standards out of politeness, but I refused to play along. Ignoring the pain in my jaw, I finished my *spritzkuchen*, then stubbornly picked up another from the plate.

"…protect us with your strong hand…"

I ate and chewed.

"…In your Son's name, we pray. Amen."

By the time Micah finished praying, three of the donuts from the plate were in my belly. I glanced at Milly and our eyes locked. She pinched her lips in disapproval, but she was the one who should be ashamed of herself for compromising with a Spathi.

While we all quickly emptied the plate of *spritzkuchen*, Hilda brought out bowls of something called *spatzle*. I must have been German in another life because it was the best macaroni and cheese I'd ever tasted. After my second bowl, I leaned back into the sofa, closed my eyes, and tuned out the conversation around me.

A few minutes later I woke with my head nestled against Micah's shoulder. I jerked upright.

The doctor winked at me. "I think it might be time to show our guests to their beds for the night, *meine liebe*."

Like zombies, we all followed Hilda down the long hallway. I couldn't wait to put my head on a pillow. Hilda directed Ben and Micah to a room on the left and Milly and me to the room opposite theirs.

The room was dark. Milly fell onto the bed, but I pulled off my boots before crawling up beside her onto the wide, soft mattress, where I closed my eyes and drifted toward sleep.

"They believe in him," I heard her whisper.

"I know."

"We have to tell them."

"Tomorrow."

I quickly fell fast asleep.

The nightmare came. I'd had it at least once a week since leaving Roslyn, but this time it was even more terrifying.

The blue sea. My mother in a print dress. The gold mountain. So tall I can't see its peak. The white sand beach. So long I can't see its beginning. A crowd of men. Their faces bright. Micah. The red dragon rises from the sea. It roars. It opens its mouth. Sharp white teeth. It devours him.

I lurched up in the bed, gasping.

"The dragon again?" Milly asked groggily.

"Yes," I breathed, trying to remember where I was.

"Just a dream," she murmured and promptly fell back to sleep.

I sank my fingers into the soft down comforter beneath me and took several deep breaths. The dream was always the same: water, my mother, gold, blood. But tonight had been different. Tonight, *I* had been the dragon who ate Micah.

Chapter Twenty-Two

I pulled my eyes open the next morning to the sound of dishes clattering in the kitchen. I wasn't sure of the time, but sunlight flooded the room, telling me I'd slept late. Ash would be impatient for his breakfast.

Milly stirred beside me. "Mornin'," she yawned.

"Morning." I wondered how Jude was doing. I climbed from the bed, pulled on my boots, and slipped from the room.

Ben and Micah's door was still closed. I headed toward the front of the house, thinking I'd sneak Ash some *spätzle* before anybody woke up, but stopped when I heard voices.

"...Sera and her friends should stay with us," Hilda was saying.

Micah replied, "It's too dangerous, for her and for you."

"He's right, my dove," the doctor answered. "We are a Europa hospital after all."

"I'm sure the 1st Cascade will be more than happy to take them in." This new voice, a woman's—probably the nurse's—pulled at my memory.

"That's the best option," Micah answered. "When Jude's ready to travel, I'll take them to Vivica Davis."

Milly came up behind me. "What are—"

"Shh!" I hissed at her, bringing my finger to my lips.

She clamped her mouth shut and leaned forward to listen with me.

"That will make it easier for you to protect her," Hilda conceded.

I frowned. *Protect me?*

"I don't know," Micah responded. "It wasn't easy when they were living at the cabin."

"Maybe if you told her the truth…," said the doctor encouragingly.

"She's not ready," Micah answered.

"She is not ready to hear it?" Hilda countered. "Or you aren't ready to tell it?"

"We must always be ready to give an answer for the hope that lies within us," the familiar female voice counseled.

"Perfect verse, Eliza," Hilda replied.

Milly's eyes rounded. "Eliza?" she mouthed.

I clenched my jaw. Eliza Cole, Micah's Spathi friend.

I strode out of the hallway, Milly at my heels. Ignoring Hilda's surprised "Good morning," I marched toward the pile of guns by the front door and snatched up an AK-12.

Eliza Cole sat beside Jude's cot. I pointed my weapon at her. "Get away from him."

Milly, fit to be tied, glared at the doctor. "*This* is your nurse?"

The Reinkanns, looking confused, stood from the sofa. "I…I'm afraid I don't understand," the doctor said. He looked at me and Milly, then at Micah.

"Seraphina." Micah stood by the fireplace, a steaming

mug of precious coffee in his hands. His tone was dark and threatening. "What are you doing?"

"Ending this ridiculous charade."

Ben walked into the room and stopped short. "What's going on?" He spotted Eliza. "Whoa." He looked at Micah, his expression tightening. "What is *she* doing here?"

"She is my nurse," the doctor answered. "And indispensable."

"She's a Spathi," Ben countered.

"So is Micah," I added.

The Reinkanns stared at me in shock. Just when I thought I'd broken their hearts with my revelation, they both burst into laughter. "Micah most certainly is not a Spathi," the doctor chuckled.

Their humor irritated me. "I saw them, along with Ken Sheridan and John Voss among others, in the old Roslyn church the night before Micah was executed."

"Executed?" Hilda blurted. She looked at Micah.

"It's a long story," Micah grumbled.

"One they deserve to hear," I retorted. "Will you tell them or should I?"

"What you should do is put the gun down and stop jumping to conclusions."

"Sera," Hilda began patiently, "there are no Spathi here."

Eliza stood from her stool. "That's not entirely true."

Micah tried to stop her. "Eliz—"

"It's okay," she interjected. "This needs to be said. I'm ashamed to admit that after the eruption and earthquake I fell into despair. My husband was gone—it was looking more and more as if God had taken him and left me behind —and I was angry and humiliated. I wanted answers. The Spathi were the closest thing I could find to Christians. I didn't agree with their methods, but they lived by a rigid set of rules that made me feel like I could earn my way into Heaven. Their hate tapped into my bitterness and, for a while, I felt purged. And then they decided to blow up a café full of soldiers."

I gripped my weapon.

"*You*," Milly accused. "You tried to kill us!"

Eliza shook her head. "While the others made plans for the café, I went for a walk to clear my head. I found myself standing outside my husband's old church and there was Micah." Tears filled her eyes. "My story spilled out of me, the Spathi, the bomb, my anger. Micah told me that God hadn't left me behind because He hated me. He'd left me behind because He loves me."

I shook my head in disgust. Nothing she said made any sense, but Christians rarely did—especially fanatical Christians. I looked at Micah. "*She* was your informant?"

He nodded.

"And the Spathi poncho I saw you with that night?"

"It was mine," Eliza responded. "A week after the bombing I worked up enough courage to attend one of Micah's meetings. Once he started talking, I realized I'd been faking it my whole life. I handed in my poncho and never looked back."

They seemed to have an answer for everything.

"Hold on," Milly spoke up. "Are you sayin'…are you sayin' that Micah *isn't* a Spathi?"

"Of course not," Hilda sputtered. "Micah is *verschlossen* —a friend of God."

Milly, Ben, and I exchanged looks. I knew they were thinking that we'd handed over an innocent person to be executed, but I'd heard Micah's speech in the church. *Death equals promotion.* Micah was a fanatic, not to mention a Skagg. I refused to lower my weapon.

We all glanced around at each other. Eliza watched me carefully while Micah sipped his coffee. Finally, the doctor spoke up. "How is this to be settled?"

Micah looked up from his mug. "Oatmeal."

"Oatmeal?" asked Ben.

"Yeah." Micah strode past me, nudging aside my weapon and heading for the kitchen. "I'm starving."

Ben shrugged. "Oatmeal."

Hilda grinned and clapped her hands. "Who wants breakfast?" She walked past me for the kitchen.

I stared after them both, angry that they weren't taking me seriously and frustrated that Micah kept talking his way out of everything. I looked over at the doctor. "He's got you all fooled."

"No," Doctor Reinkann replied. "He's got us all awake."

I scowled.

Micah and Hilda returned with bowls of steaming oatmeal. Hilda handed me one, but my hands were full with an AK-12. I could either refuse her or put down my weapon. For the sake of manners and my growling stomach, I chose the latter.

I made my stand, however, by not eating with Micah or Eliza. While the others—including Ben and Milly—gathered across the room by the fire, I sat alone on the floor by the front door.

I took my first bite and remembered Ash. "Is it possible to get something for my wolf?"

"I fed him."

I looked up at Micah in surprise.

"And you've still got all your fingers and toes?" Ben joked.

Micah shrugged. "He and I have an understanding."

"Aren't you the charmer," I grumbled.

"It's called kindness, Seraphina," Micah retorted. "Something you used to appreciate."

Doctor Reinkann cleared his throat. "Micah, what news do you have about the rebel summit?"

Ben's head popped up. "We heard rumors about that summit. Is it for real?"

"It is," the doctor answered. "Hundreds of fighters are gathering to strategize the taking of Ellensburg."

"It's a waste of time." They all looked at me. "The praetor has five times as many men and a hundred times as much firepower. The only thing the rebels will succeed in doing is getting themselves slaughtered."

Micah scowled. "You're quite the optimist."

"It's called reality, Micah. Something you used to appreciate."

He smirked and shook his head.

Hilda smiled. "God might have something to say about your version of reality, Sera."

"God certainly hasn't had much to say about all this death and destruction."

Hilda blinked at me. What I'd said was rude, but I'd had it up to my eyebrows with all their God talk.

Micah dropped his bowl onto the coffee table. "I guess manners don't mean much to you anymore either."

Angry and embarrassed, I lowered my head and focused on my oatmeal.

"Sera…" Doctor Reinkann began.

I'd heard too many religious lectures from my mom not to sense one hanging in the air. "How is the 1st Cascade doing?" I interrupted, hoping to head the doctor off.

Eliza set her spoon in her bowl. "They're the plague of

Europa. I have a brother in the 1st, and he——" She frowned at me as if suddenly realizing something. "How is *your* brother?"

Emotion tightened my throat. I swallowed hard.

"Yes," the doctor joined in. "Where is David?"

Milly cleared her throat. "David left us to join Europa."

I closed my eyes and kept breathing, deep and even. It was still hard for me to believe that my brother had betrayed me—but then that seemed to be the going trend.

Hilda turned wide eyes on me. "Is this true?"

I swirled my spoon through my oatmeal, determined not to care. "He's in Ellensburg by now."

Hilda gasped. "Lord, no!"

I looked up. She had tears in her eyes and was trembling.

The doctor shook his head. "This is not good. Not good."

I could understand them being disappointed, even sad. But terrified? Something was wrong. "What's going on?"

"Seraphina," Micah began. "The praetor is doing terrible things to kids in Ellensburg."

A tingle of alarm spread through my body. "What kind of terrible things?"

Hilda sobbed into her apron. The doctor put his arm around her shaking shoulders. "*Da, da, meine liebchen.*" He looked at me. "They took both of our boys four months ago. Only Alvin was returned."

"Alvin?" I hadn't seen either of their boys since we'd arrived last night. I'd assumed they'd both been lost to Viridea.

"Alvin stays in his room." The doctor answered with such clinical candor that I almost missed the pain in his eyes.

I looked at Micah for an explanation.

"Europa is experimenting on them," he told me.

Private Calhoun's words came back in a rush. *"Some genetic thing. Makes 'em really big and really strong. Praetor calls it the Goliath Code."*

A chill raced through me.

"They're changing them into something…not human," Eliza clarified.

My chest tightened. "You mean stronger? More powerful?"

Micah looked at Hilda and the doctor. "She needs to meet Alvin."

But I'd met Alvin and Stephen Reinkann several times. The last time, Stephen had been a typical thirteen-year-old boy, bossy and arrogant. His older brother Alvin was on David's Mathlete team at school.

Hilda's chin trembled.

The doctor sighed, then nodded. "Yes. All right."

While Eliza waited in the living room with Hilda, the rest of us followed Doctor Reinkann down the long hallway. He stopped at the room on the end. The door was closed and had a large latch with a padlock to keep it that way.

"No big movements," the doctor warned. "No loud noises."

His caution made me nervous. I searched Micah's face. What was beyond this door?

The doctor knocked softly. "Alvin?" he called sweetly. He pulled a key out of his pocket, then knocked again. "Alvin? You have guests." He opened the lock and pushed back the latch.

I heard a small squeak from inside the room. The doctor nodded at me, then eased open the door. The stench hit me like a torpedo—I almost gagged. It smelled like something had died and been left to rot. Not wanting to be rude, I resisted putting my hand over my mouth and nose as I reluctantly followed the doctor across the threshold.

The room was gloomy, with no lantern and thin curtains over the only window, but my eyes adjusted quickly to the dim light. There were books and toys scattered around the floor, along with crumpled pieces of paper and broken crayons. The walls were covered in pictures of Alvin's first steps, Alvin's first day of kindergarten, Alvin riding a bike, Alvin's Little League poster. I saw dark irregular shadows on the walls and realized they were holes, like somebody had put a fist through the drywall.

The bed was unmade. The closet door was broken— hanging from one hinge. The air was heavy and the odor powerful.

Micah stepped on a train lying in pieces on the floor, and a dull *CHOO CHOO* bounced off the walls, startling me. A chain rattled somewhere in the room and a chill raced up my spine.

"Shh," Doctor Reinkann whispered.

The stench got stronger the further in we walked. My eyes started to water. There was a large chair in the corner. I saw movement, heard more chains rattle, and realized Alvin must be sitting there. I saw him only in shadow at first. I thought he was wearing a large, furry hat. But then Doctor Reinkann eased open the curtains, flooding the room with light, and a scream lodged in my throat.

A creature stared back at me with enormous, bulging eyes that were bloodshot and oozing. His immense, misshapen head had little patches of golden hair sticking straight up from the roots. His scaly yellow skin was covered in pustules that wept a green, goopy liquid, leaving his face permanently coated in a thick mucus sheen. His flattened nose was pushed to the side and bent up at the end like a fishhook, and it, too, was leaking incessantly. His lips, set in a permanent snarl, curled back over four, sharp brown teeth. The endless stream of drool coming from his mouth explained the cloth bib that had been tied beneath his chin. He was the most horrible thing I'd ever seen.

He smiled—at least I think it was a smile—and greeted me. "Hi, Sera." The deep, rough voice broke my heart in two.

"Hey." I couldn't manage anything more.

He shifted and the putrid smell wafted toward me in a big sickening wave. I realized that Alvin Reinkann was the thing rotting in the room.

A boy with limitless possibilities had been reduced to this monstrosity.

I noticed the chain around his ankle, secured with yet another padlock and bolted to the floor beside his chair.

"We allowed him to have the run of the room for a while," the doctor explained, "but he started eating the drywall. His appetite is insatiable."

Micah looked at me. "This is what the praetor's experiment does."

Reality dawned. *David!*

I turned and ran from the room. Alvin howled in protest. I shoved past Ben and Milly, who were standing in the doorway frozen in shock, and flew down the hallway.

Micah chased me to the front door. "Seraphina! Wait!"

I pulled my coat from the hook and yanked it on, tears pouring down my face. "I have to get to Ellensburg!" I grabbed my weapon.

I tried to pull open the door, but Micah slammed it shut. Then he took hold of my arm and I spun around to face him. "I know you're worried about David," he said. "But you can't run off to Ellensburg and take on the entire guard by yourself!"

I refused to listen. I tried to shake off his grip. "I have to stop him!" Micah's fingers were like steel. "Let me go!"

"Wait for reinforcements!"

"There's no time!" I shouted.

"The rebels will be—"

I set the bore of my automatic rifle against Micah's chest. "Let me go," I ground out.

"Sera!" Milly shouted. "No!"

Everyone stared at me in shock.

Micah, however, seemed completely unfazed. "Go ahead," he said.

"I will," I yelled into his face. "I'll do it!"

"Then stop talking and pull the trigger already!" he bellowed back. Finally, he wrapped his hands over mine and pressed his thumb over my trigger finger.

I resisted. "Are you crazy?" He didn't let up. I tried to pull the gun away from him, but he only held on tighter. "What are you doing?" I cried. "Stop it!"

"I'm giving you what you want, Seraphina." With one quick jerk, he made me squeeze the trigger. The gun went off at point-blank range. *BAM!* His body jerked and my heart stopped.

Milly screamed.

"What have you done?" I whispered. "What have you—"

And then I realized he wasn't crumbling to the floor. He hadn't even staggered.

I let go of the weapon. It tumbled to my feet. Micah just stood there—calm, unmoving.

I frowned at his chest. The bullet had left a hole and a powder burn in his shirt. He should have hit the floor. He watched me closely. I jammed my fingers into the hole and tore his shirt open. There wasn't a mark on him.

My mouth went dry. I looked down at the automatic rifle and picked it up. I pointed it at the wall. And fired.

BAM!

Drywall exploded in a cloud of dust and gypsum flew everywhere.

The pieces of the puzzle began to fall into place. Micah had been uninjured in the hospital massacre, even though I knew he'd been shot several times. He'd survived the explosion at the citizenship ceremony, even though he'd been standing right next to the stage where countless others had died. He'd even survived a firing squad of Europa's finest.

My eyes slid back to his face. He was waiting for me to say something.

I said the first thing that came to my mind. "What are you?"

A flicker of hurt darkened his eyes. He opened his mouth to respond, but, before he could say a word, a mournful howl echoed outside. My breath caught. Ash. He only howled like that for one reason.

A series of rattling bangs suddenly sounded against the door behind me. I leapt toward Micah. And then a loud shout turned my blood cold.

"Open in the name of Europa!"

Chapter Twenty-Three

I willed myself not to sneeze.

Soldiers ransacked the Reinkann house, digging through drawers, turning over furniture, and throwing dishes onto the floor. They weren't going to stop looking until they'd searched in every corner and checked under every sofa cushion.

Hopefully they wouldn't look in the walls.

The five of us stood crammed into a space behind the Reinkann's fireplace, maybe two feet deep and six feet long, with our weapons slung over our shoulders. Through cracks in the mortar between the stones, I watched as Centurion Dirvis stood directly in front of me, barking out orders. "Check all of ze rooms!" he shouted. "Leave no stone unturned!"

If any of us so much as breathed hard they'd hear us.

Jude was our biggest worry. We'd had to rouse him from a heavy sleep. He was conscious, but still weak. Now he had to remain upright in a very narrow, very uncomfortable space. He stood sandwiched between Ben and Micah, who each had an arm around his waist to hold him up.

My eyes kept drifting sideways to the singed material of Micah's tee-shirt where a bullet had bounced off his chest. *Bounced off?* That was completely crazy. I kept expecting to see blood filtering through the gray fabric, something— anything—to signify that I wasn't losing my mind.

Milly had a tight grip on my right hand. Her fingers trembled, but not only because of the soldiers in the house. Like me, she had a brother in the praetor's custody; Alvin's terrifying condition was as much a possibility for Tim as it was for David. I gave her hand a reassuring squeeze.

"Zis vould go easier, Herr Doctor," Dirvis said in his usual shout, "if you vould simply tell us vhere zey are!"

"Centurion, I assure you," I heard the doctor reply, "there's no one here but us and my son."

Though I felt incredibly grateful for Doctor Reinkann's heroism, the number of empty oatmeal bowls on the coffee table behind him betrayed his lie. What price would he pay for his defiance?

Hilda and Eliza stood at the back of the room, under armed guard. Though visibly nervous, neither of them said a word. Eliza had stationed herself in front of Hilda, protecting the doctor's wife with her own body. My mind flashed back to the first Europa drop, when Eliza had back-handed a young girl over a crate of food. Eliza Cole had changed.

"Are you sure zis is your final response?" Dirvis demanded.

"Please," Dr. Reinkann pleaded. "We have done every-thing Europa has asked of us. We cure your sick. We heal your wounded. All we ask in return is that you leave us in peace."

"Peace?" Dirvis scoffed. "I see no Biotat on your hand!

Vhy should Europa give you peace ven you refuse us your allegiance?"

"I am an old man. Change is difficult—"

"Zen perhaps we can make it easier!" the centurion replied. "Bring her!"

Two soldiers dragged Hilda out from behind Eliza. "Leave her alone!" Eliza cried. One of the soldiers shoved Eliza violently back against the wall with a gun in her face, while the other hauled Hilda in front of Dirvis.

"Vill you svear your fealty to Europa, *fraulein*?" Dirvis demanded.

Hilda stuck out her chin. "I already have a King."

I felt Micah's hand slip into mine. Familiar tingles of electricity drifted from my fingers up into my arm. I turned my head. Our eyes locked. He gazed at me with a piercing intensity that made it almost impossible to look away. And then I understood. Something terrible was about to happen.

Eliza screamed. "No!"

I blinked at tears pooling in my eyes. I could hear the doctor crying hysterically. Dirvis was shouting. The soldiers were thundering through the house. Alvin was howling.

"Stop!" I heard the doctor shout.

I couldn't help myself; I looked back through the cracks in the fireplace mortar. Hilda was on her knees. Centurion Dirvis had a sword in his hand. My heart seized.

"Please!" the doctor sobbed. "Please don't do this!"

The centurion lifted the sword high over Hilda's neck. "Tell us vhere zey are, Herr Doctor, or I vill separate your vife's head from her shoulders!"

Tears slipped down my cheeks. With everything I had, I wanted to call out and save Hilda, but that would give everyone else away. Milly was breathing heavily beside me. I squeezed her hand tighter, closed my eyes, and bit into my lip until I tasted blood.

"So be it," I heard Dirvis say.

And then Hilda began to speak. "The Lord is my light and my salvation. Whom shall I fear? The Lord is the stronghold of my life. Of whom shall I be afraid?"

I opened my eyes. Hilda wasn't crying. She wasn't yelling. She wasn't even pleading for her life. A monster held a sword over her head and Hilda Reinkann was praying. In that moment, I envied her faith—a faith that could bring comfort to the doomed.

"WAIT!" the doctor shouted. "I will tell you. I will tell you everything."

I felt an instant overwhelming sense of relief. I didn't want to be responsible for Hilda's death. I couldn't blame the doctor for giving us up. I'd watched someone I loved murdered right in front of my eyes and I wouldn't wish that horror on anyone.

"They were here yesterday," the doctor continued, tears pouring down his face. "But I did not know where they had come from. At dusk, when it was time for bed, they left. I don't know which way they went. But if you are quick, you may still be able to catch them."

My heart sank. It was a terrible lie, one even Dirvis would see through. Now he would most likely kill all of them.

I looked over at Micah and frowned. He was smiling.

The room beyond the fireplace had gone silent. Even Alvin had fallen quiet. I peeked back through the mortar in time to see Centurion Dirvis lower his sword. "Gather ze men!" Dirvis shouted. "Ve must catch zem before ze sun sets!"

To my shock, the platoon gathered and left the house.

When the front door closed behind them, Hilda immediately ran to the back of the house to check on Alvin. We stayed silent in the wall to be sure the soldiers weren't trying to trick us, but, after a few minutes, Jude began to moan. He could take no more.

Doctor Reinkann pulled the bookcase back and opened the hidden door. The five of us spilled out, coughing and covered in dust. Ben and Micah helped Jude lie down on the sofa where Eliza checked his bandages. He was awake, but frail and in a lot of pain.

"Are they…are they gone?" Jude rasped.

Milly eased down beside him on the edge of the sofa to soothe him with her touch. "They're gone," she whispered. "Rest now."

Hilda hurried back into the room. "I quieted Alvin," she told her husband. "But he's very upset. I'll need to stay with him tonight." She broke into sobs. "You were brilliant, *liebchen*."

The doctor pulled her into a tight hug and kissed the top of her head. "Your strength inspired me."

Smiling broadly, Micah slapped the doctor on the back. "Joshua 2:4."

"When in doubt," Eliza said, "quote the Word."

Doctor Reinkann laughed and threw his arm around Micah's shoulders. "Had I known my faith would be so strenuously tested when you came to my door with the good news last summer, young man, I would have slammed it in your face."

Hilda patted her husband's chest. "If God is for us, my love, then who can be against us?"

I frowned. "I hate to break up this celebration, but I need to find my brother." I turned to Ben, who'd stationed himself with his weapon at the front window, watching for soldiers. "I understand if you want to stay here with Jude."

"What's your plan?" he asked.

"To save David from the Goliath Code."

"From *what?*" asked Doctor Reinkann.

"You remember the research my dad was doing on a cure for David?"

The doctor nodded. "Yes, of course."

"David thinks my dad's cure and the praetor's experiments are the same thing. That's why he left for Ellensburg. He wants the Goliath Code."

"Your brother *wants* that man to experiment on him?" Hilda exclaimed. She turned to Micah. "You cannot let this happen!"

"As I was trying to tell Seraphina—before she tried to kill me," Micah explained dryly, "she's going to need reinforcements. The rebel factions will be gathering near Liberty over the next few days, including Vivica Davis and the 1st Cascade. I'm sure Viv will be more than happy to help retrieve David."

Ben stepped away from the window. "Wait. Back up a second. Explain the trick."

"Trick?" Micah repeated.

"The one where you get shot at point-blank range and live to tell about it."

Micah shifted uncomfortably.

"It's not a trick," Doctor Reinkann answered. "Micah is one of the sealed."

"And we're s'posed to know what that is?" Milly asked.

"He's a member of the 144,000," Eliza clarified.

"Chosen by God," Hilda added.

Great, I thought. Micah had them all believing in his fanatical cause. He'd twisted their minds, just like he'd done with my grandfather. I wasn't sure how he'd managed his little trick with the AK-12, but I had no doubt it was a trick.

Ben wasn't buying it either. "Uh-huh. So, what, God stopped a speeding bullet?"

"The seal gives him special protection," Doctor Reinkann explained. "No earthly thing can harm him."

Milly laughed. "No *earthly* thing? What else is there?"

Micah gave her a serious look. "You'd be surprised."

I'd heard enough. "You're all welcome to sit around chatting about God and magic, but I'm heading to Liberty."

"Not alone." Eliza looked at Hilda. "The Ogre."

"The Ogre?" I asked.

"He lives near Liberty," Hilda explained. "He eats people and drinks their blood."

I closed my eyes, searching for patience.

"Rumor has it, he's a victim of the praetor's experiments," Micah explained. "Another Goliath."

Now that, at least, made sense. I pictured Alvin, now a gooey, monstrous blob, and hoped we'd come in contact with this Ogre of Liberty so that we could put the poor thing out of its misery.

"I'm going with you," Ben stated. "I won't do Jude any good sitting around here and I'm not abandoning David and Tim to that bastard in Ellensburg."

I nodded, more relieved than I cared to admit.

Milly looked up at Hilda from the sofa. "Will Jude be safe here?"

Hilda gave her a reassuring smile. "As safe as my own heart, *liebchen*."

Milly and Jude whispered for a moment, then she turned to me. "I'm goin', too. We need to find the boys."

Micah clapped his hands. "Great. We leave at dusk."

I scowled at him. "You're not coming." This mission was too important to drag along somebody I couldn't trust.

Micah folded his arms and sat down on the arm of the sofa. "Good luck finding the rebel camp without me."

———

WE FOLLOWED Micah into the rugged hills toward Liberty, with only the full, red moon lighting our way. I felt sure we could find the rebel camp without him, but Ben had insisted he come along for armed support. I felt sure he was more interested in Micah's supposed superpower than his firepower.

Hilda had loaded our packs with food and water before we left. Dr. Reinkann provided us with extra ammo clips. Eliza insisted on saying a prayer, and then the three of them wished us a safe journey.

Ash found us quickly and, after a feast of Hilda's *spätzle*, patrolled in large, overlapping circles through the woods. Milly and I walked together, keeping an eye on the trail behind us and listening to Ben talk with Micah ahead of us.

"If I threw you off a cliff," Ben was saying, "would you die?"

Micah pushed a low branch out of his way. "Nope."

Let's give it a try, I thought.

"No offense," Ben continued, "but why would God choose you?"

Micah laughed and clapped Ben on the shoulder. "I ask myself that same question every day."

I looked at Milly. "Does Ben have any idea how stupid he sounds?"

"Well, how would you explain it exactly?" she asked.

I gaped at her. "You don't actually believe Micah?"

"I believe the Reinkanns. They believe Micah. And if it were any other man alive, you'd believe 'em, too."

"Excuse me?"

"You're still stuck on him."

"Who, *Micah*? Don't be ridicu—"

She held up her hand. "Don't even try to deny it, Sera. I was there that day, remember? The hardest thing you ever did was hand Micah over to the praetor. And now you find out that he's not a terrorist?"

"Says Eliza," I shot out.

"Says common sense," she replied. "The Reinkanns wouldn't have a thing to do with a Spathi and you know it. The only thing holdin' you back from lettin' this go is your own guilt."

I clenched my teeth. "And what about your guilt? I was there that day, too, Milly, and I seem to recall you helping to tie Micah's hands behind his back."

Her lips tightened. "Me and the others were actin' on information that you and David provided. Besides, I'm not the one holdin' grudges."

She marched off to catch up with the boys.

I stared after my best friend with my mouth hanging open. How did Micah turn perfectly intelligent people into brainless sheep? I decided in that moment that he would not be going on the mission to rescue David and Tim. The sooner we got to Liberty and ditched him, the better.

My thoughts turned to my brother. I was afraid that I'd be too late to save David—or that he'd refuse to leave with me. It wouldn't be easy to convince him that the Goliath Code and his cure were not the same thing. I could start by telling him about Alvin; I rehearsed my speech in my head as we walked.

We made camp in the hollow of a rock face several

hours before dawn. We were still about ten miles north of Liberty, but we didn't want to risk wandering into a rebel camp in the middle of the night. We didn't make a campfire for fear it might draw unwanted attention, so Milly put her bedroll beside Ben's and huddled up with him to stay warm.

I laid my bedroll a few feet away from them and sat with my back against the rock wall, my weapon cradled in my arms. Micah had volunteered for guard duty and I intended to stay awake and guard him.

He sat several yards away, on a fallen tree, with his back to me, but we were both very aware of each other's presence. He hadn't spoken to me since we left the Reinkanns' house, which suited me just fine. I'd seen how he got into people's heads and I didn't want him messing with mine.

Milly was right. I hated to admit it, but, despite all his lies, my nagging fascination with Micah had never faded. I constantly had to remind myself of what he'd done to keep my thoughts from wandering to happier memories. Spathi or not, Micah had been a Skagg. He'd betrayed us once, he'd betray us again.

Ash padded up and settled down beside me, dropping his big head in my lap. I stroked his soft ears and struggled with my conflicted feelings. The wolf stared out into the dark night; I followed the direction of his gaze to Micah. Like Ben and Milly, he seemed won over by my nemesis. "The three of you have very poor judgment," I whispered.

At some point my eyes drifted closed and I sank into the silky, warm oblivion of sleep. I dreamed of dragons and the deep blue sea....

I lurched awake in the soft glow of dawn. I was on my side with Ash crouched in front of me, gazing into my face with concerned amber eyes. I breathed deeply, then patted him on the head. "Just a dream."

The soft sound of someone talking tickled my ears. I pushed myself up onto my elbow and looked over at Ben and Milly. They were both fast asleep. I sat up and stared out into the blossoming haze of daybreak. Micah hadn't moved. He was still sitting on top of the fallen tree. He was nodding and gesturing—definitely talking to someone.

I got to my feet. Ash followed silently beside me as I snuck closer for a better look. If Micah was attempting to betray us, I was going to shoot him again—maybe this time the bullet would leave a mark. I crept within a few feet of him, until I could make out what he was saying.

"I'll talk with him more tomorrow," he said. "If you could just open his heart to what I have to say."

After a beat, he continued. "I know he's precious to you and time is running short."

I peered past him, into the dim morning light, searching for the person he was talking to, but there was no one else there. Micah was talking to himself. I could add crazy to his growing list of oddities.

As I turned to go, I stepped on a dry branch. *SNAP!*

Micah turned. "I thought you were sleeping."

Embarrassed, I went into defensive mode. "You know, all this time I thought you were a lying traitor, but now I'm starting to think you're just plain delusional."

"I was praying."

Fanatical. Delusional. What's the difference? "Tell me why you did it, Micah."

He rolled his eyes. "Which one of my supposed crimes are we talking about?"

"Why did you defect to the Skaggs?"

"How many times do I have to tell you, Seraphina? I am not a traitor."

"Did you or did you not leave me that day and go to the Skaggs?"

He pointed at me. "Ah-ha! That's it, isn't it? That's the real issue. This isn't about the Skaggs or even the Spathi. It's about me leaving you."

"Don't flatter yourself," I spat back.

"And it's been pissing you off ever since."

"Pissing me off?" White-hot rage rose inside me. "I thought you'd been captured!" I shouted. "I *cried* over you! I joined the militia to *avenge* you! And then I see you marching with my enemy? I should have shot you the moment I saw you!"

"We both know how effective that would have been," he retorted.

I folded my arms. "Tell me the truth. No more super-hero stories."

He pushed his hand through his hair. He looked tired, as tired as I felt. "I'm one of the sealed. It's biblical. Look it up."

"I'm supposed to believe that God put a magical stamp on you and now you're immortal or invincible or something?"

"I'm not immortal, just protected for a while."

"Okay, I'll bite. Why? Why would God do that?"

"Because He needs witnesses to spread the word...the good news."

I laughed. "Good news? Have you looked around lately?"

"Have you?" he shot back. "The Earth. The sky. The entire universe. People have seen God's eternal power and divine nature in the creation since the beginning of time, Seraphina. And they still reject Him."

"Micah, the earth is dying, the sky is poisoned, and the

universe is just a useless expanse of starry ocean. There is no God. No help is coming. It's just us against Europa."

"Your mother knew better."

I froze. "You don't know anything about my mother."

His intense gaze felt like he was staring into my soul. "What happened to her in the church?"

Tears stung my eyes. I started to shake. *"She fell,"* I forced the words out. "She's buried beneath a ton of brick and—"

"Now who's the liar?"

His accusation hit me like a punch in the stomach. I dashed at the tears on my face. "Tell me something. When your god created Europa, did he single-handedly choose all the people Praetor Stanislov would slaughter? Or are the lives of individual people too insignificant for him to bother dirtying his hands over?"

"She's still alive."

"Don't say that—*don't you say that!*"

"He saved His true followers from the hour of wrath, just like He promised He would."

"I am done." I turned to leave.

"I thought you wanted the truth," he called after me.

I rounded on him. "This isn't the truth! This is a delusion created by cowardly people who are afraid of death!"

"He wants to save you, too. All He asks is that you trust Him."

"Trust him?" I sneered. "If your god is real, then he stole my mother and left me and my brother to die! And I'm supposed to *trust* that?"

"He's being patient with you. But even His patience has an end."

I gestured to the broken world around us. "This is what patience looks like?"

"This is what a last chance looks like."

"And then what, he tosses us all into hell?"

"Life is about choices, Seraphina. Every choice has a consequence. If you say you don't want God, then God will honor your choice. But realize that an eternity apart from God—completely devoid of love, justice, peace, beauty —*that* is Hell."

"*That* is crazy!"

"*That is reality!*"

We stared at each other for a moment, both of us breathing hard.

"Why are you protecting me?" I finally demanded. "I heard what you said at the Reinkann's. What are you protecting me from?"

He shook his head. "I only know that I'm supposed to keep you safe."

"So that's all this has ever been? You *protecting* me?"

He gave me a haunted look. "At first."

At first? Then what was it now?

He sighed and looked up at the sky. "I wish I knew what to say to make you understand."

Crazy or not, he felt passionate about his faith. I wasn't going to change his mind any more than he would change mine. "If it brings you comfort to believe in your god, then fine," I told him. "But enough with the sermons and magic tricks. I don't have the time or the patience to play religion with you."

I left him there and walked back to camp in the faint light of dawn. Ash waited for me by my bedroll. Ben and Milly faked sleep, trying to look as though they hadn't heard every word Micah and I had shouted at each other.

I curled up on my bedroll, pulled the blanket up over my head, and closed my eyes, hoping for a few more minutes of sleep. I was determined to forget about Micah Abrams. I had no use for a childish infatuation that couldn't stand the light of day.

My mother's face drifted behind my eyelids. I saw her vanish in the flash of a bright, white light. I squeezed my eyes tighter, determined to force the image away.

"She's not alive," I whispered to myself. "She's not."

Chapter Twenty-Four

After we ate, we packed up camp and followed Highway 97 south, toward Liberty, making sure to stay hidden in the forest. We kept the road in sight, though, and saw several Europa vehicles driving slowly past. We figured they were looking for us.

After my shouting match with Micah, I'd decided to avoid him altogether. Neither one of us was going to change the other's mind, so there was no use in constantly banging our heads together. We all had our way of dealing with the Devastation. If Micah's way was God, who was I to judge? But avoiding Micah meant walking alone.

Ben and Milly couldn't get enough of Micah's religious spiel. They were perfectly content to let me march several yards behind them if it meant they could hear all about God and salvation. I was losing two more people I loved to Jesus, which only made me hate him more.

While Ben and Milly *got saved*, I hung back and kept an eye out for foot soldiers. Every now and then I caught a flash of white fur darting through the trees. I wished Ash would just settle down and heel for a change. Of course, he'd never heeled a day in his life. Despite his total devotion to me, Ash was still a wild animal and could never abandon his true nature.

Ben slowed, falling into step beside me. "Micah says we're about an hour out. We'll stop to eat at Swauk Creek."

"Got it."

The sun felt warm on my face. I took off my coat and tied it around my hips. The sun was still a dimmer version of its former self, but, after spending a year at the top of a mountain, this was the warmest day I'd experienced in a long time. The ash from the eruption became more apparent as we edged further east. Over a year of wind and weather had eroded it into the topsoil, blending the two together and leaving behind a fertile packed clay where heartier plants were beginning to thrive.

"So, what do you think?" he asked.

I snapped a low branch off a passing tree. "About what?"

"About what Micah's saying. You know," he smirked, "about God and the end of the world."

He knew full well that I had no interest in the subject, so it was hard not to get angry with him for bringing it up. "I don't care." I tossed the branch several yards out. Ash came shooting from the woods to charge after it like a house-trained puppy.

"You have to admit, though, it is fascinating."

No, I thought, *I don't.*

Ash brought the branch back. I took it and the wolf waited eagerly for me to throw it again. I glanced up ahead at Micah. I watched the easy, confident way he talked with Milly, the way her head tilted slightly as she listened, and I knew he was convincing her. I felt my jaw tighten. Christianity had plagued my life before the Devastation and now, thanks to Micah, a new outbreak was infecting my friends.

"He says we have five more years of this mess before things get better."

"The Devastation isn't a football game. You can't put a timer on it."

"He doesn't call it the Devastation. He calls it the Tribulation. Says it's in the Bible, in Revelations."

"Revelation."

"What?"

I sighed. "Revela-*tion*. There's no 's'."

"Revelation, right. He says things are going to get worse. That some of us won't make it."

I adjusted the straps on my pack. "I'm a little too busy trying to survive to worry about where I'm headed when I die."

"But that's just it," he insisted. "We don't know when our card is gonna get punched. I mean, with everything going on, the God question seems important to answer sooner rather than later."

I hurled the branch with all my might. "Then answer it for yourself!" I snapped.

He flinched, wounded.

I felt instantly guilty. "I'm sorry. I—"

Ash's low, rumbling growl drowned out my next words. I looked down at him. Instead of chasing his stick, he'd planted his front feet and was staring off into the trees with his black lips pulled back in a snarl. At first I thought he smelled soldiers, but then a loud stomping and roaring filled my ears. The treetops in the distance shuddered. Something enormous was coming at us through the woods.

The four of us grouped together, weapons raised. Ash paced and growled in front of us. Branches cracked. Trees

SUZANNE LEONHARD

swayed. The ground shook. When I finally caught sight of it, I thought it was a bear racing toward us on its hind legs. But it was bigger than any bear I'd ever seen.

It crashed through the pines and bushes, finally stopping just inside the tree line. It stood a full fifteen feet in height, with the same misshapen head, flat nose, and bulging eyes as Alvin Reinkann. It was a Goliath.

He wore a green canvas tarp as a toga with a frayed rope tied around his waist, decorated with dangling white ornaments that rattled together as he moved.

"Where you goin', pretty birds?" His deep, gravelly voice made him sound like a bridge troll who'd just woken from a nap. To complete his monstrous look, he carried a thick tree trunk over one shoulder like a thorny club.

He stepped into our path. We got a better look at him and, more importantly, his rope belt. The white ornaments were human bones—skulls and femurs banging together like gruesome wind chimes.

"What is that?" Ben rasped.

"I'm guessing the ogre," Micah answered.

I pulled back the bolt on my AK-12. "He's a lot bigger than Alvin."

Ash had his head low and his haunches raised, ready to pounce. "Steady, boy," I told him.

I nestled my cheek against the stock of my weapon, touched my nose to the charging handle, and put the large knobby head in my crosshairs. "Time to put you out of your misery, big fella." My finger brushed the trigger. Then its eyes lit on Milly.

"Hey, Mills."

I froze.

The blue eyes. The cleft chin. The mop of blond hair. Oh, God, it couldn't be.

338

"No," Ben rasped. "No." He looked like he was about to be sick.

Micah set his hand on the barrel of my rifle, slowly redirecting it toward the ground.

A ragged sob tore from Milly's throat. She wavered—I thought she might pass out—but she steadied herself. Taking a deep breath, she set her hands on her hips. "Timothy Odette," she shouted up at the ogre. "I have been lookin' high and low for you. What're you doin' out here in these woods by yourself?"

The thing that had once been my friend looked away and lowered his head. "I's just wick-wackin' around, Mills."

"Well, you can wick-wack your behind right to Leavenworth this instant and let Doctor Reinkann take a look at you."

He brushed his hand back and forth through the bones on his belt. The creepy sound made me shiver. "Don't like doctors," he muttered.

"I don't care what you like," Milly went on. "You—" Emotion cracked her voice. "You just follow us."

I shook my head at her. "Milly, we can't go back. The praetor still has David."

Milly's eyes swam with tears. She was barely holding it together. "But Doctor Reinkann might be able to help him."

My heart raced with fear for my brother. "Tim's survived out here this long—"

"You expect me to just leave my brother out here in the wilderness to live like an animal?"

Looking confused by the conversation, Tim chewed his bottom lip and fiddled with his tree-club.

"We aren't going to leave him," Micah reassured.

"Of course we're going to leave him!" I snapped. "There's nothing we can do for him now, but there still may be time to save David. We'll get Tim on our way back to Leavenworth."

Milly lifted her chin. "Y'all go on. Me and my brother are goin' back to Leavenworth."

"Do you not see what's hanging from his belt, Milly?" Ben whispered. "Those aren't monkey bones."

"We'll be just fine." Milly looked up at Tim. "C'mon, big brother. Let's get you to the doctor."

Without sparing me a glance, she turned and walked off in the direction we'd just come.

"Look out!" Micah shouted.

He charged past me, tackling Milly to the ground just as Tim struck out with his massive tree trunk. The club flew over their heads, missing them both by inches.

I looked up at Tim. A crazed snarl twisted his bulbous face. He raised his crude club over his head, preparing for another strike. "Don't like *DOCTORS*!" he shouted.

He turned his googly eyes on Micah and took aim. Micah sidestepped the attack. The ground shook with the force of the blow as the makeshift club dug a deep furrow through the ash and dirt.

Furious that he missed again, Tim let out an earsplitting roar. The hair on my head stood on end.

"Maybe this would be a good time to run?!" Ben shouted, inadvertently drawing Tim's attention. "Whoa, now," he said. "Easy, big guy."

Milly leapt in front of the ogre. "Tim! Stop!"

Tim knocked her aside with his enormous, lumpy hand. He spotted Micah and closed in on him again.

Micah ducked behind a tall, thick pine. Tim, growling like a mad dog, swatted the tree out of the way like it was nothing. Ash charged in. He sank his teeth into Tim's bulging ankle. Tim shook the wolf off like a ragdoll.

Ben rushed up behind Tim. "Sorry, buddy." He jammed a knife into the back of his massive calf. Tim howled in pain and kicked out, knocking Ben backwards. But his attention returned to Micah.

"You!" He snorted at Micah. "You die!"

I stared up at the misshapen face of the thing that was once my trusted friend and felt my heart break. I understood Milly's desire to take him back to Doctor Reinkann for treatment, but this wasn't Tim. This wasn't the boy who'd insisted on being my brother's friend, who'd fought beside me to protect our town, who loved his sister more than anything in the world.... The Tim we knew would never want to live like this.

I blinked back hot tears and raised my weapon. "I'm sorry, Tim," I whispered. "I'm so sorry."

The crack of the gunshot echoed through the woods. I heard Milly scream.

Tim didn't fall.

Instead he turned and fixed his watery gaze on me. The bullet had scored a red gash in his forehead, but hadn't penetrated his thick skull. He bared his teeth at me and roared so loud my ears popped. "SEEEEERRRRRAAAA!"

I'd only made him angrier.

"RUN!" Micah bellowed.

As Tim bore down on me, Ben grabbed Milly's hand and sprinted off with her down the hillside. I couldn't find the will to move. Tim stopped in front of me and bent forward to glare into my eyes. His face was bulging and grotesque, covered in an oozing slime. I could feel his hot breath on my face, smell the rotting stench of it in my nose.

"You'll be tasty," he mumbled.

And then Micah was there. He charged in between me and the ogre, knocking me out of the way. Tim swung. He narrowly missed me, but Micah wasn't so lucky. A sharp branch from the tree-club plowed a deep scratch into the side of his face. He cried out in pain. Still, without missing a beat, Micah swung me up into his arms and ran with me down the hillside.

I looked back over his shoulder. Tim lumbered after us, big and awkward, but one of his steps covered five times more ground than one of Micah's.

At the bottom of the hill, we caught up with Ben and Milly. Micah dropped me to my feet and the four of us sprinted through the woods toward the highway at break-neck speed. Ash bolted ahead, leading the way.

I could hear Tim crashing through the trees, seething with monstrous rage.

We broke through the tree line and raced across Highway 97. Thick underbrush slapped at our arms and legs. We dropped down the steep bank, then stopped. Swauk Creek was rushing, deep and swollen from snow melt. Ash waited, whining, unsure of where to go next. I slid down the bank and plunged my foot in.

The water was ice cold.

Tim howled behind us.

We charged into the frigid water. It rose to my waist, cut through my clothes, and tore the breath from my lungs. I forced my numb legs through the strong current, desperate for the other side. Ash leapt in after me, paddling furiously, determined to keep up.

Milly stumbled on the slippery rocks. Ben grabbed for her. They disappeared beneath the water. After a long moment, they resurfaced, sputtering. The rushing current pulled me sideways, threatening to sweep me away. Micah caught my hand, pulling me in tight. I wrapped my arm around his neck and let him guide me to the shore.

Finally, the four of us dragged ourselves onto the opposite bank, exhausted, panting. We looked back. Tim had stopped at the water's edge. He seemed almost afraid to get his feet wet.

He looked over at us and whimpered. "Mills?"

Dripping wet and shivering, Milly dropped to her knees and stared at her brother across the rushing water. She looked small and defeated. I knelt beside her, wrapping her up in my arms.

Tim let out a mindless roar. He waved his tree trunk in the air and stomped his enormous feet. *"Traitor!"* he spat at her. *"Traitor!"*

She turned her face into my neck, sobbing.

"The praetor will pay for this, Milly," Micah said. "I swear he will pay."

"Micah," Ben said. "Your face."

I looked over at Micah. Water dripped from his dark hair, mingling with a steady stream of blood oozing from the deep cut on his cheek. He dabbed at the wound, looking puzzled. He claimed to be "sealed," protected by God, but Micah Abrams wasn't so indestructible after all.

Chapter Twenty-Five

The tiny town of Liberty, Washington, sat two miles off Highway 97, deep in the Wenatchee National Forest. Hardcore campers used the ghost town as a stopover before heading deeper into the mountains. The grinding mill still stood, along with a few of the old miners' houses and the dilapidated Meaghersville Hotel. Dredge ponds, tailing mounds, and old mining equipment left to rust in overgrown fields made the town beautiful, historic, and forgotten. The perfect place to hide a rebel summit.

While Ash patrolled the surrounding woods, the four of us lay on our bellies on a forested rise overlooking the town's only street. We all still felt the shock of our encounter with Tim, Milly more than any of us. She'd barely spoken since the creek. I added Tim's fate and Milly's pain to my long list of reasons to kill Praetor Stanislov.

Ben and I inspected the town through the scopes on our weapons. The lone street was empty—not a rebel in sight. "Looks completely deserted," I said.

"They'll be here," Micah replied. We had stopped briefly for Milly, who always carried a small med kit, to see to his face. Even in her grief, she had mechanically cleaned the gash, closing it with a few hasty stitches. But the wound still looked angry and red. "What about the houses?" he asked.

I scanned the dozen or so houses along the road. Most of them were broken-down, but even the intact buildings appeared uninhabited. I shook my head. "Nothing."

"Could be a trap," Ben murmured.

I shouldered my weapon. "Let's check the campgrounds."

We reconnoitered the woods between Williams and Boulder Creek, finding both campsites just as deserted as the town. The ash was deep there and sucked at our boots, so we reluctantly turned back toward town. We found the wolf nosing around an old mine shaft. He hadn't found anybody either. I was getting frustrated. My brother was in imminent danger; I couldn't afford to wait for a band of rebels that might never show.

Ben frowned at Micah. "Maybe you got the town wrong?"

Micah looked frustrated, too. "This is the place. We just need to wait."

The image of Tim, screaming and stomping through the forest, made my skin prickle with anxiety. It had been three days since David had left the cabin with Private Calhoun. He was certainly with the praetor by now. "I say we keep moving toward Ellensburg," I pressed.

"And then what?" Ben argued. "Take on Europa by ourselves?"

Micah shook his head. "It's their central command. There'll be hundreds of them. I know you're anxious to find David, Seraphina, but if we go in alone, we won't be able to save him or ourselves."

He was right but, in that moment, I wished I'd come alone. Then nothing could have stopped me from crashing the gates of Ellensburg.

We made camp in the mine shaft. The remainder of Hilda's *spätzle* made a hearty dinner, but it did nothing for our gloomy moods. We ate in silence on our bedrolls, by the dim glow of diffused moonlight. Before long, Ben's deep snores filled the space.

I heard the soft muffled sounds of Milly crying.

Crawling toward her bedroll, I found her huddled in a ball, shaking and shivering. I put my arm around my friend's shoulders. It broke my heart to see her in so much pain.

"Oh, Sera," she rasped. "What are we gonna do?"

I was suddenly hit by a memory of Milly walking down the hallway at Cle Elum-Roslyn high school in her cheerleader's uniform. She was always smiling, always looking like she had the world by the tail. I rarely saw Milly smile anymore; now the world had a hold of her.

"We're going to help him," I told her. "When the rebels arrive, we're going to tell Vivica what happened to Tim and that we need some men to help get him to Doctor Reinkann. Tim fought alongside most of the 1st Cascade in the Skaggs war. They'll want to help."

She cried for a few more moments, then pulled herself together. "No." She sniffled and wiped her nose on the back of her hand. "He almost killed us today. I won't risk anyone else's life. What could Reinkann do for him anyway? He can't even help his own son."

I wasn't sure what the doctor could do, but I was willing to try anything if it would make Milly feel better. "Maybe Tim—"

"Don't call him that." Milly choked back a sob. "That thing in the forest isn't Tim. It might have Tim's memories,

347

but my brother is gone. We stick with the mission. We save David. After that, we find the ogre and…and we put him down."

Her words brought a lump to my throat. She started to cry again and I held her tighter.

"I hope Micah's right," she said. "I hope there is a God. Otherwise all of this is for nothin'."

I stayed with her until she fell asleep, then I found my own bedroll. I was mentally and physically exhausted, and terrified for my brother. If the rebels weren't there by sunrise, I was leaving, with or without the others. I wouldn't wait past morning.

The night wore on. Unable to sleep, I tried not to imagine what might be happening to David, tried not to picture him deformed and raving, but the more I tried the more my mind filled with horrible thoughts and images.

I struggled to keep myself from slipping over the edge. If I fell apart now, David would be lost.

I heard a sound and opened my eyes. Something round and lumpy hovered in front of my face. I blinked and sat up, adjusting my eyes to the dim light, and realized it was a potato. I looked up into Micah's shadowed face.

"I'm all out of apples," he said.

I stared at the potato, remembering a boy who'd given me comfort when I needed it, a boy who'd protected me from bullets with his own body, a boy who'd held my hand in a pickup truck after I'd taken a man's life.

He looked me in the eye. "It's going to be all right, Seraphina."

That was all it took. My walls crumbled. Not caring who he was or what he'd done, I threw myself against him as I had before, wrapping my arms around his neck and burying my face against his shoulder. He pulled me in tight, holding me close as I cried. It felt so good to be held, cared for, protected again. In that one sweet moment I gave in to everything I'd kept tucked away in my heart for so long.

"Why did you leave me?" I cried.

"Ah, Seraphina," he breathed, "I didn't leave you. The Skaggs picked me up a few blocks from your house that night. When I refused to pledge, they put me in an internment camp near Leavenworth. I was cold and hungry and I couldn't stop thinking about you. Then they found out that I'd been friends with Steve, so they let me go."

My chin trembled. They'd let him go and he hadn't come back to me. That told me all I needed to know.

I tried to move away from him, but his arms tightened. "You're wondering why I didn't come home," he said against my forehead. "I had a chance to change their minds, to tell them the good news. At home, in Roslyn, I would have been just another enemy to them."

I looked up into his face. "What good news?"

"That we've all been separated from God because of our sin. That the punishment for sin is death. But, because God loves us, He sent His Son to take our punishment, to die in our place."

Instead of my usual revulsion, I felt a deep, quiet part of me reach out for what Micah was saying. It surprised me. "Did they believe you?"

"Some did. Some didn't. Frank Skaggs had created a special punishment for those who turned against him. Fear of that kept a lot of people from hearing me and believing."

"The brand." I had a vivid picture in my mind of John Voss with the red, blistering word TRAITOR burned into his chest.

"Right."

"So that day on Widowmaker…you weren't marching with them?"

"I was marching with them, Seraphina, but not in the way you thought. I knew a lot of those people were marching to their deaths. I had to use those last precious moments to reach as many as I could."

I stared into his dark, solemn eyes and knew in my heart he was telling the truth. He hadn't been a Spathi. He hadn't been a Skagg. Guilt washed over me like a drowning wave. I'd been wrong about him on every count and that knowledge started me crying all over again. "I'm so sorry, Micah."

He brushed away my tears as they spilled down my cheeks. "Don't be. I was the perfect replacement for your grandfather. I can't be harmed, so I took the bullet, played dead, and snuck off when they weren't looking."

My stomach tightened. "But you *can* be harmed, Micah. Your face."

"Yeah." He grunted and touched his cheek. "That was unexpected. But God knows what he's doing."

"How can you be so sure? What happened to you? Why do you believe all this?" I was desperate to understand.

He let out a slow breath. "The morning of the earthquake I woke up hungover. I got dressed, walked into my bathroom, and found myself standing on the most beautiful beach I'd ever seen. Brilliant blue water. Gorgeous, soft sand. There were thousands of men around me, speaking thousands of languages, and I understood every one of them. And then I saw the mountain…"

I sat back from him, my eyes growing wider in the dark.

"It seemed made of solid shimmering gold," he continued. "I wanted to climb it, to sit down on its peak and never move. But I was told that we had to help other people get to the top first." His stare intensified. "And then I saw the girl floating in the water."

My heart collided against my ribs.

"She was drawn to the shore, toward me. Flaming hair. Emerald eyes." He brushed his finger along my cheek. "She stole my breath away. I knew in that moment that I would give everything I had to protect her."

"And the dragon?" I asked breathlessly.

"The dragon?" He seemed confused.

I'd assumed we were having the same dream, but maybe I was wrong. "This dream turned you into a Christian?" I asked.

He shook his head. "It wasn't a dream. I could feel the sun on my face and taste the salt in the air. I was told the good news about the coming King. The truth was undeniable."

Hilda had called him chosen by God. "Is that when you were sealed?"

"Yes—me and the thousands of others with me."

"But why?"

"To serve the will of the Father."

The will of the father. I'd heard that before, first from Steve Skaggs and then from my grandfather. "What's the will of the father?" I asked.

"John 6:40," Micah replied. "For my Father's will is that everyone who looks to the Son and believes in Him shall have eternal life."

Something was happening to me—like the sound of gunfire, I could feel it in my bones. I searched his dark eyes. He believed deeply in what he said and it was getting harder for me to contradict him.

He leaned close, pressing his forehead to mine. "He's pursuing you, Seraphina," he whispered. "I can see it in your eyes. Don't let pride keep you from embracing the truth."

I could feel his breath on my lips. My heart raced. "But how do I know it's the truth?"

"Because," he replied, "it will set you free."

Like it had for Eliza and Hilda, I thought.

We sat there silently for a moment, staring into each other's eyes. I thought he might kiss me. I waited, hoping, but then he stood abruptly. "Try to get some sleep." His voice was thick with emotion. "We'll talk more tomorrow."

I watched him disappear into the dark shadows of the mine as I considered the possibilities of what he was saying. "I must be losing my mind," I whispered to myself. I stretched out on my bedroll.

Did I actually believe that all the chaos around me was all part of the grand plan of some invisible creator?

I drifted off to sleep with that question planted firmly in my mind and my nightmare returned, more detailed than ever before.

I'm floating in the middle of a deep, blue sea. Warm. Peaceful. Safe. I want to stay there forever, but a gentle, invisible force pulls me toward the shore. My feet touch down on the sandy bottom. I walk onto a soft, white beach that squishes, warm and wet, between my toes. I close my eyes, feeling the hot sun on my face, tasting the salty breeze on my tongue.

I'm not alone. Thousands of young men line the beach, standing shoulder to shoulder, each with a shining symbol on their forehead glowing bright as the sunlight. One young man stands out from the rest. Micah. He's standing in front of me, his eyes dark, solemn. "Truth, Seraphina," he whispers. "It will set you free."

A sound comes from the water. My heart seizes in my chest. An enormous red dragon rises out of the sea, roaring like a wild animal. It has seven heads covered in lethal spiked horns, glowing red eyes, sharp white teeth, and claws that slash the air like razor blades. It eyes the men on the beach and decides on Micah.

Terror knifes through me. I shout for Micah to run, but he can't; his feet are buried in the sand. The dragon moves closer. I can feel its hot, rancid breath on my face. I raise my arms and feel flames ignite my hands.

I will give everything I have to protect him.

A PIERCING NOISE pulled my eyes open. The sun was up. Blinding white light flooded the mine entrance and my mind went back to the church and the earthquake. *Endure.* I hid my face in the crook of my arm.

I heard running feet, grunts and thumps. The piercing noise came again, echoing against the walls of the mine. I recognized it now. Milly was screaming.

I bolted upright. Chaos confronted me.

Europa soldiers were everywhere. Several of them had a hold of Ben and Milly. My friends were putting up a ferocious fight. I reached for my weapon, only to find it held to the ground by a polished black boot.

"Ah-ah." The familiar voice crawled in my ears and sent fire racing through my veins. I looked up the trouser-clad leg and the ocean blue overcoat, past the brass buttons and flashy braided epaulets, and into the hateful, smiling face of Praetor Stanislov. "Good morning, Sera."

For the past year, my hatred of this man had become a living thing, something I'd fed and nurtured with the blood of his soldiers. I'd hoped the next time I saw him would be through a gunsight, but I could improvise in a pinch.

I curled my fingers around a fist-sized rock lying in the dirt beside me.

SUZANNE LEONHARD

"It is so good to see you again," the praetor cooed.

I heard snarls and yips mingled with angry shouts. Two soldiers were trying to force Ash into a cage. They'd managed to get a catch pole around his neck; he flailed at the end of it like a rabid dog. Panic rose in my chest. The wolf didn't understand what was happening and he was terrified.

"Let him go," I ground out.

"It belongs to me, my dear. I am simply retrieving my property—"

"*Let him go!*" I surged to my feet, striking the praetor on the side of the face with the rock.

Blood erupted from his cheek. He cried out in pain and the soldiers trying to wrangle Ash stopped to see what had happened.

Ash seized the opportunity and lunged. He took a chunk out of one of the soldier's arms, then raced for the woods, dragging the catch pole behind him. My heart leapt in victory as he reached the tree line.

"Run, Ash!" I screamed.

Everything went black.

Chapter Twenty-Six

My head ached. I moaned and shifted my legs. Something soft lay beneath me. I wondered if mom was up yet, making breakfast in the kitchen. No school today. I wanted to sleep forever.

Reality intruded and I cracked open my eyes.

I lay in a spacious, empty room with faded outlines on the walls where pictures had once hung. Through a large window to my left, I could see the dim orb of the sun hanging midway in the crimson sky. I'd been out for hours. Or was it days?

I remembered Milly screaming, Ben fighting, Ash running. The praetor found us in the mine. How, I wasn't sure. But I'd wanted to infiltrate Ellensburg and, although I'd hoped for a more covert entry, it seemed I'd done just that.

New mission: escape.

I needed to find David and the others.

I sat up on the cot and stared at the closed door across the room. I knew without checking that it was locked. A small plate of food waited on the floor by the bed, along with a bottle of water. I ignored them both.

I stood. The world tilted beneath me and I reached down to steady myself. Four deep depressions in the carpet showed where something like a desk had once been. I was a prisoner in somebody's former office. I steadied myself, then walked to the tall, wide window where the sun was pouring in.

Looking out, I had to brace myself against another bout of dizziness. The window, on the third floor, looked out over a complex of buildings connected by courtyards and a maze of cement paths. They'd done a painstaking job of cleaning up the ash, leaving sparkling white pavement, grassy knolls, and planters full of cheery flowers. I could even see a tall water fountain spouting brightly in the distance.

Out beyond the complex, toward the mountains, lay the real world; a desolate gray moonscape littered with destruction. It held nothing but debris, gray dunes, and broken rooftops. The ash was deep out there.

The door clicked open behind me. I turned slowly, mindful of the dizziness. A tall, muscular man walked into the room. He smiled, but it wasn't friendly. It was like the praetor's smile, cold and calculating. He stood against the far wall and stared at me without saying a word.

"I want to see my friends," I said to him.

"Of course you do."

I frowned. His voice was familiar.

He picked up the plate of food from the floor and held it out to me. "You should eat to counteract the drugs."

They'd drugged me? That explained the dizziness. I gave him a wary once over, noting the Biotat on the back of his right hand. "Where are they?"

"Your friends are fine. They have their own rooms."

"Then I want to see my brother."

He looked amused. "Why?"

"Because I'd like to know that he's all right."

He set the plate back down on the floor. "Your brother is better than all right."

I eyed him carefully. "What does that mean?" *Please tell me I'm not too late.*

He moved closer. "See for yourself."

Confused, I backed up. "Where is David?"

His hand shot out and he took a steely grip on my arm. I swallowed my fear as he yanked me forward and glared down into my face. His eyes, a glowing, otherworldly shade of blue, sent a cold chill of dread racing down my spine. "He's right here, Sera," he ground out.

That's when I recognized the nose, the mouth, the chin, the red hair—so much like my own. I took a quick shocked breath. "David?" I breathed.

He flashed me a dazzling grin and let go of my arm. "Astonishing, isn't it?" He did a slow spin. "And to think, you almost talked me out of coming."

I watched as my brother moved around the room with the grace and precision of a strutting lion. He was at least six feet tall. He had large, cut muscles that expanded and rippled as he flaunted himself, a broad, straight back, and long, powerful legs. He looked nothing like the boy he'd been and—mercifully—nothing like Tim or Alvin.

I shook my head. "I don't understand."

"It's Goliath, Sera." He clenched his fists and flexed his bulging arms. "It's everything Dad said it would be and more."

"But we found Tim in the forest and he—"

"I know about Tim," he interrupted. "It's quite sad."

I scowled at him. "Quite sad?"

"They had some problems figuring out Dad's research and had to improvise to fill in the gaps. But they resolved all that mess." He beamed. "As you can clearly see."

Busy preening, David failed to see the look of revulsion on my face. How could he just shrug off what the praetor had done to Tim?

"When I showed up," he continued, "I solved everything."

"*You* solved everything?" I felt like I might be sick. This preening behemoth was more like a distortion of David than the real thing; he was all my brother's personality flaws magnified tenfold and crammed beneath a glistening skin.

He smiled. "Come with me. I have something to show you."

With every one of my senses on high alert, I cautiously followed him out of the room. An armed guard posted outside my door fell into step behind us. We passed two more guarded doors, where I assumed Micah, Ben, and Milly were being held.

I looked up at a ceiling lit with fluorescent lights. "They have electricity here?"

"Several buildings on campus, like this one, are solar powered. We have clean water, too, from an underground reservoir."

We turned onto a broad, open staircase surrounded by large windows, and headed down to the foyer on the first floor. I saw several places where the stairs had been repaired, but no signs of catastrophic damage.

"Most of the newer buildings survived the earthquake with only minor damage," he told me. When we reached the foyer, bigger cracks could be seen in the dark marble floor. "The ash was their biggest problem," he went on. "It was over five feet deep."

He shoved open the glass exit door. It flew back against the outside wall and shattered into a thousand tiny pieces. I flinched, startled by his easy violence. Apparently, he wasn't used to his new strength.

He grinned. "Oops." He held the broken door wide for me and I stepped over the glass.

We walked along the pristine cement path. Groups of people wandered past, chatting and laughing. Some sat on the lawn, eating lunch as if everything were right with the world. I glanced up at the surrounding mountains and saw the ash reflecting silver-gray in the sunlight. *That's reality*, I thought. *All this other stuff is just Europa's sleight of hand.*

David continued filling me in, the admiration in his voice obvious. "They used firehoses to wet the ash, then snowplows to push it off campus."

The steady rumble of heavy equipment sounded in the distance.

"They're hoping to have the entire city cleared by the end of the year."

We approached the large fountain I'd seen from my window. In the center, the bronze statue of a man holding the hand of a gorilla, reminded me of the coal miner statue that had graced the courtyard of the Roslyn City Hall building. Several people relaxed nearby, enjoying the soothing sound of water.

"This is what I wanted to show you." He looked so pleased with himself and I didn't know what to expect.

I frowned at the fountain. "This?"

"Sera?" a voice called from behind me.

I looked at the thin, dark-haired man sitting on a nearby bench. I blinked. "*Dad?*"

His eyes filled with tears and I dissolved. I rushed into his arms; he pulled me into a tight hug.

"Sera, my little princess." He brushed the hair back from my face and gave me a tremulous smile. "You've grown up."

"But Seattle—"

"He wasn't there, Sera." David sounded accusatory, as if it was my fault that we'd never found him. "He's been here in Ellensburg the entire time."

"*Here?*" I looked at my dad. He nodded.

David arched his perfect brow. "He's the reason the Goliath Code worked for me."

And not for our friend, he'd failed to add.

My father grimaced. "The Goliath Code is the praetor's work, not mine."

"Don't be coy, Dad," David practically growled. "This is your victory, too."

My father gave him a weak smile. "Of course."

"Now that Sera's here," David went on, "we can be a family again."

I snorted and looked at my dad. "We're not staying here."

David's eyes darkened. "Of course we're staying."

"I'm getting our friends and leaving. And if you've got half a brain in that perfect head you've been given, you'll come with me."

David's smile twisted into a cold, hard sneer. Something completely terrifying came up in his eyes. I got a strong feeling that he was about to lunge at me.

My father rose to his feet, effectively moving between us. "Your sister needs time to adjust, David. We can't expect her to take up our cause without explaining the important work we've been doing."

"What work is that?" I asked, wary.

David seemed to relax. "Dad solved the delivery—" His

360

watch alarm beeped, interrupting him. His eyes suddenly lit up. "Gotta run." He smiled broadly. "Vitamin shot."

I watched my brother hurry off on long, strong legs and turned to my father. "Dad?" I said carefully. "What's going on?"

My father glanced at my armed guard, then nodded at me. He grabbed the cane that had been leaning against the bench. "Let's walk."

I realized he was wearing a knee brace. "You're hurt."

"Just a little present from the quake."

We started off down the path. As the armed guard fell into step behind us, my dad gave him a quick, mirthless smile that the guard didn't return. "The complex guards are harmless," Dad whispered to me. "As long as you stay clear of the gauntlet."

"Gauntlet?"

"That's what they call the road leading in and out of the complex. It's aptly named. Heavily mined. Completely impassable."

Good to know, I thought. "What are you doing in Ellensburg?"

"My team was granted use of the new genomics lab here at the university. The quake hit just after we arrived, then the ash started to fall, completely locking us in. I was desperate to get to Roslyn, Sera, to you, and mom, and David. But—" He gestured at his leg.

"Our people scouted west. There was no way through. The ash was just too deep."

"Until Praetor Stanislov arrived. About six months ago, he showed up with his troops and big trucks. He told me you and David were alive, and I…" His voice broke. "I couldn't believe it. He said that your grandfather had died, but you and David had left Roslyn with some friends."

Fury tightened my jaw. "Grandpa didn't die, Dad. The praetor killed him." I didn't even try to disguise the venom in my voice.

His expression hardened. "I know." He linked his arm through mine and moved closer. "Tim told me."

I gasped. "You talked to Tim?"

He nodded. "He was one of their first experiments."

Violence bubbled inside me.

"When the praetor cleared the ash and got the lights and water on, people started thinking he was some kind of savior. The moment we met, the guy told me that we were going to be the best of friends. That's when I knew I was in trouble."

I grunted scornfully.

"All he ever talked about was my work on the achondroplasia cure. He wanted me to begin human trials. I refused—we still had animal testing to do and the Devastation had set us back at least a year. I guess he got tired of hearing me say no. He seized my research and put his own scientists to work on it." My father's eyes pooled with tears. "He tested it on children, Sera. He used my work to cause unimaginable harm. I could hear their screams echoing down the hallways at night."

"But you were sure the cure would work. How did it go so wrong?"

"The praetor isn't what I'd call a patient man. His scientists used nanobots as accelerants. They forced massive developmental changes, which should have taken place over the course of years, to manifest in days. The human body can't adapt to complex evolutionary changes that quickly. His experiments failed, over and over again, ending in disfigurement, brain damage, even death. I told him it was the accelerant, but he insisted his Goliath Code was useless if he had to wait years for the results. He's trying to build an unstoppable army."

"For what? He's already won."

"I don't know. But I was determined not to help him do it." He paused. "And then David showed up."

I nodded, understanding. "Giving the praetor leverage over you."

"He planned to use your brother as one of his test subjects. I told David to escape, that Praetor Stanislov's Goliath Code wasn't his cure. But he didn't care." His expression filled with anguish. "Sera, he begged me to help the praetor transform him."

I squeezed his arm. I, more than anyone, understood how desperate David had been to be normal.

"I finally agreed to go over the protocols. It turned out that their mistake was a simple delivery failure, an easy fix. I insisted that I be the one to administer the treatment and that I be allowed to keep David under anesthesia for two days to spare him the pain. He woke up yesterday morning just as you see now—tall and strong." He looked despondent. "Everything he's ever wanted to be."

"But he's not the same."

"No." The word was ragged and raw. "The procedure enhances more than just physical attributes. We see heightened activity in the limbic system, resulting in lack of impulse control, amplified emotions, increased appetite, and diminished sympathetic response. The Code is buried deep, on a sequence of genes that up until recently were considered junk DNA. Honestly, I'm not even sure it's human. That's why animal trials were so important to the research."

"Are you saying it's *alien* DNA?"

He stopped and turned towards me. "What I'm saying is that the praetor is turning children into monsters. And I'm going to tell you the same thing I told your brother." He put his arm around my shoulders and spoke low in my ear. "Get out of here, Sera. Escape any way you can and never come back."

———

I SAT ALONE at a long table in the cafeteria, picking at the fried chicken and mashed potatoes on my tray. My father and I had walked the complex for almost an hour before he'd been called away to his lab. During that time, he'd told me about Ellensburg's impenetrable defenses, including the Gauntlet, the main road leading in and out of the university complex. I realized that, even with help from the rebels, we never would have made it inside alive. Now that we were here, I had no idea how we were going to get out.

The rebels had their work cut out for them; convincing the American citizens here to turn against their Europa liberators wasn't going to be easy. Ellensburg offered clean, well-lit living with fresh water and plenty of delicious imported food. At the long tables around me, people talked and laughed with soldiers as if they were old friends. I wondered if any of them knew—or cared—about the atrocities those same soldiers committed against citizens out in the real world.

I had yet to see Micah, Ben, or Milly. Not knowing what was happening to them had me on edge. My father didn't know anything about them, either. The guards seemed to lack tongues as well as personalities. I was about to climb up onto my table and demand somebody do something, when Ben and Milly entered the cafeteria.

Relief flooded through me, then white-hot anger. Ben's face was battered and swollen. Milly had bruises on her neck and a deep cut above her eyebrow. They looked exhausted, worn by battle, and it was my fault. I had asked them to come on this impossible mission for the sake of my brother. I had to get them out.

I stood and waved at them. When they spotted me, they hurried over. We hugged, then sat on opposite sides of the table.

Mindful of the armed guard standing nearby, I leaned across the table toward them. "Are you guys okay?"

Ben nodded. "Yeah."

"What about you?" Milly asked. A clump of her beautiful blonde hair had been pulled out at the scalp. "They hit you pretty hard."

"Better now that the drugs are out of my system."

She grunted. "Yeah. Wasn't that sweet of 'em?"

I glanced back at the entrance. "Where's Micah?"

Ben shook his head. "Haven't seen him."

"We thought he was with you."

Fear swirled through me. The praetor had already tried to kill Micah once.

"Don't worry," Milly added. "Micah can't be hurt, remember?"

"You're forgetting his face," Ben threw in. "You know, that big, long gash you stitched up yesterday?"

"That's different," Milly replied. "The ogre isn't human."

I blinked at her, wondering if she was onto something. Doctor Reinkann had said that Micah was protected from *earthly* harm. Goliath Tim was the furthest thing from earthly that I had ever seen.

Ben scratched at a bandage on his arm.

"What's that for?" I asked.

He scowled. "They took my blood."

"They didn't give you a blood test?" Milly asked, showing me her bandage.

"No." They didn't need to. My father had my DNA on file, like David's. I leaned closer. "We have to find Micah and get out of here," I whispered. "Tonight."

"How?" Ben whispered back. "My room's locked and guarded."

"Same here." Milly leaned in. "And what about David?"

As if on cue, a tray piled high with chicken dropped down onto the table. "How I love cafeteria food."

I felt the bench sag as my brother sat down beside me. I hadn't seen him since he'd run off for his vitamin shot. I couldn't bring myself to look at him now. His transformation, inside and out, disturbed me. I was beginning to understand how Milly felt about Tim. This wasn't my brother. My brother had vanished the moment he'd undergone the Goliath procedure and this heinous reproduction had taken his place.

Ben glared across the table at him. "This is a private conversation, pal."

"Whatever, Turner," David growled. "You've been trying to get private with my sister for a while now and I keep telling you it is not gonna happen."

Ben sat back, his eyes wide.

Milly looked confused. "And who, exactly, are you?"

"It's…" Ben shook his head, not believing what he was seeing.

"It's me, Mills." David's use of Tim's nickname for Milly was nothing but cruel.

Milly's chin trembled. "*David?*"

"Well, look at you catching on so quick. That's gotta be a new record, right?" He stuck a drumstick in his mouth and tore all the meat off in one savage bite.

"But how——" She couldn't finish.

I knew what she was thinking and my heart broke for her. How had Goliath done this for David, while leaving her own brother so destroyed?

Oblivious to her pain, David grinned. "My father, that's how. He's been living here since the eruption. Wasn't even in Seattle. Isn't that right, Sera?"

I didn't respond.

David sat back and flexed. "Hey, Ben, check out these Goliath guns."

"Yeah." Ben frowned. "Good for you."

Silent tears dripped down Milly's face. I reached over and placed my hand on hers, trying to offer some comfort.

David scowled at everyone. "What's the problem?"

"*Problem?*" Ben shot back. "They burned the cabin. Did you know that? They shot Jude. My brother almost died because of you." He stood from the table. "And I'm so very happy for you and your *Goliath guns*, but we've met a couple of people who weren't quite so lucky."

David's expression darkened and my blood ran cold. "Sit down, Ben," I whispered.

"No, Sera," Ben retorted. "Enough with the coddling. He's deserved this for a long time."

David rose to his full height, several inches taller than Ben's. "Praetor Stanislov told me you'd be jealous," he growled. "I should have known you'd make everything about you."

"No, David, this is about you. Which should make you really happy, because nobody matters more in David Donner's world than David Donner."

"Do you——" Milly bit back a sob. "Do you know what they did to Tim?"

"Tim! Tim! Tim!" David barked. "*Yes*, I know what they

did to precious Tim! And a hundred other kids after him! Pain is necessary in achieving perfection!"

The cafeteria had gone silent. The other people in the room, including the soldiers, had stopped eating to stare in our direction. My brother's face had contorted into a mask of fury. For the first time in my life, I was genuinely afraid of him.

I stood up beside him. "Calm down, David," I said gently.

"Shut up, Sera!" he shouted at me. "You don't get to tell me what to do anymore!"

"Perfection?" Ben scoffed. "Is that how you see yourself now? Because all I see is a pretty face and some big muscles wrapped around the same selfish bastard you've always been."

With a violent roar, David leapt over the table and took Ben by the throat with one hand. "I am the next evolution of mankind!" he bellowed.

Ben struggled against David's grip. His face puckered and started to turn purple.

I rushed to my brother's side. "That's enough, David!"

David ignored me, lifting Ben off the ground. "How do you like the Goliath guns now, Ben?"

I grabbed my brother's arm, trying to pry him loose, but it felt like trying to bend solid steel. I looked around at the soldiers in the room. "Do something!" I shouted. But the minute one stepped forward, the armed guard standing nearby threw the bolt on his weapon. The message was clear. *Don't interfere.*

Ben's eyes were bulging. His feet were thrashing. He was clawing at David's hands, desperate for air.

Milly screamed. "Stop, David! Stop!"

I looked around for a weapon, finally picking up my

lunch tray and slamming it across the back of my brother's head. It broke into several pieces and didn't leave a mark on him, but it did get his attention. He turned to look at me.

"STOP!" I screamed up into his face.

His smile froze my blood. "All right, Sera. I'll stop." With one twist of his wrist he snapped Ben's neck and tossed him against the far wall.

I stood there motionless, forgetting how to breathe. Milly ran to where Ben lay in a crumpled heap on the floor. She checked for a pulse, then I saw her shoulders slump. She looked back at me with tears flooding her eyes and shook her head. There was nothing she could do. Ben was dead.

Chapter Twenty-Seven

I sat on my cot in the dark, my knees pulled up to my chest, unable to cry. Watching my brother kill our friend had shattered me into a million pieces. Only rage remained.

Kind, gentle Milly had shown strength I never imagined, but I wondered if her heart could withstand this much tragedy. She had been unresponsive when I last saw her. I'd clung to her afterward, fighting separation, but in the end they'd pulled her away from me. We'd been escorted to our individual rooms. I had to get to her—get her out of Ellensburg—and, to do that, I needed Micah's help.

The door clicked open, the light turned on, and the very last person I wanted to see walked into my room, smiling—or, should I say, half smiling. The left side of the praetor's face wasn't working so well. He had a four-inch gash riding up his left cheekbone, held together with a thick black row of stitches. The resulting lopsided grin made him look like a creepy drama mask.

I did that to him, I thought. And I was going to do a whole lot worse.

David followed him into the room, his head hanging low, but that didn't fool me. He hadn't looked remorseful or ashamed after he'd killed Ben. He'd looked satisfied. I turned away now, refusing to acknowledge him.

"Poor sweet Sera," the praetor said. "To see what you have seen today would break any mortal heart."

He held out a handkerchief to me. I glared at him. "Unless that comes with a gun I'm not interested."

"Manners, Sera," the praetor warned. His misshapen smile returned. "I was delighted to hear that you and your friends had found Mr. Odette in the forest. His tracking device made it much easier to find your little hideaway in the mine."

David snorted at me and I clenched my jaw. Not only had the praetor mutilated Tim, he'd used him against us.

"Now," the praetor continued. "David has expressed his deep sorrow for losing his temper and killing your friend today. I told him that it can take time for these things to be forgiven. But he is your brother. So perhaps—"

"That monstrosity is not my brother," I seethed. "He's a *disgusting* abomination."

David drew himself to his new full height and glowered at me with fiendish blue eyes. "Careful, Sera. I'm not as easily abused as I used to be."

I leapt to my feet, heedless of his threatening stance. "The only place you were ever abused was in your own sick mind!" I shouted back at him. "You made the decision to be a victim a long time ago, David, and you've done your damnedest to live up to it!"

"And you're such a saint?" he fired back, circling me. "Tell me, dear sister, how many soldiers have you murdered in the name of patriotism?"

"I was protecting you and the others!" I shouted back. "And how did you repay me? By throwing us to our enemies the moment you caught wind of something better! We lost everything because of you, *everything*! And you couldn't care less! You're no brother of mine," I snarled. "I have a family —*and you are not a part of it!*"

"Well, now your precious family is minus one."

I curled my fingers into claws and lunged at his face. I'd tear his tongue out before I'd let one more foul word slither out of his monstrous mouth.

David brushed off my attack. He grabbed me by the throat. He lifted me off my feet and stared into my bulging eyes. "The war is over, Sera," he sneered into my face. "You lose."

I fought and kicked. It felt like striking a brick wall.

"Now, children," the praetor chastised. "Am I going to have to call a time out for the both of you? Put your sister down, David. Do it gently," he added.

David hesitated, but then did as he was told.

I choked and coughed and fell back against the wall. My father was right. Something else had been activated within David, something other than size. His strength was inhuman.

"I have come to give you some news," the praetor said to me. "Your friend Milly Odette does not carry the Goliath code in her genome."

Relief flooded through me. "Then let her go." It was too much to hope for, but I could ask.

David laughed. "You're so stupid, Sera."

The praetor flashed his lopsided smile and shook his head. "Everybody has a job, my dear. If Milly won't fit into my Goliath army, then she must fit somewhere else. And I don't think she is Europa Guard material, do you? But she is a comely young woman. She will make a welcome companion for soldiers so far from their homes. Our men do get so lonely at the front."

I shook with anger. "I'm going to kill you."

The praetor clicked his tongue. "I am sorry to disappoint you again, Sera, but you, on the other hand, are perfect for my army. So you won't be using all that venomous rage against me. You will be using it *for* me. Tonight, we will activate your Goliath Code."

Fear seized my stomach. "I want to see Micah," I blurted out.

"*Micah?*" David snarled.

The praetor appeared surprised, then he laughed. "Micah Abrams? Isn't that the young man you had me execute last spring?"

"Don't play games with me. I know you're holding him here."

The praetor shook his head at David. "I am telling you, it is so hard to find reliable executioners these days."

David clenched his teeth and cracked his knuckles. Along with every other foul thing about my brother, his hatred for Micah had only magnified.

"Alas, dear Sera, your little Jew friend is not here."

Not here? Micah hadn't been captured? This news filled me with an overwhelming combination of joy and sadness; Micah wasn't within David's reach, but he wasn't within mine, either.

"No matter. I'm sure your brother will find him for us."

David leered at me. "I can't wait."

"Good luck," I taunted. "You may be strong, David, but I'm willing to bet a bullet will put you down just like any other animal."

He grabbed for me again.

"Enough!" the praetor shouted. "Your sister needs her rest. The transformation can be quite…demanding." He flashed me his twisted smile. "Until tonight." He pivoted and left the room.

With one final leer David followed after him. "See you later, sis."

The door closed and locked, and I dropped down on my cot, the last vestiges of hope pouring out of me. So, they wanted to turn me into a monster like my brother, forced to do the praetor's bidding. I preferred death. I wished I could stop my heart from beating.

Why not? Why continue living in this desolate world when everybody I loved had been taken from me?

I looked frantically around the room for a weapon. I found one in the wooden frame of my cot. I kicked at one of the legs. It splintered into a wooden shank. Hands shaking, I got down on my knees and held the jagged tip to my throat. I would not become the praetor's toy.

"One quick thrust, Sera," I coached myself. I swallowed hard and lifted my chin.

The image of Hilda, praying with a sword poised over her head, pulled my eyes open. Hilda had been calm in the face of her own death. I'd envied her faith. It had freed her from fear.

The truth will set you free.

Micah's words the night before came back to me as soft as a gentle whisper. Suddenly, I no longer felt alone in the room.

"But can faith bring Ben back? Can it save Milly? Will it prevent me from becoming like my brother?" Tears flooded my eyes. "I'm tired, worn out by this ugly world. I've tried to do good. I've tried to be strong. But I'm surrounded by

375

enemies, and I don't know what to do." I looked up at the ceiling, tears streaming down my face. "I'm told You can set me free. That something good can come from all this destruction. I want to keep going—to keep fighting. But I can't do it alone." I bowed my head. "Help me. If You're really there…help me."

My door clicked open again. I rose to my feet, clenching the makeshift weapon in my hand.

"Sera?" my father called softly.

The glow of the moon illuminated him limping through the door toward me. I tossed the jagged piece of wood to the floor and rushed into his arms.

"Sera, I'm so sorry," he rasped. I cried against his chest.

"It's okay, dad. It's going to be all right."

He held me tighter. "You've become so strong, so brave. Your mother would be so proud of you."

"I miss her," I sobbed.

"I miss her, too," he whispered.

"I was terrible to her."

"She knew you loved her. Her choices made it hard on all of us."

I pulled back from him. It was time to tell the truth. "Dad. About Mom—"

"David told me what happened at the church."

"No. I lied."

He looked into my face. "What are you talking about?"

My chin quivered. "She didn't fall through the floor."

"Then what happened?"

I took a breath and told my father what I had never told another living soul. "She was taken. By a bright white beam of light coming down from the sky."

My father smiled and shook his head. "Sera—"

"The light poured through her and around her. And she was singing. She was…"

Suddenly, the words to the song my mother had been singing in the church, the words I hadn't been able to understand at the time, came rushing into my mind like a flood. *You are worthy to take the scroll, and to open its seals, for You were slain, and have redeemed us to God by Your blood.*

"Sera, the mind does crazy things to us when we're under stress."

"I didn't imagine it." I dashed at the tears on my face. "Other people saw the light take their families, too. Some of them think it was an enemy attack. Some of them think it was aliens. Mom…she went to church, and—"

"No, no, Sera. Don't do this. Your mom allowed herself to be manipulated by a group of people who made her think she needed something special to go to heaven. Religion, deities, beliefs about the afterlife, they all play on our natural fear of death. Faith is for cowards."

I smiled, thinking of Hilda and Doctor Reinkann. "Some of the bravest people I know are Christians, Dad. Their faith doesn't weaken them. It gives them strength. It sets them free."

It occurred to me that if Micah was right and God was in charge of everything, then He was in charge of what was about to happen to me, too. I simply needed to let go, like Hilda had done, and trust Him.

Like my brother's transformation, my procedure would be overseen by my father, which meant there was a good chance that I wouldn't end up like Tim or Alvin, that I'd turn out strong and powerful like David. But, unlike David, my transformation could be used for a greater purpose.

"After you activate my Goliath Code, I'm going to kill the praetor."

My father's eyes locked with mine. "It won't be that easy. The Biotat they're going to give you is filled with nucleic acid robots—nubots—programmed to control impulses in the brain. Those vitamin shots David's getting? It's a scopolamine derivative, used to render a person susceptible to suggestion. Stanislov is programming the Goliaths for something."

"Then I won't get the Biotat."

"Then you'll be executed."

I closed my eyes, fighting despair. It seemed my transformation would serve no real purpose after all. "Then I choose death."

"Or…"

I looked up at him.

"I have an idea," he said. "It's something I wanted to try with David, but he was so desperate for the procedure I was afraid he might alert the praetor."

"What is it?" I asked.

He gave me a steady look. "You're going to have to trust me."

I COULDN'T STOP my legs from shaking. I sat on the long gurney wearing a large white hospital gown. My hair had been pulled back into a ponytail and heart monitor sensors had been taped to my chest. Complicated, beeping equipment filled the small, brightly lit room.

My attention kept wandering to the leather restraints peeking out from beneath the gurney's sheet. Would they be using those on me?

The praetor stood nearby, observing. David was there,

too, brooding by the door. My rage at them had been temporarily replaced with mind-numbing fear.

My father wore a white lab coat with a stethoscope around his neck. "Okay, Sera." His professional tone and expression only made me more nervous. "Are you ready?"

David snorted. "There's no getting ready for this." He sneered at me. "It's gonna hurt."

"What's the matter, David?" I jabbed back. "Worried that your perfection is about to be trumped? Soon you'll be just another face in the crowd. High school all over again."

He smirked, but I could tell I'd wounded him. "I'll say goodbye to Milly for you."

With that parting shot he left the room.

My dad had to take hold of me to keep me from flying off the gurney. "I should have let Lem Richmond blow you away at the drop zone!" I screamed after him. "I'd rather have a million Bens than a brother like you!"

"Children, children," the praetor chided. "My goodness, Jason. Is this what I can look forward to from your brood? Every day will be like Hercules and Athena duking it out on Mount Olympus."

My father looked into my eyes to steady me. I took a breath and tried to calm my racing heart.

"Praetor Stanislov," Dad said, "you can tell them to begin filming now."

The praetor hit a switch near the door and the wall-sized mirror opposite me illuminated, revealing several people standing in a room on the other side, some with cameras. The praetor documented all his experiments.

My father moved in front of me to take my vitals. He listened to my heart and then reached around with his stethoscope to check my lungs. "I'm going to be starting an

IV in a moment," he said to me. "Let's just get your pulse first."

Our eyes locked. He squeezed my hand so hard I almost cried out.

"I trust our subject is ready, Doctor Donner?" the praetor inquired.

I swallowed hard and nodded.

"She's ready," he replied.

"Please proceed with the Biotat," the praetor said.

My father pulled the tattoo machine toward my side of the gurney. "Grab the hand bar," he told me.

I hesitated.

"Sera," he said firmly. "Grab the bar."

"Is there a problem?" the praetor asked.

My father turned and smiled at him. "No problem." He gave me an urgent look. "Take hold of the hand bar."

My palms sweating, I swallowed hard, thrust my arm into the machine and grabbed the bar. I squeezed my eyes shut as the needle went into action. Tears of panic burned behind my eyelids.

It was over in seconds. I removed my arm from the machine and stared at the neat black mark on the back of my hand. It looked like a bar code on a box of cookies. I tried not to imagine thousands of tiny nubots racing through my veins to take over my brain.

"You okay?" my father asked.

I nodded.

"Lie back, please."

This was it. In two days, I would wake up completely transformed. Would I be like Tim or David? Both options were equally terrifying. But, if Micah was right and God did exist, then this was all part of His plan.

I laid back on the gurney and trusted in the will of the Father.

**THE STORY CONTINUES IN
BOOK TWO: *PROPHET***

AUTHOR'S NOTE

The Goliath Code Series is based on end-times prophecies found in both the Old and New Testaments, especially Isaiah, Ezekiel, Daniel, the four Gospels, the Epistles, and Revelation. While the characters and events in the books are fictional, they are framed within the truth of the Tribulation and return of Jesus Christ. Readers are encouraged to study the Bible.

Made in United States
Orlando, FL
03 August 2023